Aliens

FROM analog

ANTHOLOGY #7

Aliens
FROM analog

Edited by Stanley Schmidt

The Dial Press

Davis Publications, Inc.
380 Lexington Avenue, New York, N.Y. 10017

COPYRIGHT NOTICES AND ACKNOWLEDGMENTS

Grateful acknowledgment is hereby made for permission to reprint the following:

First Contact by Murray Leinster; copyright 1945 by Murray Leinster, renewed; reprinted by permission of the author's Estate and the agents for the Estate, Scott Meredith Literary Agency, Inc., 845 Third Avenue, New York, New York 10022.

Green-Eyed Lady by Alison Tellure; copyright © 1981 by Davis Publications, Inc.; reprinted by permission of the author.

The Children's Hour by Lawrence O'Donnell; copyright © 1944 by Henry Kuttner, renewed by Mrs. Catherine Reggie; reprinted by permission of Harold Matson Company, Inc.

. . . And Comfort to the Enemy by Stanley Schmidt; copyright © 1969 by The Condé Nast Publications, Inc.; reprinted by permission of Scott Meredith Literary Agency, Inc.

Now Inhale by Eric Frank Russell; copyright © 1959 by Street & Smith Publications, Inc., reprinted by permission of Scott Meredith Literary Agency, Inc.

Unhuman Sacrifice by Katherine MacLean; copyright © 1958 by Street & Smith Publications, Inc.; reprinted by permission of the author.

Big Sword by Paul Ash; copyright © 1958 by Street & Smith Publications, Inc.; reprinted by permission of the author.

Wings of Victory by Poul Anderson; copyright © 1972 by The Condé Nast Publications, Inc.; reprinted by permission of Scott Meredith Literary Agency, Inc.

The Waveries by Fredric Brown; copyright © 1944 by Fredric Brown, renewed; reprinted by permission of Scott Meredith Literary Agency, Inc.

Hobbyist by Eric Frank Russell; copyright © 1947 by Eric Frank Russell, renewed; reprinted by permission of Scott Meredith Literary Agency, Inc.

Petals of Rose by Marc Stiegler; copyright © 1981 by Davis Publications, Inc.; reprinted by permission of the author.

Cover: Alan Dean Foster's "Tran." Reprinted from *Barlowe's Guide to Extraterrestrials* by permission of Wayne Barlowe and Workman Publishing.

CONTENTS

INTRODUCTION
Stanley Schmidt

Last year a movie called *E.T.* did something new for a large segment of the American public: it got their sympathies and emotions thoroughly wrapped up in the fate of a nonhuman being from a distant world. Moviegoers had met aliens before, in such films as *War of the Worlds*, but seldom as fellow creatures with wants and motivations with which humans could empathize. To science fiction *readers*, on the other hand, the new element in *E.T.* was not new at all, for the science fiction published in magazines like *Analog* (formerly called *Astounding*) has long explored a broad spectrum of possibilities for alien life and intelligence. In the best of these explorations it was taken for granted that aliens, like us, *would* have thoughts and feelings that made no less sense than ours—though it's important to realize that they might make a very different *kind* of sense. As former editor John W. Campbell used to challenge his writers, "Show me a creature that thinks as *well* as a man—but not *like* a man."

Until recently, hardly anybody *except* science fiction writers spent serious thought on the possibility of extraterrestrial life. Since human beings have begun venturing beyond the planet of their birth, and recognizing that other planets might well have given birth to other forms with comparable capabilities, interest in the subject has spread considerably. It has even become a matter of some practical importance, since our space probes—or somebody else's—could very well lead to direct contact between us and Someone Else.

Many of the stories in this small sampling of "aliens from *Analog*" are, in one way or another, about contact. The first stories about aliens were contact stories, but they tended pretty uniformly to show contact on one race or the other's home world, ending in a fight for survival and supremacy; Murray Leinster's tale of a meeting in *space*, with a bloodless and mutually beneficial solution to the resulting problems, was a real first. The nocturnal beings in ". . . And Comfort to the Enemy" grew out of John W. Campbell's and my efforts to imagine a civilization founded on such different principles from our own that we would not even recognize it as a civilization until too late; ironically, it now appears, just a few years later, that we may be starting down a similar road ourselves. Katherine MacLean shows how perfectly logical customs of one species may seem shocking and cruel to another whose customs have a different biological basis—and how failure to understand that fact can lead to great harm through the best of intentions. Marc Stiegler uncovers another aspect of such contrasts in his haunting story of urgent cooperation between species radically different not only in the character but in the lengths of their lives.

But contact and its impact on *us* are not the sole interest in these stories; the aliens themselves are as varied and intriguing as their interactions with others. Alison Tellure's entry here (one of an ongoing series of consistently high quality) tackles the daring challenge of telling a story entirely of interaction among truly alien aliens, admitting no human participants or even observers. Some of the beings you'll meet here are as truly foreign as Wink and her God, while others are as kindred spirits as those in "First Contact." Physically, they're as diverse as Paul Ash's "Big Sword" (whose name may be a bit misleading); Fredric Brown's immaterial but hardly ignorable "waveries"; and the Ythrians, Poul Anderson's answer (about which you can read more in his novel *The People of the Wind*) to the challenge of how to make an intelligent winged being that could really exist.

Science fiction writers (and, more recently, scientists) sometimes like to argue about whether alien intelligences, if they exist at all, might not operate in such utterly unexpected ways that we would find them totally incomprehensible. My strong suspicion is that an alien intelligence, like any other process in nature, can be incomprehensible only as long as you don't know the premises and logical principles upon which it is based. Once you understand those, all else follows—*if* you are willing to make the effort to follow the alien logic carefully to its conclusions. Alien as even Alison Tellure's creations are, for example, they make sense when we look at them through their own eyes. (Who knows? With enough such effort, we humans might even learn to understand each other!)

In very recent times, something new has crept into scientific debate about extraterrestrials. Since a good deal of evidence suggests that life and intelligence should arise fairly often, and contact and even travel seem easier than we used to think, *why haven't we heard from anybody yet?* Could it be that we really are alone in the universe, after all? Well, it *could* be—but the case is far from closed, and those scientists who have already assumed that "The Great Silence" means nobody is out there may be jumping the gun. It may very well be that their imaginations have simply been too limited in considering alternative explanations. For a thorough *and* imaginative discussion of how the possibilities look today, you might be interested in David Brin's article on "Xenology," in the May 1983 *Analog*. Brin is both a science fiction writer and an astrophysicist; *Analog,* I can't resist mentioning, is a monthly source of such thought-provoking articles, as well as new stories like these.

My own hunch, even as scientists puzzle over "The Great Silence," is that it would still be most surprising if we were really unique. It will be a long time before we're sure, and as long as there's still evidence to be collected, the possibilities are still out there—and even more diverse than we've yet imagined. Since at least some of them will likely turn out to approximate reality, maybe we'd better keep devoting some of our thought to this kind of speculation. It may be good practice—and it's certainly fun. ■

Stanley Schmidt

FIRST CONTACT

Murray Leinster

I.

TOMMY DORT WENT INTO THE CAPTAIN'S ROOM with his last pair of stereophotos and said:

"I'm through, sir. These are the last two pictures I can take."

He handed over the photographs and looked with professional interest at the visiplates which showed all space outside the ship. Subdued, deep-red lighting indicated the controls and such instruments as the quartermaster on duty needed for navigation of the spaceship *Llanvabon*. There was a deeply cushioned control chair. There was the little gadget of oddly angled mirrors—remote descendant of the back-view mirrors of 20th-century motorists—which allowed a view of all the visiplates without turning the head. And there were the huge plates which were so much more satisfactory for a direct view of space.

The *Llanvabon* was a long way from home. The plates, which showed every star of visual magnitude and could be stepped up to any desired magnification, portrayed stars of every imaginable degree of brilliance, in the startlingly different colors they show outside of atmosphere. But every one was unfamiliar. Only two constellations could be recognized as seen from Earth, and they were shrunken and distorted. The Milky Way seemed vaguely out of place. But even such oddities were minor compared to a sight in the forward plates.

There was a vast, vast mistiness ahead. A luminous mist. It seemed motionless. It took a long time for any appreciable nearing to appear in the vision plates, though the spaceship's velocity indicator showed an incredible speed. The mist was the Crab Nebula, six light-years long, three and a half light-years thick, with outward-reaching members that in the telescopes of Earth gave it some resemblance to the creature for which it was named. It was a cloud of gas, infinitely tenuous, reaching half again as far as from Sol to its nearest neighbor-sun. Deep within it burned two stars, a double star: one component the familiar yellow of the sun of Earth, the other an unholy white.

Tommy Dort said meditatively:

"We're heading into a deep, sir?"

The skipper studied the last two plates of Tommy's taking, and put them aside. He went back to his uneasy contemplation of the vision plates ahead. The *Llanvabon* was decelerating at full force. She was a bare half light-year from the nebula. Tommy's work was guiding the ship's course, now, but the work was done. During all the stay of the exploring ship in the nebula, Tommy Dort would loaf. But he'd more than paid his way so far.

He had just completed a quite unique first—a complete photographic record of the movement of a nebula during a period of four thousand years, taken by one individual with the same apparatus and with control exposures to detect and record any systematic errors. It was an achievement in itself worth the journey from Earth. But in addition, he had also recorded four thousand years of the history of a double star, and four thousand years of the history of a star in the act of degenerating into a white dwarf.

It was not that Tommy Dort was four thousand years old. He was, actually, in his twenties. But the Crab Nebula is four thousand light-years from Earth, and the last two pictures had been taken by light which would not reach Earth until the sixth millennium A.D. On the way here—at speeds incredible multiples of the speed of light—Tommy Dort had recorded each aspect of the nebula by the light which had left it from forty centuries since to a bare six months ago.

The *Llanvabon* bored on through space. Slowly, slowly, slowly, the incredible luminosity crept across the vision plates. It blotted out half the universe from view. Before was glowing mist, and behind was a star-studded emptiness. The mist shut off three-fourths of all the stars. Some few of the brightest shone dimly through it near its edge, but only a few. Then there was only an irregularly shaped patch of darkness astern against which stars shone unwinking. The *Llanvabon* dived into the nebula, and it seemed as if it bored into a tunnel of darkness with walls of shining fog.

Which was exactly what the spaceship was doing. The most distant photographs of all had disclosed structural features in the nebula. It was not amorphous. It had form. As the *Llanvabon* drew nearer, indications of structure grew more distinct, and Tommy Dort had argued for a curved approach for photographic reasons. So the spaceship had come up to the nebula on a vast logarithmic curve, and Tommy had been able to take successive photographs from slightly different angles and get stereo-pairs which showed the nebula in three dimensions; which disclosed billowings and hollows and an actually complicated shape. In places, the nebula displayed convolutions like those of a human brain. It was into one of those hollows that the spaceship now plunged. They had been called "deeps" by analogy with crevasses in the ocean floor. And they promised to be useful.

The skipper relaxed. One of a skipper's functions, nowadays, is to think of things to worry about, and then worry about them. The skipper of the *Llanvabon* was conscientious. Only after a certain instrument remained definitely nonregistering did he ease himself back in his seat.

"It was just barely possible," he said heavily, "that those deeps might be non-luminous gas. But they're empty. So we'll be able to use overdrive as long as we're in them."

It was a light-year and a half from the edge of the nebula to the neighborhood of the double star which was its heart. That was the problem. A nebula is a gas. It is

Murray Leinster

so thin that a comet's tail is solid by comparison, but a ship traveling on overdrive—above the speed of light—does not want to hit even a merely hard vacuum. It needs pure emptiness, such as exists between the stars. But the *Llanvabon* could not do much in this expanse of mist if it was limited to speeds a merely hard vacuum will permit.

The luminosity seemed to close in behind the spaceship, which slowed and slowed and slowed. The overdrive went off with the sudden *pinging* sensation which goes all over a person when the overdrive field is released.

Then, almost instantly, bells burst into clanging, strident uproar all through the ship. Tommy was almost deafened by the alarm bell which rang in the captain's room before the quartermaster shut it off with a flip of his hand. But other bells could be heard ringing throughout the rest of the ship, to be cut off as automatic doors closed one by one.

Tommy Dort stared at the skipper. The skipper's hands clenched. He was up and staring over the quartermaster's shoulder. One indicator was apparently having convulsions. Others strained to record their findings. A spot on the diffusedly bright mistiness of a bow-quartering visiplate grew brighter as the automatic scanner focused on it. That was the direction of the object which had sounded collision-alarm. But the object locator itself— According to its reading, there was one solid object some eighty thousand miles away—an object of no great size. But there was another object whose distance varied from extreme range to zero, and whose size shared its impossible advance and retreat.

"Step up the scanner," snapped the skipper.

The extra-bright spot on the scanner rolled outward, obliterating the undifferentiated image behind it. Magnification increased. But nothing appeared. Absolutely nothing. Yet the radio locator insisted that something monstrous and invisible made lunatic dashes toward the *Llanvabon*, at speeds which inevitably implied collision, and then fled coyly away at the same rate.

The visiplate went up to maximum magnification. Still nothing. The skipper ground his teeth. Tommy Dort said meditatively:

"D'you know, sir, I saw something like this on a liner on the Earth-Mars run once, when we were being located by another ship. Their locator beam was the same frequency as ours, and every time it hit, it registered like something monstrous, and solid."

"That," said the skipper savagely, "is just what's happening now. There's something like a locator beam on us. We're getting that beam and our own echo besides. But the other ship's invisible! Who is out here in an invisible ship with locator devices? Not men, certainly!"

He pressed the button in his sleeve communicator and snapped:

"Action stations! Man all weapons! Condition of extreme alert in all departments immediately!"

His hands closed and unclosed. He stared again at the visiplate which showed nothing but a formless brightness.

"Not men?" Tommy Dort straightened sharply. "You mean—"

"How many solar systems in our galaxy?" demanded the skipper bitterly. "How many planets fit for life? And how many kinds of life could there be? If this ship isn't from Earth—and it isn't—it has a crew that isn't human. And things that aren't human but are up to the level of deep-space travel in their civilization could mean anything!"

The skipper's hands were actually shaking. He would not have talked so freely before a member of his own crew, but Tommy Dort was of the observation staff. And even a skipper whose duties include worrying may sometimes need desperately to unload his worries. Sometimes, too, it helps to think aloud.

"Something like this has been talked about and speculated about for years," he said softly. "Mathematically, it's been an odds-on bet that somewhere in our galaxy there'd be another race with a civilization equal to or further advanced than ours. Nobody could ever guess where or when we'd meet them. But it looks like we've done it now!"

Tommy's eyes were very bright.

"D'you suppose they'll be friendly, sir?"

The skipper glanced at the distance indicator. The phantom object still made its insane, nonexistent swoops toward and away from the *Llanvabon*. The secondary indication of an object at eighty thousand miles stirred ever so slightly.

"It's moving," he said curtly. "Heading for us. Just what we'd do if a strange spaceship appeared in our hunting grounds! Friendly? Maybe! We're going to try to contact them. We have to. But I suspect this is the end of this expedition. Thank God for the blasters!"

The blasters are those beams of ravening destruction which take care of recalcitrant meteorites in a spaceship's course when the deflectors can't handle them. They are not designed as weapons, but they can serve as pretty good ones. They can go into action at five thousand miles, and draw on the entire power output of a whole ship. With automatic aim and a traverse of five degrees, a ship like the *Llanvabon* can come very close to blasting a hole through a small-sized asteroid which gets in its way. But not on overdrive, of course.

Tommy Dort had approached the bow-quartering visiplate. Now he jerked his head around.

"Blasters, sir? What for?"

The skipper grimaced at the empty visiplate.

"Because we don't know what they're like and can't take a chance! I know!" he added bitterly. "We're going to make contacts and try to find out all we can about them—especially where they come from. I suppose we'll try to make friends—but we haven't much chance. We can't trust them the fraction of an inch. We daren't! They've locators. Maybe they've tracers better than any we have. Maybe they could trace us all the way home without our knowing it! We can't risk a nonhuman race knowing where Earth is unless we're sure of them! And how can we be sure? They could come to trade, of course—or they could swoop down on overdrive with a battle fleet that could wipe us out before we knew what happened. We wouldn't know which to expect, or when!"

Tommy's face was startled.

"It's all been thrashed out over and over, in theory," said the skipper. "Nobody's ever been able to find a sound answer, even on paper. But you know, in all their theorizing, no one considered the crazy, rank impossibility of a deep-space contact, with neither side knowing the other's home world! But we've got to find an answer in fact! What are we going to do about them? Maybe these creatures will be aesthetic marvels, nice and friendly and polite—and underneath with the sneaking brutal ferocity of a Japanese. Or maybe they'll be crude and gruff as a Swedish farmer—and just as decent underneath. Maybe they're something in between. But am I going to risk the possible future of the human race on a guess that it's safe to trust them? God knows it would be worth while to make friends with a new civilization! It would be bound to stimulate our own, and maybe we'd gain enormously. But I can't take chances. The one thing I won't risk is having them know how to find Earth! Either I know they can't follow me, or I don't go home! And they'll probably feel the same way!"

He pressed the sleeve-communicator button again.

"Navigation officers, attention! Every star map on this ship is to be prepared for instant destruction. This includes photographs and diagrams from which our course or starting point could be deduced. I want all astronomical data gathered and arranged to be destroyed in a split second, on order. Make it fast and report when ready!"

He released the button. He looked suddenly old. The first contact of humanity with an alien race was a situation which had been foreseen in many fashions, but never one quite so hopeless of solution as this. A solitary Earth-ship and a solitary alien, meeting in a nebula which must be remote from the home planet of each. They might wish peace, but the line of conduct which best prepared a treacherous attach was just the seeming of friendliness. Failure to be suspicious might doom the human race—and a peaceful exchange of the fruits of civilization would be the greatest benefit imaginable. Any mistake would be irreparable, but a failure to be on guard would be fatal.

The captain's room was very, very quiet. The bow-quartering visiplate was filled with the image of a very small section of the nebula. A very small section indeed. It was all diffused, featureless, luminous mist. But suddenly Tommy Dort pointed.

"There, sir!"

There was a small shape in the mist. It was far away. It was a black shape, not polished to mirror-reflection like the hull of the *Llanvabon*. It was bulbous—roughly pear-shaped. There was much thin luminosity between, and no details could be observed, but it was surely no natural object. Then Tommy looked at the distance indicator and said quietly:

"It's headed for us at very high acceleration, sir. The odds are that they're thinking the same thing, sir, that neither of us will dare let the other go home. Do you think they'll try a contact with us, or let loose with their weapons as soon as they're in range?"

II.

The *Llanvabon* was no longer in a crevasse of emptiness in the nebula's thin substance. She swam in luminescence. There were no stars save the two fierce glows in the nebula's heart. There was nothing but an all-enveloping light, curiously like one's imagining of underwater in the tropics of Earth.

The alien ship had made one sign of less than lethal intention. As it drew near the *Llanvabon*, it decelerated. The *Llanvabon* itself had advanced for a meeting and then come to a dead stop. Its movement had been a recognition of the nearness of the other ship. Its pausing was both a friendly sign and a precaution against attack. Relatively still, it could swivel on its own axis to present the least target to a slashing assault, and it would have a longer firing-time than if the two ships flashed past each other at their combined speeds.

The moment of actual approach, however, was tenseness itself. The *Llanvabon*'s needle-pointed bow aimed unwaveringly at the alien bulk. A relay to the captain's room put a key under his hand which would fire the blasters with maximum power. Tommy Dort watched, his brow wrinkled. The aliens must be of a high degree of civilization if they had spaceships, and civilization does not develop without the development of foresight. These aliens must recognize all the implications of this first contact of two civilized races as fully as did the humans on the *Llanvabon*.

The possibility of an enormous spurt in the development of both, by peaceful contact and exchange of their separate technologies, would probably appeal to them as to the man. But when dissimilar human cultures are in contact, one must usually be subordinate or there is war. But subordination between races arising on separate planets could not be peacefully arranged. Men, at least, would never consent to subordination, nor was it likely that any highly developed race would agree. The benefits to be derived from commerce could never make up for a condition of inferiority. Some races—men, perhaps—would prefer commerce to conquest. Perhaps—perhaps!—these aliens would also. But some types even of human beings would have craved red war. If the alien ship now approaching the *Llanvabon* returned to its home base with news of humanity's existence and of ships like the *Llanvabon*, it would give its race the choice of trade or battle. They might want trade, or they might want war. But it takes two to make trade, and only one to make war. They could not be sure of men's peacefulness, nor could men be sure of theirs. The only safety for either civilization would lie in the destruction of one or both of the two ships here and now.

But even victory would not be really enough. Men would need to know where this alien race was to be found, for avoidance if not for battle. They would need to know its weapons, and its resources, and if it could be a menace and how it could be eliminated in case of need. The aliens would feel the same necessities concerning humanity.

So the skipper of the *Llanvabon* did not press the key which might possibly have blasted the other ship to nothingness. He dared not. But he dared not not fire either. Sweat came out on his face.

A speaker muttered. Someone from the range room.

"The other ship's stopped, sir. Quite stationary. Blasters are centered on it, sir."

It was an urging to fire. But the skipper shook his head, to himself. The alien ship was no more than twenty miles away. It was dead-black. Every bit of its exterior was an abysmal, nonreflecting sable. No details could be seen except by minor variations in its outline against the misty nebula.

"It's stopped dead, sir," said another voice. "They've sent a modulated short wave at us, sir. Frequency modulated. Apparently a signal. Not enough power to do any harm."

The skipper said through tight-locked teeth:

"They're doing something now. There's movement on the outside of their hull. Watch what comes out. Put the auxiliary blasters on it."

Something small and round came smoothly out of the oval outline of the black ship. The bulbous hulk moved.

"Moving away, sir," said the speaker. "The object they let out is stationary in the place they've left."

Another voice cut in:

"More frequency modulated stuff, sir. Unintelligible."

Tommy Dort's eyes brightened. The skipper watched the visiplate, with sweat-droplets on his forehead.

"Rather pretty, sir," said Tommy, meditatively. "If they sent anything toward us, it might seem a projectile or a bomb. So they came close, let out a lifeboat, and went away again. They figure we can send a boat or a man to make contact without risking our ship. They must think pretty much as we do."

The skipper said, without moving his eyes from the plate:

"Mr. Dort, would you care to go out and look the thing over? I can't order you, but I need all my operating crew for emergencies. The observation staff—"

"Is expendable. Very well, sir," said Tommy briskly. "I won't take a lifeboat, sir. Just a suit with a drive in it. It's smaller and the arms and legs will look unsuitable for a bomb. I think I should carry a scanner, sir."

The alien ship continued to retreat. Forty, eighty, four hundred miles. It came to a stop and hung there, waiting. Climbing into his atomic-driven spacesuit just within the *Llanvabon*'s air lock, Tommy heard the reports as they went over the speakers throughout the ship. That the other ship had stopped its retreat at four hundred miles was encouraging. It might not have weapons effective at a greater distance than that, and so felt safe. But just as the thought formed itself in his mind, the alien retreated precipitately still farther. Which, as Tommy reflected as he emerged from the lock, might be because the aliens had realized they were giving themselves away, or might be because they wanted to give the impression that they had done so.

He swooped away from the silvery-mirror *Llanvabon*, through a brightly glowing emptiness which was past any previous experience of the human race. Behind him, the *Llanvabon* swung about and darted away. The skipper's voice came in Tommy's helmet phones.

"We're pulling back, too, Mr. Dort. There is a bare possibility that they've some explosive atomic reaction they can't use from their own ship, but which might be destructive even as far as this. We'll draw back. Keep your scanner on the object."

The reasoning was sound, if not very comforting. An explosive which would destroy anything within twenty miles was theoretically possible, but humans didn't have it yet. It was decidedly safest for the *Llanvabon* to draw back.

But Tommy Dort felt very lonely. He sped through emptiness toward the tiny black speck which hung in incredible brightness. The *Llanvabon* vanished. Its polished hull would merge with the glowing mist at a relatively short distance, anyhow. The alien ship was not visible to the naked eye, either. Tommy swam in nothingness, four thousand light-years from home, toward a tiny black spot which was the only solid object to be seen in all of space.

It was a slightly distorted sphere, not much over six feet in diameter. It bounced away when Tommy landed on it, feet-first. There were small tentacles, or horns, which projected in every direction. They looked rather like the detonating horns of a submarine mine, but there was a glint of crystal at the tip-end of each.

"I'm here," said Tommy into his helmet phone.

He caught hold of a horn and drew himself to the object. It was all metal, dead-black. He could feel no texture through his space gloves, of course, but he went over and over it, trying to discover its purpose.

"Deadlock, sir," he said presently. "Nothing to report that the scanner hasn't shown you."

Then, through his suit, he felt vibrations. They translated themselves as clankings. A section of the rounded hull of the object opened out. Two sections. He worked his way around to look in and see the first nonhuman civilized beings that any man had ever looked upon.

But what he saw was simply a flat plate on which dim-red glows crawled here and there in seeming aimlessness. His helmet phones emitted a startled exclamation. The skipper's voice:

"Very good, Mr. Dort. Fix your scanner to look into that plate. They dumped out a robot with an infrared visiplate for communication. Not risking any personnel. Whatever we might do would damage only machinery. Maybe they expect us to bring it on board—and it may have a bomb charge that can be detonated when they're ready to start for home. I'll send a plate to face one of its scanners. You return to the ship."

Murray Leinster

"Yes, sir," said Tommy. "But which way is the ship, sir?"

There were no stars. The nebula obscured them with its light. The only thing visible from the robot was the double star at the nebula's center. Tommy was no longer oriented. He had but one reference point.

"Head straight away from the double star," came the order in his helmet phone. "We'll pick you up."

He passed another lonely figure, a little later, headed for the alien sphere with a vision plate to set up. The two spaceships, each knowing that it dared not risk its own race by the slightest lack of caution, would communicate with each other through this small round robot. Their separate vision systems would enable them to exchange all the information they dared give, while they debated the most practical way of making sure that their own civilization would not be endangered by this first contact with another. The truly most practical method would be the destruction of the other ship in a swift and deadly attack—in self-defense.

III.

The *Llanvabon*, thereafter, was a ship in which there were two separate enterprises on hand at the same time. She had come out from Earth to make close-range observations of the smaller component of the double star at the nebula's center. The nebula itself was the result of the most titanic explosion of which men have any knowledge. The explosion took place some time in the year 2946 B.C., before the first of the seven cities of long-dead Ilium was even thought of. The light of that explosion reached Earth in the year 1054 A.D., and was duly recorded in ecclesiastic annals and somewhat more reliably by Chinese court astronomers. It was bright enough to be seen in daylight for twenty-three successive days. Its light—and it was four thousand light-years away—was brighter than that of Venus.

From these facts, astronomers could calculate nine hundred years later the violence of the detonation. Matter blown away from the center of the explosion would have traveled outward at the rate of two million three hundred thousand miles an hour; more than thirty-eight thousand miles a minute; something over six hundred thirty-eight miles per second. When 20th-century telescopes were turned upon the scene of this vast explosion, only a double star remained—and the nebula. The brighter star of the doublet was almost unique in having so high a surface temperature that it showed no spectrum lines at all. It had a continuous spectrum. Sol's surface temperature is about 7,000° Absolute. That of the hot white star is 500,000°. It has nearly the mass of the Sun, but only one fifth its diameter, so that its density is one hundred seventy-three times that of water, sixteen times that of lead, and eight times that of iridium—the heaviest substance known on Earth. But even this density is not that of a dwarf white star like the companion of Sirius. The white star in the Crab Nebula is an incomplete dwarf; it is a star still in the act of collapsing. Examination—including the survey of a four-thousand-year column of its light—was worth while. The *Llanvabon* had come to make that examination. But the finding of an alien spaceship upon a similar errand had implications which overshadowed the original purpose of the expedition.

A tiny bulbous robot floated in the tenuous nebular gas. The normal operating crew of the *Llanvabon* stood at their posts with a sharp alertness which was productive of tense nerves. The observation staff divided itself, and a part went half-heartedly about the making of the observations for which the *Llanvabon* had come. The other half applied itself to the problem the spaceship offered.

It represented a culture which was up to space travel on an interstellar scale. The explosion of a mere five thousand years since must have blasted every trace of life out of existence in the area now filled by the nebula. So the aliens of the black spaceship came from another solar system. Their trip must have been, like that of the Earth ship, for purely scientific purposes. There was nothing to be extracted from the nebula.

They were, then, at least near the level of human civilization, which meant that they had or could develop arts and articles of commerce which men would want to trade for, in friendship. But they would necessarily realize that the existence and civilization of humanity was a potential menace to their own race. The two races could be friends, but also they could be deadly enemies. Each, even if unwillingly, was a monstrous menace to the other. And the only safe thing to do with a menace is to destroy it.

In the Crab Nebula the problem was acute and immediate. The future relationship of the two races would be settled here and now. If a process for friendship could be established, one race, otherwise doomed, would survive and both would benefit immensely. But that process had to be established, and confidence built up, without the most minute risk of danger from treachery. Confidence would need to be established upon a foundation of necessarily complete distrust. Neither dared return to its own base if the other could do harm to its race. Neither dared risk any of the necessities to trust. The only safe thing for either to do was destroy the other or be destroyed.

But even for war, more was needed than mere destruction of the other. With interstellar traffic, the aliens must have atomic power and some form of overdrive for travel above the speed of light. With radio location and visiplates and short-wave communication they had, of course, many other devices. What weapons did they have? How widely extended was their culture? What were their resources? Could there be a development of trade and friendship, or were the two races so unlike that only war could exist between them? If peace was possible, how could it be begun?

The men on the *Llanvabon* needed facts—and so did the crew of the other ship. They must take back every morsel of information they could. The most important information of all would be of the location of the other civilization, just in case of war. That one bit of information might be the decisive factor in an interstellar war. But other facts would be enormously valuable.

The tragic thing was that there could be no possible information which could lead to peace. Neither ship could stake its own race's existence upon any conviction of the good will or the honor of the other.

So there was a strange truce between the two ships. The alien went about its work of making observations, as did the *Llanvabon*. The tiny robot floated in bright emptiness. A scanner from the *Llanvabon* was focussed upon a vision plate from the alien. A scanner from the alien regarded a vision plate from the *Llanvabon*. Communication began.

It progressed rapidly. Tommy Dort was one of those who made the first progress report. His special task on the expedition was over. He had now been assigned to work on the problem of communication with the alien entities. He went with the ship's solitary psychologist to the captain's room to convey the news of success. The captain's room, as usual, was a place of silence and dull-red indicator lights and great bright visiplates on every wall and on the ceiling.

"We've established fairly satisfactory communication, sir," said the psychologist. He looked tired. His work on the trip was supposed to be that of measuring personal factors of error in the observation staff, for the reduction of all observations to the nearest possible decimal to the absolute. He had been pressed into service for which he was not especially fitted, and it told upon him. "That is, we can say almost anything we wish to them, and can understand what they say in return. But of course we don't know how much of what they say is the truth."

The skipper's eyes turned to Tommy Dort.

"We've hooked up some machinery," said Tommy, "that amounts to a mechanical translator. We have vision plates, of course, and then short-wave beams direct. They use frequency-modulation plus what is probably variation in wave forms—like our vowel and consonant sounds in speech. We've never had any use for anything like that before, so our coils won't handle it, but we've developed a sort of code which isn't the language of either set of us. They shoot over short-wave stuff with frequency-modulation, and we record it as sound. When we shoot it back, it's reconverted into frequency-modulation."

The skipper said, frowning:

"Why wave-form changes in short waves? How do you know?"

"We showed them our recorder in the vision plates, and they showed us theirs. They record the frequency-modulation direct. I think," said Tommy carefully, "they don't use sound at all, even in speech. They've set up a communications room, and we've watched them in the act of communicating with us. They make no perceptible movement of anything that corresponds to a speech organ. Instead of a microphone, they simply stand near something that would work as a pick-up antenna. My guess, sir, is that they use microwaves for what you might call person-to-person conversation. I think they make short-wave trains as we make sounds."

The skipper stared at him:

"That means they have telepathy?"

"M-m-m. Yes, sir," said Tommy. "Also it means that we have telepathy too, as far as they are concerned. They're probably deaf. They've certainly no idea of using sound waves in air for communication. They simply don't use noises for any purpose."

The skipper stored the information away.

"What else?"

"Well, sir," said Tommy doubtfully, "I think we're all set. We agreed on arbitrary symbols for objects, sir, by way of the visiplates, and worked out relationships and verbs and so on with diagrams and pictures. We've a couple of thousand words that have mutual meanings. We set up an analyzer to sort out their short-wave groups, which we feed into a decoding machine. And then the coding end of the machine picks out recordings to make the wave groups we want to send back. When you're ready to talk to the skipper of the other ship, sir, I think we're ready."

"H-m-m. What's your impression of their psychology?" The skipper asked the question of the psychologist.

"I don't know, sir," said the psychologist harassedly. "They seem to be completely direct. But they haven't let slip even a hint of the tenseness we know exists. They act as if they were simply setting up a means of communication for friendly conversation. But there is . . . well . . . an overtone—"

The psychologist was a good man at psychological mensuration, which is a good and useful field. But he was not equipped to analyze a completely alien thought-pattern.

"If I may say so, sir—" said Tommy uncomfortably.

"What?"

"They're oxygen breathers," said Tommy, "and they're not too dissimilar to us in other ways. It seems to me, sir, that parallel evolution has been at work. Perhaps intelligence evolves in parallel lines, just as . . . well . . . basic bodily functions. I mean," he added conscientiously, "any living being of any sort must ingest, metabolize, and excrete. Perhaps any intelligent brain must perceive, apperceive, and find a personal reaction. I'm sure I've detected irony. That implies humor, too. In short, sir, I think they could be likable."

The skipper heaved himself to his feet.

"H-m-m," he said profoundly. "We'll see what they have to say."

He walked to the communications room. The scanner for the vision plate in the robot was in readiness. The skipper walked in front of it. Tommy Dort sat down at the coding machine and tapped at the keys. Highly improbable noises came from it, went into a microphone, and governed the frequency-modulation of a signal sent through space to the other spaceship. Almost instantly the vision screen which with one relay—in the robot—showed the interior of the other ship lighted up. An alien came before the scanner and seemed to look inquisitively out of the plate. He was extraordinarily manlike, but he was not human. The impression he gave was of extreme baldness and a somehow humorous frankness.

"I'd like to say," said the skipper heavily, "the appropriate things about this first contact of two dissimilar civilized races, and of my hopes that a friendly intercourse between the two peoples will result."

Tommy Dort hesitated. Then he shrugged and tapped expertly upon the coder. More improbable noises.

The alien skipper seemed to receive the message. He made a gesture which was wryly assenting. The decoder on the *Llanvabon* hummed to itself and word-cards dropped into the message frame. Tommy said dispassionately:

"He says, sir, 'That is all very well, but is there any way for us to let each other go home alive? I would be happy to hear of such a way if you can contrive one. At the moment it seems to me that one of us must be killed.' "

IV.

The atmosphere was of confusion. There were too many questions to be answered all at once. Nobody could answer any of them. And all of them had to be answered.

The *Llanvabon* could start for home. The alien ship might or might not be able to multiply the speed of light by one more unit than the Earth vessel. If it could, the *Llanvabon* would get close enough to Earth to reveal its destination—and then have to fight. It might or might not win. Even if it did win, the aliens might have a communication system by which the *Llanvabon*'s destination might have been reported to the aliens' home planet before battle was joined. But the *Llanvabon* might lose in such a fight. If she was to be destroyed, it would be better to be destroyed here, without giving any clue to where human beings might be found by a forewarned, forearmed alien battle fleet.

The black ship was in exactly the same predicament. It too could start for home. But the *Llanvabon* might be faster, and an overdrive field can be trailed, if you set to work on it soon enough. The aliens, also, would not know whether the *Llanvabon* could report to its home base without returning. If the alien was to be destroyed, it also would prefer to fight it out here, so that it could not lead a probable enemy to its own civilization.

Neither ship, then, could think of flight. The course of the *Llanvabon* into the nebula might be known to the black ship, but it had been the end of a logarithmic curve, and the aliens could not know its properties. They could not tell from that from what direction the Earth ship had started. As of the moment, then, the two ships were even. But the question was and remained, "What now?"

There was no specific answer. The aliens traded information for information—and did not always realize what information they gave. The humans traded information for information—and Tommy Dort sweated blood in his anxiety not to give any clue to the whereabouts of Earth.

The aliens saw by infrared light, and the vision plates and scanners in the robot communication-exchange had to adapt their respective images up and down an optical octave each, for them to have any meaning at all. It did not occur to the aliens that their eyesight told that their sun was a red dwarf, yielding light of greatest energy just below the part of the spectrum visible to human eyes. But after that fact was realized on the *Llanvabon*, it was realized that the aliens, also, should be able to deduce the Sun's spectral type by the light to which men's eyes were best adapted.

There was a gadget for the recording of short-wave trains which was as casually in use among the aliens as a sound-recorder is among men. The humans wanted that, badly. And the aliens were fascinated by the mystery of sound. They were able to perceive noise, of course, just as a man's palm will perceive infrared light by the sensation of heat it produces, but they could no more differentiate pitch or tone-quality than a man is able to distinguish between two frequencies of heat-radiation even half an octave apart. To them, the human science of sound was a remarkable discovery. They would find uses for noises which humans had never imagined—if they lived.

But that was another question. Neither ship could leave without first destroying the other. But while the flood of information was in passage, neither ship could afford to destroy the other. There was the matter of the outer coloring of the two ships. The *Llanvabon* was mirror-bright exteriorly. The alien ship was dead-black by visible light. It absorbed heat to perfection, and should radiate it away again as readily. But it did not. The black coating was not a "black body" color or lack of color. It was a perfect reflector of certain infrared wave lengths while simultaneously it fluoresced in just those wave bands. In practice, it absorbed the higher frequencies of heat, converted them to lower frequencies it did not radiate—and stayed at the desired temperature even in empty space.

Tommy Dort labored over his task of communications. He found the alien thought-processes not so alien that he could not follow them. The discussion of technics reached the matter of interstellar navigation. A star map was needed to illustrate the process. It would not have been logical to use a star map from the chart room—but from a star map one could guess the point from which the map was projected. Tommy had a map made specially, with imaginary but convincing star images upon it. He translated directions for its use by the coder and decoder. In return, the aliens presented a star map of their own before the visiplate. Copied instantly by photograph, the Nav officer labored over it, trying to figure out from what spot in the galaxy the stars and Milky Way would show at such an angle. It baffled them.

It was Tommy who realized finally that the aliens had made a special star map for their demonstration too, and that it was a mirror-image of the faked map Tommy had shown them previously.

Tommy could grin, at that. He began to like these aliens. They were not human, but they had a very human sense of the ridiculous. In course of time Tommy essayed a mild joke. It had to be translated into code numerals, these into quite cryptic groups of short-wave, frequency-modulated impulses, and these went to the other ship and into heaven knew what to become intelligible. A joke which went through such formalities would not seem likely to be funny. But the aliens did see the point.

There was one of the aliens to whom communication became as normal a function as Tommy's own code-handlings. The two of them developed a quite insane friendship, conversing by coder, decoder, and short-wave trains. When technicalities in the official messages grew too involved, that alien sometimes threw in strictly nontechnical interpolations akin to slang. Often, they cleared up the confusion. Tommy, for no reason whatever, had filed a code-name of "Buck" which the decoder picked out regularly when this particular signed his own symbol to a message.

In the third week of communication, the decoder suddenly presented Tommy with a message in the message frame.

You are a good guy. It is too bad we have to kill each other.—Buck.

Tommy had been thinking much the same thing. He tapped off the rueful reply:

We can't see any way out of it. Can you?

There was a pause, and the message frame filled up again.

If we could believe each other, yes. Our skipper would like it. But we can't believe you, and you can't believe us. We'd trail you home if we got a chance, and you'd trail us. But we feel sorry about it.—Buck.

Tommy Dort took the messages to the skipper.

"Look here, sir!" he said urgently. "These people are almost human, and they're likable cusses."

The skipper was busy about his important task of thinking of things to worry about, and worrying about them. He said tiredly:

"They're oxygen breathers. Their air is twenty-eight percent oxygen instead of twenty, but they could do very well on Earth. It would be a highly desirable conquest for them. And we still don't know what weapons they've got or what they can develop. Would you tell them how to find Earth?"

"N-no," said Tommy, unhappily.

"They probably feel the same way," said the skipper dryly. "And if we did manage to make a friendly contact, how long would it stay friendly? If their weapons were inferior to ours, they'd feel that for their own safety they had to improve them. And we, knowing they were planning to revolt, would crush them while we could—for our own safety! If it happened to be the other way about, they'd have to smash us before we could catch up to them."

Tommy was silent, but he moved restlessly.

"If we smash this black ship and get home," said the skipper, "Earth Government will be annoyed if we don't tell them where it came from. But what can we do? We'll be lucky enough to get back alive with our warning. It isn't possible to get out of those creatures any more information than we give them, and we surely won't give them our address! We've run into them by accident. Maybe—if we smash this ship—there won't be another contact for thousands of years. And it's a pity, because trade could mean so much! But it takes two to make a peace, and we can't risk trusting them. The only answer is to kill them if we can, and if we can't, to make sure that when they kill us they'll find out nothing that will lead them to Earth. I don't like it," added the skipper tiredly, "but there simply isn't anything else to do!"

V.

On the *Llanvabon*, the technicians worked frantically in two divisions. One prepared for victory, and the other for defeat. The ones working for victory could do little. The main blasters were the only weapons with any promise. Their mountings were cautiously altered so that they were no longer fixed nearly dead ahead, with only a 5° traverse. Electronic controls which followed a radio-locator master-finder would keep them trained with absolute precision upon a given target regardless of its maneuverings. More, a hitherto unsung genius in the engine room devised a capacity-storage system by which the normal full-output of the ship's engines could be momentarily accumulated and released in surges of stored power far above normal. In theory, the range of the blasters should be multiplied and their destructive power considerably stepped up. But there was not much more that could be done.

The defeat crew had more leeway. Star charts, navigational instruments carrying telltale notations, the photographic record Tommy Dort had made on the six-months' journey from Earth, and every other memorandum offering clues to Earth's position, were prepared for destruction. They were put in sealed files, and if any one of them was opened by one who did not know the exact, complicated process, the contents of all the files would flash into ashes and the ash be churned past any hope of restoration. Of course, if the *Llanvabon* should be victorious, a carefully not-indicated method of reopening them in safety would remain.

There were atomic bombs placed all over the hull of the ship. If its human crew should be killed without complete destruction of the ship, the atomic-power bombs should detonate if the *Llanvabon* was brought alongside the alien vessel. There were no ready-made atomic bombs on board, but there were small spare atomic-power units on board. It was not hard to trick them so that, when they were turned on, instead of yielding a smooth flow of power, they would explode. And four men of the Earth ship's crew remained always in spacesuits with closed helmets, to fight for the ship should it be punctured in many compartments by an unwarned attack.

Such an attack, however, would not be treacherous. The alien skipper had spoken frankly. His manner was that of one who wryly admits the uselessness of lies. The skipper and the *Llanvabon*, in turn, heavily admitted the virtue of frankness. Each insisted—perhaps truthfully—that he wished for friendship between the two races. But neither could trust the other not to make every conceivable effort to find out the one thing he needed most desperately to conceal—the location of his home planet. And neither dared believe that the other was unable to trail him and find out. Because each felt it his own duty to accomplish that unbearable—to the other—act, neither could risk the possible existence of his race by trusting the other. They must fight because they could not do anything else.

They could raise the stakes of the battle by an exchange of information beforehand.

Murray Leinster

But there was a limit to the stake either would put up. No information on weapons, population, or resources would be given by either. Not even the distance of their home bases from the Crab Nebula would be told. They exchanged information, to be sure, but they knew a battle to the death must follow, and each strove to represent his own civilization as powerful enough to give pause to the other's ideas of possible conquest—and thereby increased its appearance of menace to the other, and made battle more unavoidable.

It was curious how completely such alien brains could mesh, however. Tommy Dort, sweating over the coding and decoding machines, found a personal equation emerging from the at first stilted arrays of word-cards which arranged themselves. He had seen the aliens only in the vision screen, and then only in light at least one octave removed from the light they saw by. They, in turn, saw him very strangely, by transposed illumination from what to them would be the far ultraviolet. But their brains worked alike. Amazingly alike. Tommy Dort felt an actual sympathy and even something close to friendship for the gill-breathing, bald, and dryly ironic creatures of the black space vessel.

Because of that mental kinship he set up—though hopelessly—a sort of table of the aspects of the problem before them. He did not believe that the aliens had any instinctive desire to destroy man. In fact, the study of communications from the aliens had produced on the *Llanvabon* a feeling of tolerance not unlike that between enemy soldiers during a truce on Earth. The men felt no enmity, and probably neither did the aliens. But they had to kill or be killed for strictly logical reasons.

Tommy's table was specific. He made a list of objectives the men must try to achieve, in the order of their importance. The first was the carrying back of news of the existence of the alien culture. The second was the location of that alien culture in the galaxy. The third was the carrying back of as much information as possible about that culture. The third was being worked on, but the second was probably impossible. The first—and all—would depend on the result of the fight which must take place.

The aliens' objectives would be exactly similar, so that the men must prevent, first, news of the existence of Earth's culture from being taken back by the aliens, second, alien discovery of the location of Earth, and third, the acquiring by the aliens of information which would help them or encourage them to attack humanity. And again the third was in train, and the second was probably taken care of, and the first must await the battle.

There was no possible way to avoid the grim necessity of the destruction of the black ship. The aliens would see no solution to their problems but the destruction of the *Llanvabon*. But Tommy Dort, regarding his tabulation ruefully, realized that even complete victory would not be a perfect solution. The ideal would be for the *Llanvabon* to take back the alien ship for study. Nothing less would be a complete attainment of the third objective. But Tommy realized that he hated the idea of so complete a victory, even if it could be accomplished. He would hate the idea of killing even nonhuman creatures who understood a human joke. And beyond that, he would hate the idea of Earth fitting out a fleet of fighting ships to destroy an alien culture because its existence was dangerous. The pure accident of this encounter, between peoples who could like each other, had created a situation which could only result in wholesale destruction.

Tommy Dort soured on his own brain, which could find no answer which would work. But there had to be an answer! The gamble was too big! It was too absurd that two spaceships should fight—neither one primarily designed for fighting—so that the survivor could carry back news which would set one case to frenzied preparation for war against the unwarned other.

If both races could be warned, though, and each knew that the other did not want to fight, and if they could communicate with each other but not locate each other until some grounds for mutual trust could be reached—

It was impossible. It was chimerical. It was a daydream. It was nonsense. But it was such luring nonsense that Tommy Dort ruefully put it into the coder to his gill-breathing friend Buck, then some hundred thousand miles off in the misty brightness of the nebula.

"Sure," said Buck, in the decoder's word-cards flicking into place in the message frame. "That is a good dream. But I like you and still won't believe you. If I said that first, you would like me but not believe me either. I tell you the truth more than you believe, and maybe you tell me the truth more than I believe. But there is no way to know. I am sorry."

Tommy Dort stared gloomily at the message. He felt a very horrible sense of responsibility. Everyone did, on the *Llanvabon*. If they failed in this encounter, the human race would run a very good chance of being exterminated in time to come. If they succeeded, the race of the aliens would be the one to face destruction, most likely. Millions or billions of lives hung upon the actions of a few men.

Then Tommy Dort saw the answer.

It would be amazingly simple, if it worked. At worst it might give a partial victory to humanity and the *Llanvabon*. He sat quite still, not daring to move lest he break the chain of thought that followed the first tenuous idea. He went over and over it, excitedly finding objections here and meeting them, and overcoming impossibilities there. It was the answer! He felt sure of it.

He felt almost dizzy with relief when he found his way to the captain's room and asked leave to speak.

It is the function of a skipper, among others, to find things to worry about. But the *Llanvabon*'s skipper did not have to look. In the three weeks and four days since the first contact with the alien black ship, the skipper's face had grown lined and old. He had not only the *Llanvabon* to worry about. He had all of humanity.

"Sir," said Tommy Dort, his mouth rather dry because of his enormous earnestness, "may I offer a method of attack on the black ship? I'll undertake it myself, sir, and if it doesn't work our ship won't be weakened."

The skipper looked at him unseeingly.

"The tactics are all worked out. Mr. Dort," he said heavily. "They're being cut on tape now, for the ship's handling. It's a terrible gamble, but it has to be done."

"I think," said Tommy carefully, "I've worked out a way to take the gamble out. Suppose, sir, we send a message to the other ship, offering—"

His voice went on in the utterly quiet captain's room, with the visiplates showing only a vast mistiness outside and the two fiercely burning stars in the nebula's heart.

VI.

The skipper himself went through the air lock with Tommy. For one reason, the action Tommy had suggested would need his authority behind it. For another, the skipper had worried more intensively than anybody else on the *Llanvabon*, and he was tired of it. If he went with Tommy, he would do the thing himself, and if he failed he would be the first one killed—and the taps for the Earth ship's maneuvering was already fed into the control board and correlated with the master-timer. If Tommy and the skipper were killed, a single control pushed home would throw the *Llanvabon* into the most furious possible all-out attack, which would end in the complete destruction of one ship or the other—or both. So the skipper was not deserting his post.

The outer air lock door swung wide. It opened upon that shining emptiness which was the nebula. Twenty miles away, the little round robot hung in space, drifting in an incredible orbit about the twin central suns, and floating ever nearer and nearer. It would never reach either of them, of course. The white star alone was so much hotter than Earth's sun that its heat-effect would produce Earth's temperature on an object five times as far from it as Neptune is from Sol. Even removed to the distance of Pluto, the little robot would be raised to cherry-red heat by the blazing white dwarf. And it could not possibly approach to the ninety-odd million miles which is the Earth's distance from the sun. So near, its metal would melt and boil away as vapor. But, half a light-year out, the bulbous object bobbed in emptiness.

The two spacesuited figures soared away from the *Llanvabon*. The small atomic drives which made them minute spaceships on their own had been subtly altered, but the change did not interfere with their functioning. They headed for the communication robot. The skipper, out in space, said gruffly:

"Mr. Dort, all my life I have longed for adventure. This is the first time I could ever justify it to myself."

His voice came through Tommy's space-phone receivers. Tommy wetted his lips and said:

"It doesn't seem like adventure to me, sir. I want terribly for the plan to go through. I thought adventure was when you didn't care."

"Oh, no," said the skipper. "Adventure is when you toss your life on the scales of chance and wait for the pointer to stop."

They reached the round object. They clung to its short, scanner-tipped horns.

"Intelligent, those creatures," said the skipper heavily. "They must want desperately to see more of our ship than the communications room, to agree to this exchange of visits before the fight."

"Yes, sir," said Tommy. But privately, he suspected that Buck—his gill-breathing friend—would like to see him in the flesh before one or both of them died. And it seemed to him that between the two ships had grown up an odd tradition of courtesy, like that between two ancient knights before a tourney, when they admired each other wholeheartedly before hacking at each other with all the contents of their respective armories.

They waited.

Then, out of the mist, came two other figures. The alien spacesuits were also power-driven. The aliens themselves were shorter than men, and their helmet openings were coated with a filtering material to cut off visible and ultraviolet rays which to them would be lethal. It was not possible to see more than the outline of the heads within.

Tommy's helmet phone said, from the communications room on the *Llanvabon*:

"They say that their ship is waiting for you, sir. The airlock door will be open."

The skipper's voice said heavily:

"Mr. Dort, have you seen their spacesuits before? If so, are you sure they're not carrying anything extra, such as bombs?"

"Yes, sir," said Tommy. "We've showed each other our space equipment. They've nothing but regular stuff in view, sir."

The skipper made a gesture to the two aliens. He and Tommy Dort plunged on for the black vessel. They could not make out the ship very clearly with the naked eye, but directions for change of course came from the communication room.

The black ship loomed up. It was huge, as long as the *Llanvabon* and vastly thicker. The air lock did stand open. The two spacesuited men moved in and anchored themselves with magnetic-soled boots. The outer door closed. There was a rush of air and simultaneously the sharp quick tug of artificial gravity. Then the inner door opened.

All was darkness. Tommy switched on his helmet light at the same instant as the skipper. Since the aliens saw by infrared, a white light would have been intolerable to them. The man's helmet lights were, therefore, of the deep-red tint used to illuminate instrument panels so there will be no dazzling of eyes that must be able to detect the minutest specks of white light on a navigating vision plate. There were aliens waiting to receive them. They blinked at the brightness of the helmet lights. The space-phone receivers said in Tommy's ear:

"They say, sir, their skipper is waiting for you."

Tommy and the skipper were in a long corridor with a soft flooring underfoot. Their lights showed details of which every one was exotic.

"I think I'll crack my helmet, sir," said Tommy.

He did. The air was good. By analysis it was thirty percent oxygen instead of twenty for normal air on Earth, but the pressure was less. It felt just right. The artificial gravity, too, was less than that maintained on the *Llanvabon*. The home planet of the aliens would be smaller than Earth, and—by the infrared data—circling close to a nearly dead, dull-red sun. The air had smells in it. They were utterly strange, but not unpleasant.

An arched opening. A ramp with the same soft stuff underfoot. Lights which actually shed a dim, dull-red glow about. The aliens had stepped up some of their illuminating equipment as an act of courtesy. The light might hurt their eyes, but it was a gesture of consideration which made Tommy even more anxious for his plan to go through.

The alien skipper faced them, with what seemed to Tommy a gesture of wryly humorous deprecation. The helmet phones said:

"He says, sir, that he greets you with pleasure, but he has been able to think of only one way in which the problem created by the meeting of these two ships can be solved."

"He means a fight," said the skipper. "Tell him I'm here to offer another choice."

The *Llanvabon*'s skipper and the skipper of the alien ship were face to face, but their communication was weirdly indirect. The aliens used no sound in communication. Their talk, in fact, took place on microwaves and approximated telepathy. But they could not hear, in any ordinary sense of the word, so the skipper's and Tommy's speech approached telepathy, too, as far as they were concerned. When the skipper spoke, his space phone sent his words back to the *Llanvabon*, where the words were fed into the coder and short-wave equivalents sent back to the black ship. The alien skipper's reply went to the *Llanvabon* and through the decoder, and was retransmitted by space phone in words read from the message frame. It was awkward, but it worked.

The short and stocky alien skipper paused. The helmet phones relayed his translated, soundless reply.

"He is anxious to hear, sir."

The skipper took off his helmet. He put his hands at his belt in a belligerent pose.

"Look here!" he said truculently to the bald, strange creature in the unearthly red glow before him. "It looks like we have to fight and one batch of us get killed. We're ready to do it if we have to. But if you win, we've got it fixed so you'll never find out where Earth is, and there's a good chance we'll get you anyhow! If we win, we'll be in the same fix. And if we win and go back home, our government will fit out a fleet and start hunting your planet. And if we find it we'll be ready to blast it to hell! If you win, the same thing will happen to us! And it's all foolishness! We've stayed here a month, and we've swapped information, and we don't hate each other. There's no reason for us to fight except for the rest of our respective races!"

The skipper stopped for breath, scowling. Tommy Dort inconspicuously put his own hands on the belt of his spacesuit. He waited, hoping desperately that the trick would work.

"He says, sir," reported the helmet phones, "that all you say is true. But that his race has to be protected, just as you feel that yours must be."

"Naturally!" said the skipper angrily, "but the sensible thing to do is to figure out how to protect it! Putting its future up as a gamble in a fight is not sensible. Our races have to be warned of each other's existence. That's true. But each should have proof that the other doesn't want to fight, but wants to be friendly. And we shouldn't be able to find each other, but we should be able to communicate with each other to work out grounds for a common trust. If our governments want to be fools, let them! But we should give them the chance to make friends, instead of starting a space war out of mutual funk!"

Briefly, the space sphone said:

"He says that the difficulty is that of trusting each other now. With the possible existence of his race at stake, he cannot take any chance, and neither can you, of yielding an advantage."

"But my race," boomed the skipper, glaring at the alien captain, "my race has an advantage now. We came here to your ship in atom-powered spacesuits! Before we left, we altered the drives! We can set off ten pounds of sensitized fuel apiece, right here in this ship, or it can be set off by remote control from our ship! It will be rather remarkable if your fuel store doesn't blow up with us! In other words, if you don't accept my proposal for a commonsense approach to this predicament, Dort and I blow up in an atomic explosion, and your ship will be wrecked if not destroyed—and the *Llanvabon* will be attacking with everything it's got within two seconds after the blast goes off!"

The captain's room of the alien ship was a strange scene, with its dull-red illumination and the strange, bald, gill-breathing aliens watching the skipper and waiting for the inaudible translation of the harangue they could not hear. But a sudden tensity appeared in the air. A sharp, savage feeling of strain. The alien skipper made a gesture. The helmet phones hummed.

"He says, sir, what is your proposal?"

"Swap ships!" roared the skipper. "Swap ships and go on home! We can fix our instruments so they'll do no trailing, he can do the same with his. We'll each remove our star maps and records. We'll each dismantle our weapons. The air will serve, and we'll take their ship and they'll take ours, and neither one can harm or trail the other, and each will carry home more information than can be taken otherwise! We can agree on this same Crab Nebula as a rendezvous when the double-star has made another circuit, and if our people want to meet them they can do it, and if they are scared they can duck it! That's my proposal! And he'll take it, or Dort and I blow up their ship and the *Llanvabon* blasts what's left!"

He glared about him while he waited for the translation to reach the tense small stocky figures about him. He could tell when it came because the tenseness changed. The figures stirred. They made gestures. One of them made convulsive movements. It lay down on the soft floor and kicked. Others leaned against its walls and shook.

The voice in Tommy Dort's helmet phones had been strictly crisp and professional, before, but now it sounded blankly amazed.

Murray Leinster

"He says, sir, that it is a good joke. Because the two crew members he sent to our ship, and that you passed on the way, have their spacesuits stuffed with atomic explosive too, sir, and he intended to make the very same offer and threat! Of course he accepts, sir. Your ship is worth more to him than his own, and his is worth more to you than the *Llanvabon*. It appears, sir, to be a deal."

Then Tommy Dort realized what the convulsive movements of the aliens were. They were laughter.

It wasn't quite as simple as the skipper had outlined it. The actual working-out of the proposal was complicated. For three days the crews of the two ships were intermingled, the aliens learning the workings of the *Llanvabon*'s engines, and the men learning the controls of the black spaceship. It was a good joke—but it wasn't all a joke. There were men on the black ship, and aliens on the *Llanvabon*, ready at an instant's notice to blow up the vessels in question. And they would have done it in case of need, for which reason the need did not appear. But it was, actually, a better arrangement to have two expeditions return to two civilizations, under the current arrangement, than for either to return alone.

There were differences, though. There was some dispute about the removal of records. In most cases the dispute was settled by the destruction of the records. There was more trouble caused by the *Llanvabon*'s books, and the alien equivalent of a ship's library, containing works which approximated the novels of Earth. But those items were valuable to possible friendship, because they would show the two cultures, each to the other, from the viewpoint of normal citizens and without propaganda.

But nerves were tense during those three days. Aliens unloaded and inspected the foodstuffs intended for the men on the black ship. Men transshipped the foodstuffs the aliens would need to return to their home. There were endless details, from the exchange of lighting equipment to suit the eyesight of the exchanging crews, to a final check-up of apparatus. A joint inspection party of both races verified that all detector devices had been smashed but not removed, so that they could not be used for trailing and had not been smuggled away. And of course, the aliens were anxious not to leave any useful weapon on the black ship, nor the men upon the *Llanvabon*. It was a curious fact that each crew was best qualified to take exactly the measures which made an evasion of the agreement impossible.

There was a final conference before the two ships parted, back in the communication room of the *Llanvabon*.

"Tell the little runt," rumbled the *Llanvabon*'s former skipper, "that he's got a good ship and he'd better treat her right."

The message frame flicked wordcards into position.

"I believe," it said on the alien skipper's behalf, "that your ship is just as good. I will hope to meet you here when the double star has turned one turn."

The last man left the *Llanvabon*. It moved away into the misty nebula before they had returned to the black ship. The vision plates in that vessel had been altered for human eyes, and human crewmen watched jealously for any trace of their former ship as their new craft took a crazy, evading course to a remote part of the nebula. It came to a crevasse of nothingness, leading to the stars. It rose swiftly to clear space. There was the instant of breathlessness which the overdrive field produces as it goes on and then the black ship whipped away into the void at many times the speed of light.

Many days later, the skipper saw Tommy Dort poring over one of the strange objects which were the equivalent of books. It was fascinating to puzzle over. The skipper was pleased with himself. The technicians of the *Llanvabon*'s former crew were finding out desirable things about the ship almost momently. Doubtless the aliens were as pleased with their discoveries in the *Llanvabon*. But the black ship would be enormously worth while—and the solution that had been found was by any standard much superior even to a combat in which the Earthmen had been overwhelmingly victorious.

"Hm-m-m. Mr. Dort," said the skipper profoundly. "You've no equipment to make another photographic record on the way back. It was left on the *Llanvabon*. But fortunately, we have your record taken on the way out, and I shall report most favorably on your suggestion and your assistance in carrying it out. I think very well of you, sir."

"Thank you, sir," said Tommy Dort.

He waited. The skipper cleared his throat.

"You . . . ah . . . first realized the close similarity of mental processes between the aliens and ourselves," he observed. "What do you think of the prospects of a friendly arrangement if we keep a rendezvous with them at the nebula as agreed?"

"Oh, we'll get along all right, sir," said Tommy. "We've got a good start toward friendship. After all, since they see by infrared, the planets they'd want to make use of wouldn't suit us. There's no reason why we shouldn't get along. We're almost alike in psychology."

"Hm-m-m. Now just what do you mean by that?" demanded the skipper.

"Why, they're just like us, sir!" said Tommy. "Of course they breathe through gills and they see by heat waves, and their blood has a copper base instead of iron and a few little details like that. But otherwise we're just alike! There were only men in their crew, sir, but they have two sexes as we have, and they have families, and . . . er . . . their sense of humor— In fact—"

Tommy hesitated.

"Go on, sir," said the skipper.

"Well— There was the one I called Buck, sir, because he hasn't any name that goes into sound waves," said Tommy. "We got along very well. I'd really call him my friend, sir. And we were together for a couple of hours just before the two ships separated and we'd nothing in particular to do. So I became convinced that humans and aliens are bound to be good friends if they have only half a chance. You see, sir, we spent those two hours telling dirty jokes." ■

Murray Leinster

GREEN-EYED LADY

Alison Tellure

". . . THUS YD WILLS, THUS Yd commands, thus let it be."

The hymn ended. Young Green-Eyed She, Wink to her friends, slowly let her long-held violet note fade. No priestess or soloist, the merest novice, she nonetheless took pride in her ability to emit the precise frequency of God in the holy refrain, and to maintain it with never a waver; she found a satisfaction in the skill with which she disappeared into the anonymity of the chorus. Red-Footed He was not the only friend who tuned from her spectrum, when Choirmaster wasn't looking.

A sparkling and twinkling erupted in the night, from the shadowed lawn below the City of God—the populace praising the singers, and adding their devout "amens." Wink's eyestalks stretched yearningly toward the Holy Water, peering out over that place, barely discernible in the gathering dusk, where bulked what might have been a small island. But if God had seen the hymn, Yd gave no sign.

Choirmaster dimmed until he radiated only in the infrared, but for a dull, gray-yellow pulse that rippled across his abdomen: a disappointed sigh. He quickly blanked it, and blinked a curt dismissal at his young protégés.

Matins over, they scattered to begin the long night's activities, claws clattering over limestone, blipping and glimmering idle chatter. Wink found Red at her shoulder.

"Have you seen the latest rumor?" His eyestalks extended suggestively.

"No, nor do I wish to, lazy hatchling," she replied virtuously, in disapproving blues and grays. "Have you nothing better to do than to spy upon peripheral reflections?"—That is, unreliable communications.

"Not a thing!" Red twinkled cheerfully, his habitual good humor unruffled. "Watch: there's to be a shake-up in the Servants' Corps." '

She flashed him a disgusted greenish-yellow smudge.

"Feh? . . . Always there are such rumors! Your brain must be even smaller than I have always suspected it to be. The rumors grow to brilliance, the novices waste their time jostling one another when they could be studying, and then the rumor fades away into the sensible darkness of nightly life, leaving only frustrations and broken friendships for its beacon. And why any novice ever expects the theoretical vacancies to be filled from *our* ranks, rather than from the Fishers, whom God knows have earned it, is beyond me."

"Well, naturally everyone dreams of avoiding the hazards of Fishing, and wants to skip right up to Servant status. Hope springs eternal in the mortal thorax, however irrational," he admitted in a sheepish sine wave down his middle. "Still, I saw this from a good authority: Sweetscales saw it direct from The Gimp, who happened to glimpse two Elders talking about it."

"Dim your nonsense, naming people!" she sparked tightly. "An Elder may be watching us even now!"

He reduced his intensity but slightly, an indifferent concession. "So? Let him, her, or yd watch. Want to see something else?"

"No."

"Gimp also says—" he began.

She rolled her eyes—a complex gesture, with eyestalks—then shrugged her carapace and laughed, staccato orange and silver rays fountaining outward from her braincase to disappear around behind her.

"Oh well! I can perceive that you won't be happy until you've shown me everything you know about anything, so go on; I have a few moments."

He snapped an impudent claw beneath her jaws, but returned to his gossip with relish. "The Gimp says that this time they really are going to throw out some Servants, maybe as many as seven or eight. And there really is a possibility that they won't replace them with Fishers, at least not all of them. Yd says that God's long absence from our songs and ceremonies has so alarmed the priests and Elders that they are beginning to wonder whether the current Servants have offended Yd in some way, or even whether perhaps the entire system needs a change. There were hints of an experiment. And look, everyone knows that something happens to the Fishers, out there in the wilderness. Only some of them are elevated by the experience, or unchanged. Many return . . . altered, unfit to resume life in the City of God, unfit for anything but Fishing, in fact. So why couldn't that rumored experiment be that the Elders intend to try putting novices in as Servants?"

"Your path of logic crosses deep chasms of wishful thinking, Red," she chuckled. "As for me, I look forward to my tour of duty as a Fisher."

"Yah, even if it makes you a savage?" he challenged, fringing affectionate magenta spiral patterns with jeering yellow filaments.

"What could be more devout and blessed than to spend one's life feeding God?" Wink rejoined, in pious purples and greens.

"To spend it serving Yd in comfort, right here in the City of God!"

Wink only laughed, and kept her reservations private.

But, three nights later, it was Wink herself whom a Servant of God stopped, as she creaked down the muddy path to the Lake to make a small votive offering.

"Are you Green-Eyed She?" flashed the Servant.

"Yes, honored one," Wink glimmered, almost invisibly.

"Follow me. And turn up your brights; I am getting old and can no longer see certain frequencies as well as once I could," he brusquely ordered, and turned to scuttle up a branching path with a celerity that belied his age.

Wink said, faintly, "Yes, sir! I mean, YES, SIR!"

"You needn't light up the City, hatchling, I'm not that blind yet! . . . Not yet too blind to talk, not yet so blind as to throw myself into Holy Water for God to eat, no, by God, not yet!" Wink realized he was glimmering to himself, and wisely kept dark.

For the first time in her life, she found herself inside the great stone temple that incorporated the original pier built by the Founders in ancient days. The blank, empty thoracic shells of long-ago Supreme Hierophants lined the walls leading to this most holy of sacrificial altars, standing sentinel over the ages. But the elderly Servant ushered her off into a side chamber and through a maze of passageways ending in—Wink gave one swift green blink of surprise, hastily mantled—the High Priest's office.

"This is the she," said her guide, who turned and clittered back the way they'd come.

The venerable priest looked her over for some moments in lightlessness, stalks twitching meditatively.

"Well, you are Green-Eyed She, called, I believe, Wink," he began, finally. "Choirmaster speaks well of you, praising the purity and clarity of your spectrum. He has ventured the opinion that with accelerated training, you could achieve a certain virtuosity in very fine discrimination of wavelengths. —Well, and what have you to say to that?"

"That—that I am honored by the Choirmaster, and hope to earn his words." Wink was completely taken aback by this unprecedented interview.

"I also see from your broodfoster Longstalks that you seemed to have a true and early vocation to the Service; and everyone to whom I have spoken assures me that you are not, unlike so many others, in it for the cushy berths that may be had if one survives the risks of Fishing. Eh? Are you a gambler? Do you like to see and reflect rumors about novices skipping up directly into Service? Eh?"

Wink went deep burnt sienna from embarrassment. Obviously someone had observed and reported the conversation with Red. "No, honored one. I saw such an idea once, true, but paid it no thought. And I certainly didn't reflect it on! I do not seek to avoid my duty as a Fisher. Rather, I conceive it to be an honor. One knows that all Servants of God have truly earned the privileges they enjoy, for they have all been Fishers. If a novice were to become a Servant without having first been a Fisher, the respect for the entire Service would soon decline."

The old he chuckled, little silvery sparks shivering over his carapace. "Your words look very much like ones I saw yesternight, in a very long, actinic argument. Well, we shall leave that, for the moment.

"Now I shall put you through your catechism.

"Who is God?"

The sudden switch nearly caught Wink off guard.

"God is Yd Who created world and sky, both the stars that sing and the sun that chastises, and Who fashioned mortals out of the mud and reeds of the shore of Holy Water; eternal, all wise, all powerful, all good."

"What is the purpose of life?"

"To serve God."

"Where do we go when we die?"

"Into the mud and water of Holy Lake, whence we came, for the greater glory of God, who hungers for our sake."

"If God knows no gender as mortals know it, why do we call God Yd?"

"Because Yd nurtures us, Yd's mortal hatchlings."

"Who is the Evil One?"

"The Enemy of all life, who in the beginning of time sent devil slaves against the Favored People of God; but God strengthened them and aided their counsels, and wrestled with the demons, and vanquished the Evil One."

"That's enough. All very correct. Now, what if I were to tell you that all of those things are false, that Yd created neither world nor sky, nor fashioned mortals out of mud or anything else, nor is eternal, all-wise, all-powerful, all-good; and the purpose of life is merely to live and grow and change; and while we do indeed go into Holy Lake to be consumed by God when we die, it is more to ease the burden on the Corps of Fishers than for anyone's glory; and Yd had made only one offspring in Yd's life, and that one died; and though God may once have tricked a few of the Evil One's underlings, Yd certainly never vanquished the Evil One, who is not the enemy of any *land-locked* life."

Wind had gone black with shock. "But who would dare blaspheme so—?"

"God dares."

It was nearly dawn before she lurched from the temple, dazed and quivering. Nor did she hurry to reach the cool safety of her broodhome, but trudged slowly, ruminating. Even when the eastern sky began to whiten and blaze, still she remained more absorbed in the equally blasting illumination within. Only when a fearful, sickly-green alarm blared in her eyes did she realize how late it was. Her broodfoster had come out searching for her, and now yd hustled her along, rattling with anxiety, and blinking and scolding all the way. They kept their eyes curled down below their ventral flanges, hunched against the rising sun.

After reaching the thick rock shelter of the warren, and after escaping her foster's worried lecture, she fled deep into the convoluted passageways, to her own solitary little niche—granted her upon her acceptance into the novitiate. Here she could know peace. . . .

No. Nor ever again.

For how could she have peace when the High Priest had destroyed the foundations of her universe, even as his own had been destroyed—by God Ydself—some night before?

". . . For God's recent indifference to us had been a matter of grave concern for some time," old Mottling Quickly Changing had told her, when she had partially recuperated from her first shock and bewilderment. "And the highest among us went to the altar and called out to Yd. But Yd saw us not, or refused to see. Then I ordered out the vessel, and taking two others with me to bear witness—and to row—I went in search of God, far out onto the dark waters of the Lake. Then God arose, and I quailed before Yd's vast majesty, and Yd said, 'What would you of me, little hatchling?' And I gathered my wits, and said, 'Your children desire to know by what cause you are wroth with them, and what it is they must do to regain your grace.' And God said, 'Behold, I am not wroth, but deep in thought, for the time approaches for many changes and great events.' Then Yd put me through *my* catechism, as I did you; and Yd told me—Yd showed me—wonders—terrors—and—and we rowed back, my priests and I, that black, starless night, blinded by the light."

"What did Yd tell you—?" she had dared to ask.

"I think I will let Yd tell you all about it, Ydself."

She, she was to see God, to speak to Yd, to watch Yd's slow, divine words with her own eyes! She, Wink!

"—Why *me?*" she had shimmered desperately.

"It is God's will that one go who is young, healthy, strong—that rules out most of the Servants—skilled in communication, skilled in song, whole, sound of mind—that rules out an unfortunately large percentage of Fishers and former Fishers, Servants or not—and especially one who is patient, openminded, not overly inculcated with the truisms of our society, intuitive, imaginative, and exceedingly intelligent. That rules out most of the general populace; besides, we deem it advisable to keep these new ideas within the Service, for the time being. We also add our own requirements that the candidate have a good citizenship record and a firm understanding of the concept of duty. I made inquiries among the Corps of Priests and the Corps of Broodmasters, seeking names; yours appeared most often.

"As for your entering the ranks of the Servants, it is well known that only a Servant of God may speak and understand the special words of God, is it not? You will take up your new duties as soon as you can complete the special training."

". . . Let it be as you will it, honored one," she glimmered softly. "But am I then never to become a Fisher?"

"You had truly anticipated that?"

"I had awaited it, not with pleasure, perhaps, but with . . . curiosity."

He contemplated her a moment. "The ascetic in you, no doubt. This will be an adventure far greater."

God spoke not as mortals spoke. Who could guess how the divine might meditate within itself upon the universe, or might—staggering thought—commune with other entities of its own kind? For the puny understanding of mortals, however, God had created a light-emitting organ of Yd's own holy flesh, not one that worked as mortals' did, but one large, and slow, and simple, and stilted in its expression, as befitted the stately dignity of a God.

Because of its limitations—which God had deliberately designed in as a rebuke to the pride of his people, of course—in both spectrum and subtlety of expressible forms, its codings differed not only from those of the language of the Favored People but from those of all the languages of all the other tribes they had ever conquered, converted, or otherwise made contact with. This holy coding system must each novice study, commit to memory, before he or she (never yd) could hope for advancement. Often, the candidates lost much of this knowledge during their years Fishing for God, and needs must relearn it all upon their return to the City. Periodically, over the generations, hierophantic administrators had attempted to abolish this apparently inefficient system, and, for example, send out untutored novices into the wilderness when much younger, and only begin teaching them after they had fulfilled this portion of their duty. But invariably the experiment had failed. The younger ones lacked the mature vigor needed to withstand the solitary vigils in the wild, and an ex-Fisher usually proved incapable of grasping any complex intangible concept unless he or she had already absorbed the root and essence of the idea. Therefore, the pre-adult years must span a very broad base of an eclectic eduction, only roughly sketched in; any subject of lore which might prove of use someday must be begun then.

Now the repetitious, numerical, arbitrary symbolisms of the language of God became Wink's life. Fortunately, she did not have to learn to speak it herself, since God (naturally) understood the thoughts of mortals even before they became visible; but she had to learn to understand Yd when Yd spoke. She awoke in the evening with a Servant standing over her sand pit, flashing phrases in the measured cadence of divine speech, and translating them with a brief coruscation in the common talk. She ate with the lessons still before her. She performed her devotions at the side of a translator-teacher, who herself was temporarily excused from all other duties. She eliminated her wastes, groomed her carapace and segmented limbs, deposited her as-yet-unformed and non-viable eggs in the loamy area set aside for that purpose, and digested her food with them always beaming at her, in relays. And when she shut her weary eyes in the morning to sleep, still her mind's vision saw them and sought to read them: the eternal *umber, rose, bone, umber, bone, rose, rose, umber, rose, bone* . . . the everlasting *three, two, two, three, one, three, three, four, one, three, two, four, four* . . . the unceasing *up-blurred, up-sharp, left-blurred, down-blurred, right-sharp, down-sharp* . . . the interminable and incoherent *four right-sharp rose, two left-blurred umber, one down-blurred bone.* . . .

They had moved her from her broodfoster's den into the cold stone temple. The halls thronged with other students, acolytes, and votaries; but Wink was alone, pursuing her own unique, intensive, single-minded course, living in her own private chamber, small though it was. Sometimes she yearned to escape, to clatter back to old Longstalks's apartments as fast as her six legs would carry her, to renounce the Service, to be free to joke once more with Red and the Gimp and her other friends.

Then the passion of her vocation would possess her once again. *Three left-sharp bone. . . .*

She had to abandon all her other interests. Not only did she now live in isolation from her broodmates and comrades, in itself a great psychological hardship, but even found herself forced to neglect any intellectual pursuit that did not pertain directly to her assignment of communicating with God. The High Priest could not contain his impatience with her progress, though he could not in justice fault her in comparison with what any other individual might have accomplished in the same time. But he had devoted his life to the service of God, and it grated upon him that he could not immediately provide an acolyte perfectly tailored to Yd's request.

Wink watched her childhood vanish behind her in mere days, rather than in the years she should yet have had; she watched the prospect of a normal young maturity snatched forever from her.

She did her best to keep her inner vision firmly fixed upon the High Priest's words: *". . . an adventure far greater . . ."*

The last lingering rays of light faded from the east; the stars emerged in their uncounted choral swarms, singing their high, exalted, celestial, incomprehensible song.

Slowly, Wink emerged from her dark chamber and made her way through the twisting corridors to the great cool nave. Her claws clicked on the wet flagstones and echoed against the walls as she marched down to the altar. The Servants of God awaited her there, lucent, shimmering—singing hymns, praying.

She passed them and clambered down from the altar—the dock—to the little row-boat, where already sat her two rowers, younger acolytes dark with awe. These knew no God-talk. The wooden blades dipped.

Far out onto the black water, they shipped oars. The boat bobbed. There was no sign of God. On the distant shore, the temple loomed dark; the priests had ended their rituals.

Wink resolutely kept her emotions from showing on her shell, took up her courage, and sang out God's holy name, the long purple glow, with an upper harmonic in the ultraviolet. The waters of the lake accepted it, spread it. . . .

. . . Minutes passed. Wink saw and heard nothing. She maintained the call and her prayerful state of mind. Slowly the uncomfortable certainty grew that she was being watched. Her eyestalks swiveled in all directions. Nothing. Still she gleamed in the upper frequencies, but she was beginning to dim; the strain was beginning to tell.

Suddenly it seemed that Holy Water itself chuckled—a radiating dazzle of silvery sparks expanded in concentric bands, from a point directly below the boat. Then —without Wink's having caught its approach—she found herself staring straight into a huge yellow eye, not a pincer-length away from her own green one. Another eye rose out of the water on the other side of the boat—this one was blue—and gave her its thorough attention.

Now—in the light of her own fading note—she could see beneath and surrounding her small vessel a bulk of something huge and dark. A roughly circular patch of it began to glow in the all-too-familiar rose and bone and umber, but refraction at the surface broke up the message. Timidly she dipped an eye into the water.

". . . they have chosen to send me. Welcome to my domain, small hatchling."

The mass of God fell away into the lightless depths on all sides.

Wink went utterly blank. All her coaching momentarily fled.

"Fear not. Take all time needed. My life is long." Again, pale glints of humor accompanied the statement.

At that, her wits returned.

"I abase myself before your almighty divinity," she said, as it had been drilled into her. "I present myself to the will of God."

"Your name is—?"

"I am called Green-Eyed She, Supremely Holy."

"Then, Green-Eyed She, my will is that you not so diminish your valuable self. . . . How much have they told you? Do you know what your work is to be? Has anyone said that God has blasphemed? . . . Feel free to interrupt at any time; I know that I speak too slowly for you little twinkly scooters."

Wink flashed black and orange in rapid succession, astonished and nonplussed. "The High Servant has told me that you have said many of our beliefs are not—are not quite—as we have believed. He said you wanted a young person to talk to, that none of the old Servants would do. They taught me the divine speech as swiftly as my poor weak mind was able to learn it. Now I am here, though I am still learning."

"I rather suspect they harried you, though they need not have. One of your brief generations more or less means little to me.

"Now I will clarify matters somewhat. I want you to be my messenger to your people. I wanted someone young, someone new, because I have noticed that your people have difficulty learning anything strange to them once they have passed the middle of their lives. I wanted someone intelligent because much of what I must tell you will be difficult to understand, and you must be able to explain it to even the most backward of your people in a way they can accept. And I wanted an artistic singer because I enjoy watching your songs and productions. I am often lonely and part of your duty will be to entertain me.

"These are the rules: Most of the time, I will speak, you will watch. But because I speak so awkwardly, you have my permission to flash in whenever you please; you can squeeze whole codas of reply between two of my words. And if you can guess what I am about to say, show me. I will tell you whether you are right and when you are, we can go on to the next thing. That will save some time, don't you agree?"

"Agree? Of course, God. Let it be as God wills."

"That reminds me: this God business. I suppose your High Priest told you about all that?"

"That you had said—strange and wondrous things, yes."

"Here is truth: I am not God, at least, not in the sense of a creator and regulator of matter and life, or even of the ways of natural phenomena in the world. I control nothing and have made little. Old as I am, I am but a hatchling compared to the youngest of those mountains yonder. Strong as I am, I quail before the sun even as you do, and I can no longer heave myself very far out of the water. Yet large as I am, I would be but a morsel to one who is my enemy, who dwells in the Greater Ocean."

"The Evil One," she said, taking Yd at Yd's word and interrupting.

"Yes. And yd *is* evil; that much of your faith is true. Later we will speak more, much more, of yd; now you are still relearning your concepts of myself.

"I rule your people only because you permit me to do so. Yet you gain from it also; my wisdom and—shall we say—impressive appearance—has enabled your tribe to expand its territory and rise above all other groups of your kind. My gain is that without the assistance of your society I could not long live."

Wink went black.

"Oh, do calm yourself. It is quite true. I eat a great deal. The Lake is not quite big enough to provide for all my needs. Without the labor of your Fishers—well, perhaps I would not starve; I could always reduce. But I have reached a point now where I can diminish no further in size without sacrificing some of my intellect, and I'd rather not. Yet often I have wondered how you could afford to support me."

"But, God! You are the source of all knowledge, all the arts of civilization, all supremacy in intertribal statecraft, all power—"

"Well, good. I suppose I've paid my way. But, little Green-Eyes, I thought you now understood I am no god."

"But what then am I to call you?"

". . . I hadn't thought of that. You may still refer to me as God, if you wish, to your companions, if you feel that would be politic. But within yourself you must not so think of me. Think of me, rather, as—oh, the Prisoner of the Lake. Or, perhaps, your Biggest Audience. Or, Yd Who Waits.

"Or you could call me by my real name, the one given me of old by my friends, my own kind, my long-mourned people."

"And what was that, great one?" she shone softly, suddenly awash with compassion for the divinity.

"Skysinger."

". . . Among my companions, in our own means of communication, I was accounted something of an artist/poet. And I it was who invented eyes and first discovered the glory of the stars. Thus, Skysinger. Of course, in the language of light, I have a serious speech impediment, hence this clumsy code you have striven so diligently to learn; I know I am no singer to you. Still, it would please me. . . ."

"Then I shall make so bold as to call you . . . Skysinger," she answered diffidently.

"Thank you. It has been long and long since I have had a friend to call me a friend's name.

"Now I will tell you how my people died."

Once upon a time, during the hatchling stage of the world, there lived a Giant Sea Monster. Now, this monster was the very first and only one of its kind, so it had no broodfoster yd to take care of it and love it. And everyone knows that when a hatchling grows up without an yd's fostering love, it turns out not to be a very nice person at all; and so it was with this monster.

It was neither he nor she nor yd, yet somehow all three, so it made a child all by itself. But it did not love its child, for it had never learned how; and it sent the hatchling away into exile.

But the child grew and also made children, and being somewhat foolish (by monster standards) made several of them more or less at once, and these smaller ones grew up with one another to love and enjoy, so they were different from their parent and their parent's parent. Now these new creatures—we will not call them monsters—talked and swam and explored the seas and played with thoughts and made children and enjoyed the world, until one night they realized food was getting scarcer and scarcer, and they discovered that Child—the second monster, you know—had gotten far too big and was eating far too much. They tried to show it the error of its ways, but despite its size and years it had remained rather stupid. Until it could no longer ignore the obvious; and it tried to invade the Greater Ocean where dwelt the Eldest, the First One. But that monster was prepared with many little slave-monsters, strong fighters, and together, they killed the great Child.

This left the other creatures with no immediate problems and they went about their business, though some of them wondered uneasily about the personality of their mysterious neighbor, who never came forth to join their community.

Millennia later, their bad dreams came true, and the monster attacked. First it secretly poisoned two of their kind, to gain what vantage it could; then it gathered up its warriors and invaded. The creatures had always known peace, and had no idea how to fight. They had no natural enemies in all the seas, for they were too big, too strong. . . .

No more. The monster killed them all.

All but one, who had explored far up a river in its younger nights, and who dwelt at this time in a broad Upland Lake. Now this one managed to trick the slaves of the monster into believing they had killed it, and so they reported.

Now the creature in the lake would have been very lonely and unhappy indeed, had it not the friendship of a swarm of tiny little beings who lived in the rocks around the lake, who had helped it immeasurably in driving off the fighters. It knew these little beasts for intelligent beings, though they spoke not as its own people had, and it thought that perhaps in them it had found that which might in the fullness of time be forged into a weapon capable of taking final vengeance upon the monster. For if its

Alison Tellure

little friends ever advanced to the point where they wished to sail the seas to other lands, they themselves would have the monster to contend with. So it counselled them, and they increased, and they and the creature both waxed mighty together in strength and wisdom, over the long years of the wheeling stars.

Any questions?

"It is a most peculiar experience, to hear the articles of one's faith so retold, twisted and altered, and made to appear as the myths of outland barbarian tribes, who have no real god to show."

"I hope you are not too deeply troubled, Little Green-Eyes."

"No . . . I don't *think* I am. In some ways, I feel—relief!" A pop of greenstreaked orange; surprised realization. "This story makes better sense then the old ones did, in places."

"Good. It is nearly dawn, little morsel. You had better get back home. I am sorry it takes me so long to say anything.—Oh! One more thing. My first new order to your people: Tell them to begin breeding for long and flexible mouthparts. I'll have something for them to do, generations from now, besides eat."

". . . Eh?!" A cloudy spiral of gray.

"Your pincer-claws are admirably suited for certain tasks, and indeed you can do amazingly fine work with them; I am often consumed with admiration for the offerings your artisans show me. Yet—they aren't quite fine enough for certain things I have in mind. I've thought about it and it seems to me the mouth-parts are the only appendages with any potential."

"But—but God—Skysinger—Great One—how can we 'breed for' any quality?"

"Oh, yes, you are rather hit-or-miss about passing on the genetic information, are you not. It has at least kept you adaptable. Tell me, your shes compete among themselves for the softest, sandiest places to lay their eggs, true? Would it be considered a privilege to lay them on the beaches of Holy Water?"

"Of course! But the priests do not allow it. They have always feared there would be such a stampede that the shores would soon become roiled and fouled, which would be displeasing to God."

"Tell them to build a fence around a large section of the beach, and put guards at the gate. Then let in only those shes with the longest and most supple mouth parts. When they have deposited their eggs and departed, let in only those hes with the same characteristics, to fertilize them. Then permit only the noblest and most successful and most loving yds to gather up the ripened clutches from that special beach, to brood them.

"Let it be known among all the tribes over which your tribe has jurisdiction, that God values such mouth-parts. They will soon work out a similar system on their own.

"And let it be known that the hes who hatch from these special eggs will have special procreative privileges—well, time enough for that a generation from now.

"Just tell them about the fence and the beach, Morsel. And hurry along; light touches the tops of the distant eastern hills."

Her rowers were already pulling for all they were worth.

Night followed night in an unending procession of beauty and delight, and every one filled Wink's young mind with a maelstrom of wonder, for Skysinger, even in yd's halting coded speech, spun such visions for her as to dazzle her inner eyes. Yd had personally witnessed all of mortal history, and recounted for her eyes the glories of the past, making legends live. And on other nights, yd sang of heroic deeds yet to come.

". . . great vessels of wood, with a thousand rowers . . . or perhaps—have you ever watched the skydwellers, sailing on the air? Perhaps a thousand thousand of them could be tamed and harnessed. . . ."

Or again, yd would delve into yd's own history.

"Among my kind, intelligence was directly related to size. That is one of the reasons I fear the Evil One, for yd must be unimaginably huge by now, and therefore clever beyond understanding. And that is why I puzzled for so many centuries over how you tiny things could have intelligence; yet you obviously did. Finally I realized that you had almost as many brain-cells as I, perhaps, but the cells themselves were extraordinarily small. With that hint, I solved the quandary that had long vexed me, how to increase my own intelligence without growing too large for the Lake to support. I began experiments to mutate the motherkind of which I am composed, for smaller and smaller units. It only took a few millennia. I would guess I am now about as intelligent as one of my kind eleven or twelve times my size. Whether that will be enough to out-think and defeat the Enemy, I know not."

Or yd would tell her of the many discoveries yd had made over the long centuries of solitary observation and meditation.

"The stars do indeed form a pattern, one that seems to you ephemeral creatures to be solid and unchanging. But I have lived long enough to watch some of them slowly drift across the silence. See that bright red one? No, there: the one caught in the yellow-white net of other stars. Yes. Well, I remember when it wasn't in that net; it used to be paired with the blue one to the left. And those very bright white ones in a line used to form a triangle. I've thought about it and it seems to me that some stars must be *closer* to us than others, and they move relative to one another; and that is why some of them appear to me to sail across the face of the sparkling blackness."

"Then—the sky is not the great carapace of your first High Priest, standing sentinel over the vault of the world, sending us messages of divine wisdom from the inside of its shell, which we are too stupid and corrupted to read?"

"Of course not! Childish nonsense!"

"And it is not the hollowed-out broodwarren of the world, with airvents to a greater outside world to let light in and smoke out?"

Alison Tellure

"No. Intriguing image, but I doubt it."

"Then what is it, O Skysinger the Wise?" She had progressed in her confidence with yd to such a degree that she felt almost safe in expressing a little teasing challenge now and then.

"Well—I have wondered whether perhaps the sky—is not simply sky, whether it is not air that just goes on forever. Still, there are reasons why that theory doesn't quite fit, either. . . ."

"And the stars are but another species of skydweller?"

"Oh, no. They're—at least, I *suspect* they are something quite different."

"Well, then?"

"You'll laugh at me if I tell you."

"I shall not!" Wink replied indignantly.

"You will, though."

"How would I dare?! Please tell me."

"I suspect the stars are really suns, like ours, only so remote that—"

She laughed at yd.

But some nights Skysinger seemed melancholy and weary of speaking, and then Wink sang for yd. In the course of time she went through her entire repertoire of hymns; and when yd demanded more, she hesitantly shone some of the secular folksongs of her people, with many apologies for their imperfections and unworthiness. But yd loved them, of course. Eventually, she ran out even of these. She began to compose her own, but soon discovered that the Muse does not always mass-produce upon demand. The priests sent out novices as runners to all the tribes of the Known World, to gather songs and stories for God. Thus began something of a classical fluorescence. . . .

And on some nights Skysinger and Wink simply chatted together, philosophizing, gossiping, speculating.

"If *you* are not God," Wink asked abruptly, once, "who *is?*"

They worked away at that one (always an entertaining question whenever and wherever it arises), off and on, for countless nights.

And so the nights passed, and the dawns intruded, sending them to their respective nests, she to sleep and dream, yd to ponder and reflect in lonely silence. The nights curled by like the stars, all alike, each unique. . . .

". . . I may be late tomorrow-eve, Skysinger, with your permission. A desire has taken me to speak and play once more with my broodmates and friends. I have hardly seen them for—oh, quite a long time," Wink said vaguely.

"Naturally you may do as you please. You ought not to permit me to take up so much of your life, Morsel."

"But I so enjoy our grand communions, Skysinger, my big old friend," she gently replied. "There is really no-one I would rather talk to than my poor old Prisoner of the Lake."

Next twilight she left the massive white temple through the mighty portals rather than through the pier-altar. The ways of the City of God seemed unusually crowded with jostling strangers; yet always a passage opened up before her as if a great invisible claw had brushed the people aside. As she made her way through the nighted streets—brilliantly lit by a thousand babbling conversations—a wave of gleaming purple seemed to spread before her, followed by a wave of lightlessness and blank dark carapaces. The shadows returned to the streets.

"What word bring you from God, Great Lady?" flashed out one on the edge of the crowd.

She courteously turned both eyestalks toward him. "Only that Yd is pleased with all the labors of Yd's people," she replied, benignly lavender.

Bright white lights erupted around her: huzzahs.

Wink clambered up the ancient trail to the cave where she'd been hatched and raised.

"Longstalks—! It's Wink! I'm home for a visit, but I can't stay long."

A small, glittering, clattering swarm of hatchlings swept past her and scuttled away. The largest of them came but up to her penultimate segment. Silver sparks shivered over her abdomen, in fond nostalgia.

"Longst—?" She brought up sharply. A young yd unknown to her occupied Longstalk's chamber. The brood scrambled around yd, sparkling for attention. "Who are you? Where is Longstalks?"

The young yd hunkered down, scooting backwards and lowering yd's eyes several inches in superstitious awe.

"I am Ringtail Puce." Yd seemed unwilling or unable to venture further.

"Great Lady." A reflection off the ceiling, coming from the mouth of the chamber, caught her attention; she swiveled an eye.

"Gimp!"

"I can answer your questions, Great Lady," yd continued soberly. "They beamed to me that you had come into the City."

They trudged in darkness through the tunnels to Gimp's quarters nearby.

"May I ask the Great Lady where her guards are?"

"Guards—? Do drop the Great Lady nonsense, Gimp; we're alone now."

"Nonsense, Great Lady?"

"You know me, Gimp; I'm only Wink."

"As you say, Great Lady."

With a mental sigh, Wink decided to let it pass. After all, one could not expect towering intellect from an yd.

"Where is Longstalks?"

"Longstalks has passed into Holy Water for the glory of God."

Dead—! Wink went black and lowered her upper body to the floor.

". . . When?"

"Twenty-eight nights ago."

"Why was I not told? *Why was I not told?"* she blazed.

"You were communing with God, Great Lady. Who would dare to interrupt?"

Who indeed? Her shell creaked; but the emotion remained locked inside, dark.

". . . Yd was very old," Gimp offered.

"I know, but. . . ."

"Yd was only an yd," yd replied.

"Yd was my broodfoster!"

"As you say, Great Lady."

Time passed in wordless darkness.

"Well. I'll mourn later. I have a halfnight break and I must use it well. Where are Red and Sweetscales and Smoothly and the rest of the old swarm? Take me to them; I would see foolish jests and insults once again."

"Smoothly the Rotund He has gone missioning to a new tribe dwelling beyond the Melancholy Mountains. Sweetscaled She has left the Service and joined the Corps of Warriors. And Red-Footed He has been a Fisher these three years and more. I cannot take you to any of them, Great Lady."

"Three—" *Years? Three years?* Had she been gone so long?

"Yes, Great Lady, I know that three years is longer than the normal tour of duty for a Fisher. But it is as he wishes it. He is one of those whom the life of the wilderness has claimed, and now he cannot bear to live in the City of God."

She went to the Lake not at all that night; nor the next, nor the next. She remained in her guarded temple chambers—how long had those guards been there? who had ordered them to guard her?—and grieved. By the twilight of the third night the shock had passed and she could think cogently once more.

She had been "communing with God"—and with no-one else—for over four years. She had never noticed the time passing. She felt she had lived a hundred lifetimes of scholarly acquisition of knowledge, and she did not grudge it—but she had lost so much! Track of the time, her religion, her old broodfoster, her broodmates and friends; and her proper, normal niche is her society. . . .

All I ever wanted was to live in the City of God and sing in the choir, she thought. *I only wanted the natural honors due a Servant, not to be a—a Great Lady, for God's sake!*

Yes. For God's sake. For Skysinger's sake.

And in the time she had remained absorbed, her dear broodfoster had died—for the glory of God; and Red—

He never wanted to be a Fisher at all! He feared it so! Now he had succumbed to the mysterious lure that marked so many of those with a vocation to the Service, the "savagery" he had so condemned.

How had she permitted her life to go off on such a tangent? What else had occurred while her attention had fixed so steadily upon Skysinger? Who were all those crowds of strangers? Why were her chambers guarded? (Had there been a slight tinge of sarcasm beneath Gimp's dutiful blandness? "Where are your guards, Great Lady?" "I cannot take you to them, Great Lady.") Well, she knew where to start peering out the answers. She might as well make use of the privileges she had apparently acquired. She marched from her room.

"Guard!" she flashed. "Fetch me—" She broke off and stared. The cavernous interior of the temple had become a bedlam of stroboscopic color. Priests and other Servants scurried about, slipping and iridescing frantically. For a big blue eye just about filled the arched portal over the pier, and a long questing pseudopod of colorless ropy muscle was worming its way hither and thither over the stone floor, dripping mud and frondy weeds, pushing into side-passages, probing. . . .

Oh yes. She'd dared absent herself for two, going on three, nights, and without sending any word.

"*You* I'll get to *later*," she blitzed at Skysinger. "Guard, fetch me the High Priest!" But the young he only continued to goggle at the manifestation above the altar, his eyestalks quivering.

The manifestation blinked twice at Wink's peremptory remark, than narrowed dangerously. But the tentacle ceased its wanderings and retracted, carefully backing out the way it had come, bowling over only a few more Servants in the process. Then the eye itself gradually withdrew, finally to sink into the Lake, staring at her all the while.

"Well?" Her right middle foot tapped. The guard scurried off.

Old Mottling Swiftly Changing greeted her with, "What have you brought down upon us? God is angered! We are doomed!"

"Dim that! We're nothing of the kind. I have questions."

So. She felt used. She felt a fool—twice a fool. While Skysinger had assumed the center and become the purpose of her existence—despite yd's constant protestations to the contrary, yd had always made yd's expectations felt—the orthodox priests had taken steps to defend against what they saw as a threat to their status. They had created for her a special title—one separate from the standard hierarchy—and isolated her from the populace. The guards allegedly were necessary to protect her from the demands of the importunate rabble; idle gawkers and tourists, the priests had characterized them. In fact, she suspected, her escort had probably often "protected" her from seeing old friends and people with legitimate business or with requests she would have been glad to undertake. (What harm could lie in taking prayers to Skysinger? God though yd may not be, still yd had vast wisdom.) They had kept her ignorant of events on the ground that she who communed with God ought not soil her semi-divine mind with such mundane, trifling matters. The Servants had always carried out God's commands, relayed by her, with the same pious alacrity with which their predecessors had done so throughout innumerable centuries; but they had usually managed to twist them subtly to their own advantage. For example, most of the skittering throngs out there were outlander males and females, come on pilgrimage to the City of God, in hopes of gaining entrance to God's Beach to deposit and fertilize

Alison Tellure

eggs, and of acquiring *mana* thereby. But since their clutches would be brooded by the local yds, it meant an ever-escalating concentration of the desired characteristic here in the City of God—and under the effective control of the priesthood. Had Skysinger intended this? She doubted it. It seemed to her that quite often yd evinced insufficient concern about all the ramifications and effects of yd's schemes. How much did yd really care about her people? Or was yd so consumed by yd's obsession with vengeance that none of the secondary consequences mattered to yd at all?

But first she must deal with immediacies.

"You were right about one thing, venerable one," she told the priest wryly. "When I am communing with God my mind is so free of common, trifling thoughts that I completely lose contact with mundane reality."

"It is good that your ladyship is pleased with her prodigious evolution," said Mottling Quickly Changing.

"I am *not* pleased," she flared. "Nor have I evolved, prodigiously or any other way. I have simply lost track of the time. Henceforth, priest, you will make it your business to see to it that I have time to live my real life every now and then. And let there be regular times when the people may come to see me!

"And send all those people back home! Tell them to breed on their own beaches, according to the word of God. Do not seek to molt so swiftly into a shell too large for you, old priest!"

"You forget yourself, Green-Eyed She." Dull red lightnings flickered around his words. "You forget to whom you speak."

"*You* forget to whom *you* speak. You saw God at the Gate. Yd was looking for me . . . not in anger, but in anxiety, for when Yd saw me, Yd returned peacefully into the Lake. Consider what Yd might have done had Yd *not* seen me, had Yd, for example, conceived that, for some reason, I was being kept from Yd. Consider that, and keep that image firmly in mind. Now, do you remember the blasphemous words of God, that you told me of four years ago when I was but a novice? Or have you managed to shut your inner eyes against their light entirely? For *I* remember them.

"And now consider what would happen if the populace happened to glimpse such words. How long would they continue to support and obey the Servants of God—if God is not God? How long would the outlying tribes and clans of tribes continue to submit to the domination of the City of God and its priest, if our visible, tangible god is proven no less false than their invisible, insubstantial ones, who never accept the challenge to contest for supremacy? They would say, 'Of course our gods would not accept a challenge from a mortal creature, no matter how gargantuan and great.'

"So consider carefully both of those things. And know this also." She softened the harshness of her colors. "I am no enemy to you. All in all, I appreciate my life quite as much as you do yours. While a few small things must change, those things I have mentioned, I would grieve to alter it to any large degree. I do not want your office, or any other. I believe that the City of God should continue to rule the tribes of mortals and the Servants of God should continue to rule the City, for it has always been so, and it is right. *But if I do not get my way,* there will begin to appear in the City glimmerings of dangerous reflections!"

"Great Lady, the words of her who communes with God are always observed with boundless reverence, and it is the privilege of the devout to obey them."

"That's the spirit."

Skysinger offered obstacles of a different nature.

"Where were you, Morsel? I feared something had befallen you."

"Something had—four years had passed in but a handful of days! How could you have done this to me? Did it never occur to you that I might have a life of my own to tend? Ever you claim we are friend and friend, but you treat me as a god would treat a votary."

"Little Green-Eyes, you show me nonsense. Many and many a time have I told you to do as pleased you, to live your life as you would, to give me only such time as you might without hardship; for I have lived many long millennia before you came, small one, and I shall continue to live many long centuries after you go, and my patience is vaster than my body, deeper than my lake."

"Oh, indeed, such were your hues and shapes; but your thoughts were far other. And how can a poor small mortal mind venture so close to the thought of a god without perceiving it, without bending before its strength? No, the truth is, you have dealt with me as you have dealt with my people: you have captured us, and tamed us, and forged us into that which we were not, and made tools of us, weapons for your coming war of vengeance against the Evil One.

"Who *is* the Evil One, O Skysinger, Prisoner of the Lake?"

"You know that," replied Skysinger, surprised. "I have told you that story many times."

"But I am only a mortal hatchling, Great One, and my understanding is small. Please tell me who is the Evil One."

Yd sensed a trap, of course, but decided Yd might as well feed her the lines she wanted, anyway.

"Yd is my ancient enemy, First One, Lord of Mother Sea."

"And what makes yd evil?"

"That, too, I have explained. Yd is so because—"

"I mean, *how* is yd evil? What characteristic is it that designates yd as such?"

Skysinger heaved a windy sigh; big bubbles drifted up and burst upon the surface for several dozen square meters around the boat.

"That yd destroyed those whom I loved, that yd will destroy any sapient life form other than itself, including yours; that yd cannot brook *otherness,* much less competition; that yd cannot perceive the equal reality and validity of any other entity; that yd cannot therefore understand the pain of another; that yd seeks only yd's own ends. This latter is, perhaps, the natural goal of all beings, and is not evil in an absolute sense; but it certainly makes yd uncomfortable to share a planet with."

Alison Tellure

"And whose ends do you seek, Skysinger?"

Yd had seen it coming. "My own, Morsel, and, *and*"—Yd increased brightness in order to override her attempted interruption—"I honestly believe I seek the ends of nature, of evolution if you will. (You recall what I have said of my observations of the way creature-kinds grow and change and die, just as individual beings do.) In making this alliance with your small kind, I have established your supremacy over all the world—not only merely over other tribes of your species, but over all living things on the planet. No, Morsel, not yet, perhaps, in fact; I realize that. You are still simple and weak, and have yet to extend your hegemony over all the ways of the world, and the life therein, and the very elements themselves. But that night will come, countless generations hence, Green Eyes, when this one small world will fail to contain you. I can see it as clearly as I see the stars. *If.* If you can destroy First One in the meantime. By yourselves, you cannot do it. Without my counsel, you may perhaps eventually, slowly, have begun to venture out upon the face of Mother Sea in vessels, millennia from now—and First One would become aware of you, and would inevitably put an end to you, and yd would remain lord of all yd surveys until sky and world end. With my assistance, you might possibly have a chance. And who better to ally with you in that cause than I? Am I not the Enemy's enemy? Yet by myself, I have no better chance than you.

"Since this war, one way or another, is inevitable, ought we not to devise the best odds for ourselves that we can muster? I do not guarantee our success, even as allies; but together we have the greatest hope."

"And what of my people, in the meanwhile?" Wink flared out. "In our unnumbered thousands since the beginning of time we have shaped and constrained our lives to fit your huge designs. We have worshipped you as God, and what other nameless gods may have gone unworshipped for that reason? What of my friend Red-Footed He, who has fallen into the trap he feared, and reverted to savagery in your service? What of those weary hundreds of outlanders who made a pilgrimage of who knows what trials and privations, because the priests chose to skew slightly their interpretation of a divine whim, and because you concerned yourself not with its consequences? And what, O Skysinger, of *me?* While I have conversed with you upon subjects great and petty, while I have soothed your moods and tempers with my songs, while I have thought how to please you and given no thought to anything else—all my friends have died, or gone, or changed. Gleam not to me of sky-high speculation and epic adventures I will never live to see! Even as you have no-one else to call you by a friend's name, so there is now no-one left to call me Wink!"

Yd's coded pulsing slowed and a rosy aura suffused even yd's bone-and-sienna symbols. "With your permission, then, small one, I shall use and preserve that name of friendship . . . if you accord me the name of friend?"

Wink admitted defeat at last. "You know, Skysinger, that it is my everlasting honor that you have chosen to share with me some small portion of your thoughts, just as if we were really equals. If you grant me friendship, can I do less? But surely in your wisdom you understand that no matter how high a grace it may be to see my name in your colors, still I miss the same name in the old familiar spectra of my lost comrades."

To her surprise, and indignation, silver laughter rippled beneath the waves.

"What a species I have undertaken to raise! Wink, try not to keep your inner eyes squeezed so tightly closed. Open them now and look at your thoughts; is your sorrow a soul-hunger or only a petulant melancholy?" When she remained dark yd continued. "I know your people better than you know yourselves; I have had hundreds of generations to observe you; you, Morsel, have had but the first part of a single lifetime. And I have observed that only yds truly love; the most profound attachment a he or a she can feel is a kind of shellbound sentimentalism. I have thought about it and it seems to me that it is because the hes and shes never touch; only the yds touch. The yds devote their lives to caring for people; the hes and shes devote themselves solely to abstract concepts, ideals, group-identities. This trait promises well for you in the time to come, in the plans I have for you; but do not try to dazzle me with the glare of your profound yearning for your friends. Your yearning, Green-Eyes, is but a nostalgia for the way things once were, and can never be again; for none of your kind accepts change gladly. Why this should be, I'm not certain; it may have something to do with the fact that your childhood moltings into larger carapaces are such traumatic experiences for you. It is the only thing about you that makes me doubt your complete suitability for the great project. But change and adaptation are the very substance of *my* species, and perhaps each of us can complement the other smoothly enough to promote our success in the grand alliance.

"No; dim it; don't interrupt. Consider honestly, little friend. You are angry with the priest, and you are angry with me, and for all I know you may be angry with the weather, because we have all conspired against you to steal your wonted life away. But who, I ask, has come out here every night, storm or starlight, to study and sing and philosophize? Who wakens her poor hardworking rowers earlier and earlier every twilight? Who is it who neglected her shoreside life—and for what cause, pious devotion to duty? I think not. I believe you find me quite as entertaining as I find you. Is it not so?" But Wink stubbornly refused to emit a spark. "Don't be foolish," Skysinger admonished. "I will confess to every charge you level that speaks of my manipulation and control of your species; but I am innocent of any ruination of your personal life, small one. That you must confess yourself, if you think it has been ruined."

It was true. She had to admit it—at least to herself, if not to yd. Discovering all the changes that had taken place in her absence—her absence of mind—had proven quite a shock; but that shock was now slowly diminishing. She missed the ways of her childhood, but no-one could remain forever a hatchling under the care of a broodfoster yd. Exactly how much did she truly care what those barbarian pilgrims in the City of God did in their spare time, or where they did it? And, with Red-Footed He the way he was now, they had nothing to say to one another.

As for Longstalks, she had loved yd as much as any he or she had ever loved a broodfoster. But yd was only an yd, after all.

Would she indeed return, if she could, to the nights when she was a novice in the choir, and nothing more?

No. Upon reconsideration, she would really rather continue to discuss light opera with Skysinger.

". . . Good," Skysinger said some hours later, after they'd thrashed it all out and renegotiated their arrangement. "Because you and I are just beginning our work together, Green-Eyes. I shall keep in mind your admonishment to take greater care of the consequences of my demands; but you, Wink, and your people, must accustom yourselves to the occasional changes we will make. I hope you have not too mortally offended the priests, because I have one or two little notions I'd like them to try out as soon as may be. For one thing, I have thought about it and it seems to me that what this Lake needs is a shipyard over on the far end. It's none too soon. No, I know you don't know what a shipyard is; I'll explain it all when I give you the plans to relay to your artificers and crafters. And when the priesthood calms down, why don't you talk to them about establishing a Corps of Beacon-Runners?—What is that? Why, that is a way of letting the people of the City of God learn swiftly of whatever interesting may happen, even in the farthest bounds of your tribe's dominance; do you see? And another thing, Wink, can't you get the priests to work out a better educational system? I have thought about it and it seems to me . . ."

And on they shimmered and shone at one another, rippled and rayed, scheming, coruscating, arguing aglow, long into the nights, while the stars above sang a waiting song. . . .

The rowers dipped their oars slowly, in time to the stately pulses of the dirge: deep purple, grays, blues, white. A single large bark glided after the lead boat, carrying priests and choristers.

But the ancient, awesome old High Priestess was not quite dead, not quite yet. Her spectrum was still as pure as ever.

"God!" she called out, piercingly violet. "I pray you appear unto your servant!"

A surge beneath the waves rocked the boats.

"What's all this, Morsel?"

"A state occasion, Great One. A grand sacrifice. I am High Priestess. I officiate."

"Good, I could use a snack. I am delighted that you are healed of your recent illness, Wink, and can take part once more in these social functions. I missed you."

"I am *not* healed of my illness. I am old. I am positively antique. My eyesight is failing, and soon I will no longer be able to see you, to converse with you. I have seen little glimpses of rumors among the younger Servants of God, hastily dimmed when I enter the room, to the general effect that my carapace has hardened around my brain.

"Skysinger, old friend, all the symptoms point to one little fact; the time draws ineluctably near when I will go into Holy Water for the greater glory of God."

"I see. And why are you here now, Morsel?" yd gleamed softly.

"Hmp!" A fuchsia spark. "You know perfectly well! I've no intention of becoming one more anonymous piece of flotsam in the Lake, while my empty shell goes to stand sentinel in the Temple! No; you're going to recognize who I am when I go, and say goodbye properly, and acknowledge my passing!—And, incidentally, I find the tag 'Morsel' less than tactful, under the circumstances!"

"I see."

"Stop saying 'I see'! Of course you see!" she blipped cantankerously. "I just showed you, didn't I? *You're* not the one going blind! Well, then. This is it. This is *not* a dress rehearsal. Everyone's in good spectrum today; they've been practicing for weeks."

The yellow eye snaked up out of the water and gravely surveyed the melting, glowing colors coming from the mighty boat, the proud flagship of the great building yards. "Very harmonious."

Wink stood up and teetered cautiously upon the gunwale of the smaller vessel, the traditional coracle. Skysinger noticed her hesitation.

"Green-Eyed She, our association has given me much delight over the years. I shall miss you terribly. . . . You have grown in wisdom under the wheeling sky. I suspect you have learned not only the clear sight of the mind, but even to see by the wavelengths of love that only yds heretofore have perceived. Yes, I believe you have come to love me as much as I have always loved you, little one. This achievement I honor. I acknowledge your passing with great respect. . . . And I promise you won't feel a thing."

Wink's carapace sagged just briefly; then she gathered her courage.

"Into thy maw, oh God, I commend me, body and soul," she said, somewhat ironically; and she closed her green eyes for the last time, held her breath, and jumped.

But a huge tentacle caught her before she hit the surface, to save her the instinctive panic all her kind felt in the water; and a giant claw neatly snipped the braincase from her thorax.

Then there was a great *crunch*. . . .

The state funeral procession rowed back to shore, still shining brightly, some of the mourners already beginning to argue over the selection of the new Supreme Hierophant.

And Skysinger chugged back into the dark, still depths, feeling once again an overwhelming, inexpressible loneliness . . . and perhaps a touch of indigestion. . . .

■

THE CHILDREN'S HOUR

Lawrence O'Donnell

HE SAT ON A BENCH IN THE LITTLE GROVE in front of Administration, watching the clock over the provost marshal's door jerk its long hand toward seven. Presently, when the hour struck, he would be going in that door, and up one flight of stairs, and down the corridor to the room where Lieutenant Dyke sat waiting, as he had waited so many evenings before.

Tonight might be the night that would end it. Lessing thought perhaps it would be. Something was stirring behind the intangible locks of his mind, and tonight that door might open which had resisted the skilled manipulations of hypnosis for so long. The door might swing wide tonight at last, and let the secret out which not even Lessing knew.

Lessing was a good hypnosis subject. Lieutenant Dyke had discovered that early in their class experiments in psychonamics—that astonishing means by which a soldier can learn to desensitize his own body and feel neither pain nor hunger, when pain or hunger would otherwise be intolerable. In the process of learning, dim and untrodden corridors of the mind are sometimes laid bare. But seldom in any mind was such a thing to be encountered as that block in Lessing's.

He responded well to all the usual tests. Immobility and desensitization, the trick of warping the balance center, the familiar routine of posthypnotic commands, all these succeeded without a hitch, as they had succeeded with so many others. But in Lessing's brain one barrier stood up immovable. Three months in his life were locked and sealed behind adamant walls—under hypnosis.

That was the strangest thing of all, for waking, he remembered those three months clearly. Under hypnosis—they did not exist. Under hypnosis he had no recollection that in June, July, and August of two years ago he had been living a perfectly normal existence. He was in New York, a civilian then, working in an advertising office and living the patterned life that still existed for a time after December 7, 1941. Nothing had happened to make his hypnotized memory blank out with such stubborn vehemence when asked to remember.

And so began the long sessions of searching, probing, delicately manipulating

Lessing's mind as a complicated machine is readjusted, or as muscles wasted and atrophied are gently massaged back to life.

Up to now, the dam had resisted. Tonight—

The first stroke of seven vibrated upon the evening air. Lessing got up slowly, conscious of an unaccustomed touch of panic in his mind. This was the night, he thought. There was a stirring deep down in the roots of his subconscious. He would know the truth tonight—he would look again upon the memory his mind had refused to retain—and he was illogically just a little afraid to face it. He had no idea why.

In the doorway he paused for a moment, looking back. Only the twilight was out there, gathering luminously over the camp, blurring the outlines of barracks, the bulk of the hospital distantly rising. Somewhere a train hooted toward New York an hour away. New York, that held mysteriously the memory his mind rejected.

"Good evening, sergeant," said Lieutenant Dyke, looking up from behind his desk.

Lessing looked at him a little uneasily. Dyke was a small, tight, blond man, sharp with nervous vigor, put together with taut wires. He had shown intense interest in the phenomenon of Lessing's memory, and Lessing had felt a bewildered sort of gratitude until this moment. Now he was not sure.

"Evening, sir," he said automatically.

"Sit down. Cigarette? Nervous, Lessing?"

"I don't know." He took the cigarette without knowing he had done it. This was the flood tide, he thought, and he had no mind for any other awareness than that. The dam was beginning to crumble, and behind it what flood waters, pent up in darkness, waited for release? There were almost inaudible little clicks in his mind as the bolts subconsciously, automatically clicked open. Conditioned reflex by now. His brain, responsive to Dyke's hypnotic probing, was preparing itself.

A bare light swung above Dyke's desk. His eyes turned to it, and everything else began to darken. This, too, was reflexive by now. Dyke, behind him, traced a finger back along his scalp. And Lessing went under very quickly. He heard Dyke's voice, and that changed from a sound to a strong, even suction pulling somewhere in darkness. An indefinable force that drew, and guided as it drew. The dam began to go almost at once. The gates of memory quivered, and Lessing was afraid.

"Go back. Go back. Back to the summer of '41. Summer. You are in New York. When I count ten you will remember. One. Two—" At ten Dyke's voice dropped.

Then again. And again. Until the long, difficult preparation for this moment proved itself, and James Lessing went back through time and . . .

And saw a face, white against the dark, blazing like a flame in the emptiness of the swift temporal current. Whose face? He did not know, but he knew there was a shadow behind it, darker than the blackness, shapeless and watchful.

The shadow grew, looming, leaning over him. A tinkling rhythm beat out. Words fitted themselves to it.

Lawrence O'Donnell

Between the dark and the daylight
When the night is beginning to lower
Comes a pause in the day's occupation
That is known as the children's hour—

It meant nothing. He groped through blindness, searching for reason.

And then it began to come back to him, the thing he had forgotten. A minor thing, something hardly worth remembering, surely. Something . . . no, someone— And not quite so minor, after all. Someone rather important. Someone he had met casually in a place he could not quite remember—a bar, or in the park, or at a party somewhere—very casually. Someone—yes, it had been in the park—but who? He could remember now a flickering of green around them, leaves twinkling in sunshine and grass underfoot. A fountain where they had stopped to drink. He could remember the water, clear and colorless, trickling musically away, but he could not quite remember who had . . . who it was— Everything else was coming clear except the person. Forgetfulness clung stubbornly around that figure at his side. That slender figure, smaller than himself—dark? Fair? No, dark.

"Stabbed by a white wench's black eyes."

He caught his breath suddenly, in a violent physical wrench, as memory deluged back with appalling violence. Clarissa! How could he have forgotten? How *could* he? How could even amnesia have erased *her?* He sat stunned, the shining flood all but blinding him. And somewhere under that pouring brightness was grief—but he would not let that break the surface yet.

Clarissa. What words were there to get all that vivid color into speech? When the barrier went down, it collapsed with such a blast of sudden glory that . . . that—

They had walked in the park above the Hudson, blue water marbled with deeper blue and twinkling in the sun, sliding away below them. Clear water in the fountain, tinkling down over pebbles wet and brown in the dappled shadows beneath the trees. And everything as vivid at Creation's first morning, because of Clarissa walking beside him under the shining leaves. *Clarissa*—and he had forgotten.

It was like looking back into a world a little brighter than human. Everything shone, everything glistened, every sound was sweeter and clearer; there was a sort of glory over all he saw and felt and heard. Childhood had been like that, when the newness of the world invested every commonplace with particular glamour. Glamour—yes, that was the word for Clarissa.

Not sveltness and slickness, but *glamour,* the old word for enchantment. When he was with her it had been like stepping back into childhood and seeing everything with an almost intolerable fresh clarity.

But as for Clarissa herself—who had she been? What had she looked like? And above all, how *could* he have forgotten?

He groped backward into the shapeless fog of the past. What phrase was it that had suddenly ripped the curtain? Shock had all but erased it from his mind. It was like a lightning-flash forking through the darkness and vanishing again. Darkness — blackness — black eyes — yes, that was it. "Stabbed by a white wench's black eyes." A quotation, of course, but from what? More groping. Shakespeare? Yes, "Romeo and Juliet." Why, wasn't that what—Mercutio?—had said to Romeo about Romeo's first love? The girl he loved before he met Juliet. The girl he forgot so completely—

Forgot!

Lessing sat back in his chair, letting everything else slide away for a moment in sheer amazement at the complexity of the subconscious. Something had wiped out all recollection of Clarissa from level below level of his memory, but far down in the dark, memory had clung on, disguised, distorted, hiding behind analogy and allegory, behind a phrase written by a wandering playwright three hundred years before.

So it had been impossible, after all, to erase Clarissa entirely from his mind. She had struck so deep, she had glowed so vividly, that nothing at all could quite smudge her out. And yet only Lieutenant Dyke's skill and the chance unburial of a phrase had resurrected the memory. (For one appalling moment he wondered with a shaken mind what other memories lay hidden and shivering behind other allegorical words and phrases and innocent pictures, deep in the submarine gulfs.)

So he had defeated them after all—the bodiless, voiceless people who had stood between them. The jealous god—the shadowy guardians— For a moment the glare of showering gold flashed in his mind's eye blindingly. He was, in that one shutter-flash, aware of strangers in rich garments moving against confused and unfamiliar backgrounds. Then the door slammed in his face again and he sat there blinking.

Them? Defeated *them?* Who? He had no idea. Even in that one magical glimpse before memory blanked out again he thought he had not been sure who *they* were. That much, perhaps, had been a mystery never solved. But somewhere back in the darkness of his mind incredible things lay hidden. Gods and showering gold, and people in bright clothing that blew upon a wind not—surely not—of this earth—

Bright, bright—brighter than normal eyes ever perceive the world. That was Clarissa and all that surrounded her. It had been a stronger glamour than the sheer enchantment of first love. He felt sure about that now. He who walked with Clarissa shared actual magic that shed a luster on all they passed. Lovely Clarissa, glorious world as clear — as *clarissima* indeed—as a child's new, shining world. But between himself and her, the shadowy people—

Wait. Clarissa's—aunt? Had there been an . . . an aunt? A tall, dark silent woman who damped the glory whenever she was near? He could not remember her face; she was no more than a shadow behind Clarissa's shining presence, a faceless, voiceless nonentity glowering in the background.

His memory faltered, and into the gap flowed the despair which he had been fighting

Lawrence O'Donnell

subconsciously since the lustrous flood first broke upon him. *Clarissa, Clarissa*—where was she now, with the glory around her?

"Tell me," said Lieutenant Dyke.

"There was a girl," Lessing began futilely. "I met her in a park—"

Clarissa on a glittering June morning, tall and dark and slim, with the waters of the Hudson pouring past beyond her in a smooth, blue, glassy current. *Stabbed by a white wench's black eyes.* Yes, very black eyes, bright and starry with blackness, and set wide apart in a grave face that had the remoteness and thoughtfulness of a child's. And from the moment he met that grave, bright glance they knew one another. He had been stabbed indeed—stabbed awake after a lifetime of drowsiness. (Stabbed —like Romeo, who lost both his loves . . .)

"Hello," said Clarissa.

"It didn't last very long . . . I think," he told Dyke, speaking distractedly. "Long enough to find out there was something very strange about Clarissa . . . very wonderful . . . but not long enough to find out what it was . . . I *think.*"

(And yet they had been days of glory, even after the shadows began to fall about them. For there were always shadows, just at her elbow. And he thought they had centered about the aunt who lived with her, that grim nonentity whose face he could not remember.)

"She didn't like me," he explained, frowning with the effort of remembering. "Well, no, not quite that. But there was something in the . . . in the air when she was with us. In a minute I may remember— I wish I could think what she looked like."

It probably didn't matter. They had not seen her often. They had met, Clarissa and he, in so many places in New York, and each place acquired a brilliance of its own once her presence made it *clarissima* for him. There was no sensible explanation for that glory about her, so that street noises clarified to music and dust turned golden while they were together. It was as if he saw the world through her eyes when they were together, and as if she saw it with vision clearer—or perhaps less clear—than human.

"I knew so little about her," he said. (She might almost have sprung into existence in that first moment by the river. And so far as he would ever know, now, she had vanished back into oblivion in that other moment in the dim apartment, when the aunt said—now what was it the aunt had said?)

This was the moment he had been avoiding ever since memory began to come back. But he must think of it now. Perhaps it was the most important moment in the whole strange sequence, the moment that had shut him off so sharply from Clarissa and her shining, unreal, better than normal world. . . .

What had the woman said to him?

He sat very still, thinking. He shut his eyes and turned his mind inward and backward to that strangely clouded hour, groping among shadows that slid smoothly away at his touch.

"I can't—" he said, scowling, his eyes still closed. "I can't. They were . . . negative . . . words, I think, but— No, it's no use."

"Try the aunt again," suggested Dyke. "What did she look like?"

Lessing put his hands over his eyes and thought hard. Tall? Dark, like Clarissa? Grim, certainly—or had that only been the connotation of her words? He could not remember. He slumped down in his chair, grimacing with the effort. She had stood before the mirrors, hadn't she, looking down? Had she? What were her outlines against the light? She had no outlines. She had never existed. Her image seemed to slide behind furniture or slip deftly around corners whenever his persistent memory followed it through the apartment. Here, quite clearly, the memory block was complete.

"I don't think I ever can have seen her," he said, looking up at Dyke with strained, incredulous eyes. "She just isn't there."

Yet it was her shadow between him and Clarissa in the last moment before . . . before . . . what was it that cut off all memory between that hour and this? What happened? Well, say before forgetfulness began, then. Before—Lethe.

This much he remembered—Clarissa's face in the shadowed room, grief and despair upon it, her eyes almost unbearably bright with tears, her arms still extended, the fingers curved as they had slipped from his. He could remember the warmth and softness of them in that last handclasp. And then Lethe had poured between them.

"That was it," said Lessing in a bewildered voice. He looked up. "Those were the highlights. None of them mean anything."

Dyke drew on his cigarette, his eyes narrow above its glow. "Somewhere we've missed the point," he said. "The real truth's still hidden, even deeper than all this was. Hard to know yet just where to begin probing. Clarissa, do you think?"

Lessing shook his head. "I don't think she knew." (She had walked through all those enchanted days, gravely and aloofly, a perfectly normal girl except for— What had happened? He could not quite remember yet, but that which did happen had *not* been normal. Something shocking, something terrible, buried deep down under the commonplaces. Something glorious, glimmering far beneath the surface.)

"Try the aunt again," said Dyke.

Lessing shut his eyes. That faceless, bodiless, voiceless woman who maneuvered through his memories so deftly that he began to despair of ever catching her full-face. . . .

"Go back, then," Dyke told him. "Back to the very beginning. When did you first realize that something out of the ordinary was happening?"

Lessing's mind fumbled backward through those unnaturally empty spaces of the past.

He had not even been aware, at the outset, of the one strangeness he could remember

Lawrence O'Donnell

now—that wonderful clarifying of the world in Clarissa's presence. It had to come slowly, through many meetings, as if by a sort of induced magnetism he became sensitized to her and aware as she was aware. He had known only that it was delightful simply to breathe the same air as she, and walk the same streets.

The same streets? Yes, something curious had happened on a street somewhere. Street noises, loud voices shouting— An accident. The collision just outside the Central Park entrance at Seventy-second Street. It was coming back clearly now, and with a swelling awareness of terror. They had been strolling up by the winding walk under the trellises toward the street. And as they neared it, the scream of brakes and the hollow, reverberant crash of metal against metal, and then voices rising.

Lessing had been holding Clarissa's hand. At the sudden noise he felt a tremor quiver along her arm, and then very softly, and with a curiously shocking deftness, her hand slipped out of his. Their fingers had been interlocked, and his did not relax, but somehow her hand was smoothly withdrawn. He turned to look.

His mind shrank from the memory. But he knew it had happened. He knew he had seen the circle of shaken air ring her luminously about, like a circle in water from a dropped stone. It was very like the spreading rings in water, except that these rings did not expand, but contracted. And as they contracted, Clarissa moved farther away. She was drawn down a rapidly diminishing tunnel of shining circles, with the park distorted in focus beyond them. And she was not looking at Lessing or at anything around him. Her eyes were downcast and that look of thoughtful quiet on her face shut out the world.

He stood perfectly still, too stunned even for surprise.

The luminous, concentric rings drew together in a dazzle, and when he looked again she was not there. People were running up the slope toward the street now, and the voices beyond the wall had risen to a babble. No one had been near enough to see—or perhaps only Lessing himself could have seen an aberration of his own mind. Perhaps he was suddenly mad. Panic was rising wildly in him, but it had not broken the surface yet. There hadn't been time.

And before the full, stunning realization could burst over him, he saw Clarissa again. She was coming leisurely up the hill around a clump of bushes. She was not looking at him. He stood quite still in the middle of the path, his heart thudding so hard that the whole park shook around him. Not until she reached his side did she look up, smiling, and take his hand again.

And that was the first thing that happened.

"I couldn't talk to her about it," Lessing told Dyke miserably. "I knew I couldn't from the first look at her face I got. Because *she didn't know*. To her it hadn't happened. And then I thought I'd imagined it, of course—but I knew I couldn't have imagined such a thing unless there was something too wrong with me to talk about. Later, I began to figure out a theory." He laughed nervously. "Anything, you know, to keep from admitting that I might have . . . well, had hallucinations."

"Go on," Dyke said again. He was leaning forward across the desk, his eyes piercing upon Lessing's. "Then what? It happened again?"

"Not that, no."

Not that? How did he know? He could not quite remember yet. The memories came in flashes, each complete even to its interlocking foreshadow of events to come, but the events themselves still lay hidden.

Had those shining rings been sheer hallucination? He would have believed so, he was sure, if nothing further had happened. As the impossible recedes into distance we convince ourselves, because we must, that it never really could have been. But Lessing was not allowed to forget. . . .

The memories were unraveling now, tumbling one after another through his mind. He had caught the thread. He relaxed in his chair, his face smoothing out from its scowl of deep concentration. Deep beneath the surface that discovery lay whose astonishing gleam shone up through the murk of forgetfulness, tantalizing, still eluding him, but there to be grasped when he reached it. If he wanted to grasp it. If he dared. He hurried on, not ready yet to think of that.

What had the next thing been?

The park again. Curious how memory-haunted the parks of New York were for him now. This time there had been rain, and something—alarming—had happened. What was it? He did not know. He had to grope back step by step toward a climax of impossibility that his mind shied away from touching.

Rain. A sudden thunderstorm that caught them at the edge of the lake. Cold wind ruffling the water, raindrops spattering down big and noisy around them. And himself saying, "Hurry, we can make it back to the summerhouse."

They ran hand in hand along the shore, laughing, Clarissa clutching her big hat and matching her steps to his, long, easy, running strides so that they moved as smoothly as dancers over the grass.

The summerhouse was dingy from many winters upon the rocks. It stood in a little niche in the black stone of the hillside overlooking the lake, a dusty gray refuge from the spattering drops as they ran laughing up the slope of the rock.

But it never sheltered them. The summerhouse did not wait.

Looking incredulously up the black hills, Lessing saw it glimmer and go in a luminous blurring-out, like a picture on a trick film that faded as he watched.

"Not the way Clarissa disappeared," he told Dyke carefully. "That happened quite clearly, in concentric diminishing rings. This time the thing just blurred and melted. One minute it was there, the next—" He made an expunging gesture in the air.

Dyke had not moved. His clear, piercing gaze dwelt unwavering upon Lessing.

"What did Clarissa say this time?"

Lessing rubbed his chin, frowning, "She saw it happen. I . . . I think she just said something like, 'Well, we're in for it now. Never mind, I like walking in the rain, don't you?' As if she were used to things like that. Of course, maybe she was— It didn't surprise her.''

"And you didn't comment this time either?"

"I couldn't. Not when she took it so calmly. It was a relief to know that she'd seen it too. That meant I hadn't just imagined the thing. Not this time, anyhow. But by now—''

Suddenly Lessing paused. Up to this moment he had been too absorbed in the recapture of elusive memory to look objectively at what he was remembering. Now the incredible reality of what he had just been saying struck him without warning and he stared at Dyke with real terror in his eyes. How could there be any explanation for these imaginings, except actual madness? All this could not possibly have happened in the lost months which his conscious mind had remembered so clearly. It was incredible enough that he could have forgotten, but as for *what* he had forgotten, as for the unbelievable theory he had been about to explain to Dyke, and quite matter-of-factly, drawn from hypotheses of sheer miracle—

"Go on," Dyke said quietly. "By now—what?"

Lessing took a long, unsteady breath.

"By now . . . I think . . . I began to discard the idea I was having hallucinations.''
He paused again, unable to continue with such obvious impossibilities.

Dyke urged him gently. "Go on, Lessing. You've got to go on until we can get hold of something to work from. There must be an explanation somewhere. Keep digging. Why did you decide you weren't subject to hallucinations?"

"Because . . . well, I suppose it seemed too easy an explanation," Lessing said doggedly. It was ridiculous to argue so solidly from a basis of insanity, but he searched through his mind again and came out with an answer of very tenuous logic. "Somehow madness seemed the wrong answer," he said. "As I remember now, I think I felt there was a reason behind what had happened. Clarissa didn't know, but I'd begun to see.''

"A reason? What?"

He frowned with concentration. In spite of himself the fascination of the still-unknown was renewing its spell and he groped through the murk of amnesia for the answer he had grasped once, years ago, and let slip again.

"It was so natural to her that she didn't even notice. A nuisance, but something to accept with philosophy. You were meant to get wet if you got caught in the rain away from shelter, and if the shelter were miraculously removed—well, that only emphasized the fact that you were meant to get a soaking. *Meant* to, you see.'' He paused, not at all sure just where this thread was leading, but his memory, dredging among the flotsam, had come up with that one phrase that all but dripped with significance when he saw it in full light. Revelations hovered just beyond the next thought.

"She did get wet," he went on slowly. "I remember now. She went home dripping and caught cold, and had a high fever for several days—"

His mind moved swiftly along the chain of thoughts, drawing incredible conclusions. Was something, somehow, ruling Clarissa's life with a hand so powerful it could violate every law of nature to keep her in the path its whim selected? Had something snatched her away through a tiny section of time and space to keep the street accident from her? But she had been meant to have that drenching and that fever, so—let the summerhouse be erased. Let it never have been. Let it vanish as naturally as the rain came down, so that Clarissa might have her fever . . .

Lessing shut his eyes again and ground his palms hard over them. Did he want to remember much further? What morasses of implausibility was his memory leading him into? Vanishing summerhouses and vanishing girls and . . . and . . . intervention from—outside? He took one horrified mental glance at that thought and then covered it up quickly and went on. Deep down in the murk, the gleam of that amazing discovery still drew him on, but he went more slowly now, not at all certain that he wanted to plumb the depths and see it clearly.

Dyke's voice broke in as his mind began to let go and fall slack.

"She had a fever? Go on, what came next?"

"I didn't see her for a couple of weeks. And the . . . the colors began to go out of everything—"

It had to be renewed, then, by her presence, that strange *glamour* that heightened every color, sharpened every outline, made every sound musical when they were together. He began to crave the stimulus as he felt it fade. Looking back now, he remembered the intolerable dullness of that period. It was then, probably, that he first began to realize he had fallen in love.

And Clarissa, in the interval, had discovered it too. Yes, he was remembering. He had seen it shining in her enormous black eyes on the first day he visited her again. A brilliance almost too strong to look upon, as if bright stars were interlacing their rays there until her eyes were a blaze of blackness more dazzling than any light.

He had seen her, alone, in that first meeting after her illness. Where had the aunt been? Not there, at any rate. The strange, windowless apartment was empty except for themselves. Windowless? He looked back curiously. It was true—there had been no windows. But there were many mirrors. And the carpets were very deep and dark. That was his dominant impression of the place, walking upon softness and silence, with the glimmer of reflecting distances all around.

He had sat beside Clarissa, holding her hand, talking in a low voice. Her smile had been tremulous, and her eyes so bright they were almost frightening. They were very happy that afternoon. He glowed a little, even now, remembering how happy they had been. He would not remember, just yet, that nothing was to come of it but grief.

The wonderful clarity of perception came back around him by degrees as they sat

Lawrence O'Donnell

there talking, so that everything in the world had seemed gloriously right. The room was the center of a perfect universe, beautiful and ordered, and the spheres sang together as they turned around it.

"I was closer to Clarissa then," he thought to himself, "than I ever came again. That was Clarissa's world, beautiful and peaceful, and very bright. You could almost hear the music of the machinery, singing in its perfection as it worked. Life was always like that to her. No, I never came so close again."

Machinery— Why did that image occur to him?

There was only one thing wrong with the apartment. He kept thinking that eyes were upon him, watching all he thought and did. It was probably only the mirrors, but it made him uncomfortable. He asked Clarissa why there were so many. She laughed.

"All the better to see you in, my darling." But then she paused as if some thought had come to her unexpectedly, and glanced around the reflecting walls at her own face seen from so many angles, looking puzzled. Lessing was used by then to seeing reactions upon her face that had no real origin in the normal cause-and-effect sequence of familiar life, and he did not pursue the matter. She was a strange creature, Clarissa, in so many, many ways. Two and two, he thought with sudden affectionate amusement, seldom made less than six to her, and she fell so often into such disproportionately deep and thoughtful silences over the most trivial things. He had learned early in their acquaintance how futile it was to question her about them.

"By now," he said, almost to himself, "I wasn't questioning anything. I didn't dare. I lived on the fringes of a world that wasn't quite normal, but it was Clarissa's world and I didn't ask questions."

Clarissa's serene, bright, immeasurably orderly little universe. So orderly that the stars in their courses might be forced out of pattern, if need be, to maintain her in her serenity. The smooth machinery singing in its motion as it violated possibility to spare her a street accident, or annihilating matter that she might have her drenching and her fever. . . .

The fever served a purpose. Nothing happened to Clarissa, he was fairly sure now, except things with a purpose. Chance had no place in that little world that circled her in. The fever brought delirium, and in the delirium with its strange abnormal clarity of vision—suppose she had glimpsed the truth? Or was there a truth? He could not guess. But her eyes were unnaturally bright now, as if the brilliance of fever had lingered or as if . . . as if she were looking ahead into a future so incredibly shining that its reflections glittered constantly in her eyes, with a blackness brighter than light.

He was sure by now that she did not suspect life was at all different for her, that everyone did not watch miracles happen or walk in the same glory *clarissima*. (And once or twice the world reversed itself and he wondered wildly if she could be right and he wrong, if everyone did but himself.)

They moved in a particular little glory of their own during those days. She did love him; he had no doubt of it. But her subtle exaltation went beyond that. Something wonderful was to come, her manner constantly implied, but the most curious thing was that he thought she herself did not know what. He was reminded of a child wakening on Christmas morning and lying there in a delicious state of drowsiness, remembering only that something wonderful awaits him when he comes fully awake.

"She never spoke of it?" Dyke asked.

Lessing shook his head. "It was all just beneath the surface. And if I tried to ask questions they . . . they seemed to slide right off. She wasn't consciously evading me. It was more as if she hadn't quite understood—" He paused. "And then things went wrong," he said slowly. "Something—"

It was hard to recapture this part. The bad memories were submerged perhaps a little deeper than the good ones, shut off behind additional layers of mental scar tissue. What had happened? He knew Clarissa loved him; they talked of marriage plans. The pattern of happiness had surely been set out clearly for them to follow.

"The aunt," he said doubtfully, "I think she must have interfered. I think . . . Clarissa seemed to slip out of my hands. She'd be busy when I phoned, or the aunt would say she was out. I was fairly sure she was lying, but what could I do?"

When she did see him, Clarissa had denied her neglect, reassuring him with shining glances and delicate, grave caresses. But she was so preoccupied. She did so little, really, and yet she seemed always absorbingly busy.

"If she was only watching a sparrow pick up crumbs," he told Dyke, "or two men arguing on the street, she gave all her attention to them and had none left over for me. So after awhile—I think about a week had gone by without my even seeing her—I decided to have it out with the aunt."

There were gaps— He remembered clearly only standing in the white hallway outside the apartment door and knocking. He remembered the door creaking softly open a little way. Only a little way. The chain had been on it, and it hung open only that narrow width, the chain glinting slightly from light within. It had been dim inside, light reflecting from wall to wall in the many mirrors, but from no source he could see. He could see, though, that someone was moving about inside, a figure distorted by the mirrors, multiplied by them, flickering quietly as it went about its own enigmatic business within, paying no attention to his ring at the door.

"Hello," he called. "Is that you, Clarissa?"

No answer. Nothing but the silent motion inside, visible now and then in the reflecting walls. He had called the aunt by name, then.

"Is it you, Mrs.—" *What* name? He had no idea, now. But he had called her again and again, getting angrier as the motion flickered on heedlessly. "I can see you," he remembered saying, his face against the jamb. "I know you can hear me. Why don't you answer?"

Still nothing. The motion vanished inside for a moment or two, then wavered twice

Lawrence O'Donnell

and was still again. He could not see what figure cast the reflection. Someone dark, moving silently over the thick dark carpets, paying no attention to the voice at the door. What a very odd sort of person the aunt must be. . . .

Abruptly he was struck with the unreality of the situation; that dim, flitting shape in the next room, and the unsatisfactory figure he cut, hesitating there on the threshold calling through the door. Why the devil did the woman insist on this mystery? She was too dominant, sudden, unexpected reaction. Clarissa's life to please herself—

Hot anger rose in him, a violent, sudden, unexpected reaction. "Clarissa!" he called. Then, as dim motion flickered in the mirrors again, he put his shoulder to the yielding panel, pushing hard.

The safety latch much have been flimsy. It gave with a crackling snap, and Lessing, off balance, staggered forward. The room with its many dark mirrors whirled vertiginously. He did not see Clarissa's aunt except as a swift, enigmatic movement in the glass, but quite suddenly he faced the inexplicable.

Gravity had shifted, both in direction and in force. His motion continued and he fell with nightmare slowness—Alice down the Rabbit Hole—in a spiraling, expanding orbit; it was like anaesthesia in its unlikeliness and the fact that it did not surprise him. The curious *quality* of the motion pushed everything else out of his mind for the moment. There was no one in the room with him; there were no mirrors; there was no room. Bodiless, an equation, a simplified ego, he fell toward—

There was Clarissa. Then he saw a burst of golden light flaming and falling against the white dark. A golden shower that enveloped Clarissa and carried her away.

Distantly, with the underbeat of his mind, he knew he should be surprised. But it was like half-sleep. It was too easy to accept things as they came, and he was too lazy to make the effort of awakening. He saw Clarissa again, moving against backgrounds sometimes only a little unfamiliar, at other times—he thought—wildly impossible—

Then an armored man was dropping down through warm sunlit air to the terrace, and the background was a park, with mountains rising far away. A woman was shrinking from him, two men had moved in front of her. Clarissa was there too. He could understand the language, though he did not know how he understood it. The armored man had a weapon of some sort lifted, and was crying, "Get back, Highness! I can't fire—too close—"

A young man in a long, belted robe of barbaric colors skipped backward, tugging at the coiled scarlet whip which was his belt. But neither of them seemed quite ready to make any aggressive moves, astonishment blanking their faces and staring eyes as they gaped at Lessing. Behind them the tall woman with the commanding, discontented face stood frozen by the same surprise. Lessing glanced around in bewilderment, meeting the incredulous stares of the girls flocking behind her. Clarissa was among them, and beyond her—beyond her—someone he could not quite remember. A dark figure, enigmatic, a little stooped. . . .

All of them stood transfixed. (All but Clarissa, perhaps, and perhaps the figure at her elbow—) The armored man's weapon was poised half lifted, the young robed man's whip unslung but trailing. They wore fantastic garments of a style and period Lessing had never heard of, and all their faces were strained and unhappy beneath the blankness of surprise, as if they had been living under some longstanding pressure of anxiety. He never knew what it was.

Only Clarissa looked as serene as always. And only she showed no surprise. Her black eyes under a strange, elaborate coiffure met his with the familiar twinkling of many lights, and she smiled without saying anything.

A buzzing of excitement rose among the girls. The armored man said uncertainly, "Who are you? Where did you come from? Stand back or I'll—"

"—Out of thin air!" the robed young man gasped, and gave the crimson whip a flick that made it writhe along the grass.

Lessing opened his mouth to say—well, something. The whip looked dangerous. But Clarissa shook her head, still smiling.

"Never mind," she said. "Don't bother explaining. They'll forget, you know."

If he had meant to say anything, that robbed him of all coherent thought again. It was too fantastically like . . . like . . . something familiar. Alice, that was it. Alice again, in Looking Glass Land, at the Duchess's garden party. The bright, strange costumes, the bright green grass, the same air of latent menace. In a moment someone would scream, "Off with his head!"

The robed man stepped back and braced his feet against the weight of the whip as he swung its long coil up. Lessing watched the scarlet tongue arch against the sky. ("Serpents! Serpents! There's no pleasing them!" he thought wildly.) And then the whole world was spinning with the spin of the whip. The garden was a top, whirling faster and faster under that crimson lash. He lost his footing on the moving grass and centrifugal force flung him off into unconsciousness.

His head ached.

He got up off the hall floor slowly, pushing against the wall to steady himself. The walls were still spinning, but they slowed to a stop as he stood there swaying and feeling the bump on his forehead. His mind took a little longer to stop spinning, but once it came under control again he could see quite clearly what had happened. That chain had never broken at all. He had not fallen into the dark, mirrored room within, where the shadow of the aunt flitted quietly to and fro. The door, actually, had never been opened at all. At least, it was not open now. And the position of the doormat and the long, dark scrape on the floor made it obvious that he had tried to force the door and had slipped. His head must have cracked hard against the knob.

He wondered if such a blow could send hallucinations forward as well as backward through time from the moment of collision. Because he knew he had dreamed—he must have dreamed—that the door was open and the silent shadow moving inside.

* * *

When he called Clarissa that night he was fully determined to talk to her this time if he had to threaten the guardian aunt with violence or arrest or whatever seemed, on the spur of the moment, most effective. He knew how humiliatingly futile such threats would sound, but he could think of no other alternative. And the need to see Clarissa was desperate now, after that curious Wonderland dream. He meant to tell her about it, and he thought the story would have some effect. Almost, in his bewilderment, he expected her to remember the part she herself had played, though he knew how idiotic the expectation was.

It was a little disconcerting, after his fiery resolution, to hear not the aunt's voice but Clarissa's on the telephone.

"I'm coming over," he said flatly, frustrated defiance making the statement a challenge.

"Why, of course," Clarissa sounded as if they had parted only a few hours ago.

His eagerness made the trip across town seem very long. He was rehearsing the story he would tell her as soon as they were alone. The dream had been so real and vivid, though it must have passed in the flash of a second between the time his head struck the doorknob and the time his knees struck the floor. What would she say about it? He did not know why at all, but he thought she could give him an answer to his questions, if he told her.

He rang the doorbell impatiently. As before, there was no sound from within. He rang again. No answer. Feeling eerily as if he had stepped back in time, to relive that curious dream all over again, he tried the knob, and was surprised to find the door opening to his push. No chain fastened it this time. He was looking into familiar, many-mirrored dimness as the door swung wide. While he hesitated on the threshold, not sure whether to call out or try the bell again, he saw something moving far back in the apartment, visible only in the mirrors.

For a moment the conviction that he was reliving the past made his head swim. Then he saw that it was Clarissa this time. Clarissa standing quite still and looking up with a glow of shining anticipation upon her face. It was that Christmas-morning look he had caught glimpses of before, but never so clearly as now. What she looked at he could not see, but the expression was unmistakable. Something glorious was about to happen, the lovely look implied. Something very glorious, very near, very soon—

About her the air shimmered. Lessing blinked. The air turned golden and began to shower down around her in sparkling rain. This *was* the dream, then, he thought wildly. He had seen it all before. Clarissa standing quietly beneath the golden shower, her face lifted, letting that shining waterfall pour over her slowly. But if it were the dream again, nothing further was to happen. He waited for the floor to spin underfoot—

No, it was real. He was watching another miracle take place, silently and gloriously, in the quiet apartment.

The Children's Hour

He had seen it in a dream; now it happened before his eyes. Clarissa in a shower of . . . of stars? Standing like Danae in a shower of gold—

Like Danae in her brazen tower, shut away from the world. Her likeness to Danae struck him with sudden violence. And that impossible rain of gold, and her look of rapt delight. What was it that poured down the shining torrent upon her? What was responsible for setting Clarissa so definitely apart from the rest of humanity, sheltering her at the cost of outraging natural laws, keeping the smooth machinery that protected her humming along its inaudible, omnipotent course? Omnipotent—yes, omnipotent as Zeus once was, who descended upon his chosen in that fabulous rain of gold.

Standing perfectly still and staring at the distant reflection in the glass, Lessing let his mind flash swifter and swifter along a chain of reasoning that left him at once gasping with incredulity and stunned with impossible conviction. For he thought at last he had the answer. The wildly improbable answer.

He could no longer doubt that somehow, somewhere, Clarissa's life impinged upon some other world than his. And wherever the two clashed, that other world took effortless precedence. It was difficult to believe that some dispassionate force had focused so solicitously upon her. He thought the few glimpses he had been allowed to catch spoke more of some individual intelligence watching everything she did. Some one being who understood humanity as perfectly as if it were itself very nearly human. Someone in the role of literal guardian angel, shepherding Clarissa along a path toward—what?

Certainly *Someone* had not wanted Clarissa to see the street accident, and had snatched her back through space and time to a safe distance, keeping the veil about her so that she did not even guess it had happened. *Someone* had meant her to experience the delirium of fever, and had erased the summerhouse. Someone, he began to realize, was leading her almost literally by the hand through her quiet, thoughtful, shining days and nights, casting *glamour* about her so heavily that it enveloped anyone who came intimately into its range. In her long moments of absorption, when she watched such trivial things so intently, whose voice whispered inaudibly in her ear, repeating what unguessable lessons. . . .

And how did Lessing himself fit into the pattern? Perhaps, he thought dizzily, he had a part to play in it, trivial, but in its way essential. Someone let the two of them amuse themselves harmlessly together, except when that omnipotent hand had to stretch out and push them gently back into their proper course. Clarissa's course, not Lessing's. Indeed, when anything outré had to happen, it was Clarissa who was protected. She did not guess the hiatus at the time of the street accident; she had scarcely noticed the disappearance of the summerhouse. Lessing did know. Lessing was shocked and stunned. But—Lessing was to forget.

At what point in her life, then, had Clarissa stepped into this mirrored prison with the strange aunt for jailor, and turned unknowing and unguessing into the path that

Lawrence O'Donnell

Someone had laid out for her? Who whispered in her ear as she went so dreamily about her days, who poured down in a golden torrent about this Danae when she stood alone in her glass-walled tower?

No one could answer that. There might be as many answers as the mind could imagine, and many more beyond imagination. How could any man guess the answer to a question entirely without precedent in human experience? Well—no precedent but one.

There was Danae.

It was ridiculous, Lessing told himself at this point, to imagine any connection at all in this chance likeness. And yet—how had the legend of Danae started? Had some interloper like himself, two thousand years ago, unwittingly glimpsed another Clarissa standing rapt and ecstatic under another shower of stars? And if that were possible, what right had Lessing to assume arbitrarily that the first of the Danae legend had been as true as what he was watching, and the last of it wholly false? There were so many, many legends of mortals whom the gods desired. Some of them must have had obvious explanations, but the Greeks were not a naive people, and there might, he thought, have been some basis of fact existing behind the allegory. There *must* have been some basis to explain those countless stories, pointing so insistently to some definite rock of reality beyond the fantasy.

But why this long preparation which Clarissa was undergoing? He wondered, and then unbidden into his mind leaped the legend of Semele, who saw her Olympian lover in the unveiled glory of his godhood, and died of that terrible sight. Could this long, slow preparation be designed for no other purpose than to spare Clarissa from Semele's fate? Was she being led gently, inexorably from knowledge to knowledge, so that when the god came down to her in his violence and his splendor, she could endure the glory of her destiny? Was this the answer behind that look of shining anticipation he had seen so often on her face?

Sudden, scalding jealousy enveloped him. Clarissa, glimpsing already and without guessing it, the splendor to come in which he himself could have no part . . .

Lessing struck the door a resounding blow and called, *"Clarissa!"*

In the mirror he saw her start a little and turn. The shower wavered about her. Then she moved out of sight, except for a golden flickering among the mirrors, as she approached the door.

Lessing stood there, shaking and sweating with intolerable confusion. He knew his deductions were ridiculous and impossible. He did not really believe them. He was leaping to conclusions too wild to credit, from premises too arbitrary to consider in any sane moment. Granted that inexplicable things were happening, still he had no logical reason to assume a divine lover's presence. But someone, *Someone* stood behind the events he had just been rehearsing, and of that Someone, whoever and whatever it might be, Lessing was agonizingly jealous. For those plans did not include himself. He knew they never could. He knew—

The Children's Hour

"Hello," said Clarissa softly. "Did I keep you waiting? The bell must be out of order—I didn't hear you ring. Come on in."

He stared. Her face was as serene as always. Perhaps a little glow of rapture still shone in her eyes, but the shower of gold was gone and she gave no outward sign of remembering it.

"What were you doing?" he asked, his voice slightly unsteady.

"Nothing," said Clarissa.

"But I saw you!" he burst out. "In the mirror—I saw you! Clarissa, what—"

Gently and softly a—a hand?—was laid across his mouth. Nothing tangible, nothing real. But the words did not come through. It was silence itself, a thick gag of it, pressing against his lips. There was one appalling, mind-shaking moment of that gag, and then Lessing knew that Someone was right, that he must not speak, that it would be cruel and wrong to say what he had meant to say.

It was all over in an instant, so suddenly that afterward he was not sure whether a gag had actually touched his lips, or whether a subtler gag of the mind had silenced him. But he knew he must say nothing, neither of this nor of that strange, vivid dream in which he had met Clarissa. She did not guess. She must not know—yet.

He could feel the sweat rolling down his forehead, and his knees felt shaky and his head light. He said, from a long way off,

"I . . . I don't feel well, Clarissa. I think I'd better go—"

The light above Dyke's desk swung gently in a breeze from the shaded window. Outside a distant train's hooting floated in across the post grounds, made immeasurably more distant by the darkness. Lessing straightened in his chair and looked around a little dizzily, startled at the abrupt transition from vivid memory to reality. Dyke leaned forward above his crossed arms on the desk and said gently,

"And did you go?"

Lessing nodded. He was far beyond any feeling now of incredulity or reluctance to accept his own memories. The things he was remembering were more real than this desk or the soft-voiced man behind it.

"Yes. I had to get away from her and straighten my mind out. It was so important that she should understand what was happening to her, and yet I couldn't tell her about it. She was—asleep. But she had to be wakened before it was too late. I thought she had a right to know what was coming, and I had a right to have her know, let her make her choice between me and—it. Him. I kept feeling the choice would have to be made soon, or it would be too late. *He* didn't want her to know, of course. He meant to come at the right moment and find her unquestioning, prepared for him. It was up to me to rouse her and make her understand before that moment."

"You thought it was near, then?"

"Very near."

"What did you do?"

Lessing's eyes went unfocused in remembrance. "I took her out dancing," he said, "the next night . . ."

She sat across from him at a table beside a little dance floor, slowly twirling a glass of sherry and bitters and listening to the noises of a bad orchestra echoing in the small, smoky room. Lessing was not quite sure why he had brought her here, after all. Perhaps he hoped that though he could not speak to her in words of all he suspected and feared, he could rouse her enough out of her serene absorption so that she might notice for herself how far her own world differed from the normal one. Here in this small, enclosed space shaking with savage rhythms, crowded by people who were deliberately giving themselves up to the music and the liquor, might not that serene and shining armor be pierced a little, enough to show what lay inside?

Lessing was tinkling the ice in his third collins and enjoying the pleasant haze that just enough alcohol lent to the particular, shining haze that always surrounded Clarissa. He would not, he told himself, have any more. He was far from drunk, certainly, but there was intoxication in the air tonight, even in this little, noisy, second-rate nightclub. The soaring music had a hint of marijuana delirium in it; the dancers on the hot, crowded floor exhaled excitement.

And Clarissa was responding. Her great black eyes shone with unbearable bright-ness, and her laughter was bright and spontaneous too. They danced in the jostling mob, not feeling jostled at all because of the way the music caught them up on its rhythms. Clarissa was talking much more than usual this evening, very gayly, her body resilient in his arms.

As for himself—yes, he was drunk after all, whether on the three drinks or on some subtler, more powerful intoxication he did not know. But all his values were shifting deliciously toward the irresponsible, and his ears rang with inaudible music. Now nothing could overpower him. He was not afraid of anything or anyone at all. He would take Clarissa away—clear away from New York and her jailor aunt, and that shining Someone who drew nearer with every breath.

There began to be gaps in his memory after awhile. He could not remember how they had got out of the nightclub and into his car, or just where they intended to go, but presently they were driving up the Henry Hudson Parkway with the river sliding darkly below and the lights of Jersey lying in wreaths upon the Palisades.

They were defying the—the pattern. He thought both of them knew that. There was no place in the pattern for this wild and dizzying flight up the Hudson, with the cross-streets reeling past like spokes in a shining wheel. Clarissa, leaning back in the bend of his free arm, was in her way as drunk as he, on nothing more than two sherries and the savage rhythms of the music, the savage excitement of this strange night. The intoxication of defiance, perhaps, because they were running away. From some-thing—from Someone. (That was impossible, of course. Even in his drunkenness he knew that. But they could try—)

"Faster," Clarissa urged, moving her head in the crook of his arm. She was glitteringly alive tonight as he had never seen her before. Very nearly awake, he thought in the haze of his reeling mind. Very nearly ready to be told what it was he must tell her. The warning—

Once he pulled up deliberately beneath a street light and took her in his arms. Her eyes and her voice and her laughter flashed and sparkled tonight, and Lessing knew that if he thought he had loved her before, this new Clarissa was so enchanting that . . . that . . . Yes, even a god might lean out from Olympus to desire her. He kissed her with an ardor that made the city whirl solemnly around them. It was delightful to be drunk and in love, and kissing Clarissa under the eyes of the jealous gods. . . .

There was a feeling of . . . of wrongness in the air as they drove on. The pattern strove to right itself, to force them back into their ordained path. He could feel its calm power pressing against his mind. He was aware of traffic imperceptibly edging him into streets that led back toward the apartment they had left. He had to wrench himself out of it, and then presently the northbound way would be closed off for repairs, and a detour went off along other streets that took them south again. Time after time he found himself driving past descending street numbers toward downtown New York, and swung around the block in bewildered determination not to return.

The pattern must be broken. It *must* be. Hazily he thought that if he could snap one thread of it, defy that smooth, quiet power in even so small a way as this, he would have accomplished his purpose. But alone he could not have done it. The omnipotent machinery humming in its course would have been irresistible—he would have obeyed it without knowing he obeyed—had not Clarissa shared his defiance tonight. There seemed to be a power in her akin to the power of that omnipotence, as if she had absorbed some of it from long nearness to the source.

Or was it that Someone stayed his hand rather than strike her forcibly back to her place in the pattern, rather than let her guess—yet—the extent of his power?

"Turn," said Clarissa. "Turn around. We're going wrong again."

He struggled with the wheel. "I can't . . . I can't," he told her, almost breathless. She gave him a dazzling dark glance and leaned over to take the wheel herself.

Even for her it was hard. But slowly she turned the car, while traffic blared irritably behind them, and slowly they broke out of the pattern's grip again and rounded another corner, heading north, the lights of Jersey swimming unfocused in the haze of their delirium.

This was no normal drunkenness. It was increasing by leaps and bounds. This, thought Lessing dimly, is *His* next step. He won't let her see what he's doing, but he knows he's got to stop us now, or we'll break the pattern and prove our independence.

The tall, narrow buildings shouldering together along the streets were like tall trees in a forest, with windows for motionless leaves. No two windows on the same level, or quite alike. Infinite variety with infinitesimal differences, all of them interlacing and glimmering as they drove on and on through the stony forest. Now Lessing could see among the trees, and between them, not transparently but as if through some new dimension. He could see the streets that marked off this forest into squares and oblongs, and his dazed mind remembered another forest, checkered into squares—Looking Glass Land.

He was going south again through the forest.

"Clarissa—help me," he said distantly, wrestling again with the wheel. Her small white hands came out of the dark to cover his.

A shower of light from a flickering window poured down upon them, enveloping Clarissa as Zeus enveloped Danae. The jealous god, the jealous god— Lessing laughed and smacked the wheel in senseless triumph.

There was a light glimmering ahead through the trees. He would have to go softly, he warned himself, and tiptoed forward over the . . . the cobbled road. Without surprise he saw that he was moving on foot through a forest in darkness, quite alone. He was still drunk. Drunker than ever, he thought with mild pride, drunker, probably, than any mortal ever was before. Any mortal. The gods, now—

People were moving through the trees ahead. He knew they must not see him. It would shock them considerably if they did; he remembered the garishly dressed people of his other dream, and the young man with the whip. No, it would be better to stay hidden this time if he could. The forest was wheeling and dipping around him behind a haze of obscurity, and nothing had very much coherence. The ringing in his ears was probably intoxication, not actual sound.

The people were somberly clad in black, with black hoods that covered their hair and framed pale, intolerant faces. They were moving in a long column through the trees. Lessing watched them go by for what seemed a long while. Some of the women carried work bags over their arms and knitted as they walked. A few of the men read from small books and stumbled now and then on the cobblestones. There was no laughter.

Clarissa came among the last. She had a gay little face beneath the black cap, gayer and more careless than he had ever seen her in this . . . this world. She walked lightly, breaking into something like a dance step occasionally that called down upon her the frowns of those who walked behind. She did not seem to care.

Lessing wanted to call to her. He wanted to call so badly that it seemed to him she sensed it, for she began to fall behind, letting first one group pass her and then another, until she walked at the very end of the column. Several girls in a cluster looked back a few times and giggled a little, but said nothing. She fell farther back. Presently the procession turned a corner and Clarissa stopped in the middle of the road, watching them go. Then she laughed and performed a solemn little pirouette on one toe, her black skirts swinging wide around her.

Lessing stepped from behind his tree and took a step toward her, ready to speak her name. But he was too late. Someone else was already nearer than he. Someone else— Clarissa called out gaily in a language he did not know, and then there was a flash of crimson through the trees and a figure cloaked from head to heels in bright red came up to her and took her into its embrace, the red folds swinging forward to infold them both. Clarissa's happy laughter was smothered beneath the stooping hood.

Lessing stood perfectly still. It might be another woman, he told himself fiercely. It might be a sister or an aunt. But it was probably a man. Or—

He squinted slightly—nothing focused very well in his present state, and things tended to slip sidewise when he tried to fix his eyes upon them—but this time he was almost sure of what he saw. He was almost sure that upon Clarissa's lifted face in the dimness of the woods a light was falling softly—from the hood above her. A light, glowing from within the hood. A shower of light. Danae, in her shower of gold. . .

The woods tilted steeply and turned end for end. Lessing was beyond surprise as he fell away, spinning and whirling through darkness, falling farther and farther from Clarissa in the woods. Leaving Clarissa alone in the embrace of her god.

When the spinning stopped he was sitting in his car again, with traffic pouring noisily past on the left. He was parked, somewhere. Double-parked, with the motor running. He blinked.

"I'll get out here," Clarissa told him matter-of-factly. "No, don't bother. You'll never find a parking place, and I'm so sleepy. Good night, darling. Phone me in the morning."

He could do nothing but blink. The dazzle of her eyes and her smile was a little blinding, and that haze still diffused all his efforts to focus upon her face. But he could see enough. They were exactly where they had started, at the curb before her apartment house.

"Good night," said Clarissa again, and the door closed behind her.

There was silence in the office after Lessing's last words. Dyke sat waiting quietly, his eyes on Lessing's face, his shadow moving a little on the desktop under the swinging light. After a moment Lessing said, almost defiantly,

"Well?"

Dyke smiled slightly, stirring in his chair. "Well?" he echoed.

"What are you thinking?"

Dyke shook his head. "I'm not thinking at all. It isn't time yet for that—unless the story ends there. It doesn't, does it?"

Lessing looked thoughtful. "No. Not quite. We met once more."

"Only once?" Dyke's eyes brightened. "That must be when your memory went, then. That's the most interesting scene of all. Go on—what happened?"

Lessing closed his eyes. His voice came slowly, as if he were remembering bit by bit each episode of the story he told.

Lawrence O'Donnéll

"The phone woke me next morning," he said. "It was Clarissa. As soon as I heard her voice I knew the time had come to settle things once and for all—if I could. If I were allowed. I didn't think—*He*—would let me talk it out with her, but I knew I'd have to try. She sounded upset on the phone. Wouldn't say why. She wanted me to come over right away."

She was at the door when he came out of the elevator, holding it open for him against a background of mirrors in which no motion stirred. She looked fresh and lovely, and Lessing marveled again, as he had marveled on waking, that the extraordinary drunkenness of last night had left no ill effects with either of them this morning. But she looked troubled, too; her eyes were too bright, with a blinding blackness that dazzled him, and the sweet serenity was gone from her face. He exulted at that. She was awakening, then, from the long, long dream.

The first thing he said as he followed her into the apartment was,

"Where's your aunt?"

Clarissa glanced vaguely around. "Oh, out, I suppose. Never mind her. Jim, tell me—did we do something wrong last night? Do you remember what happened? Everything?"

"Why I . . . I think so." He was temporizing, not ready yet in spite of his decision to plunge into these deep waters.

"What happened, then? Why does it worry me so? Why can't I remember?" Her troubled eyes searched his face anxiously. He took her hands. They were cold and trembling a little.

"Come over here," he said. "Sit down. What's the matter, darling? Nothing's wrong. We had a few drinks and took a long ride, don't you remember? And then I brought you back here and you said good night and went in."

"That isn't all," she said with conviction. "We were—fighting something. It was wrong to fight—I never did before. I never knew it was there until I fought it last night. But now I do know. What was it, Jim?"

He looked down at her gravely, a tremendous excitement beginning to well up inside him. Perhaps, somehow, they had succeeded last night in breaking the spell. Perhaps *His* grip had been loosened after all, when they defied the pattern even as briefly as they did.

But this was no time for temporizing. Now, while the bonds were slack, was the moment to strike hard and sever them if he could. Tomorrow she might have slipped back again into the old distraction that shut him out. He must tell her now— Together they might yet shake off the tightening coils that had been closing so gently, so inexorably about her.

"Clarissa," he said, and turned on the sofa to face her. "Clarissa, I think I'd better tell you something." Then a sudden, unreasoning doubt seized him and he said irrelevantly, "Are you sure you love me?" It was foolishly important to be reassured just then. He did not know why.

Clarissa smiled and leaned forward into his arms, putting her cheek against his shoulder. From there, unseen, she murmured, "I'll always love you, dear."

For a long moment he did not speak. Then, holding her in one arm, not watching her face, he began.

"Ever since we met, Clarissa darling, things have been happening that—worried me. About you. I'm going to tell you if I can. I think there's something, or someone, very powerful, watching over you and forcing you into some course, toward some end I can't do more than guess at. I'm going to try to tell you exactly why I think so, and if I have to stop without finishing, you'll know I don't stop on purpose. I'll have been stopped."

Lessing paused, a little awed at his own daring in defying that Someone whose powerful hand he had felt hushing him before. But no pad of silence was pressed against his lips this time and he went on wonderingly, expecting each word he spoke to be the last. Clarissa lay silent against his shoulder, breathing quietly, not moving much. He could not see her face.

And so he told her the story, very simply and without references to his own bewilderment or to the wild conclusions he had reached. He told her about the moment in the park when she had been drawn away down a funnel of luminous rings. He reminded her of the vanishment of the summerhouse. He told of the dreamlike episode on the hallway here, when he called irrationally into the mirrored dimness, or thought he called. He told her of their strange, bemused ride uptown the night before, and how the pattern swung the streets around under their wheels. He told her of his two vivid dreams through which she—yet not she—had moved so assuredly. And then, without drawing any conclusions aloud, he asked her what she was thinking.

She lay still a moment longer in his arms. Then she sat up slowly, pushing back the smooth dark hair and meeting his eyes with the feverish brilliance that had by now become natural to her.

"So that's it," she said dreamily, and was silent.

"What is?" he asked almost irritably, yet suffused now with a sense of triumph because the Someone had not silenced him after all, had slipped this once and let the whole story come out into open air at last. Now at last he thought he might learn the truth.

"Then I was right," Clarissa went on. "I *was* fighting something last night. It's odd, but I never even knew it was there until the moment I began to fight it. Now I know it's always been there. I wonder—"

When she did not go on, Lessing said bluntly, "Have you ever realized that . . . that things were different for you? Tell me, Clarissa, what is it you think of when you . . . when you stand and look at something trivial so long?"

She turned her head and gave him a long, grave look that told him more plainly

　　　　　　　　　　　　　　　　　　　　　　　　　　　　　Lawrence O'Donnell

than words that the whole spell was not yet dissolved. She made no answer to the question, but she said,

"For some reason I keep remembering a fairy story my aunt used to tell me when I was small. I've never forgotten it, though it certainly isn't much of a story. You see—"

She paused again, and her eyes brightened as he looked, almost as if lights had gone on behind them in a dark room full of mirrors. The look of expectancy which he knew so well tightened the lines of her face for a moment, and she smiled delightedly, without apparent reason and not really seeming to know she smiled.

"Yes," she went on. "I remember it well. Once upon a time, in a kingdom in the middle of the forest, a little girl was born. All the people in the country were blind. The sun shone so brightly that none of them could see. So the little girl went about with her eyes shut too, and didn't even guess that such a thing as sight existed.

"One day as she walked alone in the woods she heard a voice beside her. 'Who are you?' she asked the voice, and the voice replied, 'I am your guardian.' The little girl said, 'But I don't need a guardian. I know these woods very well. I was born here.' The voice said, 'Ah, you were born here, yes, but you don't belong here, child. You are not blind like the others.' And the little girl exclaimed, 'Blind? What's that?'

" 'I can't tell you yet,' the voice answered, 'but you must know that you are a king's daughter, born among these humble people as our king's children sometimes are. My duty is to watch over you and help you to open your eyes when the time comes. But the time is not yet. You are too young—the sun would blind you. So go on about your business, child, and remember I am always here beside you. The day will come when you open your eyes and see.' "

Clarissa paused. Lessing said impatiently, "Well, did she?"

Clarissa sighed. "My aunt never would finish the story. Maybe that's why I've always remembered it."

Lessing started to speak. "I don't think—" But something in Clarissa's face stopped him. An exalted and enchanted look, that Christmas-morning expression carried to fulfillment, as if the child were awake and remembering what many-lighted, silver-spangled glory awaited him downstairs. She said in a small, clear voice,

"It's true. Of course it's true! All you've said, and the fairy tale too. Why, *I'm* the king's child. Of course I am!" And she put both hands to her eyes in a sudden childish gesture, as if half expecting the allegory of blindness to be literal.

"Clarissa!" Lessing said.

She looked at him with wide, dazzled eyes that scarcely knew him. And for a moment a strange memory came unbidden into his mind and brought terror with it. Alice, walking with the Fawn in the enchanted woods where nothing has a name, walking in friendship with her arm about the Fawn's neck. And the Fawn's words when they came to the edge of the woods and memory returned to them both. How it started away from her, shaking off the arm, wildness returning to the eyes that had looked as serenely into Alice's as Clarissa had looked into his. *"Why—I'm a Fawn,"* it said in astonishment. *"And you're a Human Child!"*

Alien species.

"I wonder why I'm not a bit surprised?" murmured Clarissa. "I must have known it all along, really. Oh, I wonder what comes next?"

Lessing stared at her, appalled. She was very like a child now, too enraptured by the prospect of—of what?—to think of any possible consequences. It frightened him to see how sure she was of splendor to come, and of nothing but good in that splendor. He hated to mar the look of lovely anticipation on her face, but he must. He had wanted her to help him fight this monstrous possibility if she could bring herself to accept it at all. He had not expected instant acceptance and instant rapture. She *must* fight it—

"Clarissa," he said, "think! If it's true . . . and we may be wrong . . . don't you see what it means? He . . . they . . . won't let us be together, Clarissa. We can't be married."

Her luminous eyes turned to him joyously.

"Of course we'll be married, darling. *They're* only looking after me, don't you see? Not hurting me, just watching. I'm sure they'll let us marry whenever we like. I'm sure they'd never do anything to hurt me. Why darling, for all we know you may be one of us, too. I wonder if you are. It almost stands to reason, don't you think? Or why would They have let us fall in love? Oh, darling—"

Suddenly he knew that someone was standing behind him. *Someone*— For one heart-stopping moment he wondered if the jealous god himself had come down to claim Clarissa, and he dared not turn his head. But when Clarissa's shining eyes lifted to the face beyond his, and showed no surprise, he felt a little reassurance.

He sat perfectly still. He knew he could not have turned if he wanted. He could only watch Clarissa, and though no words were spoken in that silence, he saw her expression change. The rapturous joy drained slowly out of it. She shook her head, bewilderment and disbelief blurring the ecstasy of a moment before.

"No?" she said to that standing someone behind him. "But I thought— Oh, no, you mustn't! You wouldn't! It isn't fair!" And the dazzling dark eyes flooded with sudden tears that doubled their shining. "You can't, you can't!" sobbed Clarissa, and flung herself forward upon Lessing, her arms clasping his neck hard as she wept incoherent protest upon his shoulder.

His arms closed automatically around her while his mind spun desperately to regain its balance. What had happened? Who—

Someone brushed by him. The aunt. He knew that, but with no sense of relief even though he had half-expected that more awesome Someone at whose existence he could still only guess.

The aunt was bending over them, pulling gently at Clarissa's shaking shoulder. And

Lawrence O'Donnell

after a moment Clarissa's grip on his neck loosened and she sat up obediently, though still catching her breath in long, uneven sobs that wrung Lessing's heart. He wanted desperately to do or say whatever would comfort her most quickly, but his mind and his body were both oddly slowed, as if there were some force at work in the room which he could not understand. As if he were moving against the momentum of that singing machinery he had fancied he sensed so often—moving against it, while the other two were carried effortlessly on.

Clarissa let herself be pulled away. She moved as bonelessly as a child, utterly given up to her grief, careless of everything but that. The tears streaked her cheeks and her body drooped forlornly. She held Lessing's hands until the last, but when he felt her fingers slipping from his the loss of contact told him, queerly, as nothing else quite had power to tell, that this was a final parting. They stood apart over a few feet of carpet, as if inexorable miles lay between them. Miles that widened with every passing second. Clarissa looked at him through her tears, her eyes unbearably bright, her lips quivering, her hands still outstretched and curved from the pressure of his clasp.

This is all. You have served your purpose—now go. Go and forget.

He did not know what voice had said it, or exactly in what words, but the meaning came back to him clearly now. *Go and forget.*

There was strong music in the air. For one last moment he stood in a world that glittered with beauty and color because it was Clarissa's, glittered even in this dark apartment with its many, many mirrors. All about him he could see reflecting Clarissas from every angle of grief and parting, moving confusedly as she let her hands begin to drop. He saw a score of Clarissas dropping their curved hands—but he never saw them fall. One last look at Clarissa's tears, and then . . . and then—

Lethe.

Dyke let his breath out in a long sigh. He leaned back in his creaking chair and looked at Lessing without expression under his light eyebrows. Lessing blinked stupidly back. An instant ago he had stood in Clarissa's apartment; the touch of her fingers was still warm in his hands. He could hear her caught breath and see the reflections moving confusedly in the mirrors around them—

"Wait a minute," he said. "Reflections—Clarissa—I almost remembered something just then—" He sat up and stared at Dyke without seeing him, his brow furrowed. "Reflections," he said again. "Clarissa—lots of Clarissas—but no aunt! I was looking at two women in the mirror, but I didn't see the aunt! I never saw her—not once! And yet I . . . wait . . . the answer's there, you know . . . right there, just in reach, if I could only—"

Then it came to him in a burst of clarity. Clarissa had seen it before him; the whole answer lay in that legend she had told. The Country of the Blind! How could those sightless natives hope to see the king's messenger who watched over the princess as she walked that enchanted wood? How could he remember what his mind had never been strong enough to comprehend? How could he have *seen* that guardian except as a presence without shape, a voice without words, moving through its own bright sphere beyond the sight of the blind?

"Cigarette?" said Dyke, creaking his chair forward.

Lessing reached automatically across the desk. There was no further sound but the rustle of paper and the scratch of a match, for a little while. They smoked in silence, eying one another. Outside feet went by upon gravel. Men's voices called distantly, muffled by the night. Crickets were chirping, omnipresent in the dark.

Presently Dyke let down the front legs of his chair with a thump and reached forward to grind out his unfinished cigarette.

"All right," he said. "Now—are you still too close, or can you look at it objectively?"

Lessing shrugged. "I can try."

"Well, first we can take it as understood—at least for the moment—that such things as these just don't happen. The story's full of holes, of course. We could tear it to pieces in ten minutes if we tried."

Lessing looked stubborn. "Maybe you think—"

"I haven't begun to think yet. We haven't got to the bottom of the thing, naturally. I·don't believe it really happened exactly as you remember. Man, how could it? The whole story's still dressed up in a sort of allegory, and we'll have to dig deeper still to uncover the bare facts. But just as it stands—what a problem! Now I wonder—"

His voice died. He shook out another cigarette and scratched a match abstractedly. Through the first cloud of exhaled smoke he went on,

"Take it all as read, just for a minute. Unravel the allegory in the allegory—the king's daughter born in the Country of the Blind. You know, Lessing, one thing strikes me that you haven't noticed yet. Ever think how completely childish Clarissa seems? Her absorption in trivial things, for instance. Her assumption that the forces at work about her must be protective, parental. Yes, even that glow you spoke of that affected everything you saw and heard when you were with her. A child's world is like that. Strong, clear colors. Nothing's ugly because they have no basis for comparison. Beauty and ugliness mean nothing to a child. I can remember a bit from my own childhood—that peculiar enchantment over whatever interested me. Wordsworth, you know—'Heaven lies about us in our infancy,' and all the rest. And yet she was adult enough, wasn't she? Past twenty, say?"

He paused, eying the tip of his cigarette. "You know," he said, "it sounds like a simple case of arrested development, doesn't it? Now, now, wait a minute! I only said *sounds* like it. You've got sense enough to recognize a moron when you see one. I don't say Clarissa was anything like that. I'm just getting at something—

"I'm thinking about my own little boy. He's eleven now, and getting adjusted, but when he first started school he had an I.Q. way above the rest of the class, and they

Lawrence O'Donnell

bored him. He didn't want to play with the other kids. Got to hanging around the house reading until my wife and I realized something had to be done about it. High I.Q. or not, a kid needs other kids to play with. He'll never learn to make the necessary social adjustments unless he learns young. Can't grow up psychically quite straight unless he grows up with his own kind. Later on a high I.Q. will be a fine thing, but right now it's almost a handicap to the kid.'' He paused. ''Well, see what I mean?''

Lessing shook his head. ''I can't see anything. I'm still dizzy.''

''Clarissa,'' said Dyke slowly, ''might—in the allegory, mind you, not in any real sense—be the king's daughter. She might have been born of . . . well, call it royal blood . . . into a race of inferiors, and never guess it until she began to develop beyond their level. Maybe the . . . the king felt the same as I did about my own child—she needed the company of inferiors . . . of children—while she was growing up. She couldn't develop properly among—adults. Adults, you see, so far developed beyond anything we know that when they're in the same room with you, you can't even remember what they looked like.''

It took Lessing a good minute after Dyke stopped speaking to realize just what he meant. Then he sat up abruptly and said, ''Oh, no! It can't be that. Why, I'd have known—''

''You ought,'' Dyke remarked abstractedly, ''to watch my kid play baseball. While he's playing, it's the most important thing in life. The other kids never guess he has thoughts that go beyond the game.''

''But . . . but the shower of gold, for instance,'' protested Lessing. ''The presence of the god . . . even the—''

''Wait a minute! Just wait, now. You remember yourself that you jumped at conclusions about the god. Made him up completely out of a glimpse of what looked like a golden shower, and the memory of the Danae legend, and the feeling of a presence and a purpose behind what happened. If you'd seen what looked like a burning bush instead of a shower, you'd have come up with a completely different theory, involving Moses maybe. As for the presence and the visions—'' Dyke paused and gave him a narrowed look. He hesitated a moment. ''I'm going to suggest something about those later on. You won't like it. First, though, I want to follow this . . . this allegory on through. I want to explain fully what *might* lie beyond this obvious theory on Clarissa. Remember, I don't take it seriously. But neither do I want to leave it dangling. It's fascinating, just as it stands. It seems very clearly to indicate—in the allegory—the existence of *homo superior,* here and now, right among us.''

''Supermen?'' Lessing echoed. With an obvious effort he forced his mind into focus and sat up straighter, looking at Dyke with a thoughtful frown. ''Maybe. Or maybe—Lieutenant, do you ever read Cabell? In one of his books somewhere I think he has a character refer to a sort of super-race that impinges on ours with only one . . . one facet. He uses the analogy of geometry, and suggests that the other race might be represented by cubes that show up as squares on the plane geometric surface of our world, though in their own they have a cubic mass we never guess." He frowned more deeply, and was silent.

Dyke nodded. "Something like that, maybe. Fourth dimension stuff—people restricting themselves into our world temporarily, and for a purpose." He pulled at his lower lip and then repeated, "For a purpose. That's humiliating! I'm glad I don't really believe it's true. Even considering the thing academically is embarrassing enough. *Homo superior,* sending his children among us—to play."

He laughed. "Run along, children! I wonder if you see what I'm driving at. I'm not sure myself, really. It's too vague. My mind's human, so it's limited. I'm set in patterns of anthropomorphic thinking, and my habit-patterns handicap me. We have to feel important. That's a psychological truism. That's why Mephistopheles was always supposed to be interested in buying human souls. He wouldn't have wanted them, really—impalpables, intangibles, no use at all to a demon with a demon's powers."

"Where do the demons come in?"

"Nowhere. I'm just talking. *Homo superior* would be another race without any human touching points at all—as adults. Demons, in literature, were given human emotions and traits. Why? Muddy thinking. They wouldn't have them, any more than a superman would. Tools!" Dyke said significantly, and sat staring at nothing.

"Tools?"

"This . . . this world." He gestured "What the devil do we know about it? We've made atom smashers and microscopes. And other things. Kid stuff, toys. My boy can use a microscope and see bugs in creek water. A doctor can take the same microscope, use stains, isolate a germ and do something about it. That's maturity. All this world, all this—matter—around us, might be simply tools that we're using like kids. A superrace—"

"By definition, wouldn't it be too super to understand?"

"In toto. A child can't completely comprehend an adult. But a child can more or less understand another child—which is reduced to the same equation as his own, or at least the same common denominator. A superman would have to grow. He wouldn't start out mature. Say the adult human is expressed by x. The adult superman is xy. A superchild—undeveloped, immature—is xy/y. Or in other words, the equivalent of a mature specimen of *homo sapiens*. *Sapiens* reaches senility and dies. *Superior* goes on to maturity, the true superman. And that maturity—"

They were silent for awhile.

"They might impinge on us a little, while taking care of their own young," Dyke went on presently. "They might impose amnesia on anyone who came too close, as you did—might have done. Remember Charles Fort? Mysterious disappearances, balls

Lawrence O'Donnell

of light, spaceships, Jersey devils. That's a side issue. The point is, a superchild could live with us, right here and now, unsuspected. It would appear to be an ordinary adult human. Or if not quite ordinary—certain precautions might be taken." Again he fell silent, twirling a pencil on the desk.

"Of course, it's inconceivable," he went on at last. "All pure theory. I've got a much more plausible explanation, though as I warned you, you won't like it."

Lessing smiled faintly. "What is it?"

"Remember Clarissa's fever?"

"Of course. Things were different after that—much more in the open. I thought—maybe she saw things in the delirium for the first time that she couldn't be allowed to see head-on, in normal life. The fever seemed to be a necessity. But of course—"

"Wait. Just possibly, you know, you may have the whole thing by the wrong end. Look back, now. You two were caught in a rainstorm, and Clarissa came out of it with a delirium, right? And after that, things got stranger and stranger. Lessing, did it ever occur to you that you were both caught in that storm? Are you perfectly sure that it wasn't *yourself* who had the delirium?"

Lessing sat quite still, meeting the narrowed gaze. After a long moment he shook himself slightly.

"Yes," he said. "I'm sure."

Dyke smiled. "All right. Just thought I'd ask. It's one possibility, of course." He waited.

Presently Lessing looked up.

"Maybe I did have a fever," he admitted. "Maybe I imagined it all. That still doesn't explain the forgetfulness, but skip that. I know one way to settle at least part of the question."

Dyke nodded. "I wondered if you'd want to do that. I mean, right away."

"Why not? I know the way back. I'd know it blindfolded. Why, she may have been waiting for me all this time! There's nothing to prevent me going back tomorrow."

"There's a little matter of a pass," Dyke said. "I believe I can fix that up. But do you think you want to go so soon, Lessing? Without thinking things over? You know, it's going to be an awful shock if you find no apartment and no Clarissa. And I'll admit I won't be surprised if that's just what you do find. I think this whole thing's an allegory we haven't fathomed yet. We may never fathom it. But—"

"I'll have to go," Lessing told him. "Don't you see that? We'll never prove anything until we at least rule out the most obvious possibility. After all, I might be telling the simple truth!"

Dyke laughed and then shrugged faintly.

Lessing stood before the familiar door, his finger hesitating on the bell. So far, his memory had served him with perfect faith. Here was the corridor he knew well. Here was the door. Inside, he was quite sure, lay the arrangement of walls and rooms where once Clarissa moved. She might not be there any more, of course. He must not be disappointed if a strange face answered the bell. It would disprove nothing. After all, two years had passed.

And Clarissa had been changing rather alarmingly when he saw her last. The fever had seemed to speed things up.

Well, suppose it were all true. Suppose she belonged to the super-race. Suppose she impinged upon Lessing's world with only one facet of her four-dimensional self. With that one facet she had loved him—they had that much of a meeting ground. Let her have a deeper self, then, than he could ever comprehend; still she could not yet be fully developed into her world of solid geometry, and while one facet remained restricted into the planar world which was all he knew, she might, he thought, still love him. He hoped she could. He remembered her tears. He heard again the sweet, shy, ardent voice saying, "I'll always love you—"

Firmly he pressed the bell.

The room was changed, Mirrors still lined it, but not—not as he remembered. They were more than mirrors now. He had no time to analyze the change, for a motion stirred before him.

"Clarissa—" he said. And then, in the one brief instant of awareness that remained to him, he knew at last how wrong he had been.

He had forgotten that four dimensions are not the outermost limits of conceivable scope. Cabell had unwittingly led him astray: there are dimensions in which a cube may have many more than six sides. Clarissa's dimension—

Extensions are possible in dimensions not entirely connected with space—or rather, space is merely a medium through which these extensions may be made. And because humans live upon a three-dimensional planet, and because all planets in this continuum are three-dimensional, no psychic tesseract is possible—except by extensions.

That is, a collection of chromosomes and genes, arranged on earth and here conceived, cannot in themselves form the matrix for a superman. Nor can a battery give more than its destined voltage. But if there are three, six, a dozen batteries of similar size, and if they are connected in series—

Until they are connected, until the linkage is complete, each is an individual. Each has its limitations. There are gropings, guided fumblings through the dark, while those in charge seek to help the scattered organism in fulfilling itself. And therefore the human mind can comprehend the existence of a superbeing up to the point that the connection is made and the batteries become one unit, of enormous potential power.

On earth there was Clarissa and her nominal aunt—who could not be comprehended at all.

On a remote planet in Cygnae Taurus, there was a Clarissa too, but her name there was something like Ezandora, and her mentor was a remote and cryptic being who was accepted by the populace as a godling.

On Seven Million Four Twenty Eight of Center Galaxy there was Jandav, who carried with her a small crystal through which her guidance came.

In atmospheres of oxygen and halogen, in lands ringed with the shaking blaze of crusted stars beyond the power of our telescopes—beneath water, and in places of cold and darkness and void, the matrix repeated itself, and by the psychic and utterly unimaginable power and science of *homo superior,* the biological cycle of a race more than human ran and completed itself and began again. Not entirely spontaneously, at the same time, in many worlds, the pattern that was Clarissa was conceived and grew. The batteries strengthened.

Or to use Cabell's allegory, the Clarissa Pattern impinged one facet upon earth, but it was not one facet out of a possible six—but one out of a possible infinity of facets. Upon each face of that unimaginable geometric shape, a form of Clarissa moved and had independent being, and gradually developed. Learned and was taught. Reached out toward the center of the geometric shape that was—or one day would be—the complete Clarissa. One day, when the last mirror-facet sent inward to the center its matured reflection of the whole, when the many Clarissas, so to speak, clasped hands with themselves and fused into perfection.

Thus far we can follow. But not after the separate units become the complete and tremendous being toward which the immaturity of Clarissa on so many worlds was growing. After that, the destiny of *homo superior* has no common touching point with the understanding of *homo sapiens.* We knew them as children. And they passed. They put away childish things.

"Clarissa—" he said.

Then he paused, standing motionless in silence, looking across that dark threshold into that mirrory dimness, seeing—what he saw. It was dark on the landing. The staircases went up and down, shadowy and still. There was stasis here, and no movement anywhere in the quiet air. This was power beyond the need for expression of power.

He turned and went slowly down the stairs. The fear and pain and gnawing uneasiness that had troubled him for so long were gone now. Outside, on the curb, he lit a cigarette, hailed a taxi, and considered his next movements.

A cab swung in. Further along the street, the liquid, shining blackness of the East River glissaded smoothly down to the Sound. The rumble of an El train came from the other direction.

"Where to, sergeant?" the driver asked.

"Downtown," Lessing said. "Where's a good floor show?" He relaxed pleasantly on the cushions, his mind quite free from strain or worry now.

This time the memory block was complete. He would go on living out his cycle, complacent and happy as any human ever is, enjoying life to his capacity for enjoyment, using the toys of earth with profound satisfaction.

"Nightclub?" the driver said. "The new Cabana's good—"

Lessing nodded. "O.K. The Cabana." He leaned back, luxuriously inhaling smoke. It was the children's hour. ∎

... AND COMFORT TO THE ENEMY

Stanley Schmidt

CARLA FELT THE CHILL OF APPROACHING WINTER *more than I did. I had been here for nearly a year, and for all that time the twenty-year winter had been advancing stealthily as the Little Sun hurtled away toward aphelion. I was used to the cold. But Carla had only come out from Earth to join me a few days ago, after my boss finally decided to make my assignment here permanent. Spending all that time in Florida had done little to prepare her for the bleak hills and cold air here.*

Today I was showing her Centaurus Historical Park, jointly maintained by humans and Redskins as a memorial to their first meeting here a few decades earlier. The climb from the quaint little Mayflower *village was strenuous enough to take her mind off the cold, and she showed revived interest as we strolled among the historic boulders on the hilltop. Hardly anyone else was there, either human or Redskin (a corruption of "Reska" which happened to fit), so we could read the plaques set in the rockfaces at our leisure.*

Carla paused for a long time in front of the one which told how the first Redskins here had had to be rescued from their own laws against antagonizing alien races—laws which to civilized humans seemed almost incredibly harsh. Finally she said quietly, "Mike, I think that's why I feel uneasy about them."

"Huh?" I said, surprised, "Who?"

"The Redskins." She drew her sweater tighter around her shoulders and motioned toward the plaque. "They were going to slaughter their own people because one of them might *have trivially annoyed a human. I know there's been no trouble since, but I can't help thinking there's something sinister about them that may show up someday. Humans* wouldn't *treat their own like that!"*

I put my arm around her and tried to think how to dispel her vague worries. Thoughts like that weren't going to make frontier life any easier for her. Before I found words, an unmistakably accented voice behind us said quietly, "Please don't be too sure of that."

Carla jumped a foot and whirled around with a little shriek to find herself facing a Redskin. He was shorter than Carla, hairless, his skin toughened and darkened almost to brown by age and work, and his face might have been drawn by a human caricaturist. But I hoped Carla would recognize his smile and the twinkle in his eyes.

Just in case, I hastened to introduce her. "Carla, this is Kirlatsu, a good friend of mine from the day I landed here and a real old-timer on the Reska spaceways. Kirlatsu, my wife, Carla."

Kirlatsu extended his hand and Carla took it, a trifle timidly. "Very happy to meet you, Carla," he told her. "I'm sorry if I startled you. But I overheard your comment, and I wouldn't want Mike's wife to get the wrong idea. Our colonization laws are extreme—but so were the events that produced them. I know. I was there.

"I knew Ngasik well. Our paths crossed in several sirla *during our* dlazöl, *and though he was four years older, we were close friends on Slepo IV . . ."*

· The last time Kirlatsu actually saw Ngasik was the night the first tunnel ship came. When dusk fell they and a few other young men of Sirla Tsardong still sat—as usual—around a flickering campfire, plying Ngasik for the tales he told so well at the end of a hard day's work. His supply was seemingly inexhaustible—nobody could remember hearing him repeat a yarn—and his gift of gab held listeners enthralled for hours. But tonight stories were not forthcoming.

Instead Ngasik's gaze kept wandering off to the uninvited new ship, a hundred yards away at the other end of the clearing. The big gibbous moon and fireflies flitting in and out of the forest gave enough light to make out its ludicrous outline, with the top half a mirror image of the bottom, but little more. Its crew had retired into it for the night, and a couple of ports still glowed in its side. Ngasik would stop in mid-sentence, stare wistfully at those ports, and murmur things like, "They've come all the way out here just to do away with the one way of life that really suited me!"

Finally one of the others laughed at him. "Come on, Ngasik! This doesn't come as a shock to anybody. We've been hearing progress reports on tunnel-ship development for a couple of years now. And why should you care? You're no criminal."

Ngasik couldn't see exactly who had spoken, but he glared across the fire at the voice. "For some of us," he said coolly, "space was the one place we could find something like independence. What's it going to be with government inspectors coming out in their own ships to check up on us all the time?"

"Safer," his critic muttered. A couple of people on the other side of the fire got up and went to their huts. Kirlatsu, here on his first job, did not yet find alien wilderness as congenial as Ngasik. He suggested mildly, "The only reason we haven't had them from the start is that warp ships are too expensive to run without a big payload, and we didn't know there was another way. Maybe it's a good idea. Suppose some sirla met another race with an advanced technology and decided to stir up trouble. If that had happened before there were tunnel ships to patrol the colonies . . ."

"Frankly," Ngasik interrupted, "I don't think anybody seriously expects that to happen. I've been in space four years—some people for sixteen. No sign of alien intelligence. The old philosophers were right. We're probably unique, a long shot that hit once."

By ones and twos, members of the circle gave up on getting the usual stories and drifted off to their huts. Eventually only Ngasik and Kirlatsu remained. Lacking the distraction of Ngasik's narrative, Kirlatsu grew more and more conscious of the wild noises from the surrounding forest, and they made him uncomfortable. They seemed even louder and more persistent than usual tonight—especially those deep, wavering, chilling howls. And the bugs were intensely annoying—the dome of fence-field over the camp was fine for keeping out big prowling animals, but nearly worthless against small crawling and flying things. Kirlatsu found himself swatting at them constantly. Finally, losing his temper, he raised a heavily shod foot and stamped viciously at a beetlelike thing on the ground, so big it must have found a "soft" place in the field between two generators to get in. As it died, it emitted a long moan, high-pitched and falling. To Kirlatsu it sounded exactly like, ". . . Shot that hit once."

"Did you hear that?" he gasped.

Ngasik shrugged. "Mimic," he said. "Not uncommon. I've seen a couple of those around lately. Didn't know they did that, though."

Kirlatsu stood up. "My imagination's running away with me," he said apologetically. "Good night, Ngasik." He went off to his hut, a modest but comfortable structure of native rock and wood, and locked himself in. Shortly he heard Ngasik extinguishing the fire and going off to his own hut, and stretched out to try to sleep.

It's not *just my imagination*! Kirlatsu thought defensively as sleep continued to elude him. *There's something different in the air tonight. Something's brewing. Those noises really* are *worse*. The forest seemed to scream at him. A plaintive, agitated series of those howls sounded nearby. Another seemed to answer it from far off.

Suddenly there were sounds *very* nearby—the rustles and thumps of large animals moving in the grass, and a familiar chattering. Kirlatsu knew even before he jumped up to look out his window that they were tsapeli, but he had never known them to come this close to camp before.

He saw three dark forms prowling just at the edge of the invisible dome. They stopped. Standing very still, they cautiously began to look intently around the camp. Three pairs of eyes began to glow faint green, and then gradually grew and brightened until they were piercing white searchlights. One of them nearly blinded Kirlatsu when it looked right at his hut window. Then the eyes dimmed again and the tsapeli were running toward the invisible shell, hurling themselves against it, bouncing off and trying again.

Kirlatsu began to feel very uncomfortable. He knew—intellectually, at least—that the tsapeli couldn't get through that wall. But the very idea that they would *try* was alarming. In the three months since the sirla established itself here, he had thought of the tsapeli as picturesque creatures of the night, rather eerie with their searchlight eyes and mantis faces, but not dangerous as long as nobody went outside at night and chased them. Now they were making a deliberate effort to break into camp.

He was relieved to hear Ngasik's voice outside, summoning any and all to help him chase the pests off. Young men made brave by fence-field, flashlights, and numbers swarmed from their huts. Kirlatsu joined them.

In the flashlight beams the tsapeli could be seen more clearly. Monkeylike, with prehensile tail and four hands of which they could walk on two or four, they were as large as adult Reska. Smooth black fur covered them almost completely, even most of the head—a small sphere housing mouth, nostrils, and a pair of triangular "wings" with eyes at the tips and ears farther in.

They stood their ground, all three chattering at once and staring back at the Reska with eyes glowing at full strength. After a moment of that, Ngasik started a noise-making and hand-waving campaign. He was obviously enjoying himself until he saw that the tsapeli were just waving back and chattering louder.

And then a metallic gleam at the far end of the clearing revealed at least a dozen tsapeli surrounding the *Tsulan*, the government tunnel ship that had come in this afternoon.

Just at that moment Tsardong-li, local boss of Sirla Tsardong, popped out of his hut demanding to know what was going on. He didn't finish asking before he saw for himself. He yelped, "Get those critters away from here—and away from that ship!"

"We're working on it," Ngasik told him cheerfully. "They don't seem very anxious to go."

"Well, *make* them go!" Tsardong-li ordered. "All of you—take guns outside if you have to. Just get rid of them. Don't come back until they're gone!"

Within two minutes a very hesitant Kirlatsu was running back out of his hut with gun and key in hand and joining the group streaming out of the dome—while Tsardong-li stayed inside to shout useless encouragements. Each man approached the shell on the run, pointing his key straight ahead so it canceled just enough fence-field to let him through. The tsapeli tried to find the holes they saw Reska coming through, and had to be chased away with shots.

Faced with actual weapon fire, they finally turned and fled, bounding away on all fours—straight toward the larger group around the *Tsulan*. As the Reska converged on the ship, all the tsapeli gathered there turned to face them, staring blindingly. Their chattering changed to shrill sirenlike noises. Just before he began shooting, Kirlatsu could barely hear a fresh chorus of howls start up in the nearby forest.

As soon as the shooting started, the tsapeli began jumping wildly around, but made no move to leave. Between their blazing eyes and their erratic jumping, decent aim was impossible and the Reska scored few hits. The only consolation, Kirlatsu thought wryly, was that the tsapeli weren't shooting back.

Then he heard the rustle of wings and looked up to see dozens of big, sharp-beaked, beacon-eyed "birds" emerging from the forest and swooping down among the Reska. Suddenly the Reska were too busy warding off birds—none too successfully—to keep

Stanley Schmidt

up very steady firing. The flying things were diving quickly and unpredictably, in-flicting nasty stabs and poking at Reska weapons, keys, and lights.

Just as he managed to shoot a bird that was coming after him, Kirlatsu saw Ngasik's gun knocked from his hand by another. Immediately four or five tsapeli ran out, oblivious of birds and gunfire, and surrounded Ngasik. Kirlatsu saw them coming and so did another Reska who was momentarily free. They both opened fire on the same tsapeli and blasted him to a pulp. Then they had their hands full of birds again, while the other tsapeli who had rushed Ngasik grabbed him and quickly subdued his struggles. Carrying him easily, they vanished into the forest. Two others roughly grabbed up the remains of the demolished tsapeli and followed them.

In less than a minute no tsapeli was in sight, but the birds continued their diving and slashing for some ten minutes. Their numbers never seemed to diminish—when one was shot down, another came out of the forest. Then, as abruptly as they had come, the survivors scattered and vanished.

The Reska were too badly shaken by the experience, and too riddled with physical injuries, to attempt pursuit. Instead they returned, as fast as if pursued themselves, to the safety of the dome. They neither saw nor heard any more of Ngasik that night, and could only reconstruct its events later.

Ngasik gave up struggling almost immediately; it was a waste of energy. His captors were all too capable of keeping viselike grips on him even while plunging through the pitch-dark forest on winding trails nearly overgrown with smelly bushes. To Ngasik's diurnal eyes their speed seemed reckless, but for the nocturnal tsapeli that was normal lighting. The powerful beams their eyes could produce were reserved for short periods of unusually critical observation. Quite likely they had been evolved less as sensory aids than as weapons against other nocturnal animals.

Between jolts, as his four bearers ran unevenly over the rough ground, Ngasik found himself reflecting that his deliberate abduction by four of them in cooperation was rather odd behavior for jungle beasts. Moreover, they were still chattering inter-mittently, in ways no Reska could hope to imitate, but Ngasik began to feel strongly that they were talking among themselves. Maybe his comment to Kirlatsu at the campfire had been a bit presumptuous. From a practical point of view, he wasn't at all sure that being the first Reska to be captured by intelligent alien savages was especially preferable to being captured by unintelligent alien monsters.

In the darkness and traveling on feet not his own, Ngasik found it very hard to estimate distances, but he guessed that they went perhaps a mile before they stopped. He wished he had been able to tell more about the route. All members of the sirla carried two-way radio handsets in the field, and if the tsapeli didn't take his he would try to call Kirlatsu at the first chance. But not knowing where he was, relative to camp, would make it very hard to help the sirla plot his rescue.

He could see only that they had paused in front of one of those huge fungoid growths sirla workers had often seen in the forest and sometimes mistaken for rocks. This one was at least ten feet high and surrounded by thorny bushes. A tsapeli hurried forward from the rear of the procession and looked ready to rush right into the bushes. He did, in fact, but they parted with a loud rustle at his approach, exposing a gaping opening. The bushes stayed apart as the rest of the procession followed him into the cavernous interior of the fungoid, and snapped back together as soon as the last tsapeli was inside.

There were many more fireflies inside than out, but not nearly enough for Ngasik. The tsapeli put him down, letting him stand on his own feet but keeping tight holds on his arms. At first he could see nothing except the lazily flying points of light. His strongest initial impression was the powerful mixture of odors that filled the place, most of them recognizably organic and many almost nauseating. But as seconds passed his eyes adjusted enough so he could make out the forms standing around him, some erect and some down on all fours, and another door leading to deeper darkness at the back of the room. Next to that door a birdlike thing perched on what looked like a defoliated tree branch, so still that Ngasik wasn't sure if it were alive. But he was quite relieved to see that it had a short, innocuous-looking beak, quite unlike those vicious things that had joined the attack on the Reska back at the clearing.

The first tsapeli in crowded close to the side walls, and Ngasik could see well enough to feel slightly sick as the two carrying the badly wounded one came in and crossed in front of him. They carried their burden with utter lack of care—though the victim was in such bad shape that he was probably beyond caring. Only part of his face, marked with a distinctive white crescent, was recognizably intact. Most of his body was bloody and practically shredded. The left eye was thoroughly smashed.

One of the carriers emitted a short burst of loud chatter as they crossed the room. The tsapeli holding Ngasik followed them to a far corner, dragging Ngasik along. They paused next to a big, shapeless sack resting in a recess in the wall. Another tsapeli emerged from the back room and joined them. The newcomer quickly looked the victim over, with apparent disinterest, and then watched as each of Ngasik's captors used one hand to help pull a long slit open at the top of the sack.

Ngasik quickly looked away and then back. The sack was partly filled with a dark, vile-smelling liquid, richly populated with writhing wormlike things of many shapes and sizes. Battling nausea, though he was not normally squeamish, he forced himself to watch as the victim was dumped unceremoniously into that mess, landing with a dull splash. Then his captors let the sack snap shut again, and all the tsapeli walked unconcernedly away from it. Most of them left through the front door, exchanging chatter as they went. The one from the back room and Ngasik's bodyguards, again gripping him with both hands, stayed.

The one from the back room moved around in front of Ngasik. Without warning, his eyes glowed brightly and swept Ngasik from head to toe. The examination lasted perhaps ten seconds; then darkness returned and Ngasik felt something slimy slapped on his arm, followed by a faint tickling sensation where it was. He had shut his eyes when the tsapeli's had suddenly started glowing, so he could almost immediately see the big leechlike thing sucking on his skin. Automatically, he yelled, "Hey, get that thing off me!"

Not very surprisingly, they ignored him. He didn't bother to yell again. After two or three long minutes, the same tsapeli disengaged the leech and carried it through the second door. Oddly, there were no fireflies in the back room, and the tsapeli with the leech used a little green light from his eyes. Ngasik could faintly see an unusual variety of small fungoids growing on the floor and walls back there, but he couldn't tell what the tsapeli was doing.

In a few minutes the keeper of the leech returned, emitted a piercing sirenlike burst, and then chattered briefly to the others. In a few seconds a very large and ugly carnivore, its entire body slightly luminescent, came bounding in through the front door. Ngasik stiffened. His captors let go of him and walked casually out the front door.

He glanced after them in surprise, then looked warily back at the saber-toothed carnivore. The one remaining tsapeli motioned meaningfully at the beast, chattered briefly, and left Ngasik alone with it.

Ngasik and the big meat-eater watched each other motionlessly for several minutes. Finally Ngasik nerved himself to try a dash for the door.

The carnivore got there first, blocking the door with its body. A blood-curdling rumble arose from deep down its wide-open throat. Ngasik changed his mind about leaving.

It was an hour before he worked up the courage to try sneaking across to the back room. Again the carnivore talked him out of it.

"O.K.," he muttered, "I'll stay. Can't say as I care for your hospitality, though."

He tried to sleep, but with little success. For one thing, he couldn't feel very secure with that watchdog in the room. For another, he kept hearing snatches of the eerie howling, outside but closer than he had ever heard it before.

Morning broke tranquil and innocuous at the Reska camp. Dead birds had been removed by scavengers and the nocturnal hordes were quiet. The tall grass in the clearing and the trees of the surrounding forest waved gently in erratic breezes, flashing bright green under clear purple sky. Beads of dew still glistened on the grass, and the tiny yellow and white diurnal arthropods so numerous in grassy clearings were out in full force. The only slightly unfamiliar note was the crop of large, flat-topped "mushrooms" which had sprung up overnight among the huts.

Kirlatsu stood by his hut and watched, with a feeling he had been spared until now, as the work crews of the sirla started out for the day. As communications specialist—radio tech, in less bombastic language—he would probably stay close to camp all day. But most of the other groups—explorers, miners, fur trappers, gatherers of plants already found useful—were going out into the fields and forests as if nothing had happened last night.

Well—*almost* as if nothing had happened. Today every man was armed, which was not standard operating procedure. Most had taken their weapons out spontaneously. Then Tsardong-li had made it mandatory.

Most of the men wore bandages. And Ngasik was not with his group.

Kirlatsu idly kicked one of the new mushrooms and noticed that it was too tough to care. Then he looked up and noticed Dzukarl, the Arbiter from Reslaka, hurrying toward him from the *Tsulan*. Dzukarl, Kirlatsu reflected, was the focus of Ngasik's resentment of the tunnel ships. Kirlatsu wasn't sure where he stood in that matter. He hadn't really understood why his friend was so bothered by the new ships. But then Ngasik *had* been in space a lot longer than he had . . .

Dzukarl stopped in front of him and demanded crisply, "Where's Tsardong-li?"

"In his hut, I suppose, sir."

"I want to talk to him."

"Yes, sir." Kirlatsu called the boss on his handset and relayed the message. A minute later Tsardong-li approached.

Without waiting for him to arrive, Dzukarl snapped, "Tsardong-li, what was all the infernal racket last night?"

"Wild animals," Tsardong-li answered calmly as he joined them. "Big things we call 'tsapeli.' We've seen them before. A bit more restless than usual last night . . . I think your ship shook them up."

"A bit more restless!" Kirlatsu blurted out, incredulous that Tsardong-li was treating the incident so lightly. "They got Ngasik—" Then he saw Tsardong-li glaring at him with personalized fury, realized he was out of line, and shut up.

Dzukarl turned to Kirlatsu. "Oh, really? They got one of your men, did they? Tell me about it, young fellow."

Horribly embarrassed and afraid of what Tsardong-li would do to him later, but at the same time worried about Ngasik and afraid to defy an Arbiter, Kirlatsu told. When he finished, Dzukarl turned back to Tsardong-li and said coolly, "You didn't mention any of that."

Tsardong-li stammered a little and Dzukarl added accusingly, "Sounds like intelligent behavior to me."

"Or pack behavior," Tsardong-li said, "which seems a lot more likely. Anyway, we're planning a rescue operation."

"*Planning?*" Dzukarl echoed in shocked tones. "And meanwhile your men are going about their jobs as if nothing's wrong, while one of them is out there in the jungle, maybe being—"

Kirlatsu's radio buzzed sharply. Dzukarl cut off in midsentence to listen as Kirlatsu received the call.

Ngasik's voice came through clearly enough to recognize and understand easily. There was noticeable noise, but not too much: he was well within the range of these little transceivers. "This is the first chance I've had to call," he said. He sounded drowsy. "I'm not hurt—yet. Don't know what they have in mind for me. They have a big ugly monster guarding me, but nobody's paying much attention now that the sun's up. Can't go anywhere, though. This watchdog's a light sleeper, and he's got an extra pair of eyelids he can use for sunglasses if he has to."

Kirlatsu asked anxiously, "Where are you, Ngasik?"

"I don't know. I'm in one of those big forest fungoids—the real big ones. It's hollow. But I can't tell where it is, except it's *maybe* a mile or two from camp."

Dzukarl asked, "Are those things intelligent?"

The radio voice laughed curtly. "I don't know. I have the feeling they may be savages on the *brink* of intelligence—but I mean *savages!* Kirlatsu, you know that one that was shot up so badly? Listen to what they did to him . . ." Kirlatsu listened with a sense of horror as Ngasik told about the bag of maggots, or whatever they were. Ngasik finished, "Not even the crudest, most vicious savages on Reslaka would treat their dead that way."

Tsardong-li asked, "Can you tell us anything to help us find you and get you out of there?"

"Please don't—not yet, anyway. You come charging in here with a swarm of armed men and that may be just what it takes to make the tsapeli decide to dump me in a handy maggot bag. I think I have a better idea."

"What?"

"Look, I'm going to have to keep these reports short. I'll tell you if it works. I'll try to call every day, if I stay that long, but I want to be sure my radio power cell gets lots of rest. O.K.? Better stop for now . . ." Kirlatsu's receiver went silent.

Nobody said anything for a few seconds. Then Dzukarl told Tsardong-li, "You should have reported this when it happened. Frankly, I think we got these patrol ships going just in time. I have an ugly hunch we have our first culture-contact crisis developing here. I've half a mind to order you off the planet right now."

"And leave Ngasik?" Tsardong-li snapped. "Besides, I don't think you could. The only laws anybody ever bothered to pass on the subject are pretty explicit about real danger from a culture at least comparable to our own. I hardly think these subhumans qualify."

Dzukarl didn't answer right away, because it was obvious that Tsardong-li also knew the law—such as it was. As it turned out, he didn't answer at all, for at that moment they were interrupted again.

The nearest mushroom said, "Excuse me, gentlemen. May I have your attention for a few moments?"

After a day of fitful sleep, during which he woke several times but never saw the bird on the branch move, Ngasik finally decided it was time to stay awake and get ready to try his escape "plan." It was risky, but it just might let him get out quickly enough to avoid injury.

Virtually all wild animals feared fire. It seemed reasonable that savages who had not yet learned to control and use it would also fear it. By kindling a bonfire, Ngasik hoped to get his captors so confused and excited that they wouldn't notice if he bolted into the forest.

Kindling a bonfire might not be easy. Because of the watchdog, he would have to do it right in the middle of the floor. There was practically no fuel available—unless the fungus itself burned easily, which Ngasik was a little afraid it might. But it might not take much. He could spare some of the uncomfortable clothes the Reska wore here as protection against the alien environment . . .

His lighter worked well. Darkness had barely become complete outside when the small pile of fabrics burst into leaping orange flames, crackling loudly and filling the room with smoke. For a tense moment Ngasik thought the floor was going to catch, but then he saw it turning dark and wet around the fire. The watchdog leaped up, yelping wildly, and shut the dark membranes over its eyes. It glared menacingly at Ngasik, then glanced at the fire and dashed noisily out the front door.

Ngasik tried to follow, but as he started the painful crawl through the unyielding guard bushes he met several tsapeli on the run. He backed into the room, choking on the smoke, and stood aside as two of the tsapeli came in, following by a lumbering, armor-skinned quadruped with a huge pointed snout. At a signal from one tsapeli, the quadruped walked up and methodically sprayed the fire with white foam from its snout. The other tsapeli walked—*walked*, not ran—around the fire and did something to the still-motionless bird's head. Immediately the bird flapped its stubby wings and moved onto the tsapeli's shoulder. Almost without stopping, the tsapeli continued around the dying fire. He stopped in front of Ngasik, looked straight at him and gabbled something.

The bird squawked, "That's a no-no."

Ngasik blinked, then shrugged. If one intelligent species here, why not another, physically capable of both tsapeli and Reska speech and for some reason willing to act as a go-between? But then, how had it learned Resorka?

Ngasik hoped to get a chance to speak to the bird alone. For now, he would have to be content with conversing through it.

The Resorka-speaking bird was only one of two surprises of the moment. Ngasik commented wryly on the other. "You guys didn't seem exactly terrified of my fire."

The bird chattered like a tsapeli, then the tsapeli himself chattered for a while, then the bird spoke again in Resorka. "No. We don't use it any more—outlawed it long ago as dangerous and unnecessary—but that's hardly cause for irrational fear of it. When one gets started accidentally, we put it out and go about our business. Yours wasn't accidental."

The other tsapeli said something which the bird didn't translate and went back to the dark corner where they had dumped their dead—or at least mortally wounded —compatriot. The one with the bird on his shoulder went along.

Ngasik didn't, since nobody dragged him and he had seen more than enough of what was in that corner. He looked toward the door and toyed with the idea that this might be his chance to escape. Then the armor-plated animal, finished putting out the fire, lumbered out. The bushes parted for it and Ngasik saw his watchdog pacing back and forth outside. He dropped the idea of running for now. He started mulling over what the bird had said about not using fire "anymore," but then he was startled by a third tsapeli voice behind him.

He whirled and stared. A tsapeli with a familiar white crescent on his face stood in front of the niche in the wall, chattering away with the others. His fur was wet, but he looked unscarred and in robust health. Ngasik recognized dizzily that his idea of what went on in that sack was in for some drastic revision.

The three tsapeli stood talking incomprehensibly, with frequent obvious allusions to Ngasik, for some minutes. Meanwhile another came in the front door and offered Ngasik a tray of uncooked local food. Ngasik looked at it with a mixture of disgust and hunger, noticed that this was the same tsapeli who had introduced him to the leech and the watchdog, and decided not to eat. He had found a potable spring in a corner, which the watchdog was willing to share with him, and for a while that would be enough.

The one with the food put the tray down but stayed where he was. He said something to the others and they came over to join him. The wet one with the crescent stepped forward and scrutinized Ngasik with the aid of his eyelights. When he finished, he looked into Ngasik's face, his eyes still glowing dull green, and demanded—through the bird—"Where did you creatures come from?"

Ngasik resented being called a creature by this creature, but nevertheless started trying to phrase an answer that would convey a modicum of truth to these primitives. "You've seen the stars in the sky?" he began. "Each of them is a giant ball of fire, very far away. Around many of them revolve worlds, like yours. My people come from such a world, so far away it takes light almost seventy years to get here from there—"

"O.K., O.K.!" the crescent-faced tsapeli interrupted. "Another planet of another star. Why not just say so? You've got it backwards, anyway—the stars go around the planets. Anyway *ours* does."

"How do you know that?" Ngasik asked.

The tsapeli jabbered among themselves. Finally one of them announced authoritatively, "It is taught by our philosophers. As for planets associated with other stars, we're not sure there are such things. Yet I suppose it is reasonable that if our sun goes around a planet, others could, too. Although they would have to be exceedingly far away, since we can't see such motion . . ."

"I said ours was seventy light-years away. That's pretty far."

"That's confusing, too. How can light take time to go anywhere? Vision is instantaneous. Anyway, suppose we buy your story. Then how did you get here?"

Ngasik groaned. How could he possibly hope to explain spacewarp to beings with no technology at all—beings who thought light traveled instantaneously? He could remember the concise rote definitions given to young Reska during dlazöl, but even they would help little. Some of the words probably were not even translatable. But it was all he could do.

"Our ships," he began, "bend space around themselves to provide more convenient geodesics . . ."

Mild furor broke out among the tsapeli. As Ngasik had expected, not much was getting through. The remainder of the night's interrogation was a spectacular exercise in futility, one big conversational impasse with only a few welcome leaks. But though little was accomplished, it went on until a couple of hours before dawn.

When the tsapeli finally left, and the watchdog came back in, Ngasik fought down his desire for sleep. Now was his chance to talk to the "parrot." He moved close to its perch and whispered, "Are you a prisoner of theirs, too?"

But the bird just spouted a tsapeli sentence of the same length and waited for a reply, though no tsapeli was present. Ngasik gave up and went to sleep, despite the renewed howling outside.

The parrot understood nothing. All it could do was translate.

Ngasik's morning call came later than expected. Kirlatsu, agitated by the events of yesterday and this morning, was tremendously relieved when he finally heard it. He listened with disappointment as Ngasik told how his fire trick had flopped, but he hardly heard the details. He was too brimming with his own startling news. As soon as he felt an opening in the conversation, he burst out, "Ngasik, there *is* intelligent life on the planet!"

"Oh, really?" Ngasik said calmly. "Do tell."

Kirlatsu did. "Yesterday morning we found some new things growing on the ground, mushroom-shaped with flat tops that turn out to be loudspeakers. They started talking to us!"

"Hm-m-m? What did they say?"

"You certainly are taking this calmly," Kirlatsu observed.

"Sorry. Afraid I'm getting blasé in my old age. Well, what did the mushrooms have to say for themselves?"

"A lot of it was gibberish at first, but it improved. When we got over the first shock and started answering them, they seemed to learn from what we said and changed their approach accordingly. The slant, that is, the way they presented it. As for the content, they seemed to know what they wanted to say and they weren't going to be swayed from it. The gist of it was that we don't belong here and we'd better get off the continent or something terrible will happen to us."

"Like what?"

"They're very vague on that. They also had the cheery news that if we do leave this continent and go to another one we'll probably run into the same kind of threats, but that's our problem. Then this morning they changed their tune. Instead of the

Stanley Schmidt

continent, now they want us to get off the *planet*. They demand an immediate promise to that effect, and convincing evidence that we're starting to carry it out.''

"Aha!" Ngasik said suddenly. "I'm beginning to see the light, I think."

"Huh?"

"Wait. You finish your story first. What was Tsardong-li's reaction?"

"He said he wasn't going to be bullied by a toadstool, and stubbed his toe kicking the nearest one. What did you mean by 'aha'?"

"I think I'm starting to see connections. You say they switched from 'continent' to 'planet' this morning. Well, last night I was talking to some of the tsapeli through a bird they have that can translate between tsapeli and Resorka. The one that was so demolished in the fight—he came out of that bag of worms healed instead of eaten —asked me where we came from. They had a little trouble swallowing the idea that we were from a planet of a distant star, but I think they finally did. And this morning your mushrooms are talking planets instead of continents. Sounds suspiciously like your mushrooms are just propagandists planted there by the tsapeli and kept up to date by them."

"That's a bit much. Still, how did *any* of them learn our language? And can they do anything more than threaten?"

"I don't know. As for the language, they must have had spies. The mimic-beetles, maybe? I just know I'm starting to think there's more here than meets the eye."

"So is Dzukarl. He's about ready to order the sirla off the planet, but Tsardong-li's standing pat on the letter of the law—which, as he points out, makes no provision for gabby mushrooms. But Dzukarl's getting plenty nervous. Since your fire didn't faze them, are you ready to have us try to rescue you?"

Ngasik hesitated briefly before answering, "No, I still think it's too risky. I don't have any more ideas to try just now, and I'd sure like to get out of here—the eyestrain's something fierce. But unless you have something real clever and foolproof all worked out, I think I'm safer biding my time than trying anything rash."

When Ngasik's inquisitors—the Leechkeeper and Crescentface—returned at dusk, they seemed to exude exasperation. Crescentface opened the conversation with, "Why haven't your people responded to our ultimatum?"

Thereby pretty well confirming Ngasik's suspicion about the mushrooms. The tsapeli were the free agents here—probably the *only* free agents. Deal successfully with them and problems like birds and mushrooms would be solved in the bargain.

Ngasik laughed humorlessly. "I can hardly say, seeing how much contact with them you've allowed me. But one reason might be that you haven't given them any *reason* why they should leave."

"But they *must!*" the Leechkeeper said emphatically. Ngasik noted with mild surprise that they didn't seem to think it odd that he knew what the ultimatum was. "Can't they see that? Before they . . . you . . . came, everything was normal. All nature was in harmony. Your coming introduced a clashing note. You brought discord

and destruction. If you stay it will just get worse. Everything will . . . collapse—"
His voice drifted off and his tail twitched nervously. Ngasik could see that he realized
he was not making himself clear.

Ngasik could sympathize somewhat with that frustration, but that didn't change the
fact that the Leechkeeper's plea sounded like nothing more than superstitious fear of
the vaguest kind. There was nothing in it substantial enough for Ngasik to seize on
and try to clarify. He said, "I'm sorry. But I could never persuade them to leave on
the basis of that. Tsardong-li is a hard-boiled egg. He'd have to have neat, specific,
compelling reasons, succinctly phrased and preferably expressed in cash terms to the
nearest decimal."

"There *are* compelling reasons!" the Leechkeeper insisted. "I just don't know how
to explain them to you. I don't think the translator is equipped—" He gave up. Ngasik
recalled his own attempts to tell where he had come from, and how, and for a moment
he felt sure he understood the Leechkeeper's feeling. Perhaps there really were reasons
why the Reska produced far-reaching disturbances here. Perhaps even Tsardong-li
could be moved by them—if he could be told, to his satisfaction, what they were. But
if he couldn't there was no chance.

All Ngasik could do was to repeat, "I'm sorry. Maybe the danger isn't as great as
you think. Surely we can't be *that* terrible a threat to you. We haven't even—"

Suddenly—to the momentary confusion of the translator-parrot—Crescentface interrupted with a fierce stamp of his foot and lashing of his tail. "The danger is real,"
he said hotly, "and we haven't overestimated it. If we can't make you understand it,
that's too bad. We meant you no harm and we hoped to avoid it, but we have no
choice left. We don't make threats we can't follow up. Our warnings were simple
statements of fact." Then he switched to his own language, untranslated, for five
seconds, and stamped angrily out, emitting a series of siren screams as he passed
through the door.

Ngasik was left alone with the Leechkeeper, hopelessly confused and for the first
time actually fearful of what was happening. He asked the Leechkeeper, "What's the
matter with him? Where's he going?"

The Leechkeeper said only, "They were warned. You can't expect us to sit idle
and watch our way of life be destroyed."

An unprecedentedly chilling chorus of howls had already started outside, some of
them just outside the door. Ngasik still didn't know what kind of animals produced
the howls, though he had heard them often and had seen many animals, but suddenly
he was practically positive they were instruments of long-distance communication for
the tsapeli. Something was being plotted out there. Under the howls, briefly, he faintly
heard a buzzing of wings, far smaller and faster than the razor-beaked birds that had
attacked the Reska the night he was captured.

He protested, "But nobody's trying to destroy your way of life! Listen—"

The Leechkeeper interrupted dully, "Whether you kill us maliciously or accidentally, we're just as dead."

Ngasik tried to explain that there was no reason to believe any such thing was going to happen. Privately, he wasn't so sure. Even as he talked, he remembered his pavement-encrusted home planet and how different it was now from the wilderness most of it had been a few centuries earlier. He himself had chosen space and wild planets in preference to the noise and pollution that came with the comforts of home. It could happen here, too—not overnight, of course.

Just minutes later, he was interrupted by the sound of huge wings outside. The Leechkeeper said, "Come with me," and went through the door with the parrot still on his shoulder. Ngasik hesitated a moment and then followed. He really had no more than a fleeting illusion of a choice.

The Leechkeeper led him a few dozen feet to a clearing tightly hemmed in by trees. The full moon hanging above the clearing showed an enormous "bird" on the ground, wings partly spread and filling a great deal of the clearing. The bird was leaning awkwardly forward, and Crescentface was climbing into a deep pouch just below its throat. The Leechkeeper indicated that Ngasik should climb in next to him. Ngasik hesitated, but only until Crescentface gave a siren burst and the watchdog came charging from among the trees. Finally the Leechkeeper climbed in and slipped something in the parrot's mouth.

Ngasik, trying to get used to the excessive warmth and snug fit of the pouch, which came up to his chin when he stood full-length in it, asked his tsapeli escorts, "Where are we going?"

Crescentface said, "To the capital."

"Capital?" Ngasik echoed sharply. "Of what?"

"The continent." And then the parrot went limp. The Leechkeeper tucked it down inside the pouch and shouted something. The big bird leaned back, raising its passengers several feet, and started flapping its expansive wings. All three passengers stood with their heads above the pouch, watching the moonlit clearing fall below. Then they hung between the stars and the dark trees, rapidly gaining speed and altitude.

Ngasik, for the first time really shocked by events, took out his radio and tried frantically to get a call through to Kirlatsu. The tsapeli were watching, of course, but at least they couldn't understand what he said with the parrot drugged. He wanted somebody of the sirla to know what was happening.

But no answer came.

Kirlatsu heard, but was quite unable to answer. The disease which had started raging through the Reska camp only minutes earlier, striking with terrifying suddenness and simultaneity, had just got to him. He was in the initial stage of severe nausea and violent muscle spasms, and had no idea how he would be in ten minutes. Some were already dead; others were still passing through a varied succession of agonizing symptoms. A few seemed to be making a partial recovery already, and still fewer, immune or at least delayed in their reaction, had not yet been struck.

And Ngasik's fading voice from Kirlatsu's radio was saying, "They *were* behind the mushrooms' threats, and they insist they weren't kidding. Don't know what they mean, but you'd better watch out . . ."

Thanks for the advice, Kirlatsu thought wryly. Gradually he began to feel better, passing into a phase characterized by great, but finite, weakness and misery. But by the time he was able to reach and use his radio, Ngasik was out of range.

There was no point in even attempting a reply now. Later—if he lived long enough—Kirlatsu could build a new transmitter powerful enough to reach Ngasik's handset, and a receiver capable of picking Ngasik's weak signal out of overwhelming noise. The techniques were routine but would take time, and Kirlatsu was in no condition to even start them now.

Instead he called Dzukarl, aboard the *Tsulan*, and gasped out the essentials of what had happened to Ngasik. He finished with a personal comment. "I'm afraid you were right. They are dangerous. We should have listened to their . . ." He heard motions inside the ship that sounded like somebody getting ready to come out. "Don't come out!" he warned quickly. "There's . . . sickness out here. Or do you have it on the ship, too?"

"None that I know," Dzukarl said.

Kirlatsu started to feel a new pounding sensation in his eyes and ears. "It struck suddenly," he explained. "Just a few minutes ago. It sounds silly, but . . . Ngasik said the tsapeli were repeating their threats just before it happened." The pain was getting worse. Kirlatsu just hoped this would pass like the first painful phase. He added, "Some of us are dead already. Keep the ship sealed."

Dzukarl snapped, "Is Tsardong-li alive?" Kirlatsu strained to see. The boss had fallen just a few yards away, but Kirlatsu couldn't tell whether he was alive or not. Dzukarl repeated his question more loudly.

Kirlatsu said weakly, "I don't know." Then he saw Tsardong-li's arm creeping out toward his own radio, reaching it, snapping it on, then lying exhausted from the effort.

"Yes," Tsardong-li said, just loud enough for his radio to hear.

"Listen," the Arbiter said, "I'm telling you once more: take your sirla off this planet before it's too late. We'll bring you aboard and take you home in quarantine under expert medical care."

Tsardong-li found strength to snarl, "No! I'm not going to be beat that easily. I have my own medics." (*If any of them are still alive*, Kirlatsu thought sourly.) "And I'm still not convinced that anything here comes under your jurisdiction."

Dzukarl muttered something under his breath. "If it doesn't," he said aloud, "it's high time it did. Whether the tsapeli are a legally civilized race or not, messing with them is like playing with fire. Tsardong-li, you're about to become a precedent. Stay if you insist. I'm rushing a full report on the situation here back to Reslaka. When

I come back, I'll have a warrant to take everybody who's still alive off here. You won't gain anything except a few more weeks of this and making me waste some fuel."

He broke contact. A mushroom midway between Kirlatsu and Tsardong-li asked, "Do I understand correctly that one group of you is leaving as requested—but plans to return?"

Kirlatsu, annoyed and disgusted, grunted. Had he been in more articulate shape, the grunt would have been a select morsel of Resorka profanity, but the mushroom took it for assent. It said, "I wouldn't advise that."

That was all Kirlatsu heard, for already the *Tsulan* was readying its engines. Moments later it flashed away into the night sky.

The big bird flew for hours, and for all Ngasik knew, it might have covered hundreds of miles. In its initial climb it rapidly reached such a speed that the passengers could no longer stand the wind in their faces and took refuge completely inside the pouch. Judging from feel, the bird must have early climbed into a fast stream and just ridden it without exertion for most of the trip. Then the wind on an exposed face might not have been too severe, but the temperature would have been. There was enough heat loss through the outer wall at those altitudes to make Ngasik begin to appreciate the bird's body heat.

Finally he felt a strong sensation of descent and deceleration. The tsapeli at his sides stood up and stuck their heads out the top of the pouch. Ngasik followed suit. The wind that hit his face was cold and strong, but a welcome relief after being cramped in the dark warmth of the passenger pouch for so long.

The sky was already beginning to redden with approaching dawn, and visibility was far better for diurnal eyes than when they took off. The Leechkeeper pointed with apparent pride to a region off to the right, making noises which did Ngasik little good without the parrot's help. But he did gather that that area was the "capital."

It was a plateau rimmed by steep slopes. Gray morning mists swirled skyward from a lake sunk in the middle of it. From the air, the forests which covered it looked indistinguishable from those around the sirla encampment. On the ground, after the big bird landed in a small clearing near the lake, Ngasik recognized minor differences in vegetation, but only minor ones. The "capital" was just virtually unbroken forest like all the other temperate parts of the planet.

The tsapeli led Ngasik past two of the fungoid "houses" and stopped at the third one. The interior was a single room, smaller than his previous prison, and with no extra doors or furniture other than a familiar luminous watchdog. The tsapeli indicated that he was to stay and then left, hurrying to their lodgings before the full daylight.

Ngasik, tired after the long, uncomfortable flight on an empty stomach, fell asleep almost immediately. He woke several times during the day and tried the radio, but always without success.

* * *

. . . **And Comfort to the Enemy**

Night, of course, brought visitors. Crescentface and the Leechkeeper, with the parrot on his shoulder, entered first, followed by a large stranger with more of an easygoing air than any of the other tsapeli Ngasik had met. The stranger carried a closed container, evidently carved from some fruit, under one arm. A strip of skin shaved bare above his upper lip created an effect that struck Ngasik as whimsically comical.

Crescentface gestured elaborately toward the stranger and introduced him. The parrot translated everything except the unpronounceable name, which had some resemblance to an improbable consonant cluster: "His Honor, Bdwdlsplg, First Person of the National Assembly of Sorcerers."

Bdwdlsplg wrinkled his upper lip in a way that Ngasik interpreted as a smile of sorts. "I'm afraid the bird didn't render my title very well," he apologized. "I gather it isn't really very translatable. Fortunately it's not really very important, either. My pleasure to meet you." He uncovered the container he carried and held it out to Ngasik. "You must be hungry. You'll find this nutritious and, I hope, palatable."

This time Ngasik took the food—not because he was put at ease by Bdwdlsplg's relative suavity, but simply because he had decided that for some reason the tsapeli considered him rather special. Maybe it was nothing more than the fact that he was the one bird in the hand supposed to be worth several elsewhere. Whatever the cause, they seemed unlikely to murder him—yet, anyway. His decision was also influenced, of course, by a hunger that had become overpowering.

The container held some fruit and a few small animals, none of them cooked. Yet some of them tasted remarkably as if they *had* been cooked. There were also a couple of smaller containers, one containing a thin liquid and the other a sort of pudding. Ngasik was about to try the pudding when he noticed several of the little white arthropods he had seen in clearings lodged in its surface.

Bdwdlsplg saw him staring at them and explained, "They make the pudding for us. It's our main staple crop, and the bug colonies plant it, take care of it, and harvest it, thereby saving us all that trouble. They convert it to this form, and all we have to do is gather it from their hives. Very satisfying form of agriculture. Naturally the pudding always has a few of the bugs scattered through it, so rather than pick them out we just bred them for flavor."

Ngasik nodded numbly and tasted it. Actually, it wasn't bad. His upbringing included a mild prejudice against bugs in his food, but several days of fasting made that easy to overcome. He settled down to eating Bdwdlsplg's gifts without complaint.

"Now," said Bdwdlsplg, "to business. We're going to be asking you a good many questions. Before we start, do you have any you'd like to ask us? We'll be glad to answer—within reason."

"Yes," Ngasik responded immediately and with renewed irritation. "What happened to my shipmates? And don't tell me nothing did. I have my own . . . er . . . *magical* . . . ways of knowing that something did."

Stanley Schmidt

Bdwdlsplg wrinkled his lips again and made some noises that might have been laughter. "Your magic isn't as impressive as you might think. I'll admit we don't understand all the details, any more than you understand everything you've seen here. But it's pretty obvious that your technology is built on applying the fundamental principles of nature—the ones you shouldn't even have to understand—from scratch. Trying to imitate in a few years what nature has developed over millions, instead of just learning to use it and build on it. What a colossally obtuse way to try to build a civilization—when evolution has already done most of the work for you, and better than you'll ever do it yourself!"

Hold on! Ngasik thought. *Who's looking down on whose civilization? You're the savages here . . . aren't you?* He said coldly, "It's served us well. What about my shipmates—or don't you want to answer?"

"Oh, I'll answer. Are you through eating? Your friends, I regret, have contracted a particularly virulent disease, custom tailored for them. You contributed, by the way—the fluid sample Syglgdm took from you showed us what was needed."

Ngasik remembered the leech, but found the possibility of doing such a thing—and the implications of what else the tsapeli could do—a bit much to assimilate all at once. For now he accepted it and asked, "Why?"

"A last resort. They were offered a chance to leave unharmed. It was necessary for them to leave because they were disrupting the local life patterns."

"How? Mining a few minerals, harvesting a few plants? I can't believe that what little we took could have any large-scale, long-range harmful effects."

"The arrival of a second ship strongly suggested that things would get worse before they got better."

That Ngasik could not deny. "If you would confront us directly—*explain* the difficulty—maybe we could negotiate."

"There are no concessions for us to make. You don't understand the delicacy of the situation. The emergence of intelligence naturally tends to unbalance the—ecology. Do you have that word?" Bdwdlsplg had hesitated to use it, but it came through translation all right. Ngasik nodded, and Bdwdlsplg went on, "Presumably your odd devices did; certainly our tailored life forms did. Restoring and maintaining a viable balance was a hard-earned accomplishment. The new balance is so delicate, so precarious, that we have to be extremely careful about introducing new forms. The very presence of an unplanned alien element here, even quite a small one, could quite conceivably precipitate chaos.

"We realize that you probably *intend* no such thing, but you quite literally threaten our entire way of life. Therefore, we can't tolerate your presence. If you won't go willingly, and promptly, we're forced to take extreme measures. Exterminate those who are here, deter survivors who might want to come later. All without personal malice."

Part of Ngasik, even with his superficial acquaintance with ecology, could see their viewpoint. What they said might be literally true. But still, those were his shipmates, his sirla, being exterminated!

That issue was too big and confusing to grasp on the spur of the moment. He kept tossing it around mentally while a detached part of his mind asked numbly, "You say you don't even need to know the laws of physics and chemistry and—"

The translation evidently wasn't getting through. Bdwdlsplg interrupted, "I guess those are the ones. But we're just now beginning to see that maybe there are times when it would be nice to have them."

"But how—"

Bdwdlsplg held up one hand, palm forward, and wrinkled his shaved lip again. "It's my turn to ask questions now. You say you're from the stars . . ."

Dzukarl, under quarantine aboard the *Tsulan* and miserable enough just from his trembling weakness and horrible itching, winced at the scowl on Aingao's face on his phonescreen. Aingao, as Chairman of the Overgovernment of Reslaka, with jurisdiction transcending all sirla and geographic units, was not one to be offended lightly. He glared out of the screen at the Arbiter and demanded, "You're *sure* the ship was fully sealed?"

Dzukarl gulped. "Yes, sir. For several hours before the outbreak in the sirla camp. Since the onset was so sudden in the camp but seemed to miss us altogether, we assumed the disease-causing agent arrived suddenly and worked almost at once. Maybe we were wrong. I can hardly imagine the pathogen getting through the *Tsulan*'s seals. But it obviously got aboard some time and struck while we were at space."

"Hm-m-m. I gather you haven't made much progress toward isolating the germ and finding a cure?"

"No, sir. One of our medical officers died almost immediately. The other seems to be immune and has been working very diligently to get a handle on the disease. As soon as we landed he had additional, highly sophisticated, instruments sent aboard through a sterilizing chamber to help him."

"What has he learned so far?"

Dzukarl lowered his eyes from the screen. "Er . . . very little, sir. Actually, there's no lead at all yet." He added hastily, "But I'm sure something will turn up. Meanwhile, there is a sirla in a very ticklish spot with more or less intelligent natives on a world they are trying to exploit. One man has been captured. And . . . er . . . there is a remote possibility that the plague is a biological weapon used by the natives."

"*What?*" Aingao almost shouted.

"I'm afraid you heard me, sir. I can hardly accept it myself, but the aborigines *were* making threats shortly before the plague struck, to the effect that something unpleasant would happen if the Reska didn't get off the planet forthwith."

Aingao frowned. "Aborigines talking about getting off planets? Forgive me, Dzukarl, but that hardly sounds consistent."

Dzukarl shook his head miserably. "I know it's confusing, sir. I'm confused myself.

But let's figure it out later. Right now, I believe it's urgent that Sirla Tsardong be taken off that planet—and kept off. I tried to persuade Tsardong-li, but he refused. Said there was no developed race there so I had no basis for authority. Technically, he's right. But I think the case is special. I request a warrant giving me special authority to order removal."

Aingao chewed on his upper lip, pondering the request. Dzukarl elaborated on it: "Moreover, sir, I believe the probable urgency is extreme. Tunnel ships are too slow because of acceleration and deceleration time. And there will likely be considerable danger upon arrival. I would like to return by warp ship, and take a sizable armed division with me."

Aingao groaned. "I'm afraid I find your requests basically reasonable. But the *expense* of using a warp ship just for transport! And the *morality* of letting diseased men from the *Tsulan* travel with healthy soldiers . . . of sending healthy men to a plague world—"

He was interrupted by a sharp buzz in his own office. "Excuse me," he said. "Something urgent coming in." He leaned out of the field of view for several minutes, his voice becoming too low for Dzukarl to understand what he said. When he returned to Dzukarl's screen he was very pale. "Maybe it doesn't matter," he said weakly. "Your plague seems to be spreading like wildfire from your 'sealed' ship. Deaths have already been reported as much as forty miles from the spaceport. And you've been in port less than two hours!"

"Sir," Dzukarl said tightly, "I hate to mention it, but—"

Aingao nodded. "I know. In that time one ship has cleared here on an interplanetary run and another on an interstellar trade route. The interplanetary we can probably intercept, but the *interstellar* . . ." He stared blankly into space, shaking his head slowly.

There came a day when Ngasik found a signal on his radio, weak but intelligible. He listened intently, both relieved and concerned, as Kirlatsu explained, "I've built some new equipment so we could talk to you. I would have done it sooner, but I've been sick. Most of us have been sick. We had hoped to find where you were and plot a safe way to rescue you, but I'm afraid that's impossible now. There aren't enough of us left alive and well."

Ngasik felt spiritual sickness as he visualized his sirla decimated by plague, but physically he was still in good shape. Bdwdlsplg had even provided him with a diurnal watchdog so he could get some exercise in sunlight. He told Kirlatsu, "The plague is artificial. The tsapeli took a fluid sample from me and used it to *invent* a plague to exterminate the Reska. Probably some of us are immune—I haven't got it yet." (He realized abruptly that that was odd—the disease was based on *his* body fluids, and yet *he* seemed immune. Had they done something else to prevent his getting it?) "It might be a good idea for the survivors there to seal themselves in the ship. They may be after you shortly with a new strain designed to catch those who resisted the first batch. They're very anxious to eradicate us.''

"They may not have to bother," Kirlatsu said bitterly. "This one's still spreading, finally attacking individuals we thought were immune."

So maybe my time will *come*, Ngasik thought.

Kirlatsu had paused, but Ngasik said nothing. After a while Kirlatsu said pensively, "So the tsapeli caused this! They must know how to cure it, too—but they'd rather just watch us suffer and die. Ngasik . . . why are they doing this to us?''

"It's hard to explain," Ngasik said slowly. "To really understand it—to be sure whether it makes sense even from their standpoint—I'd have to know more about ecology than the little I remember from my dlazöl.

"It turns out that our 'obvious savages,' ironically, have almost a pure technocracy organized on a continent-wide basis. Their technology is entirely biological, but very advanced. The new life forms they create—and they can make them to order over-night—make it necessary to control the ecology very closely. Their entire culture depends on keeping that running smoothly. It has to be handled by people who understand it, so the modern descendants of the 'sorcerer' class who learned the tricks of manipulating life control the main branch of their government. The government has to be continent-wide because ecological interactions interlock strongly over an entire land mass.

"They claim that our coming here upsets things enough so the whole system could collapse—so they want to get rid of us, by foul means if not fair." He added wryly, "And they have the gall to hint they'd like to know our secrets of interstellar flight!''

Kirlatsu, his radio voice crackly even with the new long-distance equipment, asked, "How about the folks back home? Did the *Tsulan* take the plague there?''

Ngasik shut his eyes. "I don't know," he said. "I'm not sure how easy or hard that would be. But the tsapeli have hinted that they wouldn't mind exterminating the Reska altogether—to be very sure we give them no more trouble."

Kirlatsu said nothing, but Ngasik heard his slow, heavy breathing and knew nothing more to say to him. He broke contact.

As he tried to get back to sleep, an idea began to form in his mind—and then a decision.

Thirteen of the original hundred Reska were still alive in the sirla camp when the warp ship landed. Kirlatsu looked at it, puzzled, as it settled down, nearly filling the clearing, and became silent. He had figured the *Tsulan* might return eventually—though by the time it could get back there might be nobody alive to meet it—but certainly not this soon. And a warp ship was a surprise in any case.

He watched to see who would come out of it. In a few minutes Dzukarl emerged and walked slowly toward the camp, carrying a key to let him inside the dome. As he came close, Kirlatsu saw with a sinking sensation that he was thin and covered with the white spots that came in a late stage of the plague.

Dzukarl stopped near Kirlatsu and said, "I want to talk to Tsardong-li." His voice was weak, but had the old air of authority.

Kirlatsu said, "Tsardong-li is dead."

"I'm sorry." Brief pause. "I bring orders to remove Sirla Tsardong from Slepo IV. If possible, I am to attempt also to rescue the man who was taken prisoner. We are prepared to fight the tsapeli—"

"Don't you know when you're licked?" Kirlatsu interrupted bitterly. "Oh, we'll be glad to go back with you. All thirteen—" Then he was interrupted by the long-distance radio.

"What's going on?" Ngasik demanded anxiously. His voice was distorted by the noise filters, but Kirlatsu had little trouble understanding it. "I thought I heard a ship going over a little while ago. Is somebody—"

"This is Dzukarl," the Arbiter broke in. "I came back with a warp ship to take you all off the planet. Can you tell me where to bring a rescue party?"

"No," Ngasik answered promptly. "And you can't afford to try to find me. You went back to Reslaka. Did the plague—"

"Yes." Dzukarl nodded glumly. "It's spreading wildly over Reslaka—and the colonies, carried by ships which left port before we knew the *Tsulan* was contagious. I would never have believed a disease could spread so fast—and work so fast. I'm half afraid it could wipe us out before we find a cure."

"It could," Ngasik said bluntly. "That's what it's supposed to do."

Kirlatsu saw Dzukarl turn pale. The Arbiter said weakly, "What?"

"The tsapeli developed the plague to exterminate the Reska. Naturally they would want to make it fast-working. Otherwise we might be able to discover a cure before it had finished its job."

Dzukarl said fiercely, "O.K., they may wipe us out, but at least we can take them with us! I brought along weapons and troops. A lot of them are sick, but not too sick to go down fighting!"

"Where's the point in that?" Ngasik asked very quietly. It suddenly seemed to Kirlatsu, somehow, that the quiet in his friend's voice now was more suggestive of new-found strength than of defeat. "Suppose you bomb the whole planet—which you probably aren't equipped to do anyway. You destroy all the tsapeli. But that doesn't save the Reska—*because only the tsapeli know how to cure the plague!*

"Face it, Dzukarl—the chance of our medics finding a cure in time to stop something that works that fast is infinitesimal. If you exterminate the tsapeli, you may soothe your sense of honor—but you practically *guarantee* our extinction."

"Does it really matter?" Dzukarl asked. "Aren't we doomed either way?"

"No!" Ngasik practically shouted. "I've been living among the tsapeli, starting to learn about them. I know what their reason for doing this is. All they really want is to keep Reska off this planet—for reasons which make sense to them. Their purpose will be served if the Reska just leave and never come back. It doesn't really matter if you go away cured, just so you go away. If you come back, you can be hit with a fresh plague.''

"You mean," Dzukarl asked, confused, "they're willing to just *give* us the cure?"

"Of course not. We've made them angry and distrustful. But there is something we have and they want. They want it badly enough to risk giving you the cure in return for it. I've made a deal with them.''

"You've *what?*''

"They want to know how to build starships—and they claim they can work *one* alien into their ecology, under close supervision. I've agreed to stay and teach them.'' There was a numb silence at Kirlatsu's end of the line. Ngasik added, ''I warned them there's a lot to learn, and it will take a long time. After all, they're starting from nothing.''

"But," Dzukarl spluttered, "but . . . but, that's *treason!*''

"No!'' Kirlatsu shouted, suddenly understanding. "No, it isn't, really. And under the circumstances, I can't see that we have any choice—except nonsurvival.''

"Neither can I," Ngasik said. ''The cure will work much as the disease. Your camp and ships will be 'infected,' and the effects should start showing up very shortly. Then you leave, fast, to show good faith. When you go home, the cure will spread just as the disease did. If they don't keep their word—if any trickery shows up—I've made it clear to the tsapeli that you can get word to me without even entering the atmosphere here. In which case I've promised to kill myself, which they emphatically don't want. Otherwise, surviving Reska can be cured and stay far away from Slepo.''

Kirlatsu was full of an odd mixture of hope, relief, and gratitude—and concern. "But, Ngasik," he said, "have you thought of what you're letting yourself in for? The danger, the loneliness—''

"I'll manage," Ngasik assured him, sounding almost cheerful. "I'll keep alive; I may even find small pleasures in learning what makes these characters tick. In any case, if I can save a few billion lives it's worth it. Good-bye, Kirlatsu.''

"Good-bye, Ngasik.'' Kirlatsu broke contact and went straight to his hut. Dzukarl was still confused, but he could wait a while for an explanation. Right now Kirlatsu wanted to start remembering what it felt like to have a future.

"They kept their part of the bargain," Kirlatsu finished, "and we checked the plague before it wiped us out—but not before it killed forty-one percent of the race. With damage so great and widespread, the Overgovernment of Reslaka decided—virtually without opposition—that extreme precautions were necessary in the future.''

"To prevent more trouble with the plague?" Carla asked. "Or the tsapeli?'' She shuddered, remembering some of the gorier details of Kirlatsu's story.

Kirlatsu shook his head. "No. That was the least of our worries. Slepo IV was put strictly off limits, of course. The radical precautions were just those laws you were wondering about—to guard against trouble with races not yet imagined. You see, the really deadly thing about the tsapeli wasn't that they could start plagues.''

"It wasn't?"

"No. If we'd known *they had a highly technical culture, we wouldn't have tangled with them. If we had, Dzukarl could have forced us off even under the puny laws we had then. What we learned from the tsapeli—and it came as a terrible shock to all of us—was that a highly developed and dangerous culture might be very far from obvious . . . until it's too late. We were most anxious to see that we never fell into that trap again."*

Carla suddenly seemed to understand. She murmured an apology to Kirlatsu for what she had said earlier. And I thought of something Kirlatsu had not cleared up.

"But were you really out of this *trap?" I asked. "Weren't you—aren't* you—*afraid of what the tsapeli will do when Ngasik teaches them, and they come into space after you?"*

Kirlatsu smiled slyly. "Not terribly," he said. "You see, Ngasik was just a cook—with a gift of gab." ■

NOW INHALE

Eric Frank Russell

HIS LEG IRONS CLANKED AND his wrist chains jingled as they led him into the room. The bonds on his ankles compelled him to move at an awkward shuffle and the guards delighted in urging him onward faster than he could go. Somebody pointed to a chair facing the long table. Somebody else shoved him into it with such force that he lost balance and sat down hard.

The black brush of his hair jerked as his scalp twitched and that was his only visible reaction. Then he gazed across the desk with light gray eyes so pale that the pupils seemed set in ice. The look in them was neither friendly nor hostile, submissive nor angry; it was just impassively and impartially cold, cold.

On the other side of the desk seven Gombarians surveyed him with various expressions: triumph, disdain, satisfaction, boredom, curiosity, glee and arrogance. They were a humanoid bunch in the same sense that gorillas are humanoid. At that point the resemblance ended.

"Now," began the one in the middle, making every third syllable a grunt, "your name is Wayne Taylor?"

No answer.

"You have come from a planet called Terra?"

No response.

"Let us not waste any more time, Palamin," suggested the one on the left. "If he will not talk by invitation, let him talk by compulsion."

"You are right, Eckster." Putting a hand under the desk Palamin came up with a hammer. It had a pear-shaped head with flattened base. "How would you like every bone in your hands cracked finger by finger, joint by joint?"

"I wouldn't," admitted Wayne Taylor.

"A very sensible reply," approved Palamin. He placed the hammer in the middle of the desk, positioning it significantly. "Already many days have been spent teaching you our language. By this time a child could have learned it sufficiently well to understand and answer questions." He favored the prisoner with a hard stare. "You have pretended to be abnormally slow to learn. But you can deceive us no longer. You will now provide all the information for which we ask."

"Willingly or unwillingly," put in Eckster, licking thin lips, "but you'll provide it anyway."

"Correct," agreed Palamin. "Let us start all over again and see if we can avoid painful scenes. Your name is Wayne Taylor and you come from a planet called Terra?"

"I admitted that much when I was captured."

"I know. But you were not fluent at that time and we want no misunderstandings. Why did you land on Gombar?"

"I've told my tutor at least twenty times that I did it involuntarily. It was an emergency landing. My ship was disabled."

"Then why did you blow it up? Why did you not make open contact with us and invite us to repair it for you?"

"No Terran vessel must be allowed to fall intact into hostile hands," said Taylor flatly.

"Hostile?" Palamin tried to assume a look of pained surprise but his face wasn't made for it. "Since you Terrans know nothing whatever about us what right have you to consider us hostile?"

"I wasn't kissed on arrival," Taylor retorted. "I was shot at coming down. I was shot at getting away. I was hunted across twenty miles of land, grabbed, and beaten up."

"Our soldiers do their duty," observed Palamin virtuously.

"I'd be dead by now if they were not the lousiest marksmen this side of Cygni."

"And what is Cygni?"

"A star."

"Who are you to criticize our soldiers?" interjected Eckster, glowering.

"A Terran," informed Taylor as if that were more than enough.

"That means nothing to me," Eckster gave back with open contempt.

"It will."

Palamin took over again. "If friendly contact were wanted the Terran authorities would send a large ship with an official deputation on board, wouldn't they?"

"I don't think so."

"Why not?"

"We don't risk big boats and important people without knowing what sort of a reception they're likely to get."

"And who digs up that information?"

"Space scouts."

"Ah!" Palamin gazed around with the pride of a pygmy who has trapped an elephant. "So at last you admit that you are a spy?"

"I am a spy only in the estimation of the hostile."

"On the contrary," broke in a heavily jowled specimen seated on the right, "you are whatever we say you are—because we say it."

"Have it your own way," conceded Taylor.

"We intend to."

"You can be sure of that, my dear Borkor," soothed Palamin. He returned attention to the prisoner. "How many Terrans are there in existence?"

"About twelve thousand millions."

"He is lying," exclaimed Borkor, hungrily eying the hammer.

"One planet could not support such a number," Eckster contributed.

"They are scattered over a hundred planets," said Taylor.

"He is still lying," Borkor maintained.

Waving them down, Palamin asked, "And how many ships have they got?"

"I regret that mere space scouts are not entrusted with fleet statistics," replied Taylor coolly. "I can tell you only that I haven't the slighest idea."

"You must have *some* idea."

"If you want guesses, you can have them for what they are worth."

"Then make a guess."

"One million."

"Nonsense!" declared Palamin. "Utterly absurd!"

"All right. One thousand. Or any other number you consider reasonable."

"This is getting us nowhere," Borkor complained.

Palamin said to the others, "What do you expect? If we were to send a spy to Terra would we fill him up with top-secret information to give the enemy when caught? Or would we tell him just enough and only enough to enable him to carry out his task? The ideal spy is a shrewd ignoramus, able to take all, unable to give anything."

"The ideal spy wouldn't be trapped in the first place," commented Eckster maliciously.

"Thank you for those kind words," Taylor chipped in. "If I had come here as a spy, you'd have seen nothing of my ship, much less me."

"Well, exactly where were you heading for when forced to land on Gombar?" invited Palamin.

"For the next system beyond."

"Ignoring this one?"

"Yes."

"Why?"

"I go where I'm told."

"Your story is weak and implausible." Palamin lay back and eyed him judicially. "It is not credible that a space explorer should bypass one system in favor of another that is farther away."

"I was aiming for a binary said to have at least forty planets," said Taylor. "This system has only three. Doubtless it was considered relatively unimportant."

"What, with us inhabiting all three worlds?"

"How were we to know that? Nobody has been this way before."

"They know it now," put in Eckster, managing to make it sound sinister.

"This one knows it," Palamin corrected. "The others do not. And the longer they

Eric Frank Russell

don't, the better for us. When another life form starts poking its snout into our system we need time to muster our strength."

This brought a murmur of general agreement.

"It's your state of mind," offered Taylor.

"What d'you mean?"

"You're taking it for granted that a meeting must lead to a clash and in turn to a war."

"We'd be prize fools to assume anything else and let ourselves be caught unprepared," Palamin pointed out.

Taylor sighed. "To date we have established ourselves on a hundred planets without a single fight. The reason: we don't go where we're not wanted."

"I can imagine that," Palamin gave back sarcastically. "Someone tells you to beat it and you obligingly beat it. It's contrary to instinct."

"Your instinct," said Taylor. "We see no sense in wasting time and money fighting when we can spend both exploring and exploiting."

"Meaning that your space fleets include no warships?"

"Of course we have warships."

"Many?"

"Enough to cope."

"Pacifists armed to the teeth," said Palamin to the others. He registered a knowing smile.

"Liars are always inconsistent," pronounced Eckster with an air of authority. He fixed a stony gaze upon the prisoner. "If you are so careful to avoid trouble, why do you *need* warships?"

"Because we have no guarantee that the entire cosmos shares our policy of live and let live."

"Be more explicit."

"We chevvy nobody. But someday somebody may take it into their heads to chevvy us."

"Then you will start a fight?"

"No. The other party will have started it. We shall finish it."

"Sheer evasion," scoffed Eckster to Palamin and the rest. "The technique is obvious to anyone but an idiot. They settle themselves upon a hundred planets—if we can believe that number, which I don't! On most there is no opposition because nobody is there to oppose. On the others the natives are weak and backward, know that a struggle is doomed to failure and therefore offer none. But on any planet sufficiently strong and determined to resist—such as Gombar for instance—the Terrans will promptly treat that resistance as unwarranted interference with themselves. They will say they are being chevvied. It will be their moral justification for a war."

Palamin looked at Taylor. "What do you say to that?"

Giving a deep shrug, Taylor said, "That kind of political cynicism has been long out of date where I come from. I can't help it if mentally you're about ten millennia behind us."

"Are we going to sit here and allow ourselves to be insulted by a prisoner in chains?" Eckster angrily demanded of Palamin. "Let us recommend that he be executed. Then we can all go home. I for one have had enough of this futile rigmarole."

Another said, "Me, too." He looked an habitual me-tooer.

"Patience," advised Palamin. He spoke to Taylor. "You claim that you were under orders to examine the twin system of Halor and Ridi?"

"If by that you mean the adjacent binary, the answer is yes. That was my prescribed destination."

"Let us suppose that instead you had been told to take a look over our Gombarian system. Would you have done so?"

"I obey orders."

"You would have come upon us quietly and surreptitiously for a good snoop around?"

"Not necessarily. If my first impression had been one of friendliness, I'd have presented myself openly."

"He is dodging the question," insisted Eckster, still full of ire.

"What would you have done if you had been uncertain of our reaction?" continued Palamin.

"What anyone else would do," Taylor retorted. "I'd hang around until I'd got the measure of it one way or the other."

"Meanwhile taking care to evade capture?"

"Of course."

"And if you had not been satisfied with our attitude you'd have reported us as hostile?"

"Potentially so."

"That is all we require," decided Palamin. "Your admissions are tantamount to a confession that you are a spy. It does not matter in the least whether you were under orders to poke your inquisitive nose into this system or some other system, you are still a spy." He turned to the others. "Are we all agreed?"

They chorused, "Yes."

"There is only one proper fate for such as you," Palamin finished. "You will be returned to your cell pending official execution." He made a gesture of dismissal. "Take him away."

The guards took him by simple process of jerking the chair from under him and kicking him erect. They tried to rush him out faster than he could go; he stumbled in his leg irons and almost fell. But he found time to throw one swift glance back from the doorway and his strangely pale eyes looked frozen.

* * *

Eric Frank Russell

When the elderly warder brought in his evening meal, Taylor asked, "How do they execute people here?"

"How do they do it where you come from?"

"We don't."

"You don't?" The warder blinked in amazement. Putting the tray on the floor, he took a seat on the bench beside Taylor and left the heavily barred grille wide open. The butt of his gun protruded from its holster within easy reach of the prisoner's grasp. "Then how do you handle dangerous criminals?"

"We cure the curable by whatever means are effective no matter how drastic, including brain surgery. The incurable we export to a lonely planet reserved exclusively for them. There they can fight it out between themselves."

"What a waste of a world," opined the warder. In casual manner he drew his gun, pointed it at the wall and pressed the button. Nothing happened. "Empty," he said.

Taylor made no remark.

"No use you snatching it. No use you running for it. The armored doors, multiple locks and loaded guns are all outside."

"I'd have to get rid of these manacles before I could start something with any hope of success," Taylor pointed out. "Are you open to bribery?"

"With what? You have nothing save the clothes you're wearing. And even those will be burned after you're dead."

"All right, forget it." Taylor rattled his irons loudly and looked disgusted. "You haven't yet told me how I'm to die."

"Oh, you'll be strangled in public," informed the warder. He smacked his lips for no apparent reason. "All executions take place in the presence of the populace. It is not enough that justice be done, it must also be seen to be done. So everybody sees it. And it has an excellent disciplinary effect." Again the lip-smacking. "It is quite a spectacle."

"I'm sure it must be."

"You will be made to kneel with your back to a post, your arms and ankles tied behind it," explained the warder in tutorial manner. "There is a hole drilled through the post at the level of your neck. A loop of cord goes round your neck, through the hole and around a stick on the other side. The executioner twists the stick, thereby tightening the loop quickly or slowly according to his mood."

"I suppose that when he feels really artistic he prolongs the agony quite a piece by slackening and retightening the loop a few times?" Taylor ventured.

"No, no, he is not permitted to do that," assured the warden, blind to the sarcasm. "Not in a final execution. That method is used only to extract confessions from the stubborn. We are a fair-minded and tender-hearted people, see?"

"You're a great comfort to me," said Taylor.

"So you will be handled swiftly and efficiently. I have witnessed many executions and have yet to see a sloppy, badly performed one. The body heaves and strains against its bonds, the eyes stick out, the tongue protrudes and turns black and complete collapse follows. The effect is invariably the same and is a tribute to the executioner's skill. Really you have nothing to worry about, nothing at all.''

"Looks like I haven't, the way you put it," observed Taylor dryly. "I'm right on top of the world without anything to lose except my breath." He brooded a bit, then asked, *"When* am I due for the noose?"

"Immediately after you've finished your game," the warder informed.

Taylor eyed him blankly. "Game? What game? What do you mean?"

"It is conventional to allow a condemned man a last game against a skilled player chosen by us. When the game ends he is taken away and strangled."

"Win or lose?"

"The result makes no difference. He is executed regardless of whether he is the winner or the loser."

"Sounds crazy to me," said Taylor frowning.

"It would, being an alien," replied the warder. "But surely you'll agree that a person facing death is entitled to a little bit of consideration if only the privilege of putting up a last-minute fight for his life."

"A pretty useless fight."

"That may be. But every minute of delay is precious to the one concerned." The warder rubbed hands together appreciatively. "I can tell you that nothing is more exciting, more thrilling than a person's death-match against a clever player."

"Is that so?"

"Yes. You see, he cannot possibly play in normal manner. For one thing, his mind is obsessed by his impending fate while his opponent is bothered by no such burden. For another, he dare not let the other win—and he dare not let him lose, either. He has to concentrate all his faculties on preventing a decisive result and prolonging the game as much as possible. And, of course, all the time he is mentally and morally handicapped by the knowledge that the end is bound to come."

"Bet it gives you a heck of a kick," said Taylor.

The warder sucked his lips before smacking them. "Many a felon have I watched playing in a cold sweat with the ingenuity of desperation. Then at last the final move. He has fainted and rolled off his chair. We've carried him out as limp as an empty sack. He has come to his senses on his knees facing a crowd waiting for the first twist."

"It isn't worth the bother," decided Taylor. "No player can last long."

"Usually they don't but I've known exceptions, tough and expert gamesters who've managed to postpone death for four or five days. There was one fellow, a professional *alizik* player, who naturally chose his own game and contrived to avoid a decision for sixteen days. He was so good it was a pity he had to die. A lot of video-watchers were sorry when the end came."

"Oh, so you put these death-matches on the video?"

"It's the most popular show. Pins them in their chairs, I can tell you."

"Hm-m-m!" Taylor thought a bit, asked, "Suppose this video-star had been able to keep the game on the boil for a year or more, would he have been allowed to do so?"

"Of course. Nobody can be put to death until he has completed his last game. You could call it a superstition, I suppose. What's more, the rule is that he gets well fed while playing. If he wishes he can eat like a king. All the same, they rarely eat much."

"Don't they?"

"No—they're so nervous that their stomachs refuse to hold a square meal. Occasionally one of them is actually sick in the middle of a game. When I see one do that I know he won't last another day."

"You've had plenty of fun in your time," Taylor offered.

"Quite often," the warder admitted. "But not always. Bad players bore me beyond description. They give the video-watchers the gripes. They start a game, fumble it right away, go to the strangling post and that's the end of them. The greatest pleasure for all is when some character makes a battle of it."

"Fat chance I've got. I know no Gombarian games and you people know no Terran ones."

"Any game can be learned in short time and the choice is yours. Naturally you won't be permitted to pick one that involves letting you loose in a field without your irons. It has to be something that can be played in this cell. Want some good advice?"

"Give."

"This evening an official will arrange to arrange the contest after which he will find you a suitable partner. Don't ask to be taught one of our games. No matter how clever you may try to be your opponent will be better because he'll be handling the familiar while you're coping with the strange. Select one of your own planet's games and thus give yourself an advantage."

"Thanks for the suggestion. It might do me some good if defeat meant death—but victory meant life."

"I've told you already that the result makes no difference."

"There you are then. Some choice, huh?"

"You can choose between death in the morning and death the morning after or even the one after that." Getting up from the bench, the warder walked out, closed the grille, said through the bars, "Anyway, I'll bring you a book giving full details of our indoor games. You'll have plenty of time to read it before the official arrives."

"Nice of you," said Taylor. "But I think you're wasting your time."

Left alone, Wayne Taylor let his thoughts mill around. They weren't pleasant ones. Space scouts belonged to a high-risk profession and none knew it better than themselves. Each and every one cheerfully accepted the dangers on the ages-old principle that it always happens to the other fellow, never to oneself. But now it had happened and to him. He ran a forefinger around the inside of his collar which felt a little tight.

When he'd dived through the clouds with two air-machines blasting fire to port and starboard he had pressed alarm button D. This caused his transmitter to start flashing a brief but complicated number giving his co-ordinates and defining the planet as enemy territory.

Earlier and many thousands of miles out in space he had reported his intention of making an emergency landing and identified the chosen world with the same co-ordinates. Button D, therefore, would confirm his first message and add serious doubts about his fate. He estimated that between the time he'd pressed the button and the time he had landed the alarm-signal should have been transmitted at least forty times.

Immediately after the landing he'd switched the delayed-action charge and taken to his heels. The planes were still buzzing around. One of them swooped low over the grounded ship just as it blew up. It disintegrated in the blast. The other one gained altitude and circled overhead, directing the search. To judge by the speed with which troops arrived he must have had the misfortune to have dumped himself in a military area full of uniformed goons eager for blood. All the same, he'd kept them on the run for six hours and covered twenty miles before they got him. They'd expressed their disapproval with fists and feet.

Right now there was no way of telling whether Terran listening-posts had picked up his repeated D-alarm. Odds were vastly in favor of it since it was a top priority channel on which was kept a round-the-clock watch. He didn't doubt for a moment that, having received the message, they'd do something about it.

The trouble was that whatever they did would come too late. In this very sector patrolled the *Macklin,* Terra's latest, biggest, most powerful battleship. If the *Macklin* happened to be on the prowl, and at her nearest routine point, it would take her ten months to reach Gombar at maximum velocity. If she had returned to port, temporarily replaced by an older and slower vessel, the delay might last two years.

Two years was two years too long. Ten months was too long. He could not wait ten weeks. In fact it was highly probable that he hadn't got ten days. Oh, time, time, how impossible it is to stretch it for a man or compress it for a ship.

The warder reappeared, shoved a book between the bars. "Here you are. You have learned enough to understand it."

"Thanks."

Lying full length on the bench he read right through it swiftly but comprehensively. Some pages he skipped after brief perusal because they described games too short, simple and childish to be worth considering. He was not surprised to find several games that were alien variations of ones well known upon Terra. The Gombarians had playing cards, for instance, eighty to a pack with ten suits.

Alizik proved to be a bigger and more complicated version of chess with four hundred squares and forty pieces per side. This was the one that somebody had dragged

Eric Frank Russell

out for sixteen days and it was the only one in the book that seemed capable of such extension. For a while he pondered *alizik,* wondering whether the authorities—and the video audience—would tolerate play at the rate of one move in ten hours. He doubted it. Anyway, he could not prevent his skilled opponent from making each answering move in five seconds.

Yes, that was what he really wanted: a game that slowed down the other fellow despite his efforts to speed up. A game that was obviously a game and not a gag because any fool could see with half an eye that it was possible to finish it once and for all. Yet a game that the other fellow could not finish, win or lose, no matter how hard he tried.

There wasn't any such game on the three worlds of Gombar or the hundred worlds of Terra or the multimillion worlds yet unfound. There couldn't be because, if there were, nobody would play it. People like results. Nobody is sufficiently cracked to waste time, thought, and patience riding a hobbyhorse that got nowhere, indulging a rigmarole that cannot be terminated to the satisfaction of all concerned including kibitzers.

But nobody!

No?

"When the last move is made God's Plan will be fulfilled; on that day and at that hour and at that moment the universe will vanish in a mighty thunderclap."

He got off the bench, his cold eyes expressionless, and began to pace his cell like a restless tiger.

The official had an enormous pot belly, small, piggy eyes and an unctuous smile that remained permanently fixed. His manner was that of a circus ringmaster about to introduce his best act.

"Ah," he said, noting the book, "so you have been studying our games, eh?"

"Yes."

"I hope you've found none of them suitable."

"Do you?" Taylor surveyed him quizzically. "Why?"

"It would be a welcome change to witness a contest based on something right out of this world. A genuinely new game would give a lot of satisfaction to everybody. Providing, of course," he added hurriedly, "that it was easy to understand and that you didn't win it too quickly."

"Well," said Taylor, "I must admit I'd rather handle something I know than something I don't."

"Good, good!" enthused the other. "You prefer to play a Terran game?"

"That's right."

"There are limitations on your choice."

"What are they?" asked Taylor.

"Once we had a condemned murderer who wanted to oppose his games-partner in seeing who could be the first to catch a sunbeam and put it in a bottle. It was nonsensical. You must choose something that obviously and beyond argument can be accomplished."

"I see."

"Secondly, you may not select something involving the use of intricate and expensive apparatus that will take us a long time to manufacture. If apparatus is needed, it must be cheap and easy to construct."

"Is that all?"

"Yes—except that the complete rules of the game must be inscribed by you unambiguously and in clear writing. Once play begins those rules will be strictly followed and no variation of them will be permitted."

"And who approves my choice after I've described it?"

"I do."

"All right. Here's what I'd like to play." Taylor explained it in detail, borrowed pen and paper and made a rough sketch. When he had finished the other folded the drawing and put it in a pocket.

"A strange game," admitted the official, "but it seems to me disappointingly uncomplicated. Do you really think you can make the contest last a full day?"

"I hope so."

"Even two days perhaps?"

"With luck."

"You'll need it!" He was silent with thought a while, then shook his head doubtfully. "It's a pity you didn't think up something like a better and trickier version of *alizik*. The audience would have enjoyed it and you might have gained yourself a longer lease on life. Everyone would get a great kick out of it if you beat the record for delay before your execution."

"Would they really?"

"They sort of expect something extra-special from an alien life form."

"They're getting it, aren't they?"

"Yes, I suppose so." He still seemed vaguely dissatisfied. "Oh, well, it's your life and your struggle to keep it a bit longer."

"I'll have only myself to blame when the end comes."

"True. Play will commence promptly at midday tomorrow. After that it's up to you."

He lumbered away, his heavy footsteps dying along the corridor. A few minutes later the warder appeared.

"What did you pick?"

"Arky-malarkey."

"Huh? What's that?"

"A Terran game."

"That's fine, real fine." He rubbed appreciative hands together. "He approved it, I suppose?"

"Yes, he did."

"So you're all set to justify your continued existence. You'll have to take care to avoid the trap."

"What trap?" Taylor asked.

"Your partner will play to win as quickly and conclusively as possible. That is expected of him. But once he gets it into his head that he can't win he'll start playing to lose. You've no way of telling exactly when he'll change his tactics. Many a one has been caught out by the sudden switch and found the game finished before he had time to realize it."

"But he must keep to the rules, mustn't he?"

"Certainly. Neither you nor he will be allowed to ignore them. Otherwise the game would become a farce."

"That suits me."

Somewhere outside sounded a high screech like that of a bobcat backing into a cactus. It was followed by a scuffle of feet, a dull thud, and dragging noises. A distant door creaked open and banged shut.

"What goes?" said Taylor.

"Lagartine's game must have ended."

"Who's Lagartine?"

"A political assassin." The warder glanced at his watch. "He chose *ramsid,* a card game. It has lasted a mere four hours. Serves him right. Good riddance to bad rubbish."

"And now they're giving him the big squeeze?"

"Of course." Eying him, the warder said, "Nervous?"

"Ha-ha," said Taylor without mirth.

The performance did not commence in his cell as he had expected. A contest involving an alien life form playing an alien game was too big an event for that. They took him through the prison corridors to a large room in which stood a table with three chairs. Six more chairs formed a line against the wall, each occupied by a uniformed plug-ugly complete with hand gun. This was the knock-down-and-drag-out squad ready for action the moment the game terminated.

At one end stood a big, black cabinet with two rectangular portholes through which gleamed a pair of lenses. From it came faint ticking sounds and muffled voices. This presumably contained the video camera.

Taking a chair at the table, Taylor sat down and gave the armed audience a frozen stare. A thin-faced individual with the beady eyes of a rat took the chair opposite. The potbellied official dumped himself in the remaining seat. Taylor and Rat-eyes weighed each other up, the former with cold assurance, the latter with sadistic speculation.

Upon the table stood a board from which arose three long wooden pegs. The left-hand peg held a column of sixty-four disks evenly graduated in diameter, the largest at the bottom, smallest at the top. The effect was that of a tapering tower built from a nursery do-it-yourself kit.

Wasting no time, Potbelly said, "This is the Terran game of Arky-malarkey. The column of disks must be transferred from the peg on which it sits to either of the other two pegs. They must remain graduated in the same order, smallest at the top, biggest at the bottom. The player whose move completes the stack is the winner. Do you both understand?"

"Yes," said Taylor.

Rat-eyes assented with a grunt.

"There are three rules," continued Potbelly, "which will be strictly observed. You will make your moves alternately, turn and turn about. You may move only one disk at a time. You may not place a disk upon any other smaller than itself. Do you both understand?"

"Yes," said Taylor.

Rat-eyes gave another grunt.

From his pocket Potbelly took a tiny white ball and carelessly tossed it onto the table. It bounced a couple of times, rolled across and fell off on Rat-eyes' side.

"You start," he said.

Without hesitation Rat-eyes took the smallest disk from the top of the first peg and placed it on the third.

"Bad move," thought Taylor, blank of face. He shifted the second smallest disk from the first peg to the second.

Smirking for no obvious reason, Rat-eyes now removed the smallest disk from the third peg, placed it on top of Taylor's disk on the second. Taylor promptly switched another disk from the pile on the first peg to the empty third peg.

After an hour of this it had become plain to Rat-eyes that the first peg was not there merely to hold the stock. It had to be used. The smirk faded from his face, was replaced by mounting annoyance as hours crawled by and the situation became progressively more complicated.

By bedtime they were still at it, swapping disks around like crazy, and neither had got very far. Rat-eyes now hated the sight of the first peg, especially when he was forced to put a disk back on it instead of taking one off it. Potbelly, still wearing his fixed, meaningless smile, announced that play would cease until sunrise tomorrow.

The next day provided a long, arduous session lasting from dawn to dusk and broken only by two meals. Both players worked fast and hard, setting the pace for each other and seeming to vie with one another in effort to reach a swift conclusion. No onlooker could find cause to complain about the slowness of the game. Four times Rat-eyes

Eric Frank Russell

mistakenly tried to place a disk on top of a smaller one and was promptly called to order by the referee in the obese shape of Potbelly.

A third, fourth, fifth and sixth day went by. Rat-eyes now played with a mixture of dark suspicion and desperation while the column on the first peg appeared to go up as often as it went down. Though afflicted by his emotions he was no fool. He knew quite well that they were making progress in the task of transferring the column. But it was progress at an appalling rate. What's more, it became worse as time went on. Finally, he could see no way of losing the game, much less winning it.

By the fourteenth day Rat-eyes had reduced himself to an automaton wearily moving disks to and fro in the soulless, disinterested manner of one compelled to perform a horrid chore. Taylor remained as impassive as a bronze Buddha and that fact didn't please Rat-eyes either.

Danger neared on the sixteenth day though Taylor did not know it. The moment he entered the room he sensed an atmosphere of heightened interest and excitement. Rat-eyes looked extra glum. Potbelly had taken on added importance. Even the stolid, dull-witted guards displayed faint signs of mental animation. Four off-duty warders joined the audience. There was more activity than usual within the video cabinet. Ignoring all this, Taylor took his seat and play continued. This endless moving of disks from peg to peg was a lousy way to waste one's life but the strangling-post was lousier. He had every inducement to carry on. Naturally he did so, shifting a disk when his turn came and watching his opponent with his pale gray eyes.

In the midafternoon Rat-eyes suddenly left the table, went to the wall, kicked it good and hard and shouted a remark about the amazing similarity between Terrans and farmyard manure. Then he returned and made his next move. There was some stirring within the video cabinet. Potbelly mildly reproved him for taking time off to advertise his patriotism. Rat-eyes went on playing with the surly air of a delinquent whose mother has forgotten to kiss him.

Late in the evening, Potbelly stopped the game, faced the video lenses and said in portentious manner, "Play will resume tomorrow—the seventeenth day!"

He voiced it as though it meant something or other.

When the warder shoved his breakfast through the grille in the morning, Taylor said, "Late, aren't you? I should be at play by now."

"They say you won't be wanted before this afternoon."

"That so? What's all the fuss about?"

"You broke the record yesterday," informed the other with reluctant admiration. "Nobody has ever lasted to the seventeenth day."

"So they're giving me a morning off to celebrate, eh? Charitable of them."

"I've no idea why there's a delay," said the warder. "I've never known them to interrupt a game before."

"You think they'll stop it altogether?" Taylor asked, feeling a constriction around his neck. "You think they'll officially declare it finished?"

"Oh, no, they couldn't do that." He looked horrified at the thought of it. "We mustn't bring the curse of the dead upon us. It's absolutely essential that condemned people should be made to choose their own time of execution."

"Why is it?"

"Because it always has been since the start of time."

He wandered off to deliver other breakfasts, leaving Taylor to stew over the explanation. "Because it always has been." It wasn't a bad reason. Indeed, some would consider it a good one. He could think of several pointless, illogical things done on Terra solely because they always had been done. In this matter of unchallenged habit the Gombarians were no better or worse than his own kind.

Though a little soothed by the warder's remarks he couldn't help feeling more and more uneasy as the morning wore on without anything happening. After sixteen days of moving disks from peg to peg it had got so that he was doing it in his sleep. Didn't seem right that he should be enjoying a spell of aimless loafing around his cell. There was something ominous about it.

Again and again he found himself nursing the strong suspicion that officialdom was seeking an effective way of ending the play without appearing to flout convention. When they found it—if they found it—they'd pull a fast one on him, declare the game finished, take him away and fix him up with a very tight necktie.

He was still wallowing in pessimism when the call came in the afternoon. They hustled him along to the same room as before. Play was resumed as if it had never been interrupted. It lasted a mere thirty minutes. Somebody tapped twice on the inside of the video cabinet and Potbelly responded by calling a halt. Taylor went back to his cell and sat there baffled.

Late in the evening he was summoned again. He went with bad grace because these short and sudden performances were more wearing on the nerves than continual daylong ones. Previously he had known for certain that he was being taken to play Arkymalarkey with Rat-eyes. Now he could never be sure that he was not about to become the lead character in a literally breathless scene.

On entering the room he realized at once that things were going to be different this time. The board with its pegs and disks still stood in the center of the table. But Rat-eyes was absent and so was the armed squad. Three people awaited him: Potbelly, Palamin, and a squat, heavily built character who had the peculiar air of being of this world but not with it.

Potbelly was wearing the offended frown of someone burdened with a load of stock in a nonexistent oil well. Palamin looked singularly unpleased and expressed it by snorting like an impatient horse. The third appeared to be contemplating a phenomenon on the other side of the galaxy.

"Sit," ordered Palamin, spitting it out.

Taylor sat.

"Now, Marnikot, you tell him."

The squat one showed belated awareness of being on Gombar, said pedantically to Taylor, "I rarely look at the video. It is suitable only for the masses with nothing better to do."

"Get to the point," urged Palamin.

"But having heard that you were about to break an ages-old record," continued Marnikot, undisturbed, "I watched the video last night." He made a brief gesture to show that he could identify a foul smell at first sniff. "It was immediately obvious to me that to finish your game would require a minimum number of moves of the order of two to the sixty-fourth power minus one." He took flight into momentary dreamland, came back and added mildly, "That is a large number."

"Large!" said Palamin. He let go a snort that rocked the pegs.

"Let us suppose," Marnikot went on, "that you were to transfer these disks one at a time as fast as you could go, morning, noon and night without pause for meals or sleep, do you know how long it would take to complete the game?"

"Nearly six billion Terran centuries," said Taylor as if talking about next Thursday week.

"I have no knowledge of Terran time-terms. But I can tell you that neither you nor a thousand generations of your successors could live long enough to see the end of it. Correct?"

"Correct," Taylor admitted.

"Yet you say that this is a Terran game?"

"I do."

Marnikot spread hands helplessly to show that as far as he was concerned there was nothing more to be said.

Wearing a forbidding scowl, Palamin now took over. "A game cannot be defined as a genuine one unless it is actually played. Do you claim that this so-called game really is played on Terra?"

"Yes."

"By whom?"

"By priests in the Temple of Benares."

"And how long have they been playing it?" he asked.

"About two thousand years."

"Generation after generation?"

"That's right."

"Each player contributing to the end of his days without hope of seeing the result?"

"Yes."

Palamin fumed a bit. "Then *why* do they play it?"

"It's part of their religious faith. They believe that the moment the last disk is placed the entire universe will go bang."

"Are they crazy?"

"No more so than people who have played *alizik* for equally as long and to just as little purpose."

"We have played *alizik* as a series of separate games and not as one never-ending game. A rigmarole without possible end cannot be called a game by any stretch of the imagination."

"Arky-malarkey is not endless. It has a conclusive finish." Taylor appealed to Marnikot as the undisputed authority. "Hasn't it?"

"It is definitely finite," pronounced Marnikot, unable to deny the fact.

"So!" exclaimed Palamin, going a note higher. "You think you are very clever, don't you?"

"I get by," said Taylor, seriously doubting it.

"But we are cleverer," insisted Palamin, using his nastiest manner. "You have tricked us and now we shall trick you. The game is finite. It can be concluded. Therefore it will continue until it reaches its natural end. You will go on playing it days, weeks, months, years until eventually you expire of old age and chronic frustration. There will be times when the very sight of these disks will drive you crazy and you will beg for merciful death. But we shall not grant that favor—and you will continue to play." He waved a hand in triumphant dismissal. "Take him away."

Taylor returned to his cell.

When supper came the warder offered, "I am told that play will go on regularly as from tomorrow morning. I don't understand why they messed it up today."

"They've decided that I'm to suffer a fate worse than death," Taylor informed.

The warder stared at him.

"I have been very naughty," said Taylor.

Rat-eyes evidently had been advised of the new setup because he donned the armor of philosophical acceptance and played steadily but without interest. All the same, long sessions of repetitive motions ate corrosively into the armor and gradually found its way through.

In the early afternoon of the fifty-second day Rat-eyes found himself faced with the prospect of returning most of the disks to the first peg, one by one. He took off the clompers he used for boots. Then he ran barefooted four times around the room, bleating like a sheep. Potbelly got a crick in the neck watching him. Two guards led Rat-eyes away still bleating. They forgot to take his clompers with them.

By the table Taylor sat gazing at the disks while he strove to suppress his inward alarm. What would happen now? If Rat-eyes had given up for keeps it could be argued that he had lost, the game had concluded and the time had come to play okey-chokey with a piece of cord. It could be said with equal truth that an unfinished game remains an unfinished game even though one of the players is in a mental home giving his hair a molasses shampoo.

If the authorities took the former view his only defense was to assert the latter one. He'd have to maintain with all the energy at his command that since he had not won or lost his time could not possibly have come. It wouldn't be easy if he had to make his protest while being dragged by the heels to his doom. His chief hope lay in Gombarian unwillingness to outrage an ancient convention. Millions of video viewers would take a poor look at officialdom mauling a pet superstition. Yes, man, there were times when the Idiot's Lantern had its uses.

He need not have worried. Having decided that to keep the game going would be a highly refined form of hell, the Gombarians had already prepared a roster of relief players drawn from the ranks of minor offenders whose ambitions never rose high enough to earn a strangling. So after a short time another opponent appeared.

The newcomer was a shifty character with a long face and hanging dewlaps. He resembled an especially dopey bloodhound and looked barely capable of articulating three words, to wit, "Ain't talking, copper." It must have taken at least a month to teach him that he must move only one disk at a time and never, never, never place it upon a smaller one. But somehow he had learned. The game went on.

Dopey lasted a week. He played slowly and doggedly as if in fear of punishment for making a mistake. Often he was irritated by the video cabinet, which emitted ticking noises at brief but regular intervals. These sounds indicated the short times they were on the air.

For reasons best known to himself Dopey detested having his face broadcasted all over the planet and near the end of the seventh day he'd had enough. Without warning he left his seat, faced the cabinet and made a number of swift and peculiar gestures at the lenses. The signs meant nothing to the onlooking Taylor. But Potbelly almost fell off his chair. The guards sprang forward, grabbed Dopey, and frogmarched him through the door.

He was replaced by a huge-jowled, truculent character who dumped himself into the chair, glared at Taylor and wiggled his hairy ears. Taylor, who regarded this feat as one of his own accomplishments, promptly wiggled his own ears back. The other then looked fit to burst a blood vessel.

"This Terran sneak," he roared at Potbelly, "is throwing dirt at me. Do I *have* to put up with that?"

"You will cease to throw dirt," ordered Potbelly.

"I only wiggled my ears," said Taylor.

"That is the same thing as throwing dirt," Potbelly said mysteriously. "You will refrain from doing it and you will concentrate upon the game."

And so it went on with disks being moved from peg to peg hour after hour, day after day, while a steady parade of opponents arrived and departed. Around the two-hundredth day Potbelly himself started to pull his chair apart with the apparent intention of building a camp fire in the middle of the floor. The guards led him out. A new referee appeared. He had an even bigger paunch and Taylor promptly named him Potbelly Two.

How Taylor himself stood the soul-deadening pace he never knew. But he kept going while the others cracked. He was playing for a big stake while they were not. All the same, there were times when he awoke from horrid dreams in which he was sinking through the black depths of an alien sea with a monster disk like a millstone around his neck. He lost count of the days and once in a while his hands developed the shakes. The strain was not made any easier by several nighttime uproars that took place during this time. He asked the warder about one of them.

"Yasko refused to go. They had to beat him into submission."

"His game had ended?"

"Yes. The stupid fool matched a five of anchors with a five of stars. Immediately he realized what he'd done he tried to kill his opponent." He wagged his head in sorrowful reproof. "Such behavior never does them any good. They go to the post cut and bruised. And if the guards are angry with them they ask the executioner to twist slowly."

"Ugh!" Taylor didn't like to think of it. "Surprises me that none have chosen my game. Everybody must know of it by now."

"They are not permitted to," said the warder. "There is now a law that only a recognized Gombarian game may be selected."

He ambled away. Taylor lay full length on his bench and hoped for a silent, undisturbed night. What was the Earth-date? How long had he been here? How much longer would he remain? How soon would he lose control of himself and go nuts? What would they do with him if and when he became too crazy to play?

Often in the thought-period preceding sleep he concocted wild plans of escape. None of them were of any use whatever. Conceivably he could break out of this prison despite its grilles, armored doors, locks, bolts, bars and armed guards. It was a matter of waiting for a rare opportunity and seizing it with both hands. But suppose he got out, what then? Any place on the planet he would be as conspicuous as a kangaroo on the sidewalks of New York. If it were possible to look remotely like a Gombarian, he'd have a slight chance. It was not possible. He could do nothing save play for time.

This he continued to do. On and on and on without cease except for meals and sleep. By the three-hundredth day he had to admit to himself that he was feeling somewhat moth-eaten. By the four-hundredth he was under the delusion that he had been playing for at least five years and was doomed to play forever, come what may. The four-twentieth day was no different from the rest except in one respect of which he was completely unaware—it was the last.

* * *

Eric Frank Russell

At dawn of day four twenty-one no call came for him to play. Perforce he waited a couple of hours and still no summons. Maybe they'd decided to break him with a cat-and-mouse technique, calling him when he didn't expect it and not calling him when he did. A sort of psychological water torture. When the warder passed along the corridor Taylor went to the bars and questioned him. The fellow knew nothing and was as puzzled as himself.

The midday meal arrived. Taylor had just finished it when the squad of guards arrived accompanied by an officer. They entered the cell and removed his irons. Ye gods, this was something! He stretched his limbs luxuriously, fired questions at the officer and his plug-uglies. They took no notice, behaved as if he had stolen the green eye of the little yellow god. Then they marched him out of the cell, along the corridors and past the games room.

Finally they passed through a large doorway and into an open yard. In the middle of this area stood six short steel posts each with a hole near its top and a coarse kneeling-mat at its base. Stolidly the squad tramped straight towards the posts. Taylor's stomach turned over. The squad pounded on past the posts and toward a pair of gates. Taylor's stomach turned thankfully back and settled itself.

Outside the gates they climbed aboard a troop-carrier which at once drove off. It took him around the outskirts of the city to a spaceport. They all piled out, marched past the control tower and onto the concrete. There they halted.

Across the spaceport, about half a mile away, Taylor could see a Terran vessel sitting on its fins. It was far too small for a warship, too short and fat for a scoutship. After staring at it with incredulous delight he decided that it was a battleship's lifeboat. He wanted to do a wild dance and yell silly things. He wanted to run like mad toward it but the guards stood close around and would not let him move.

They waited there for four long, tedious hours, at the end of which another lifeboat screamed down from the sky and landed alongside its fellow. A bunch of figures came out of it, mostly Gombarians. The guards urged him forward.

He was dimly conscious of some sort of exchange ceremony at the halfway mark. A line of surly Gombarians passed him, going the opposite way. Many of them were ornamented with plenty of brass and had the angry faces of colonels come fresh from a general demotion. He recognized one civilian, Borkot, and wiggled his ears at him as he went by.

Then willing hands helped him through an air lock and he found himself sitting in the cabin of a ship going up. A young and eager lieutenant was talking to him but he heard only half of it.

". . . Landed, snatched twenty and beat it into space. We cross-examined them by signs . . . bit surprised to learn you were still alive . . . released one with an offer to exchange prisoners. Nineteen Gombarian bums for one Terran is a fair swap, isn't it?"

"Yes," said Taylor, looking around and absorbing every mark upon the walls.

"We'll have you aboard the *Thunderer* pretty soon . . . *Macklin* couldn't make it with that trouble near Cygni . . . got here as soon as we could." The lieutenant eyed him sympathetically. "You'll be heading for home within a few hours. Hungry?"

"No, not at all. The one thing they didn't do was starve me."

"Like a drink?"

"Thanks, I don't drink."

Fidgeting around embarrassedly, the lieutenant asked, "Well, how about a nice, quiet game of draughts?"

Taylor ran a finger around the inside of his collar and said, "Sorry, I don't know how to play and don't want to learn. I am allergic to games."

"You'll change."

"I'll be hanged if I do," said Taylor. ■

UNHUMAN SACRIFICE

Katherine MacLean

"DAMN! HE'S ACTUALLY DOING IT. Do you hear that?"

A ray of sunlight and a distant voice filtered down from the open arch in the control room above. The distant voice talked and paused, talked and paused. The words were blurred, but the tone was recognizable.

"He's outside preaching to the natives."

The two engineers were overhauling the engines, but paused to look up toward the voice.

"Maybe not," said Charlie, the junior engineer. "After all, he doesn't know their language."

"He'd preach anyway," said Henderson, senior engineer and navigator. He heaved with a wrench on a tight bolt, the wrench slipped, and Henderson released some words that made Charlie shudder.

On the trip, Charlie had often dreamed apprehensively that Henderson had strangled the passenger. And once he had dreamed that he himself had strangled the passenger and Henderson too.

When awake the engineers carefully avoided irritating words or gestures, remained cordial toward each other and the passenger no matter what the temptation to snarl, and tried to keep themselves in a tolerant good humor.

It had not been easy.

Charlie said, "How do you account for the missionary society giving him a ship of his own? A guy like that, who just gets in your hair when he's trying to give you advice, a guy with a natural-born talent for antagonizing people?"

"Easy," Henderson grunted, spinning the bolt. He was a stocky, square-built man with a brusque manner and a practiced tolerance of other people's oddities. "The missionary society was trying to get rid of him. You can't get any farther away than where they sent us!"

The distant voice filtered into the control room from the unseen sunlit landscape outside the ship. It sounded resonant and confident. "The poor jerk thinks it was an honor," Henderson added. He pulled out the bolt and dropped it on the padded floor with a faint thump.

"Anyhow," Charlie said, loosening bolt heads in a circle as the manual instructed, "he can't use the translator machine. It's not ready yet, not until we get the rest of their language. He won't talk to them if they can't understand."

"Won't he?" Henderson fitted his wrench to another bolt and spun it angrily. "Then what is he doing?" Without waiting for an answer he replied to his own question. "*Preaching*, that's what he is doing!"

It seemed hot and close in the engine room, and the sunlight from outside beckoned.

Charlie paused and wiped the back of his arm against his forehead. "Preaching won't do him any good. If they can't understand him, they won't listen."

"We didn't listen, and that didn't stop him from preaching to *us!*" Henderson snapped. "He's lucky we found a landing planet so soon, he's lucky he didn't drive us insane first. A man like that is a danger to a ship." Henderson, like Charlie, knew the stories of ships which had left with small crews and returned with a smaller crew of one or two red-eyed maniacs and a collection of corpses. Henderson was a conservative. He preferred the regular shipping runs, and ships with a regular-sized crew and a good number of passengers. Only an offer of triple pay and triple insurance indemnity had lured him from the big ships to be co-engineer on this odd three-man trip.

". . . I didn't mind being preached at." Charlie's tone was mild, but he stared upward in the direction of the echoing voice with a certain intensity in his stance.

"Come off it, you twerp. We only have to be sweet to each other on a trip when we're cabinbound. Don't kid old Harry, you didn't like it."

"No," said Charlie dreamily, staring upward with a steady intensity. "Can't say that I did. He's not such a good preacher. I've met better in bars." The echoing voice from outside seemed to be developing a deeper echo. "He's got the translator going, Harry. I think we ought to stop him."

Charlie was a lanky redhead with a mild manner, about the same age as the preacher, but Henderson, who had experience, laid a restraining hand on his shoulder.

"I'll do it," said Henderson, and scrambled up the ladder to the control room.

The control room was a pleasant shading of grays, brightly lit by the sunlight that streamed in through the open archway. The opening to the outside was screened only by a billowing curtain of transparent Saran-type plastic film, ion-coated to allow air to pass freely, but making a perfect and aseptic filter against germs and small insects. The stocky engineer hung a clear respirator box over a shoulder, brought the tube up to his mouth, and walked through the plastic film. It folded over him and wrapped him in an intimate tacky embrace, and gripped to its own surface behind him, sealing itself around him like a loose skin. Just past the arch he walked through a frame of metal like a man-sized croquet wicket and stopped while it tightened a noose around the trailing films of plastic behind him, cutting him free of the doorway curtain and sealing the break with heat.

Without waiting for the plastic to finish wrapping and tightening itself around him, the engineer went down the ramp, trailing plastic film in gossamer veils, like ghostly battle flags.

They could use this simple wrapping of thin plastic as an airsuit air lock, for the air of the new world was rich and good, and the wrapping was needed only to repel strange germs or infections. They were not even sure that there were any such germs; but the plastic was a routine precaution for ports in quarantine, and the two engineers were accustomed to wearing it. It allowed air to filter by freely, so that Henderson could feel the wind on his skin, only slightly diminished. He was wearing uniform shorts, and the wind felt cool and pleasant.

Around the spaceship stretched grassy meadow and thin forest, and beyond that in one direction lay the blue line of the sea, and in another the hazy blue-green of distant low mountains. It was so like the southern United States of Charlie's boyhood that the young engineer had wept with excitement when he first looked out of the ship. Harry Henderson did not weep, but he paused in his determined stride and looked around, and understood again how incredibly lucky they had been to find an Earth-type planet of such perfection. He was a firm believer in the hand of fate, and he wondered what fate planned for the living things of this green planet, and why it had chosen him as its agent.

Down in the green meadow, near the foot of the ramp, sat the translator machine, still in its crate and on a wheeled dolly but with one side opened to expose the controls. It looked like a huge box, and it was one of the most expensive of the new inductive language analyzers, brought along by their passenger in the hope and expectation of finding a planet with natives.

Triumphant in his success, the passenger, the Revent Winton, sat cross-legged on top of the crate, like a small king on a large throne. He was making a speech, using the mellow round tones of a trained elocutionist, with the transparent plastic around his face hardly muffling his voice at all.

And the natives were listening. They sat around the translator box in a wide irregular circle, and stared. They were bald, with fur in tufts about their knees and elbows. Occasionally one got up, muttering to the others, and hurried away; and occasionally one came into the area and sat down to listen.

"Do not despair," called Revent Winton in bell-like tones. "Now that I have shown you the light, you know that you have lived in darkness and sin all your lives, but do not despair . . ."

The translator machine was built to assimilate a vast number of words and sentences in any tongue, along with fifty or so words in direct translation, and from that construct or find a grammatical pattern and print a handbook of the native language. Meanwhile, it would translate any word it was sure of. Henderson had figured out the meaning of a few native words the day before and recorded them in, and the machine was industriously translating those few words whenever they appeared, like a deep bell, tolling the antiphony to the preacher's voice. The machine spoke in an enormous bass that was Henderson's low tones recorded through a filter and turned up to twenty times normal volume.

"I . . . LIGHT . . . YOU . . . YOU . . . LIVED . . . DARK . . . LIFE . . ."

The natives sat on the green grass and listened with an air of patient wonder.

"Revent Winton." Harry tried to attract his attention.

Winton leaned toward the attentive natives, his face softened with forgiveness. "No, say to yourselves merely: I have lived in error. Now I will learn the true path of a righteous life."

The machine in the box below him translated words into its voice of muted thunder. "SAY YOU . . . I . . . LIVED . . . I . . . PATH . . . LIFE . . ."

The natives moved. Some got up and came closer, staring at the box, and others clustered and murmured to each other, and went away in small groups, talking.

Henderson decided not to tell the Revent what the machine had said. But this had to be stopped.

"Revent Winton!"

The preacher leaned over and looked down at him benevolently. "What is it, my son?" He was younger than the engineer, dark, intense and sure of his own righteousness.

"MY SON," said the translator machine in its voice of muted thunder. The sound rolled and echoed faintly back from the nearby woods, and the natives stared at Henderson.

Henderson muttered a bad word. The natives would think he was Winton's son! Winton did not know what it had said.

"Don't curse," Winton said patiently. "What is it, Harry?"

"Sorry," Henderson apologized, leaning his arms on the edge of the crate. "Switch off the translator, will you?"

"WILL YOU . . ." thundered the translator. The preacher switched it off.

"Yes?" he asked, leaning forward. He was wearing a conservative suit of knitted dark-gray tights and a black shirt. Henderson felt badly dressed in his shorts and bare hairy chest.

"Revent, do you think it's the right thing to do, to preach to these people? The translator isn't finished, and we don't know anything about them yet. Anthropologists don't even make a suggestion to a native about his customs without studying the whole tribe and the way it lives for a couple of generations. I mean, you're going off half cocked. It's too soon to give them advice."

"I came to give them advice," Winton said gently. "They need my spiritual help. An anthropologist comes to observe. They don't meddle with what they observe, for meddling would change it. But I am not here to observe, I am here to help them. Why should I wait?"

Winton had a remarkable skill with syllogistic logic. He always managed to sound as if his position were logical, somehow, in spite of Henderson's conviction that he was almost always entirely wrong. Henderson often, as now, found himself unable to argue.

"How do you know they need help?" he asked uncertainly. "Maybe their way of life is all right."

"Come, now," said the preacher cheerfully, swinging his hand around the expanse of green horizon. "These are just primitives, not angels. I'd be willing to guess that they eat their own kind, or torture, or have human sacrifices."

"Humanoid sacrifices," Henderson muttered.

Winton's ears were keen. "Don't quibble. You know they will have some filthy primitive custom or other. Tribes on Earth used to have orgies and sacrifices in the spring. It's spring here—the Great Planner probably intended us to find this place in time to stop them."

"Oy," said Henderson and turned away to strike his forehead with the heel of his hand. His passenger was planning to interfere with a spring fertility ceremony. If these natives held such a ceremony—and it was possible that they might—they would be convinced that the ceremony insured the fertility of the earth, or the health of the sun, or the growth of the crops, or the return of the fish. They would be convinced that without the ceremony summer would never return and they would all starve. If Winton interfered, they would try to kill him.

Winton watched him, scowling at the melodrama of his gesture.

Henderson turned back to try to explain.

"Revent, I appeal to you, tampering is dangerous. Let us go back and report this planet, and let the government send a survey ship. When the scientists arrive, if they find that we have been tampering with the natives' customs without waiting for advice, they will consider it a crime. We will be notorious in scientific journals. We'll be considered responsible for any damage the natives sustain."

The preacher glared. "Do you think that I am a coward, afraid of the anger of atheists?" He again waved a hand, indicating the whole sweep of the planet's horizon around them. "Do you think we found this place by accident? The Great Planner sent me here for a purpose. I am responsible to Him, not to you or your scientist friends. I will fulfill His purpose." He leaned forward, staring at Henderson with dark fanatical eyes. "Go weep about your reputation somewhere else."

Henderson stepped back, getting a clearer view of the passenger, feeling as if he had suddenly sprouted fangs and claws. He was still as he had appeared before, an intense brunet young man, wearing dark tights and dark shirt, sitting cross-legged on top of a huge box, but now he looked primitive somehow, like a prehistoric naked priest on top of an altar.

"Anthropology is against this kind of thing," Henderson said.

Winton looked at him malevolently from his five-foot elevation on the crate and the extra three feet of his own seated height. "You aren't an anthropologist, are you, Harry? You're an engineer?"

"That's right," Henderson admitted, hating him for the syllogism.

Winton said sweetly. "Then why don't you go back to the ship and work on the engine?"

"There will be trouble," Henderson said softly.

"I am prepared for trouble," the Revent Winton said equally softly. He took a large old-fashioned revolver out of his carry case and rested it on his knee.

The muzzle pointed midway between the engineer and the natives.

Henderson shrugged and went back up the ramp.

"What did he do?" Charlie was finishing his check of the fuel timers, holding a coffee cup in his free hand.

Angrily silent, Harry cut an exit slit from the plastic coating. He ripped off the gossamer films of plastic, wadded them up together and tossed them in a salvage hopper.

"He told me to mind my own business. And that's what I am going to do."

The preacher's impressive voice began to ring again from the distance outside, and, every so often, like a deep gong, the translator machine would speak a word in the native dialect.

"The translator is still going," Charlie pointed out.

"Let it. He doesn't know what it is saying." Sulkily, Henderson turned to a library shelf, and pulled out a volume, *The E. T. Planet: A Manual of Observation and Behavior on Extraterrestrial Planets, with Examples.*

"What is it saying?"

"Almost nothing at all. All it translated out of a long speech the creep made was 'I life path.' "

The younger engineer lost his smile. "That was good enough for others. Winton doesn't know what the box is saying?"

"He thinks it's saying what he is saying. He's giving out with his usual line of malarky."

"We've got to stop it!" Charlie began to climb the ladder.

Henderson shrugged. "So go out and tell him the translator isn't working right. I should have told him. But if I got close to him now, I'd strangle him."

Charlie returned later, grinning. "It's O.K. The natives are scared of Winton, and they like the box; so they must think that the box is talking sense for itself, and Winton is gibbering in a strange language."

"He is. And it is," Henderson said sourly. "They are right."

"You're kind of hard on him." Charlie started searching the shelves for another copy of the manual of procedure for survey teams. "But I can see what you mean. Anyhow, I told Winton that he was making a bad impression on the natives. It stopped him. It stopped him cold. He said he would put off preaching for a week and study the natives a little. But he said we ought to fix up the translator so that it translates what he says." Charlie turned, smiling, with a book in one hand. "That gives us time."

"Time for what?" Henderson growled without looking up from his book. "Do you think we can change Winton's mind? That bonehead believes that butting into people's lives is a sacred duty. Try talking any bonehead out of a Sacred Duty! He'd butt into a cannibal banquet! I hope he does. I hope they eat him!"

"Long pig," Charlie mused, temporarily diverted by the picture. "Tastes good to people, probably would taste foul to these natives, they're not the same species."

"He says he's planning to stop their spring festival. If it has sacrifices or anything he doesn't like, he says he'll stop it."

Charlie placed his fists on the table and leaned across toward Henderson, lowering his voice. "Look, we don't know even if the natives are going to have any spring festival. Maybe if we investigate we'll find out that there won't be one, or maybe we'll find out that Winton can't do them any harm. Maybe we don't have to worry. Only let's go out and investigate. We can write up reports on whatever we find, in standard form, and the journals will print them when we get back. Glory and all like that." He added, watching Henderson's expression, "Maybe, if we have to, we can break the translator."

It was the end of the season of dry. The river was small and ran in a narrow channel, and there were many fish near the surface. Spet worked rapidly, collecting fish from fish traps, returning the empty traps to the water, salting the fish.

He was winded, but pleased with the recollection of last night's feast, and hungry in anticipation of the feast of the evening to come. This was the season of the special meals, cooking herbs and roots and delicacies with the fish. Tonight's feast might be the last he would ever have, for a haze was thickening over the horizon, and tomorrow the rains might come.

One of the strangers came and watched him. Spet ignored him politely and salted the fish without looking at him directly. It was dangerous to ignore a stranger, but to make the formal peace gestures and agreements would be implying that the stranger was from a tribe of enemies, when he might already be a friend. Spet preferred to be polite, so he pretended not to be concerned that he was being watched.

The haze thickened in the sky, and the sunlight weakened. Spet tossed the empty trap back to its place in the river with a skillful heave of his strong short arms. If he lived through the next week, his arms would not be strong and short, they would be weak and long. He began to haul in another trap line, sneaking side glances at the stranger as he pulled.

The stranger was remarkably ugly. His features were all misfit sizes. Reddish brown all over like a dead leaf, and completely bald of hair at knees and elbows, he shone as if he were wet, covered all over with a transparent shininess, like water, but the water never dripped. He was thick and sturdy and quick-moving, like a youngling, but did not work. Very strange, unlike reality, he stood quietly watching, without attacking Spet, although he could have attacked without breaking a peace gesture. So he was probably not of any enemy tribe.

It was possible that the undripping water was an illusion, meant to indicate that the stranger was really the ghost of someone who had drowned.

The stranger continued to watch. Spet braced his feet against the grass of the bank and heaved on the next trap line, wanting to show his strength. He heaved too hard, and a strand of the net gave way. The stranger waded out into the water and pulled in the strand, so that no fish escaped.

It was the act of a friend. And yet when the net trap was safely drawn up on the bank, the brown stranger stepped back without comment or gesture, and watched exactly as before—as if his help was the routine of one kinfolk to another.

That showed that the brown one was his kin and a member of his family. But Spet had seen all of his live kinfolk, and none of them looked so strange. It followed reasonably that the brown one was a ghost, a ghost of a relative who had drowned.

Spet nodded at the ghost and transferred the fish from the trap to the woven baskets and salted them. He squatted to repair the broken strand of the net.

The brown ghost squatted beside him. It pointed at the net and made an inquiring sound.

"I am repairing the trap, Grandfather," Spet exclaimed, using the most respectful name for the brown ghost relative.

The ghost put a hand over his own mouth, then pointed at the ground and released its mouth to make another inquiring noise.

"The ground is still dry, Grandfather," Spet said cordially, wondering what he wanted to know. He rose and flung the trap net out on its line into the river, hoping that the brown ghost would admire his strength. Figures in dreams often came to tell you something, and often they could not speak, but the way they looked and the signs they made were meant to give you a message. The brown ghost was shaped like a youngling, like Spet, as if he had drowned before his adult hanging ceremony. Perhaps this one came in daylight instead of dreams, because Spet was going to die and join the ghosts soon, before he became an adult.

The thought was frightening. The haze thickening on the horizon looked ominous.

The brown ghost repeated what Spet had said, almost in Spet's voice, blurring the words slightly. *The ground is still dry, Grandfather*. He pointed at the ground and made an inquiring noise.

"Ground," said Spet, thinking about death and every song he had heard about it. Then he heard the ghost repeat the word, and saw the satisfaction of his expression, and realized that the ghost had forgotten how to talk, and wanted to be taught all over again, like a newborn.

That made courtesy suddenly a simple and pleasant game. As Spet worked, he pointed at everything and said the word, he described what he was doing, and sometimes he sang the childhood work songs that described the work.

The ghost followed and helped him with the nets, and listened, and pointed at things he wanted to learn. Around his waist coiled a blind silver snake that Spet had not noticed at first, and the ghost turned the head of the snake toward Spet when he sang, and sometimes the ghost talked to the snake himself, with explanatory gestures.

It was very shocking to Spet that anyone would explain things to a snake, for snakes are wise, and a blind snake is the wise one of dreams—he who knows everything.

Katherine MacLean

The blind snake did not need to be explained to. Spet averted his eyes and would not look at it.

The ghost and he worked together, walking up the riverbank, hauling traps, salting fish and throwing the traps back, and Spet told what he was doing, and the ghost talked down to the snake around his waist, explaining something about what they were doing. Once the brown ghost held the blind silver snake out toward Spet, indicating with a gesture that he should speak to it.

Terrified and awed, Spet fell to his knees. "Tell me, Wisest One, if you wish to tell me, will I die in the hanging?"

He waited, but the snake lay with casual indifference in the ghost's hand and did not move or reply.

Spet rose from his knees and backed away. "Thank you, O Wise One."

The ghost spoke to the snake, speaking very quietly, with apologetic gestures and much explanation, then wrapped it again around his waist and helped Spet carry the loads of salted fish, without speaking again or pointing at anything.

It was almost sundown.

On the way back to his family hut, Spet passed the Box That Speaks. The black gibbering spirit sat on top of it and gibbered as usual, but this time the box stopped him and spoke to him, and called him by his own name, and asked questions about his life.

Spet was carrying a heavy load of salted fish in two baskets hung on a yoke across one sturdy shoulder. He was tired. He stood in the midst of the green meadow that in other seasons had been a river, with the silver hut of the ghosts throwing a long shadow across him. His legs were tired from wading in the river, and his mind was tired from the brown ghost asking him questions all day; so he explained the thing that was uppermost in his mind, instead of discussing fishing and weather. He explained that he was going to die. The ceremony of hanging, by which the almost-adults became adults, was going to occur at the first rain, five younglings were ready, usually most of them lived, but he thought he would die.

The box fell silent, and the ghost on top stopped gibbering, so Spet knew that it was true, for people fall silent at a truth that they do not want to say aloud.

He made a polite gesture of leave-taking to the box and went toward his family hut, feeling very unhappy. During the feast of that evening all the small ones ate happily of fish and roots and became even fatter, and the thin adults picked at the roots and herbs. Spet was the only youngling of adult-beginning age, and he should have been eating well to grow fat and build up his strength, but instead he went outside and looked at the sky and saw that it was growing cloudy. He did not go back in to the feast again; instead he crouched against the wall of the hut and shivered without sleeping. Before his eyes rested the little flat-bottomed boats of the family, resting in the dust behind the hut for the happy days of the rain. He would never travel in those boats again.

Hanging upside down was a painful way to become an adult, but worth it, if you lived. It was going to be a very bad way to die.

Hurrying and breathless with his news, Revent Winton came upon the two engineers crouched at the riverbank.

"I found out . . ." he began.

"*Shhh,*" one said without turning.

They were staring at a small creature at the edge of the water.

Winton approached closer and crouched beside them. "I have news that might interest you." He held his voice to a low murmur, but the triumph sounded in it like a rasp cutting through glass, a vibration that drew quick speculative glances from the engineers. They turned their attention back to the water's edge.

"Tell us when this is over. Wait."

The young preacher looked at what they were staring at and saw a little four-legged creature with large eyes and bright pointed teeth struggling feebly in the rising water. The young engineer, Charlie, was taking pictures of it.

"Its feet are stuck," Winton whispered. "Why don't you help it?"

"It's rooting itself," Henderson murmured back. "We're afraid that loud noises might make it stop."

"Rooting itself?" Winton was confused.

"The animal has two life stages, like a barnacle. You know, a barnacle is a little fish that swims around before it settles down to being just kind of a lump of rock. This one has a rooted stage that's coming on it now. When the water gets up to its neck it rolls up underwater and sticks its front legs out and starts acting like a kind of seaweed. Its hind feet are growing roots. This is the third one we've watched."

Winton looked at the struggling little creature. The water was rising toward its neck. The large bright eyes and small bared teeth looked frightened and uncomprehending. Winton shuddered.

"Horrible," he murmured. "Does it know what is happening?"

Henderson shrugged. "At least it knows the water is rising, and it knows it must not run away. It has to stand there and dig its feet in." He looked at Winton's expression and looked away. "Instinct comes as a powerful urge to do something. You can't fight instinct. Usually it's a pleasure to give in. It's not so bad."

Revent Paul Winton had always been afraid of drowning. He risked another glance at the little creature that was going to turn into a seaweed. The water had almost reached its neck, and it held its head high and panted rapidly with a thin whimpering sound.

"Horrible." Winton turned his back to it and pulled Henderson farther up the bank away from the river. "Mr. Henderson, I just found out something."

He was very serious, but now he had trouble phrasing what he had to say. Henderson urged him, "Well, go on."

"I found it out from a native. The translator is working better today."

"Charlie and I just recorded about four hundred words and phrases into it by distance pickup. We've been interviewing natives all day." Henderson's face suddenly grew cold and angry. "By the way, I thought you said that you weren't going to use the translator until it is ready."

"I was just checking it." Winton actually seemed apologetic. "I didn't say anything, just asked questions."

"All right." Henderson nodded grudgingly. "Sorry I complained. What happened? You're all upset, man!"

Winton evaded his eyes and turned away; he seemed to be looking at the river, with its banks of bushes and trees. Then he turned and looked in the direction of the inland hills, his expression vague. "Beautiful green country. It looks so peaceful. God is lavish with beauty. It shows His goodness. When we think that God is cruel, it is only because we do not understand. God is not really cruel."

"All right, so God is not really cruel," Henderson repeated cruelly. "So what's new?"

Winton winced and pulled his attention back to Henderson.

"Henderson, you've noticed that there are two kinds of natives—tall, thin ones that are slow, and quick, sturdy, short ones that do all the hard work. The sturdy ones we see in all ages, from child size up. Right?"

"I noticed."

"What did you think it meant?"

"Charlie and I talked about it." Henderson was puzzled. "Just a guess, but we think that the tall ones are aristocrats. They probably own the short ones, and the short ones do all the work."

Thick clouds were piled up over the far hills, accounting for the slow rise in the river level.

"The short ones are the children of the tall thin ones. The tall thin ones are the adults. The adults are all sick, that is why the children do all the work."

"What . . ." Henderson began, but Winton overrode his voice, continuing passionately, his eyes staring ahead at the hills.

"They are sick because of something they do to themselves. The young ones, strong and healthy, when they are ready to become adults they . . . they are hung upside down. For days, Henderson, maybe for more than a week, the translator would not translate how long. Some of them die. Most of them . . . most of them are stretched, and become long and thin." He stopped, and started again with an effort. "The native boy could not tell me why they do this, or how it started. It has been going on for so long that they cannot remember."

Abruptly and, to Henderson, shockingly, the preacher dropped to his knees and put his hands together. He tilted his head back with shut eyes and burst into prayer.

"O Lord, I do not know why You waited so long to help them to the true light, but I thank You that You sent me to stop this horrible thing."

Quickly he stood up and brushed his knees. "You'll help me, won't you?" he asked Henderson.

"How do we know it's true?" Henderson scowled. "It doesn't seem reasonable."

"Not reasonable?" Winton recovered his poise in sudden anger. "Come now, Harry, you've been talking as if you knew some anthropology. Surely you remember the puberty ceremonies. Natives often have initiation ceremonies for the young males. It's to test their manhood. They torture the boys, and the ones who can take it without whimpering are considered to be men, and graduated. Filthy cruelty! The authorities have always made them stop."

"No one around here has any authority to order anyone else to stop," Harry grunted. He was shaken by Winton's description of the puberty ceremony, and managed to be sarcastic only from a deep conviction that Winton had been always wrong, and therefore would continue to be wrong. It was not safe to agree with the man. It would mean being wrong along with Winton.

"No authority? What of God?"

"Well, what *of* God?" Henderson asked nastily. "If He is everywhere, He was here before you arrived here. And He never did anything to stop them. You've only known them a week. How long has God known them?"

"You don't understand." The dark-haired young man spoke with total conviction, standing taller, pride straightening his spine. "It was more than mere luck that we found this planet. It is my destiny to stop these people from their ceremony. God sent me."

Henderson was extremely angry, in a white-faced way. He had taken the preacher's air of superiority in the close confines of a spaceship for two months, and listened patiently to his preaching without letting himself be angry, for the sake of peace in the spaceship. But now he was out in the free air again, and he had had his fill of arrogance and wanted no more.

"Is that so?" he asked nastily. "Well, I'm on this expedition, too. How do you know that God did not send *me*, to stop *you?*"

Charlie finished taking pictures of the little animal under water as it changed, and came back up the bank, refolding the underwater lens. He was in time to see Winton slap the chief engineer in the face, spit out some profanity that would have started him on an hour of moral lecture if he had heard either of them emit such words. He saw Winton turn and run, not as if he were running away, but as if he were running to do something, in sudden impatience.

Ten minutes later Henderson had finished explaining what was bothering the preacher. They lay on the bank lazily looking down into the water, putting half attention into locating some other interesting life form, and enjoying the reflection of sunset in the ripples.

"I wish I could chew grass," Henderson said. "It would make it just like watching a river when I was a kid. But the plastic stuff on my face keeps me from putting anything into my mouth.''

"The leaves would probably be poisonous anyhow.'' Charlie brushed a hand through the pretty green of the grass. It was wiry and tough, with thin round blades, like marsh grass. "This isn't really grass. This isn't really Earth, you know.''

"I know, I wish I could forget it. I wonder what that creep Winton is doing now.'' Henderson rolled on his back and looked lazily at the sky. "I've got one up on him now. I got him to act like a creep right out in the open. He won't be giving me that superior, fatherly bilge. He might even call me Henderson now instead of Harry.''

"Don't ask too much.'' Charlie clipped a piece of leaf from a weed and absently tried to put it into his mouth. It was stopped by the transparent plastic film that protected him from local germs and filtered the air he breathed.

He flicked the leaf away. "How did that creep get to be a missionary? Nothing wrong with him, except he can't get on with people. Doesn't help in his line of work to be like that.''

"Easy, like I said,'' said Henderson, staring into the darkening pink and purple of the sky. "They encouraged him to be a missionary so he would go far, far away. Don't ever tell him. He thinks that he was chosen for his eloquence.'' Henderson rolled back onto his stomach and looked at the river. It was a chilly purple now, with silver ripples. "More clouds over the mountains. And those little clouds overhead might thicken up and rain. If the river keeps rising, there might be a flood. We might have to move the ship.''

"Winton said that the native mentioned a flood.'' Charlie got up lazily and stretched. "Getting dark out here anyhow. We'll have to find out more about that interview.''

They went in search of the preacher.

What he told them was disturbing, and vague.

"That was Spet,'' Henderson said. "That was the one I was learning words from all afternoon. And he told you he was going to die?''

Winton was earnest and pale. He sat crouched over the chart table as if his resolution to act had frightened him. "Yes. He said he was going to die. He said that they were going to hang him upside down in a tree as soon as the next rain starts. Because he is old enough.''

"But he said that other young males live through it? Maybe he's wrong about dying. Maybe it's not as tough as it sounds.''

"He said that many die,'' Winton said tonelessly. His hands lay motionless on the table. He was moved to a sudden flare of anger. "Oh, those stupid savages. Cruel, cruel!'' He turned his head to Henderson, looking up at him without the usual patronizing expression. "You'll fix the translator so that it translates me exactly, won't you? I don't want to shoot them to stop them from doing it. I'll just stop them by explaining that God doesn't want them to do this thing. They will have to understand me.''

He turned his head to Charlie, standing beside him. "The savages call me Enaxip. What does that mean? Do they think I'm a god?"

"It means Big Box," Henderson cut in roughly. "They still think that the box is talking. I see them watch the box when they answer, they don't watch you. I don't know what they think you are."

That night it did not rain. Winton allowed himself to fall asleep near dawn.

To Spet also it made a difference that it did not rain.

The next day he fished in the river as he always had.

The river was swollen and ran high and swiftly between its banks and fishing was not easy at first, but the brown ghost returned, bringing another one like himself, and they both helped Spet with pulling in the fish traps. The new ghost also wanted to be told how to talk, like a small one, and they all had considerable amusement as the two ghosts acted out ordinary things that often happened, and Spet told them the right words and songs to explain what they were doing.

One of them taught him a word in ghost language, and he knew that he was right to learn it, because he would soon be a ghost.

When Spet carried the fish back along the path to his family hut that evening, he passed the Box That Speaks. It spoke to him again, and again asked him questions.

The spirit covered with black that usually gibbered on top of the box was not there. Nothing was on top of the box, but the brown ghost who had just been helping him fish stood beside the box and spoke to it softly each time it asked Spet a question. The box spoke softly back to the ghost after Spet answered, discussing his answers, as if they had a problem concerning him.

Spet answered the questions politely, although some of them were difficult questions, asking reasons for things he had never thought needed a reason, and some were questions it was not polite to ask. He did not know why they discussed him, but it was their business, and they would tell him if they chose.

When he left them, the brown ghost made a gesture of respect and mutual aid in work, and Spet returned, warmed and pleased by the respect of the relative-ghost.

He did not remember to be afraid until he was almost home.

It began to rain.

Charlie came up the ramp and into the spaceship, and found Henderson pacing up and down, this thick shoulders hunched, his fists clenched, and his face wrinkled with worry.

"Hi." Charlie did not expect an answer. He kicked the lever that tightened the noose on the curtain plastic behind him, watched the hot wire cut him loose from the curtain and seal the curtain in the same motion. He stood carefully folding and smoothing his new wrapping of plastic around himself, to make sure that the coating he had worn outside was completely coated by the new wrapping. All outside dust and germs had to be trapped between the two layers of sterile germproof plastic.

He stood mildly smoothing and adjusting the wrappings, watching Henderson pace with only the very dimmest flicker of interest showing deep in his eyes. He could withdraw his attention so that a man working beside him could feel completely unwatched and as if he had the privacy of a cloak of invisibility. Charlie was well-mannered and courteous, and this was part of his courtesy.

"How're things?" he asked casually, slitting open his plastic cocoon and stepping out.

Henderson stopped pacing and took a cigar from a box on the table with savage impatience in his motions. "Very bad," he said. "Winton was right."

"Eh?" Charlie wadded up the plastic and tossed it into the disposal hopper.

"The natives, they actually do it." Henderson clenched the cigar between his teeth and lit it with savage jerky motions. "I asked Spet. No mistake in the translator this time. He said, yes, they hang the young men upside down in trees after the first spring rain. And yes, it hurt, and yes, sometimes one died, and no, he didn't know why they had to do this or what it was for. Ha!" Henderson threw the cigar away and began to pace again, snarling.

"Oh, yes, the translator was working fine! Generations of torturing their boys with this thing, and the adults can't remember how it started, or why, and they go on doing it anyway."

Charlie leaned back against the chart table, following his pacing with his eyes. "Maybe," he said mildly, "there's some good reason for the custom."

"A good reason to hang upside down for a week? Name one!"

Charlie did not answer.

"I just came from the native village," he said conversationally, as though changing the subject. "Winton has started. He's got the translator box right in the center of their village now, and he's sitting on top of it telling them that God is watching them, and stuff like that. I tried to reason with him, and he just pointed a gun at me. He said he'd stop the hanging ceremony even if he had to kill both of us and half the natives to do it."

"So let him try to stop them, just by talking." Henderson, who had stopped to listen, began to pace again, glowering at the floor. "That flapping mouth! Talking won't do it. Talking by itself never does anything. I'm going to do it the easy way. I'm going to kidnap Spet and keep them from getting him. Charlie, tribes only do things at the right season, what they call the right season. We'll turn Spet loose after the week is up, and they won't lay a hand on him. They'll just wait until next year. Meanwhile they'll be seeing that the trees aren't angry at them or any of that malarky. When they see that Spet got away with it, they'll have a chance to see a young male who's becoming a healthy adult without being all stretched out and physically wrecked. And maybe next year Spet will decide to get lost by himself. Maybe after looking at how Spet looks compared with an adult who was hanged, some of the kids due for hanging next year would duck into the forest and get lost when it's due."

"It's a good dream," Charlie said, lounging, following Henderson's pacing with his eyes. "I won't remind you that we swore off dreaming. But I'm with you in this, man. How do we find Spet?"

Henderson sat down, smiling. "We'll see him at the stream tomorrow. We don't need to do anything until it starts raining."

Charlie started rummaging in the tool locker. "Got to get a couple of flashlights. We have to move fast. Have to find Spet in a hurry. It's already raining, been raining almost an hour."

Darkness and rain, and it was very strange being upside down. Not formal and ceremonial, like a story-song about it, but real, like hauling nets and thatching huts, and eating with his brothers. The world seemed to be upside down. The tree trunk was beside him, strong and solid, and the ground was above him like a roof being held up by the tree, and the sky was below his feet and very far away—and, looking down at the clouds swirling in the depth of the sky, he was afraid of falling into it. The sky was a lake, and he would fall through it like a stone falling through water. If one fell into the sky, one would fall and fall for a long time, it looked so very deep.

Rain fell upward out of the sky and hit him under the chin. His ankles and wrists were tightly bound, but did not hurt, for the elders had used a soft rope of many strands tied in a way that would not stop circulation. His arms were at his sides, his wrists bound to the same strand that pulled at his ankles, and the pull on his arms was like standing upright, carrying a small weight of something. He was in a standing position, but upside down. It was oddly comfortable. The elders had many generations of experience to guide them, and they had chosen a tall tree with a high branch that was above the flood. They had seemed wise and certain, and he had felt confidence in them as they had bound and hung him up with great gentleness, speaking quietly to each other. Then they had left him, towing their little flat-boats across the forest floor that was now a roof above his head, walking tall and storklike across the dim-lit glistening ground, which looked so strangely like a rough, wet ceiling supported by the trunks of trees.

The steady rain drummed against the twigs and small spring leaves, splashing in the deepening trickles of water that ran along the ground. Spet knew that somewhere the river was overflowing its banks and spreading into the forest and across meadows to meet and deepen the rain water. In the village the street would be muddy, and the children would be shouting, trying already to pole the boats in the street, wild with impatience for the rising of the river, to see again the cold swift flow of water and watch the huts of the town sag and flow downward, dissolve and vanish beneath the smooth surface.

For a month in the time of floods everyone would live in boats. His tribe would paddle and pole up the coast, meeting other tribes, trading baskets and fishhooks, salt fish for salt meat, and swapping the old stories and songs with new variations brought from far places. Last time they had been lucky enough to come upon a large animal caught in the flood, swimming and helpless to resist the hunters. The men of the

Katherine MacLean

enemy tribe had traded the skin for half the roast meat on a raft, and sung a long story-song that no one had heard before. That was the best feast of all.

Then the horde of small boats would come home to the lakes that were the draining meadows and forest, and take down the sick and dying young men who had been hanging in the trees, and tend and feed them and call them "elder." They would then travel again for food, to fight through storms to salt the meat of drowned animals and hunt the deep sea fish caught in the dwindling lakes. When the rains had stopped and the land began to dry, they would return to the damp and drying land to sing and work and build a village of the smooth fresh clay left by the flood.

But Spet would not see those good times again. He hung in his tree upside down with the rain beating coolly against his skin. It was growing too dark to see more than the dim light of the sky. He shut his eyes, and behind his shut eyes were pictures and memories, and then dreams.

Here he is. How do we get him down. Did you bring a knife. How do we get up to him. It's slippery. I can't climb this thing. Wait, I'll give you a boost.

A flash of light, too steady for lightning, lasting a full second. Spet awoke fully, staring into the darkness, looking for the light which now was gone, listening to the mingled voices in the strange language.

"Don't use the flashlight, it will frighten him."

"Going to try to explain to him what we're doing?"

"No, not right away. He'll come along. Spet's a pal of mine already."

"Man, do these trees have roots. As big as the branches!"

"Live mangroves."

"You're always claiming the South has everything. What are mangroves?"

"Florida swamp trees. They root straight into deep water. Give a hand here."

"Keeps raining like this and they're going to need their roots. How high can we climb just on the roots, anyhow?"

"Think you're kidding? Why else would they have roots like this? This territory must be under water usually, deep water. This flat land must be delta country. We're just in the dry season."

"What do you mean delta country? I'm a city boy, define your terms."

"I mean, we're at the mouth of one of those big wandering rivers like the Mississippi or the Yellow River that doesn't know where it's going to run next, and splits up into a lot of little rivers at the coast, and moves its channel every spring. I noticed that grass around the ship looked like salt-water grass. Should have thought about it."

A dark figure appeared beside Spet and climbed past him toward the branch where the rope was tied. The next voice was distant. *"You trying to tell me we landed the ship in a river bed? Why didn't you say something when we were landing?"*

"Didn't think of it then." That voice was loud and close.

"It's a fine time to think of it now. I left the ship wide open. You up there yet?"

"Uh huh. I'm loosening the rope. Going to lower him slow. Catch him and keep him from landing on his head, will you?"

"Ready. Lower away."

The voices stopped and the world began to spin, and the bole of the tree began to move past Spet's face.

Suddenly a pair of wet arms gripped him, and the voice of the brown ghost called, *"Got him."*

Immediately the rope ceased to pull at Spet's ankles, and he fell head-first against the brown ghost and they both tumbled against slippery high roots and slid down from one thick root to another until they stopped at the muddy ground. The ghost barked a few short words and began to untie the complex knots from Spet's ankles and wrists.

It was strange sitting on the wet ground with its coating of last year's leaves. Even right side up the forest looked strange, and Spet knew that this was because of death, and he began to sing his death song.

The brown ghost helped him to his feet and said clearly in ordinary words, "Come on, boy, you can sing when we get there."

His friend dropped down from a low branch to the higher roots of the tree, slipped and fell on the ground beside them.

In Spet's language the standing one said to the other, "No time for resting, Charlie, let's go."

It was very dark now, and the drips from the forest branches poured more heavily, beating against the skin. The ghost on the ground barked a few of the same words the relative-ghost had made when he had fallen, and got up.

The two started off through the forest, beckoning Spet to follow. He wondered if he were a ghost already. Perhaps the ghosts had taken him to be a ghost without waiting for him to die. That was nice of them, and a favor, possibly because they were kinfolk. He followed them.

The rain had lightened and became the steady, light-falling spray that it would be for the next several days. Walking was difficult, for the floor of the forest was slippery with wet leaves, and the mud underneath was growing soft again, remembering the time it had been part of the water of the river, remembering that the river had left it there only a year ago. The ghosts with him made sputtering words in ghost talk, sometimes tripped and floundered and fell, helped each other up and urged him on.

The forest smelled of the good sweet odors of damp earth and growing green leaves. The water and mud were cooling against his hurting feet, and Spet unaccountably wanted to linger in the forest, and sit, and perhaps sleep.

The floods were coming, and the ghosts had no boats with them.

"Come on, Spet. We go to big boat. Come on, Spet."

Why did they stumble and flounder through the forest without a boat? And why were they afraid? Could ghosts drown? These ghosts, with their perpetually wet appearance—if they had drowned once, would they be forced to relive the drowning, and be caught in the floods every year? A bad thing that happened once had to happen again and again in dreams. And your spirit self in the dream lived it each time as something new. There is no memory in the dream country. These ghosts were dream people, even though they chose to be in the awake world. They were probably bound by the laws of the dream world. They would have to re-enact their drowning. Their boat was far away, and they were running toward the watercourse where the worst wave of the flood would come.

Spet understood suddenly that they wanted him to drown. He could not become a ghost, like these friendly brown ghosts, and live in their world, without first dying.

He remembered his first thoughts of them, that they carried the illusion of water over them because they had once drowned. They wanted him to be like them. They were trying to lure him through waters where he would stumble and drown as they had. Naturally as they urged him on their gestures were nervous and guilty. It is not easy to urge a friend onward to his death. But to be shaped like a young one, merry, brown, and covered with water, obviously he had to be drowned as they were drowned, young and merry, before the hanging had made a sad adult of him.

He would not let them know that he had guessed their intention. Running with them toward the place where the flood would be worst, he tried to remember on what verse he had stopped singing his death song, and began again from that verse, singing to stop the fear-thoughts. The rain beat coolly against his face and chest as he ran.

Each man in his own panic, they burst from the forest into the clearing. The engineers saw with a wave of relief that the spaceship was still there, a pale shaft upright in the midst of water. Where the meadow had been was a long narrow lake, reflecting the faint light of the sky, freckled with drifting spatters of rain.

"How do we get to it?" Charlie turned to them.

"How high is the water? Is the ramp covered?" Henderson asked practically, squinting through the rain.

"Ramp looks the same. I see grass sticking up in the water. It's not deep."

Charlie took a careful step and then another out into the silvery surface. Spongy grass met his feet under the surface, and the water lapped above his ankles, but no higher.

"It's shallow."

They started out toward the ship. It took courage to put their feet down into a surface that suggested unseen depth. The shallow current of water tugged at their ankles and grew deeper and stronger.

"Henderson, wait!"

The three stopped and turned at the call. The path to the village was close, curving away from the forest toward the distant riverbank, a silvery road of water among dark bushes. A dark figure came stumbling along the path, surrounded by the silvery shine of the rising water. Ripples spread from his ankles as he ran.

He came to the edge where the bushes stopped and the meadow began, saw the lake-appearance of it, and stopped. The others were already thirty feet away.

"Henderson! Charlie!"

"Walk, it's not deep yet. Hurry up." Charlie gestured urgently for him to follow them. They were still thirty feet out, standing in the smooth silver of the rising water. It was almost to their knees.

Winton did not move. He looked across the shining shallow expanse of water, and his voice rose shrilly. "It's a lake, we need boats."

"It's shallow," Charlie called. The rain beat down on the water, speckling it in small vanishing pockmarks. The two engineers hesitated, looking back at Winton, sensing something wrong.

Winton's voice was low, but the harshness of desperation made it as clear as if he had screamed.

"Please. I can't swim—"

"Go get him," Henderson told Charlie. "He's got a phobia. I'll herd Spet to the ship, and then head back to help you."

Charlie was already splashing in long strides back to the immobile figure of the preacher. He started to shout when he got within earshot.

"Why didn't you say so, man? We almost left you behind!" He crouched down before the motionless fear-dazed figure. "Get on, man. You're getting taxi service."

"What?" asked Winton in a small distant voice. The water lapped higher.

"Get on my back," Charlie snapped impatiently. "You're getting transportation."

"The houses dissolved, and they went off in boats and left me alone. They said that I was an evil spirit. I think they did the hangings anyway, even though I told them it was wrong." Winton's voice was vague, but he climbed on Charlie's back. "The *houses* dissolved."

"Speak up, stop mumbling," muttered Charlie.

The spaceship stood upright ahead in the center of the shallow silver lake that had been a meadow. Its doors were open, and the bottom of the ramp was covered by water. Water tugged against Charlie's lower legs as he ran, and the rain beat against their faces and shoulders in a cool drumming. It would have been pleasant, except that the fear of drowning was growing even in Charlie, and the silver of the shallow new lake seemed to threaten an unseen depth ahead.

"There seems to be a current," Winton said with an attempt at casual remarks. "Funny, this water looks natural here, as if the place were a river, and those trees look like the banks."

Charlie said nothing. Winton was right, but it would not be wise to tell a man with a phobia about drowning that they were trying to walk across the bed of a river while the water returned to its channel.

"Why are you running?" asked the man he carried.

"To catch up with Henderson."

Once they were inside the spaceship with the door shut they could ignore the water level outside. Once inside, they would not have to tell Winton anything about how it was outside. A spaceship made a good submarine.

Katherine MacLean

The water level was almost to Charlie's knees and he ran now in a difficult lurching fashion. Winton pulled up his feet nervously to keep them from touching the water. The plastic which they wore was semipermeable to water and both of them were soaked.

"Who is that up ahead with Henderson?"

"Spet, the native boy."

"How did you persuade him to stay away from the ceremony?"

"We found him hanging and cut him down."

"Oh." Winton was silent a moment trying to absorb the fact that the engineers had succeeded in rescuing someone. "It's a different approach. I talked, but they wouldn't listen." He spoke apologetically, hanging on to Charlie's shoulders, his voice jolting and stopping as Charlie tripped over a concealed tuft of grass or small bush under the water. "They didn't even answer—or look at me. When the water got deep they went off in little boats and didn't leave a boat for me."

Charlie tripped again and staggered to one knee. They both briefly floundered waist deep in the water, and then Charlie was up again, still with a grip on his passenger's legs, so that Winton was firmly on his back.

When he spoke again, Winton's tone was casual, but his voice was hysterically high in pitch. "I asked them for a boat, but they wouldn't look at me."

Charlie did not answer. He respected Winton's attempt to conceal his terror. The touch of water can be a horrifying thing to a man with a phobia of drowning. He could think of nothing to distract Winton's attention from his danger, but he hoped desperately that the man would not notice that the water had deepened. It is not possible to run in water over knee height. There was no way to hurry now. The rain had closed in, in veiling curtains, but he thought he saw the small figures of Henderson and the native in the distance reach the ramp which led to the spaceship.

If the flood hit them all now, Henderson and Spet could get inside, but how would he himself get this man with a phobia against water off his back and into the water to swim? He could visualize the bony arms tightening around his throat in a hysterical stranglehold. If a drowning man gets a clutch on you, you are supposed to knock him out and tow him. But how could he get this nonswimming type off his back and out where he could be hit? If Winton could not brace himself to walk in water up to his ankles, he was not going to let go and try to swim in water up to his neck. He'd flip, for sure! Charlie found no logical escape from the picture. The pressure of the strong bony arms around his throat and shoulders and the quick, irregular breathing of the man he was carrying made him feel trapped.

The water rose another inch or so, and the drag of it against his legs became heavier. The current was pulling sidewise.

"You're going slowly." Winton's voice had the harsh rasp of fear.

"No hurry." With difficulty, Charlie found breath to speak in a normal tone. "Almost there."

The curtain of rain lifted for a moment and he saw the spaceship, dark against the sky, and the ramp leading to its open door. The ramp was very shrunken, half covered by the rising water. It seemed a long away ahead.

As he watched, a light came on.

In the archway of the spaceship, Henderson flipped a switch and the lights went on.

Spet was startled. Sunlight suddenly came from the interior of the hut and shone against the falling rain in a great beam. Rain glittered through the beam in falling drops like sparks of white fire. It was very unlike anything real, but in dreams sunlight could be in one place and rain another at the same time, and no one in the dream country was surprised. And these were people who usually lived in the dream country, so apparently they had the power to do it in the real world also.

Nevertheless, Spet was afraid, for the sunlight did not look right as it was, coming out in a great widening beam across the rippling rain-pocked water. Sunlight did not mix well with rain.

"Sunlight," Spet said apologetically to his relative-ghost.

The brown ghost nodded and led him down the slope of the ramp through the strange sparkling sunlight, with the ramp strange and hard underfoot.

"Don't go inside until I return," the ghost said, mouthing the words with difficulty. The ghost placed his hands around the railing of the ramp. "You hang on here and wait for me," said the brown ghost of someone in his family, and waded down into the water.

Spet followed him down into the comfortable water until his sore feet were off the end of the ramp and in the cooling soft mud, and then he gripped the rail obediently and waited. The water lapped at his waist like an embrace, and the wind sang a death song for him.

The bright glare of the strange sunlight on dancing water was beautiful, but it began to hurt his eyes. He closed them, and then heard a sound other than the wind. Two sounds.

One sound he recognized as the first flood crest crashing through the trees to the north, approaching them, and he knew he must hurry and drown before it arrived, because it was rough and hurtful.

The other sound was the strange voice of the black spirit which usually gibbered on top of the Box That Speaks. Spet opened his eyes and saw that the gibbering spirit was riding on the shoulders of the brown ghost, as he and his friend, the other brown ghost, moved through the waist-deep water toward Spet and the ramp.

The black spirit gibbered at him as they passed, and Spet felt a dim anger, wondering if it would bring bad luck to him with its chants, for its intentions could not be the same as the friendly ghosts.

"Spet, come up the ramp with us. It's dry inside. Don't look like that, there's nothing to be afraid of now, we'll go inside and shut the door, it will keep the water away, it won't get in. . . . Come along, Spet."

Katherine MacLean

The black spirit suddenly leaped down on the ramp with a strange scream. *"Aaaaiiii! . . . He's turning into a seaweed. Quick, get him out of the water! Help!"*

The spirit with the black skin and white face possibly wanted him for his own dark spirit world. He was coming down the ramp at Spet, screaming. He was too late, though, Spet knew that he was safe for the dim land of the drowned with the friendly ghosts who had come for him. He felt his feet sending roots down into the mud, moving and rooting downward, and a wild joy came over him, and he knew that this was the right thing for him, much more right and natural than it would have been to become a tall sad adult.

He had been feeling a need for air, panting and drawing the cold air into his lungs. Just as the clawed hands of the dark spirit caught hold of his neck, Spet had enough air, and he leaned over into the dark and friendly water, away from the painful beauty of the bright lights and moving forms. The water closed around him, and the sound of voices was lost.

He could still feel the grip of the spirit's bony arms around his neck, pulling upward, but he had seen the brown ghosts running toward them, and they would stop it from doing him any harm, so he dismissed the fear from his mind and bent deeper into the dark, and plunged his hands with spread fingers deep into the mud, and gripped his ankles, as if he had always known just how to do this thing. His hands locked and became unable to unfold. They would never unfold again.

He felt the soft surge that was the first flood wave arriving and passing above him and ignored it, and, with a mixture of terror and the certainty of doing right, he opened his mouth and took a deep breath of cold water.

All thought stopped. As the water rushed into his lungs, the rooted sea creature that was the forgotten adult stage of Spet's species began its thoughtless pseudo-plant existence, forgetting everything that had ever happened to it. Its shape changed.

The first wave of the flood did not quite reach up to the edge of the ship's entrance. It caught the two engineers as they dragged a screaming third human up the ramp toward the entrance, but it did not quite reach into the ship, and when it passed the three humans were still there. One of them struck the screaming one, and they carried him in.

Winton was hysterical for some time, but Henderson seemed quite normal. He worked well and rationally in compiling a good short survey report to carry to the planetary-survey agency, and when the waters dried around the spaceship he directed the clearing of mud from the jets and the overhaul of the firing chambers without a sign of a warp in his logic.

He did not want to speak to any native, and went into the ship when they appeared.

Winton was still slightly delirious when they took off from the planet, but, once in space, he calmed down and made a good recovery. He just did not talk about it. Henderson still seemed quite normal, and Charlie carefully did not tell Winton that Henderson kept a large bush in a glass enclosure in the engine room.

Ever since that time Henderson has been considered a little peculiar. He is a good enough risk for the big liners, for they have other engineers on board to take over if he ever cracks. He has no trouble getting jobs, but wherever he goes he brings with him an oversized potted plant and puts it in the engine room and babies it with water and fertilizer. His fellow officers never kid him about it, for it is not a safe subject.

When Henderson is alone, or thinks he is alone, he talks to the potted bush. His tone is coaxing. But the bush never answers.

Charlie runs into him occasionally when their ships happen to dock at the same space port around the same planet. They share a drink and enjoy a few jokes together, but Charlie takes care not to get signed onto the same ship as Henderson. The sight of Henderson and his potted bush together make him nervous.

It's the wrong bush, but he'll never tell Henderson that. ■

BIG SWORD
Paul Ash

HE WAS TALLER THAN THE TALLEST by nearly an inch, because the pod that hatched him had hung on the Tree more than twenty days longer than the rest, kept from ripening by all the arts at the People's command. The flat spike sheathed in his left thigh was, like the rest of him, abnormally large: but it was because he represented their last defense that they gave him the name, if a thought-sign can be called that, of "Big Sword."

He was a leader from his birth, because among the People intelligence was strictly proportional to size. They had two kinds of knowledge: Tree-knowledge, which they possessed from the moment they were born; and Learned-knowledge, the slow accumulation of facts passed on from one generation to another with the perfect accuracy of transmitted thought, which again was shared by all alike. The Learned-knowledge of the People covered all the necessities that they had previously experienced: but now they were faced with a wholly new danger and they needed somebody to acquire the Learned-knowledge to deal with it. So they made use of the long-known arts that could delay ripening of the pods on the Tree. These were not used often, because neighboring pods were liable to be stunted by the growth of an extra-large one, but now there was the greatest possible need for a leader. The Big Folk, after two years of harmlessness, had suddenly revealed themselves as an acute danger, one that threatened the life of the People altogether.

Tree-knowledge Big Sword had, of course, from the moment of his hatching. The Learned-knowledge of the People was passed on to him by a succession of them sitting beside him in the treetops while his body swelled and hardened and absorbed the light. He would not grow any larger: the People made use of the stored energy of sunlight for their activities, but the substance of their bodies came from the Tree. For three revolutions of the planet he lay and absorbed energy and information. Then he knew all that they could pass on to him, and was ready to begin.

A week later he was sitting on the edge of a clearing in the forest, watching the Big Folk at their incomprehensible tasks. The People had studied them a little when they first appeared in the forest, and had made some attempt to get in touch with them, but without success. The Big Folk used thought all right, but chaotically: instead of an ordered succession of symbols there would come a rush of patterns and half-patterns, switching suddenly into another set altogether and then returning to the first, and at any moment the whole thing might be wiped out altogether. Those first students of the People, two generations ago, had thought that there was some connection between the disappearance of thought and the vibrating wind which the Big Folk would suddenly emit from a split in their heads. Big Sword was now certain that they were right, but the knowledge did not help him much. After the failure of their first attempts at communication the People, not being given to profitless curiosity, had left the Big Folk alone. But now a totally unexpected danger had come to light. One of the Big Folk, lumbering about the forest, had cut a branch off the Tree.

When they first arrived the Big Folk had chopped down a number of trees—ordinary trees—completely and used them for various peculiar constructions in the middle of the clearing, but that was a long time ago and the People had long since ceased to worry about it. Two generations had passed since it happened. But the attack on the Tree itself had terrified them. They had no idea why it had been made and there was no guarantee that it would not happen again. Twelve guardians had been posted round the Tree ready to do anything possible with thought or physical force to stave off another such attack, but they were no match for the Big Folk. The only safety lay in making contact with the Big Folk and telling them why they must leave the Tree of the People alone.

Big Sword had been watching them for two days now and his plan was almost ready. He had come to the conclusion that a large part of the difficulty lay in the fact that the Big People were hardly ever alone. They seemed to go about in groups of two or three and thought would jump from one to another at times in a confusing way: then again you would get a group whose thoughts were all completely different and reached the observer in a chaotic pattern of interference. The thing to do, he had decided, was to isolate one of them. Obviously the one to tackle would be the most intelligent of the group, the leader, and it was clear which one filled that position: he stood out among his companions as plainly as Big Sword. There were one or two factors to be considered further, but that evening, Big Sword had decided, he would be ready to act.

Meanwhile the Second Lambdan Exploratory Party had troubles of their own. Mostly these were the professional bothers that always accompany scientific expeditions; damaged equipment, interesting sidelines for which neither equipment nor workers happened to be available, not enough hours in the day. Apart from that there was the constant nag of the gravitation, twenty percent higher than that of Earth; and the effect, depressing until you got used to it, of the monochromatic scenery, laid out in darker and lighter shades of black and gray. Only the red soil and red rocks varied that monotony, with an effect which to Terrestrial eyes was somewhat sinister. Nevertheless, the Expedition were having fewer troubles than they expected. Lambda, apparently, was a thoroughly safe planet. Whatever those gray-and-black jungles might look like it appeared that they had nothing harmful in them.

At thirty light-years away from Earth most personal troubles had got left behind. John James Jordan, however, the leader of the party, had brought his with him. His most urgent responsibility was in the next cabin, in bed and, it was to be hoped, asleep.

There was no doubt about it, a man who made his career in space had no business to get married. Some men, of course, could take their wives with them: there were three married couples on the expedition, though they were with the first party at base on the coast. But for a spaceman to marry a woman and leave her at home didn't make sense.

He wondered, now, what he had thought he was doing. Marriage had been a part of that hectic interval between his first expedition and his second, when he had arrived home to find that space exploration was News and everybody wanted to know him. He had been just slightly homesick, that first time. The idea of having somebody to come back to had been attractive.

The actual coming back, three years later, had not been so good. He had had time to realize that he scarcely knew Cora. Most of their married life seemed to have been spent at parties: he would arrive late, after working overtime, and find Cora already in the thick of it. He was going to have more responsibility preparing for the third expedition: he was going to have to spend most of his time on it. He wondered how Cora was going to take it. She had never complained when he wasn't there, during the brief period of their married life: but somehow what he remembered wasn't reassuring.

Just the same, it was a shock to find that she had divorced him a year after his departure—one of the first of the so-called "space divorces." It was a worse shock, though, to find that he now had a two-year-old son.

The rule in a space divorce was that the divorced man had the right to claim custody of his children, providing that he could make adequate arrangements for them during his absence. That would have meant sending Ricky to some all-year-round school. There was no sense to that. Cora's new husband was fond of him. Jordan agreed to leave Ricky with his mother. He even agreed, three years later on his next leave, not to see Ricky—Cora said that someone had told the little boy that her husband was not his real father and contact with somebody else claiming that position was likely to upset him.

Once or twice during his Earth-leaves—usually so crammed with duties that they made full-time exploration look like a holiday—Jordan got news of Cora. Apparently she was a rising star in the social world. He realized, gradually, that she had married him because for a brief time he had been News, and could take her where she wanted to be. He was vaguely relieved that she had got something out of their marriage: it was nice that somebody did. He was prepared to grant her doings the respect due to the incomprehensible. Nevertheless he was worried, for a moment, when he heard that she had been divorced yet again and remarried—to a prominent industrialist this time. He wondered how Ricky had taken it.

His first actual contact with Cora in about seven years came in the form of a request from her lawyer that he should put his signature to an application for entrance to a school. Merely a formality. The insistence on that point roused his suspicions and he made some inquiries about the school in question.

Half an hour after getting answers he had found Cora's present address, booked a passage on the Transequatorial Flight, and canceled his engagements for the next twenty-four hours.

He was just in time to get aboard the flier. He had taken a bundle of urgent papers with him and he had three hours of flight in which to study them, but he hardly tried to do so. His conscience felt like a Lothornian cactus-bird trying to break out of the egg.

Why on Earth, why in Space, why in the Universe hadn't he taken some sort of care of his son?

He had never visited Antarctica City before and he found it depressing. With great ingenuity somebody had excavated a building-space in the eternal ice and filled it with a city which was an exact copy of all the other cities. He wondered why anybody had thought it worth while.

Cora's house seemed less a house than an animated set for a stereo on The Life of the Wealthy Classes. It had been decorated in the very latest style—he recognized one or two motifs which had been suggested by the finds of the First Lambdan Expedition, mingled with the usual transparent furniture and electrified drapes. He was contemplating a curious decorative motif, composed of a hooked object which he recognized vaguely as some primitive agricultural implement and what looked like a pile-man's drudge—but of course that particular mallet-shape had passed through innumerable uses—when Cora came in.

Her welcome was technically perfect: it combined a warm greeting with just a faint suggestion that it was still open to her to have him thrown out by the mechman if it seemed like a good idea. He decided to get the business over as soon as possible.

"What's the matter with Ricky, Cora? Why do you want to get rid of him?"

Cora's sparkle-crusted brows rose delicately.

"Why, Threejay, what a thing to say?"

The idiotic nickname, almost forgotten, caught him off balance for a moment, but he knew exactly what he wanted to say.

"This school you want to send him to is for maladjusted children. It takes complete responsibility, replacing parents—you wouldn't be allowed to see him for the next three years at least."

"It's a very fine school, Threejay. Camillo insisted we should send him to the best one available."

Camillo must be the new husband.

"Why?" repeated Jordan.

The welcome had drained right out of Cora's manner. "May I ask why this sudden uprush of parental feeling? You've never shown any interest in Ricky before. You've left him to me. I'm not asking you to take any responsibility. I'm just asking you to sign that form.''

"Why?''

"Because he's unbearable! Because I won't have him in the house! He pries round—there's no privacy. He finds out everything and then uses it to make trouble. He's insulted half our friends. Camillo won't have him in the house and neither will I. If you don't want him to go to that school, perhaps you'll suggest an alternative.''

Jordan was shaken, but tried not to show it. "I'd like to see him, Cora.''

As swiftly as it had arisen Cora's rage sank out of sight. "Of course you can see him, Threejay!'' She turned to the wall-speaker and murmured briefly into it. "Who knows, maybe the sight of a really, truly father is all he needs! You can just have a nice fatherly chat with him before you have to catch your flier back, and then he'll settle down and turn into a model citizen.''

The door slid open and a boy came quietly in. He was a very neat and tidy boy, small for his age, with a serious, almost sad expression. He said gently, "Good morning, Cora.''

Cora spoke over her shoulder. "Ricky, dear, who do you think this is?''

Ricky looked at the visitor and his eyes widened.

"You . . . you're Dr. Jordan, aren't you? You wrote that book about Cranil—it's called *The Fossil Planet*. And I saw you on the stereo two nights ago. You were talking about that place where all the forests are gray and black. And—'' Ricky stopped with his mouth half open. His face went blank.

"That's who I am,'' said Jordan gravely.

"I know.'' Ricky swallowed. "But you're here . . . I mean . . . this sounds silly, but I suppose . . . I mean, you wouldn't be my father, would you?''

"Don't put on an act, Ricky,'' said Cora harshly. "You know perfectly well he's your father.''

Ricky turned rather white. He shook his head. "No, honestly. I knew my father's name was Jordan, but I just didn't connect it up. I say—'' he stopped short.

"Yes, Ricky?''

"I suppose you wouldn't have time to talk to me a little? About Lambda, I mean. Because I really am interested—not just kid stuff. I want to be a xenobiologist.''

Cora laughed, a delicate metallic sound.

"Why be so modest, Ricky? After all, he's your father. He's apparently decided it's time he took an interest in you. He's due back to that place that fascinates you so much in a week or two, so I don't see how he'll do that unless he takes you with him. Why not ask him to?''

Ricky went scarlet and then very pale. He looked quickly away, but not before Jordan had had time to see the eager interest in his face replaced by sick resignation.

"Why shouldn't you take him, Threejay?'' went on Cora. "These Mass-Time ships have lots of room. You've decided that it's time you were responsible for him instead of me. Those books he reads are full of boys who made good in space. Why don't you—''

"Yes, why don't I?" said Jordan abruptly.

"Don't!" said Ricky sharply. "Please, don't! Honestly, I know it's a joke . . . I mean I don't read that kid stuff now . . . but—''

"No joke," said Jordan. "As Cora says, there's lots of room. Do you want to come?''

And I'd had my psycho check only the week before, reflected Jordan, and they didn't find a thing.

He noticed suddenly that a report was moving through the scanner on his desk—the latest installment of Woodman's researches on the sexual cycles of Lambdan fresh-water organisms. He'd intended to read that tonight instead of mulling over all this stuff about Ricky.

He pushed the switch back to the beginning, but it was no use. He remembered how he had felt—how Cora's needling had made him feel—and how Ricky had looked when he grasped that the proposal was serious. No chance at all of backing out then—not that he had wanted to. It was true that, with Mass-time flight, there was plenty of room; one feature of the drive was that within certain limits the bigger the ship the faster it would go. And he had complete authority over the selection of personnel for this second expedition, which was to reinforce the team already settled on Lambda. Ricky's inclusion was taken with a surprising lack of concern by the rest of the staff. And it had looked as though his insane action was working out all right. Until the last two days Ricky had been no trouble at all.

If anything, Ricky had been too desperately anxious to keep out of the way and avoid being a nuisance, but he had seemed completely happy. Jordan's project of getting to know him had never got very far, because his time was fully occupied, but Ricky had spent the weeks before blast-off mainly in the Interstellar Institute, chaperoned by young Woodman, who had taken a fancy to him. Jordan had taken time out once or twice during that period to worry over the fact that he was hardly seeing the boy, but once they got aboard ship it would be different.

Once aboard ship, absorbed in checking stores and setting up projects to go into operation as soon as they landed, it was—once the party's settled and working, it'll be different. He'd have some time to spare.

Unfortunately that hadn't been soon enough. He should have paid some attention to Cora. She wouldn't have got worked up like that over nothing. She had said Ricky made trouble. He'd done that all right. And Jordan had known nothing about it till it attained the dimensions of a full-blown row.

Rivalry on the expedition was usually friendly enough. Unfortunately Cartwright and Penn, the two geologists, didn't get on. They had different methods of working and each was suspicious of the value of the other's work. But without Ricky they wouldn't have come to blows on it.

Paul Ash

Quite accidentally the riot had been started by Ellen Scott. As soil specialist she had an interest in geology. Talking to Cartwright she had happened to say something about the date of the Great Rift. Cartwright had shot out of his chair.

"Ellen—where did you get that idea? Who told it to you?"

Ellen looked surprised.

"I thought you did, Peter. The Great Rift's your pet subject. If you didn't, I suppose it was Penn."

"I haven't mentioned it to anyone. I only worked it out a couple of days ago. It's in my notes now, on my desk. Penn must have been going through them. Where is he?"

"Calm down, Peter!" Ellen got to her feet in astonishment. "Probably he worked it out too—you may have mentioned something that set him on the track. He must have mentioned it to me in the last few days, I think . . . that is, if he was the one who told me." She looked puzzled. "I don't remember discussing it with him. No, I believe—" she broke off suddenly and refused to say any more. Cartwright, un-mollified, strode off to look for Penn. Dr. Scott departed in search of Ricky.

"Ricky, do you remember a day or two ago we were talking about the Great Rift?"

Ricky looked up from the microscope he was using.

"Sure," he said. "Why?" His smile faded and he began to look worried. "What's happened?"

"You remember you said something about the date—that it was about fifteen thousand years ago? You did say that, didn't you?"

Ricky's expression had faded to a watchful blank, but he nodded.

"Well, who told you that? How did you know?"

"Somebody said it," said Ricky flatly. He did not sound as though he expected to be believed.

Ellen Scott frowned.

"Listen, Ricky. Dr. Cartwright's got the idea that somebody must have looked through the papers on his desk and read that date. He says he didn't mention it to anyone. There may be trouble. If you did get curious and took a look at his notes—well, now is the time to say so. It's not a good thing to have done, of course, but nobody'll pay much attention once it's cleared up."

"I didn't look," said Ricky wretchedly. "I don't remember how I knew, but I didn't look. Honestly not."

Unfortunately by that time Cartwright and Penn had already started arguing which ended with both of them crashing through the wall of the dining cabin—which had not been built to take assaults of that kind—and throwing Barney the cook into a kind of hysterics. After that Jordan came on the scene.

Ricky had come and told him about it all. At least, he'd said that he had somehow learned that the date of the Great Rift had been fixed, and had mentioned it to Dr.

Scott while they were talking about geology. He didn't know how he had learned it. He denied looking through Cartwright's papers.

It was something that he had told the story, but then he must have thought that Ellen Scott would if he didn't.

Jordan's thoughts wandered off to Ellen for a moment. She was another person who believed that people who chose to work on alien planets must avoid personal ties. How right she was.

Nothing more had happened. Cartwright and Penn seemed to be on somewhat better terms, having purged their animosity. But Ricky had been going round with a haunted and hopeless look on his face and Jordan was going crazy trying to think up an approach to the matter which would not drive the boy still further away from him. But if he really made a habit of prying into private papers—and Cora had accused him of just that, after all—something must be done about it.

But what?

Jordan sighed, turned the viewer back to the beginning again and started to concentrate on Woodman's report. He had read three frames when the silence was split by a terrified bellow from the direction of the forest.

"Uelph! Uelph! Dewils. Uelph!"

Jordan shot through the door, grabbing a flashlight on the way. It was hardly needed: three moons were in the sky and their combined light was quite enough to show him the huge shape blundering among the cabins.

"Barney!" he shouted. "Stand still! What's the matter?"

Barney—seventeen stone on Earth, over twenty on Lambda—came to a halt and blinked at the flashlight. He put up a huge hand, feeling at his face. He seemed to be wearing some sort of mask or muffler over his mouth—otherwise he was draped in flannelette pajamas of brilliant hue and was barefooted. He ripped off the muffler—whatever it was—and threw it away. His utterance was a little clearer, but not much.

"Dewils in a voresh. Caught eee. Woot ticky tuff on a wouth."

He was gasping and sweating and Jordan was seriously worried. Barney was a superb cook, but he was apt to get excited and the extra gravitation of Lambda produced a slight strain on his heart. At that moment Ricky appeared like a silent shadow at his father's elbow.

"What's the matter with him?" As usual the boy looked neat and alert, although at the moment he was wearing pajamas and a robe. Jordan gestured towards his cabin.

"Take Barney in there and see what's sticking his mouth up." Several other people had appeared by this time, including Ellen Scott in a brilliant robe and Woodman in rumpled pajamas. Jordan sent Ellen to switch on the overhead floods and organized a search party.

Half an hour later Barney's mouth had been washed free from the gummy material which had been sticking his lips together and he was in some shape to explain.

"I woke up suddenly lying out in the forest. All damp it was." He groaned faintly. "I can feel my lumbago coming on already. I was lyin' flat on my back and there was somethin' over my arms—rope or somethin'. My mouth was all plastered up and there was a thing sittin' on my chest. I got a glimpse of it out of the crack of me eyes, and then it went. There was more of them round. They was shoutin'."

"Shouting?" repeated Jordan. "You mean just making a noise?"

"No sir, they was shouting in English. I couldn't hear what, but it was in words all right. They said 'People.' That was the only word I got, but that's it right enough. 'People.' Then I got my arms free and started to swipe around. I got hold of one of them and it stung me and I let it go."

He pointed to a neat puncture wound in the flesh at the base of his thumb. Jordan got out antiseptics and bathed it.

"I got up and ran back," Barney went on. "I was only a little way into the forest—I could still see the lights here. I ran as hard as I could but me feet kept slippin'." The light of remembered panic was in his eyes. "They stuck somethin' over me mouth—I couldn't breathe. It took me hours to get it off. I dunno what it was."

"It was a leaf," said Woodman. He produced a large leaf, perhaps twenty inches long: it was dark gray and one surface was smeared with a dully shining substance. "It's been coated with some kind of vegetable gum."

"But how did you get into the forest, Barney?" demanded Dr. Scott.

Barney shook his head miserably.

"He walked," said another of the party. "On his own. Tracks of his feet in the mud. You've been sleepwalking, Barney."

"Then where did he get the gag?" demanded Woodman. "This gum comes from a plant which is quite rare and there aren't any within a hundred yards of the clearing. Besides, we found the place where he'd been lying. A couple of saplings were bent over and the ends shoved in the mud—those were used to hold his arms down, I reckon. No, he was attacked all right, but what did it?"

"I suppose," said Dr. Scott slowly, "this couldn't have been somebody's idea of a joke?"

There was a brief silence. Ricky looked up suddenly and caught his father's eye. His face went rigid, but he said nothing.

"We shall have to assume it wasn't," said Jordan. "That means precautions. We always assumed that Lambda was a safe planet. Apparently we were wrong. Until we know what happened no one goes out alone. Those of you who have observations to make outside will have to work in pairs and with your radios turned on. We'll arrange for a monitor on all the individual frequencies. The floods had better stay on tonight and we'll have a patrol—three men keeping in touch. Two hours for each of us. Doc, will you see to Barney?"

The medical officer nodded and took Barney off to his cabin, and its specially strengthened bunk. Jordan looked thoughtfully at his son.

"You'd better get back to bed, Ricky. Unless you have anything to contribute."

Ricky was standing stiffly upright. "I haven't," he said.

"Get along, then. Now about this patrol—"

Jordan put himself on the first shift of the patrol—he wouldn't be able to sleep. Why in Space had he brought Ricky? Either he had brought him into danger or—worse—Ricky was somehow at the bottom of this. He spent a good deal of time running errands for Barney. He had not seemed to mind it, but how did you tell what a boy was thinking? Might he have thought it funny to send big Barney lumbering in panic through the forest? And how could he have done it?

Jordan remembered that Ricky had once been found reading the article on Hypnosis in the Terrestrial Encyclopedia.

And if Ricky was innocent, what could be at the bottom of that ludicrous and inefficient attack?

In the top of the tallest tree available, Big Sword waited for daylight and brooded over the failure of his plan.

It was easy enough to get the biggest of the Big Folk into the forest. He had discovered that for part of the time they lay folded out flat in their enclosures, with their eyes shut, and during this time they were more sensitive to suggestion than when they were active. Big Sword, whose own eyes had an internal shutter, found eyelids rather fascinating: he had been tempted to experiment with Barney's but had refrained. He thought bitterly that he might as well have done so.

He had summoned twelve of the People and all of them thinking together had got the Big Person to its feet and walking. It had occurred to Big Sword that the receptiveness of the Big Person might be improved if they got it to lie down again. He had further decided that, in view of the blanking-out of thought when the creatures began to blow through their face-split, this aperture had better be shut.

That, he now knew, had been a mistake. No sooner was the gummed leaf in place on the Big Person's face than its eyes had popped open and showed every sign of coming right out of its face. There had been just warning enough in its thoughts for the band of People to hop out of range, except for Big Sword, who had had to use his spike for the first time in his life, to get free. Then the great arms had swung dangerously about and the creature had thrashed to its feet. After that there was no hope of making contact. Its mind was in a turmoil, making the People actively uncomfortable: they had retreated as far as they could, until the interwoven lives of trees and other forest creatures were sufficiently interposed to reduce the Big Person's thoughts to a comfortable intensity.

Big Sword had been surprised by the low level of intelligence shown by the Big Person. It had made no effort at all to understand him—its thoughts were a much worse muddle than any of the others he had investigated. Perhaps he had made a mistake? Perhaps size among these monsters was not directly connected with intelligence? Or perhaps it was an inverse relationship?

Big Sword was suddenly desperately thirsty and tired. He slid into the rain-filled

Paul Ash

cup of an enormous leaf—to soak up water through the million mouths of his skin and make his plans afresh.

The camp next morning was subdued and rather weary. Nobody had got their full sleep. Now there was all the awkward business of rearranging a full-time research program so that nobody should have to go into the forest alone. The lurking menace which last night had provided a formidable thrill this morning was nothing more than a vague, dreary uneasiness. Furthermore there was always the possibility that it would turn out to be nothing more than the work of an ingenious kid with a distorted sense of humor. And nobody liked to think what that would do to Jordan.

The working parties dispersed. Those whose work took them to the laboratory sheds tried to concentrate on it. Ricky, who had decided that this was not a morning for wrestling with lessons, slipped off to see if Barney wanted any odd jobs done, and was sent to pick fresh beans in the hydroponics shed.

The mechanical job helped to keep his mind steady. Having once got out of a nightmare, it was creeping round him again. This time with a difference.

There had got to be an explanation somewhere.

When he had left the house in Antarctica he had seemed to leave all his troubles behind. No more need to keep a continual watch on himself, in case he let something out. No more temptation, when in spite of himself he had put his foot in it again, to come out with something really startling and see what they could do about it. He was free. He had been free for months.

Then it started happening all over again. He had heard all sorts of scientific gossip—people here talked shop all the time. How was he to know what he'd heard and what he hadn't? How could he stop this happening again, now that whatever it was had followed him out here?

There was just one ray of hope. He couldn't possibly have had anything to do with what happened to Barney. If he could only find out what did that, some real solid explanation he could show everybody, then he might somehow be able to tell someone of the way he seemed to pick up knowledge without noticing it, knowledge he had no right to have—

Anyway, doing something was better than just sitting and waiting for things to go wrong again.

He delivered the beans to the kitchen and wandered out. The raw, red earth of the clearing shone like paint in the sun. In places he could still see the traces of Barney's big feet, going and coming, leading into the forest. There, among the black leaves and blacker shadows, lurked some real, genuine, tangible menace you could go for with a stick. There was a good supply of sticks stacked by his father's cabin for the benefit of the working parties. Ricky provided himself with one.

Big Sword had finished drinking—or bathing, whichever way you looked at it—and had climbed out of the diminished pool in the leaf-cup to spread his membranes in the sun. He looked like a big bat, lying spread out on the leaf. The black webs that stretched between his arms and legs and his sides would snap back into narrow rolls when he wanted to move, but when he extended them to catch the sunlight they covered a couple of square feet. They absorbed all the light in the visible range and well into the ultraviolet and infrared. Like most organisms on Lambda, Big Sword supported himself by a very efficient photosynthesis.

He had only just begun to make up for the wear and tear of the night—continuous activity in the dark was exhausting—when he felt the call out of the forest.

"Longfoot is going, Big Sword. Longfoot is going on the Journey. You wished to see. Come quickly!"

Big Sword's membranes snapped into thin ridges along his arms and legs and he bounded off among the trees. The Long Journey was mysterious to him, as it was to all of the People before the urge actually came to them—but the rest were content to leave it as a mystery. Big Sword wanted to know more.

He came in flying leaps to the edge of the forest, where the trees stopped short on the edge of the Great Rift. Some twenty or so of the People were gathered on the edge of the sheer cliff. Longfoot sat among them, his legs twitching occasionally with the urge to be off. As Big Sword arrived Longfoot shot to his feet, eager to depart.

"Where are you going?" demanded Big Sword. "What will you find over there, Longfoot? Why do you want to cross the waste, with no water and no shade? You will be dried to a stick before you get halfway across."

But Longfoot's mind was shut off; he had no longer any interest in Big Sword, or the People, or the danger to the Tree. He did not know why he had to go down on to the waste of boulders and small stones, but the urge could no longer be resisted. He dropped over the edge of the cliff, bouncing from ledge to ledge until he reached the bottom, and set off across the wide, rock-strewn plain, along the lines of shadow cast by the newly risen sun.

Big Sword watched him sadly. He himself was nearly a year away from feeling that call which had come to Longfoot, and the thought of his own journeying did not trouble him yet. He had been warned early of the dangers of going out on to the waste and, with the habit of logical thought strongly cultivated in him, he was troubled about what would happen. The waste stretched almost as far as he could see—at least twelve miles. At the end of it was the dark line which might have been a far-off continuation of the Forest. But why Longfoot should have wished to go there, or the many thousands of the People who had made that journey before him, Big Sword could not see.

He went back into the forest and found another perch on the edge of the clearing. Few of the Big People were in sight. He was conscious of vague alarms emanating from those who were within reach—it was an emotion foreign to his experience, but he disliked it. He wondered how to set about detaching a specimen from the group, since the direct method had proved unsuitable.

He became suddenly and sharply aware that one had detached itself already and was coming slowly toward him.

Paul Ash

Ricky had seen the little black figure sail out of the shadows and land on an equally black leaf. It took all his concentration to make it out when it had stopped moving, but he at last managed to fix its position. Slowly, casually, he wandered towards it, observing it out of the corner of his eye.

Its body was a blob perhaps four inches long and its head about half of that, joined on by a short neck. It rested on its bent fore-limbs and the hind legs stuck up like those of a grasshopper; they looked to be at least twice as long as trunk and head together. As he sidled closer Ricky could make out the big convex eyes, gray with black slitlike pupils, filling more than half the face. Ricky knew the fauna list of Lambda by heart; this creature was not on it. It must be one of Barney's "little devils" all right.

The creature sat quietly on its big leaf as he approached, with no sign of having noticed him. Now it was just within his reach if he stretched up. One more step and he would be right under it—ahhhh!

He had only begun to grab when Big Sword bounced over his head, landed lightly on the ground behind him and leaped sideways into another tree.

Ricky turned, slowly, and began his careful stalk again. He was murmuring softly to himself, coaxing words derived from rabbit- and guinea-pig owners of his acquaintance: "Come on, come on! Come to uncle. He won't hurt you. Nothing to be afraid of. Come on, you little brute. Come—"

Big Sword sailed away from his grasping hand to land on a branch ten feet farther into the forest.

Ricky had entirely forgotten the prohibition on leaving the clearing; he had forgotten everything except the desire to get hold of this creature, to have it close enough to examine, to hold it gently in his hands and get it tame. His stick lay forgotten on the earth outside the forest.

Big Sword was getting irritated and slightly flustered. It was easy enough to avoid getting caught, but he didn't wish to play tag with this creature, he wanted to tame it, to make it understand him. And its mind seemed to be shut. What was more, every so often it would begin that infuriating blowing process which seemed to drain away its thoughts out of his reach. To know when it was going to grab he had to watch it the whole time. Finally he took refuge on a branch ten feet above its head and sat down to consider.

Ricky, at the bottom of the tree, was experiencing all the emotions of a dog which has treed a squirrel and now has to persuade it to come within reach. Apparently he was licked. If only the little beast would drop on to that branch there—where that applelike object was—and begin to eat it, perhaps, so that it could forget he was there . . . Suddenly, the little brute did. At least, it dropped to the lower branch and put its long-fingered hands on the round knob. Ricky's mouth opened in amazement.

His hands itched, but he kept them firmly at his sides. Perhaps he had been standing there so long that it had forgotten about him and thought he was part of the landscape.

Perhaps if he spread his arms out very, very slowly it would take them for branches and—

Something like a small explosion happened inside his head. He blinked and gasped, forgetting all about immobility. He froze again hastily, expecting the creature to be out of sight. But it was still there.

Big Sword observed this reaction to his vehement negative with stirrings of hope. The idea of doing what this creature wanted, as a means of starting communication by demonstration, had seemed a singularly forlorn one. But the Big Creature had clearly noticed *something*.

Big Sword decided that it was time to try a suggestion of his own. He thought — hard—on the proposition that the Big Creature should turn around and look the other way.

The Big Creature ducked its head and blinked its eyes again. Big Sword got the impression that these reactions were caused by the strength of his thought. He tried again, gently.

Something was getting through. Weakly, faintly he felt a negative reply. The Big Creature refused to turn its back.

Big Sword put out another suggestion. Let the Big Creature take one step sideways, away from him.

Hesitantly, the Big Person did. Big Sword copied its direction in a joyful leap and ended on a level with the creature's head.

The next thought reached him, fuzzy but comprehensible. "If you understand me, put your hands on top of your head."

Watching suspiciously for any sudden move, Big Sword obeyed. The posture was not one he could keep up for long without losing his balance, but he felt the sudden surge of excitement in the Big Creature and was encouraged.

"Now watch! I shall sit down on the ground. Do you understand what that means? I'm going to sit down."

The Big Creature folded up in an awkward way; its knees were on the wrong side of its body, but Big Sword recognized the operation. He followed it with a thought of his own.

"I will spread my membranes out."

The Big Creature's astonishment was a dazzling shock and he put out a protest. In reply came something which could be an apology. He sharpened his thoughts and put out the next one with all the clearness at his command.

"We have proved that we can make contact. Now we have to practice thinking to and fro until we understand clearly."

He had just felt the other's incoherent agreement when the interruption began. Another of the Big Creatures came lumbering between the trees.

"Ricky! Scatter my stuffing, what are you doing here? You'll be in the doghouse for sure. Do you want Barney's little black devils to carry you away?"

Ricky scrambled to his feet in alarm.

"Sorry, Dr. Woodman, I forgot. I was . . . looking at things and I came in here without thinking. I'm awfully sorry."

"No harm done. Come out before we have any more alarms and excursions."

Big Sword felt an impulse of despair from the Big Creature which he had at last succeeded in taming; it seemed to regret this interruption even more than he did. It was anxious that the second Big Creature should not see him, so he remained still, one dark shape among many and effectively invisible; but he sent a thought after the tame one: "Come again! I will be on the edge of the clearing. Come again!" and was nearly knocked over by the energy of its reply.

Woodman marched Ricky firmly out of the forest.

"Now you're here you may as well be useful. I want to go up to my pet pool and I can't find a chaperone. If I've timed it rightly, we should find something interesting up there."

Ricky summoned up a show of polite interest. Normally he would have been delighted.

"Is it the pseudohydras again?"

"That's right. Remember when we saw them catching those things like two-tailed torpedoes?"

"Yes, but you said all the ones in the pool had been eaten now."

"They have. Here we are. Don't lean over like that—they won't like your shadow. Lie down. So!"

Ricky lay on his belly and stared down into the transparent water. Except where it was shadowed it reflected the brilliant blue of the sky, the only thing on Lambda that had a familiar color. He felt, suddenly, stirrings of homesickness, but they vanished quickly. Homesick, when the most wonderful thing possible had just happened? Nonsense!

He concentrated on the pseudohydras. They lived just where the pool overflowed into a small brown stream. Each consisted mainly of a network of branching white threads, up to six inches long, issuing from a small blobby body anchored on the stones. There were perhaps fifty of them, and together their tentacles made a net across the mouth of the stream which nothing larger than a wheat-grain could escape. The sluggish waters of the stream must all pass through this living mesh, carrying anything unlucky enough to swim out of the pool; the tentacles were immensely sticky and could hold struggling creatures several times the size of the pseudohydra's own body, until the flesh of the tentacles had flowed slowly around them and enclosed them in a capsule whose walls slowly digested them away.

"See there?" whispered Woodman.

Here and there one of the tentacles ended in a transparent, hard-edged blob. Small dark cigar-shaped objects jerked uneasily within it, perhaps a dozen in each little case.

"It's caught some more torpedoes!" whispered Ricky. "Little tiny ones this time."

"Not caught," answered Woodman. "I thought they'd be ripe today! Watch that one—it's nearly ready to split."

A few minutes later the capsule indicated did split. The tiny torpedo shapes, three or four millimeters long, spilled out into the water. They hovered uncertainly, veering here and there under the uneven propulsion of the water-jets emerging from the two-pronged hind end. Ricky gasped.

"It's let them go! And look—there's one rubbing against a tentacle and not getting caught. What's happened?"

Two of the little torpedo shapes came together. They jerked uncertainly round each other, then swiveled to lie parallel. They moved off together.

Others were paired already. One pair separated as Ricky watched them. Two little torpedoes shot off crazily. One came right under his eyes and he saw that it was emitting a faint milky stream.

Woodman's hand came down, holding a pipette. The torpedo veered off. Woodman sucked up a drop of water and held out the pipette.

"There," he said softly. Tiny specks, barely visible, floated in the drop.

"Eggs," said Woodman.

"Eggs! But—these are babies. The other ones were much bigger."

"So they were, Ricky. Do you know what these are going to hatch into? More torpedoes? Not on your life! Unless there's something else crazy about the life cycle, these will hatch into little pseudohydras."

Ricky rolled over to stare at him. "But what are the big torpedoes, then?"

"This is how I see it. You know about the reproductive cycles in Coelenterates, back on Earth? Especially hydroids like Obelia and so on? The sessile ones reproduce by budding for a while. Then they start to produce buds which don't turn out like the parents. Those break off and go swimming away on their own. They feed and get big and in the end they produce eggs or sperm, and the fertilized eggs produce a new sessile generation. Well, here the free-living forms—the torpedoes—are ready to lay eggs as soon as they're released. They mate a few minutes after hatching and lay eggs as soon as they're fertilized. But after that they aren't finished. They go swimming around the pool and feed and get fat. And when they're full grown, they come swimming back to the old pseudohydras, and the pseudohydras eat them and use the food to produce a whole new crop of little torpedoes. Get it?"

Ricky scowled. "What a disgusting animal."

"Nonsense! It's a beautiful piece of natural economy. Don't be a snob, Ricky. Just because no terrestrial organism evolved this way you think it's unethical. Some Earth creatures beat pseudohydra hollow for nastiness—think of some of the parasites. Think of the barnacles, degenerate males parasitic on the female. There just aren't any ethics in evolution except that the species shall survive, if you call that an ethic."

Ricky looked at him doubtfully. "We've evolved. And we bother about other species, too."

Woodman nodded. "We try to—some of us. But our survival has meant that a good many other species didn't."

Something else occurred to Ricky. "This sort of whatsit—alternate generations—has evolved lots of times on Earth, hasn't it?"

"Sure. Dozens of different lines evolved it independently, not to mention all the Lambdan forms that have it, and a few on Arcturus III, and some on Roche's—it's one of the basic dodges, apparently. One stage makes the most of the *status quo* and the other acts as an insurance against possible changes. Once a well-balanced set of hereditary characters has appeared it can repeat itself fast by asexual reproduction, without the disorganization of chromosome reassortment and so on. On the other hand, should conditions change, a sexually produced population has a much better chance of showing up a few adaptable forms. Some lines of life have dropped the sexual stage, just as some have dropped the asexual, but it probably doesn't pay in the long run."

"How does a stage get dropped?"

Woodman considered. "I suppose the first stage might go like this: one single asexual stage—one of these pseudohydras, for instance—happens to get isolated. Say all the rest in the pool die off. It can produce its little torpedoes, but there are no mates for them. The pseudohydra goes on reproducing asexually—you've seen how they split down the middle—and in the end a mutant form occurs which doesn't waste its substance producing useless torpedoes and that breeds faster than the others and in the end replaces them. That's just one way it could happen. In one of the African lakes there used to be annual swarms of jellyfish, all male. One single asexual stage must have got trapped in that lake, God knows how long ago, and it went on producing those useless male jellyfish century after century, while asexual reproduction kept the species going."

"What happened to it?"

Woodman scowled. "Silly fools polluted the lake with industrial waste and the jellyfish died out. Come on, it's time for lunch."

Ellen Scott put away the last of her soil samples and scowled thoughtfully at her apparatus. Tensions in the camp were mounting and everyone was snapping at everybody else. One party had decided that Barney's adventure was somehow due to Ricky, and wanted to call off the precautions that hindered their work. The other stuck to it that Ricky could not have organized it and that precautions were still necessary. Anyway, who in the other party was prepared to tell Doc that there was no danger in the forest except for his son?

Ellen told herself that she was neutral. She didn't know whether or not Ricky was behind their troubles and didn't much care, if only he would leave off tearing his father's nerves to pieces. She had heard a little gossip about him on Earth after it had been announced that he was to join the expedition, and though she had discounted it at the time, after the business of Cartwright's report she was inclined to believe it.

People whose work lay in space had no business with marriage and children. She had decided that for herself years ago. You could run planetary research properly, or you could run a family properly. Not both. Children were part of life on Earth; the settled pattern of security, with which she had grown so bored, was necessary to them. When they were older, perhaps—Ricky had seemed perfectly happy at first.

But what on Lambda was the matter with him now? He'd been going around in a dream ever since the night of Barney's adventure. Starting suddenly to talk to himself, breaking off with equal suddenness and an air of annoyance. He didn't seem now to be particularly worried by the suspicions floating around the camp, although he seemed the sort of sensitive boy to be desperately upset by them. In fact over that affair with Cartwright he had been upset, and this affair was worse.

And Jordan was obviously heading for a nervous breakdown if this went on much longer.

Ricky, lying in his cabin and theoretically taking his afternoon rest—imposed because of Lambda's longer day—had come to the conclusion that it was time to tell his father about his Research. Despite his absorption in his overwhelming new interest, he was vaguely aware that the grown-ups were getting bothered. For another he could now "talk" fluently with Big Sword and haltingly with the rest of the People; he knew what they wanted and there was no excuse for delaying any longer. Besides, the results of Research were not meant to be kept to oneself, they were meant to be free to everyone.

He allowed himself to think for a moment about the possibilities of his newly discovered power. Of course, people had been messing about with telepathy for centuries, but they had never got anywhere much. Perhaps only a fully developed telepath, coming of a race to which telepathy was the sole method of communication, could teach a human being how to control and strengthen his wayward and uncertain powers. Or perhaps, thought Ricky, the people who were really capable of learning the trick got into so much trouble before they could control it that they all simply shut it off as hard as they could, so that the only ones who tried to develop it were those in whom it never became strong enough to do anything useful. He himself had now, at last, learned how to shut off his awareness of other minds; it was the first necessity for clear reception that one should be able to deafen oneself to all minds except one. It occurred to him that he'd better make that point clear straight off: that he was not going to eavesdrop on anyone else's thoughts. Never again.

But obviously the thing had terrific potentialities for research, not only into the difficult and thorny problem of the connection between mind and matter, or into contact with alien races. Why, he could probably find out what really went on in the minds of terrestrial animals, those that had minds; and he could find out what it was that people experienced in a Mass-Time field, which they could never properly remember afterwards, and—oh, all sorts of things! Ricky got up from his bunk. His father ought to be free at this moment; it was the one time of day he kept to himself, unless an emergency happened. Quite unconsciously Ricky opened his mind to thoughts from that direction, to see whether it was a good time to visit his father's cabin.

The violence of the thought he received nearly knocked him over. What on Lambda was stirring old Doc J. up to such an extent? And—bother, he was talking to somebody—Woodman, apparently. Ricky, unlike Big Sword, could still pick up thought at the moment when it drained into the level of speech, but even for him it was highly indistinct. He strained, trying to catch the cause of all this commotion. Woodman had found something—something unpleasant—something—

Ricky dashed out of the cabin door and crossed the half-dozen yards that separated his hut from his father's. Just outside the voices were clearly distinct; Woodman was speaking excitedly and loudly.

"It was absolutely devilish! Oh, I suppose it was physical—some sort of miasma—in fact it nearly knocked me down, but it felt just exactly as though somebody were standing and hating me a few yards off. Like that feeling you get after space 'flu, as though nobody loves you, only this was magnified about a million times—the most powerful depressant ever, and absolutely in the open air, too."

"Where was this?"

"The eighth sector—just about here."

He was evidently pointing to a map. Cold with apprehension, Ricky deliberately tried to probe into his father's mind, to see just what they were looking at. The picture was fuzzy and danced about, but he could see the pointer Jordan was using—the ivory stylus he always carried, and—yes, that was the clearing in the forest that housed the Tree itself! The guards about it had been all too successful in their efforts to keep intruders away.

Jordan laughed harshly. "Do you remember that we scheduled this planet as safe?" He got to his feet. "First Barney encounters devils and now you've discovered the Upas Tree. You're sure this gas or whatever it is came from the plants?"

"I'm certain it was this one particular tree. It's by itself in the middle of an open space. The feeling began when I was six feet from it. It has big pods—they may secrete the toxic stuff. Though it must be intermittent—I collected a branch once before and didn't feel anything. Perhaps it's seasonal."

"Well, it'll have to come down." Ricky, horrified, felt his father's savage satisfaction at coming across an enemy he could deal with. "Ellen wants to push her soil examinations out in that direction—it's the only sector we haven't covered yet and a good many people want to work there."

Ricky straightened from his crouching position under the window and appeared like a jack-in-the-box over the sill.

"You mustn't, Doc! Honestly you mustn't. That Tree's terribly important. It's only—"

"Ricky!" Jordan lunged to his feet, scattering objects across his desk. "Were you listening to my conversation?"

Ricky turned white. "Yes, I was, but—"

"Go to your cabin."

Woodman made a move to intervene, but Jordan brushed it aside.

"I'll speak to you later. For the moment, you'll go to your cabin and stay there, until I have time to deal with you."

Woodman thought that Ricky was about to make some further protest, but after a moment's tension he turned and bolted.

Jordan picked up the stylus with a trembling hand.

"I'll come with you and investigate this thing at once, Woodman. We'll need masks and an air-sampler, and we may as well take one of those portable detection kits. Can you draw them from the store, please, and be ready in ten minutes. Get a blaster, too."

Woodman thought of arguments and decided against them. Old Jordan had been stewing up for something like this for the last week and it was probably better to let him get it out of his system. When it came to the point Jordan wouldn't start destroying things without careful consideration; he was too good a scientist for that. Woodman didn't know why Ricky was so concerned, but he himself would take good care that a possibly unique specimen wasn't damaged in a hurry. He went for the equipment.

Jordan hesitated at the entrance to Ricky's cabin. He heard a slight movement within, and moved on. He was still trembling with a fury that he only half understood, and knew that he was in no state to conduct a delicate interview, or even to think straight. Better leave the boy alone until he had got things sorted out in his own mind.

Ricky, lying tense on his bunk, "listened" with all his power. Old Woodman didn't really approve of this expedition, made in such a hurry. Good. Doc. J. was half aware that his own brain wasn't working straight. Good again. Ricky spared a moment to wish that he had given more thought to his father during the last week, but it was too late for that now. Even if Jordan didn't take a blaster to the Tree straight off the People were still perched on the thin edge of disaster. For the first time since he had understood what Big Sword wanted him to do, Ricky began to doubt whether it could be done. Were people going to listen to him? Were Doc. J. and Woodman and Miss Ellen and the rest of them really any different from Cora and Camillo and all the other people on Earth who didn't even try to understand?

No, there was only one way to make the People safe—if it would work. And he'd *got* to take it. Because this was his own fault for not telling Doc. J. sooner. He'd acted like a silly kid, wanting to keep his secret to himself just a little longer. Well, now he was not going to act like a silly kid. He was going to put things right, if he could—righter than they were before. With any luck it would be hours before anyone missed him. He might even be able to do what he wanted and call back on his transmitter to explain before they found that he had gone.

Ricky was already out of the clearing before Jordan, who had started out with Woodman, turned back to speak to Dr. Scott.

"Ellen, I've left Ricky in his cabin. We had a . . . disagreement. I think he's better left to himself just now, but would you mind going to his cabin in an hour or so, to see that he's all right?"

"Of course, John. But what—?"

"No time now. I'll explain later. Thank you, Ellen. Good-by."

There was no undergrowth in the forest but the branches were extremely thick and the darkness beneath them almost complete. Jordan, following Woodman through the trees at the slow pace enforced by these conditions, felt his anger drain away and a deep depression take its place. What sort of showing had he made, either as a father or as the head of the expedition? This particular episode was quite idiotic. There was nothing in Woodman's report to call for this immediate dash into the forest. He should at least have stopped to find out what Ricky knew about it—and now that he was cooling off, Ricky's anxiety seemed more and more puzzling. If it weren't that to turn back would make him look even more of a fool than he did already, he would have given up and gone to find out what the boy knew.

In front of him Woodman came to a halt.

"That's it, sir! That's the Tree! But—there's no feeling about it now."

Jordan brushed past him.

"Stay here. Be ready to put your mask on." He walked slowly forward until he was right under the branches of the Tree.

On either side of the clearing, sitting in the treetops, the Guardians consulted anxiously.

"We must not try to drive them away," the Contact said. "Yes, we must do as he suggested."

Jordan looked up at the branches and dared them to depress him.

"I don't feel anything," he said at last. "Woodman, are you certain this is the right tree?"

"Well, I was, sir." Woodman approached it in growing doubt. "All these little clearings are so much alike, I could have—no, it is the right one! I tied my handkerchief to this branch for a marker, before I bolted. Here it is."

The Guardians gave the telepathic equivalent of a sigh and started on the next line of defense.

"You know, sir—" Woodman was carefully deferential—"I've never seen another specimen like this. After all, this little bit of the Forest is pretty well cut off—the Rift on one side, the Mountains on the other and the River in the south. This type of soil doesn't even extend as far as the River. You might get forms here which were unique—relics, or species evolved since the Rift opened. I don't feel we ought to destroy it without very good reason."

Jordan scowled up at the nearest pod.

"I wasn't proposing to destroy it here and now! If the thing is a potential menace we must find out about it, that's all. I must say I don't . . . what's that?"

The sound of snapping twigs could be heard back along the path. Woodman started down it with Jordan at his heels; it was so dark that he was almost on top of Dr. Scott before he saw her.

"John! Thank goodness. Listen, you've got to come back at once. It's . . . it's Ricky. He's gone. I went to his cabin like you said, and he wasn't there. He isn't anywhere in camp. He's gone."

There was a flurry in the camp, but it was an organized flurry. Jordan, white and sick-looking, nevertheless had himself well under control. Important facts were sorted out quickly.

Three parties working on the east side of the clearing could swear that Ricky had not passed them.

Various delicate gadgets which responded violently to the movement of humans anywhere near them were rigged in the wood to the north, which was taboo in consequence. They showed no sign of disturbance.

That left the south and the west. South was a stretch of about eight miles of forest, unbroken until it reached the big river. West was about half a mile of forest, fairly well explored, and then the Great Rift.

"There'd be no sense in going that way." Jordan laid a pointer on the map to indicate the Rift; he noticed in a detached way that his hand was quite steady. "It doesn't lead anywhere. There's just one place he could be making for, if we assume him to have an intelligible plan, and that is the First Base on the coast. The one way he could possibly get there would be to get to the river and float down it on one of the log-rafts—we saw plenty of them coming down while we were at the base."

"But the rapids—" said somebody.

"Has anyone reason to suppose that Ricky knew about the rapids?" Beads of sweat stood out on Jordan's forehead. No one answered. "We have to find him before he gets there. Unless any of you can suggest another way he might be trying to go."

Nobody cared to suggest that Ricky, if he had flung off in blind panic, might be headed nowhere in particular under the shade of the black trees. On the south side the paths went only for half a mile or so, and if he left them he could be lost within a hundred yards of the camp. They had already tried to pick up the tracker he was supposed to carry, but he had evidently switched it off or thrown it away.

The geologist, Penn, spoke suddenly from the back of the group.

"How about the Rift? It interested him. He might try to get across."

"That's possible," said Jordan. "On the Rift he'd be relatively easy to spot. That's why I propose to leave it till later. We have only one heliflier. If he's gone through the forest to the River we have to catch him at once. He's been gone two and a half hours. If he went straight to the nearest point of the river he might be there by now. The heliflier's the only chance. I can patrol the whole stretch and spot him as soon as he comes to it. If he hasn't reached it by dawn, I'll go back and fly over the Rift. If he does happen to be there, he won't take much harm in that time."

"There are two helifliers," someone suggested.

"No," said Jordan sharply. "The other is unsafe."

Not all the party were to join the hunt at once.

"There are only a few profitable lines," said Jordan. "We don't want everybody exhausted at the same time. This may be more than one day's search. And some of you have long-term observations to continue." He raised his hand, stilling a protest. "If to take all of you would increase the . . . the speed with which we are likely to find Ricky by one percent, or half that, I'd take you all. But I won't ruin several months' work for nothing."

In the end several parties set out through the trees south and one went west. Jordan had already taken the one serviceable heliflier and departed. They had arranged an automatic sound-signal to go off every half hour in the clearing, in case Ricky was lost and trying to find his way back, and there were flares and a searchflight for when it became dark.

Ellen Scott had been left behind as part of the "reinforcements." She managed to catch Woodman before his party left.

"You used the second heliflier, didn't you? What's wrong with it?"

Woodman grimaced. "It failed to co-operate over landing. I got down intact by the skin of my incisors and had to walk home—we fetched it finally on the truck. I found a rough patch on one of the power planes and cleaned it up. That may or may not have been the cause of the trouble. We haven't got checking equipment here and nobody's tried it out the hard way. Leave it alone, Ellen. When those things are good they're very very good. Once they act up—leave them alone. It wouldn't be any use over the Forest and Doc. J. won't miss anything on the River."

"How about the Rift?"

"Why should he go there? He was upset but he wasn't crazy. No, he must have set out for the base camp—probably thinks he'll be treated as a hero if he gets there. I'll give him heroics next time we meet."

Ellen was occupied for the next hour with various laboratory jobs to be done for members of the search party. Reports came in every few minutes over the radio, but they were all negative. The ground was hard dry. If Ricky had stuck to the broken trails, he would leave no sign. Even off them, he was small enough to walk under the trees where a grown man would have had to push his way through. There were three chances: to see him from the air, to get a fix on his radio, and to come upon him among the trees. And however systematic the searchers were they knew perfectly well that they could only do that by chance.

Unless one could guess where he had gone. Jordan thought he had guessed.

Ellen prowled restlessly about. What would Ricky have done? Nothing had been taken from his room; had he set out without any equipment at all?

She went to the kitchen. Barney was muddling around among his store-cupboards, in a very bad mood. He had wanted to go with the search parties and had been turned down.

"Barney," said Ellen quickly, "did Ricky take any food?"

"That's what I'm trying to check, Miss. There's some biscuits gone, I think. He could have taken them, or it could have been anyone this afternoon. And I think one of the big canteens has gone, but I suppose a search party took it."

"They didn't," said Ellen sharply. "There are always plenty of streams, apart from the pools in the leaves. They only took small water bottles."

"One of the big canteens has gone," repeated Barney obstinately. "And one of the water bottles isn't, if you take my meaning—Ricky did not take one of those, I mean, I've accounted for them. The canteen I can't account for. But Ricky wouldn't lumber himself up with that," he added morosely. "He couldn't carry it if it was more than half full, and he knows about the streams as well as anybody. No, I reckon someone pinched it for a collecting tin or something. That's how it goes in this place, and now we can see what comes of it. You can't keep a proper check on anything—"

But Dr. Scott had gone.

She waited, fuming, until the party which had gone west came back.

"Yes, we looked over the Rift all right," said the leader morosely. "Hell, Ellen, the whole place is a heat-trap. With the haze and flickers visibility is about twenty yards. Even from the air you wouldn't see anything, unless maybe when the shadows get longer and before they get too long. Jordan wouldn't see anything if he did fly over it now. Besides, why should the kid have gone into that oven?"

Ellen turned away. Why should Ricky have gone that way? But why should he have taken a big canteen, unless he was going to cross a waterless area? If he had taken it, of course. But there were plenty of containers in the stores for scientific work.

Ricky had been interested in the Rift, certainly. He had been asking questions about it yesterday—one of the few times lately he had shown interest in anything at all.

But visibility in the Rift was bad now. When the shadows were longer—

Jordan called over the radio. He had been flying up and down the river and the adjacent forest for the last hour and a half. Ricky had been gone about four hours.

There were three hours of daylight left.

Two hours later the situation was unchanged. To the parties in the forest night would make little difference; they were using lights already. Jordan proposed to stay in the air—one or other of the moons would be in the sky most of the night. There was about one hour of daylight left.

Ellen Scott listened to his report, and those of the search parties. Then she went briskly to the place where the one remaining heliflier was parked. She found another member of the expedition contemplating it gloomily.

"Come away from there, Phil," she said severely.

"Oh, hell, Ellen, there's a seventy-five-percent chance the thing's all right. Woodman said he'd fixed up a rough plane, didn't he?" The man turned away nevertheless. "What in Space did Jordan want to bring that kid here for?"

Ten minutes later he shot out of his cabin, where he had been dispiritedly collecting

Paul Ash

together the makings of a drink, in time to see the heliflier rise gently into the air and disappear towards the west.

Although the shadows were beginning to lengthen, the Rift was like a furnace. The water in the canteen was hot. Ricky and Big Sword sat in the slightly cooler earth on the north of a boulder and contemplated the forest lying away to the left—not the forest they knew, but the strange trees of the farther side.

Big Sword's goggle eyes did not register emotion, but Ricky could feel the stir of curiosity in him. Big Sword was already reaching out to new streams, new treetops, new bare places that would be warm in the sun. For himself Ricky could only think about the two miles remaining to be walked.

He had hopelessly underestimated the time it would take him to pick his way through eight miles of boulders, too hot for the hand, walking on sliding shingle; he had managed less than two miles an hour. But now he had to get on. He stirred himself, got Big Sword perched again on his shoulder and re-strapped the canteen, lighter now but still a burden.

He had gone perhaps a dozen strides when the shadow of the heliflier came up behind and settled over his head.

Ricky started to run. There was no sense to it, and Big Sword disliked the effects, but he ran just the same, with the water sloshing about on his back. The shadow of the flier slid forward a hundred yards and it began to come down over a comparatively level place. Ricky swerved sideways. He heard the shout echo among the boulders, but the echo of combined relief and exasperation in his mind rang louder.

"Ricky! Stop and talk! Whatever it is, I'll help. There's no sense in running. If I get in touch with your father, there'll be another flier and several people here in twenty minutes. Stop! Listen to me, will you, you—"

The shouts echoed on for a moment, but the thought had stopped.

Dr. Scott came whirling up through hot red mists to find herself lying beside a fire. A very hot fire, in a stone fireplace. It didn't make sense. Warm water was being sloshed across her face and there was a murmur of voices—two of them.

"She hit her head. That's all. She fainted. She'll come round in a minute. Then you'll hear her. It isn't sleep, no—not exactly. What's the matter? Why don't you—"

The second voice was no more than a vague murmur of curiosity; it was beginning to sound irritated as well.

Ellen remembered that she had been running among a lot of boulders and had twisted her foot. No doubt she had hit her head when she fell; certainly it ached. But what had she been doing that for?

She opened her eyes.

Ricky's anxious face hung directly above her and he was pouring water from his cupped hand on to her forehead. Beside him was—

Ellen winced and shut her eyes.

"Dr. Scott. Please!" Ricky sounded worried. "Are you hurt?"

"Delirious, I think," said Ellen faintly. She opened her eyes again. "Where did it go?"

Ricky's face was a study in doubt and other emotions. Ellen put a hand to the aching spot on the back of her head and began very cautiously to sit up.

"Come on, Ricky," she said firmly. "Who were you talking to?"

"Aloud?" said Ricky, in tones of surprise. "Oh, so that's why he couldn't hear."

Ellen shut her eyes again. "I'm the one with concussion, not you," she pointed out. "Who couldn't hear?"

"Well, his *name's* Big Sword," said Ricky doubtfully. "More or less, that is. He says he's coming back, anyway."

Ellen opened her eyes once more. They focused on the region of Ricky's right ear. Laid gently over it was a skinny black hand with four long, many-jointed fingers. A slender arm stole into view, attached to what might have been a medium-sized potato that had happened to grow black. On top of this was perched a head about the size of a large egg. The greater part of this was occupied by two large light-gray eyes with slit pupils and dully shining surfaces. They goggled at her solemnly.

Once again she was aware of a vague murmur of curiosity, not divisible into words.

Ellen drew a deep breath. "Ricky, this . . . this friend of yours. Why did you bring him here?"

Ricky studied her face earnestly. "It was my idea, not his, Dr. Scott. I wanted to get to the forest over there. To the other side of the Rift."

"But why?"

Ricky shook his head.

"It wasn't that at all. It was my idea, I tell you, not Big Sword's. He didn't . . . didn't hypnotize me. He wouldn't have done it to Barney except that he couldn't think of anything else to do. And I've absolutely got to get there now!"

Ellen sat up and stared at him. "All right, Ricky. Listen, you tell me the reason. If it's a good one . . . well, I must let your father know you're safe. But I won't tell him where you are. I'll fly you to the forest, and then back. How about that?"

Ricky breathed a sigh of relief. "Yes," he said. "Is Doc. J. very worried?"

"Worried? Listen, make it quick. I'm going to call him in ten minutes, whatever. What are you doing here?"

Ricky sighed and closed his eyes for a moment. "The idea began with the jellyfish, really," he said. "The male jellyfish in the lake."

The heliflier had completed the fifth sweep down the river to the Sea; back up the river to the rapids, where many rafts of floating vegetation broke up and re-formed, making Jordan's heart jump as he hovered above them; on up the river to the point he had fixed as farthest east. It was no good to fly over the forest; he had found that he could not pick up the search parties when he knew they were directly below him. The River was his only hope.

Nearly time to make another report. His hand was on the button of the radio when the speaker came suddenly to life.

"Calling all search parties. John Jordan please answer. Can you hear?"

Jordan's voice came out as a harsh croak. "I hear. Is he—"

"Ricky's safe. He's with me now. Turn everyone home. But—listen. He had a good reason for going off as he did. He had something to do and it's not finished. So I'm not going to tell you where we are."

Jordan shouted something incoherent, but her voice overrode him.

"It's important, John. I don't know if it will come off, but he must have a chance to try. You can probably find out where we are, but—don't come. Do you understand?"

"Ellen, is he really all right? And are you?"

"Sure I'm all right. We're going to remain all right. We'll be back some time next morning. Oh, and Ricky says"—her voice broke off for a moment—"Ricky says he is very sorry to have worried you, honestly he is, but it was urgent, and will you please not do anything to damage that Tree." There was a moment's silence. "John? You haven't done something to it already?"

"I haven't, no."

"Don't let anyone touch it. Good night, John. Sleep well."

"Ellen—"

The speaker clicked and was silent.

The helifliers were designed for sleeping in, in an emergency, but they were not air-conditioned. Ellen felt the compress on her head, which had long ceased to be cold, and envied bitterly Ricky's ability to sleep under these conditions. A faint gleam of light from button-sized surfaces a couple of yards off showed that Big Sword was still sitting and watching as he had been doing ever since they lay down. Ellen wished bitterly that she had had the sense to lie beside the refrigerator so that she could get more cold water without having to lift her aching head.

The gray buttons moved. She felt small, strong fingers tugging gentle at the compress. She lifted the pressure of her head and felt it go. There was a sound of faint movement and the click of the refrigerator door, with a momentary blast of lovely cold air. A few minutes later the compress, beautifully cold now, was poked carefully back under her head. She felt the thistledown touch of skinny fingers against her cheek.

"Thank you," she murmured, and then, remembering, she repeated it inside her head, "Thank you, Big Sword."

They had flown at dawn and the heliflier sat among the boulders at the foot of the cliff. Ellen and Ricky sat beside it, shivering a little in the morning cold, and waited.

Ellen looked at Ricky's intent face. He could not hear strange members of the People distinctly, she had gathered, but he could usually detect their presence.

"What does it feel like?" she asked abruptly.

"Hearing thoughts?" Ricky considered. "It feels like thinking. You can't really tell other thoughts from your own—unless they've been specially directed. That's what made it all so very difficult."

"I see." Ellen sighed. What on Earth, or off it, could Ricky's future be? True telepaths would not fit in Earth's scheme of things.

"I used to pick up thoughts all the time," Ricky went on. "I didn't know that until I found out how to shut them off. It was a sort of fuzzy background to my thinking. Do you know, I think all real thinkers must be people with no telepathy, or else they learn to shut it right off. Now I can do that I think much clearer."

"So you don't overhear thoughts accidentally now?" Ellen felt encouraged.

"No, I don't. I only get directed thoughts. I'm not going to overhear anyone ever again, it's just a nuisance."

"Stick to that. I don't think uncontrolled telepathy is much good to a human being."

"It isn't. I tell you what, I think there are two ways of evolving communication, telepathy and communication between senses; and people who are good at the one aren't good at the other. I'll never be a real good communicator like the People, my mind doesn't work the right way. But I'll be good enough to be useful for research. I'm going to—" Ricky broke off, seized his companion's arm and pointed.

Ellen looked up at the cliff. It was about thirty feet high, here, with only a couple of six-inch ledges to break the sheer drop. Black foliage overhung it in places.

"There!" whispered Ricky. Slowly there came into view a black head the size of an egg—a black head in which eyes shone gray.

"Is he coming back?" whispered Ellen. "Has he given up, then?"

There was a faint rustling among the leaves. Ricky's grip tightened painfully on her arm.

A second black head appeared beside the first.

"You see," said Ricky anxiously, "I didn't really think you'd just go and destroy the Tree straight off, but I couldn't be sure. And everyone was angry with me about one thing or another and I didn't know if they'd listen."

"Speaking for myself," said Woodman, "there were one or two moments when if I'd had a blaster handy the Tree would have been done for there and then."

"So you were just taking out insurance," said Jordan.

"Yes, because if we found other Trees the species would continue anyway. Big Sword and I meant to ask you to help about that, later—the Journey, I mean—only then I thought we'd better try that straight away in case I was stopped later. I thought if I could *show* people it was better than telling them."

"Isn't Big Sword coming?" said another of the party. The whole of the expedition, including even Barney, was seated around a square table raised on trestles in the center of the clearing. Ricky nodded.

"As soon as we're ready," he said. "Now, if you like. But he says if too many

Paul Ash

people think at him at once it may hurt, so he wants you to be ready to start talking if I give the signal.''

"What about?" said Cartwright.

"Anything. Anything at all. Shall I call him?"

There was half a minute's expectant silence. Then lightly as a grasshopper Big Sword flew over Ellen's head and landed with a slight bounce in the center of the table.

There was a simultaneous forward movement of heads as everybody bent to look at him, and he sat up and goggled out of pale bulging eyes. Then—

Most of them felt the sharp protest of discomfort before Ricky waved his hand. Nobody had really thought out what to say and there was a moment of silence, then somebody began to talk about the weather, the statistician began on the multiplication table, Jordan found himself muttering, " 'Twas brillig, and the slithy toves . . . "—after a minute or so only Ricky was still silent.

"He says he'll go to one person after another, but the rest keep talking," reported Ricky presently. "You can ask him to do things if you like."

Solemnly Big Sword went round the table, sitting for a few moments in front of each person, snapping out his membranes, revolving to present his back view, and then going on.

"That's him!" said Barney as Big Sword came to a halt in front of him. "But how did he sting me?"

The spindly hand whipped to Big Sword's flat thigh and flashed back holding a flat gray spike two and a half inches long. He held it out and Barney fingered the point in a gingerly fashion.

"That's the sword, is it?" murmured Woodman. "Do they secrete it, Ricky?"

"I think so, but I haven't asked him."

Woodman breathed out a long sigh.

"This," he said, "is the answer to a biologist's prayer."

Big Sword bounced suddenly back into the middle of the table. "He's tired," said Ricky. "He says he'll send someone else another day." Ricky yawned uncontrollably as Big Sword took a flying leap off the table and hopped across the clearing. He had had a hard day the day before and a very early start this morning and a lot of excitement since.

"Can we just have the story straight?" said the statistician suddenly. "The biological story, I mean. You people may have been able to follow it through all the interruptions, but I didn't. I gathered that Ricky had discovered the female of the species, but that's all. How did they get lost?"

"I'll tell it," said Jordan, looking at Ricky, who was nodding sleepily, "and Ricky can correct me. Big Sword's people are the active and intelligent offspring of an organism which to all intents and purposes is a large tree. They are produced by an asexual budding process inside pods. When they are a year or so old they are seized by the urge to migrate across the Rift. They never knew why, and probably none of them ever got across. It occurred to Ricky that alternation of generations usually turns out to have sex at the bottom of it. Big Sword's People couldn't reproduce themselves—they simply hatched from the Tree. So Ricky thought that there might be another Tree on the other side of the Rift which produced females. And when I very foolishly considered destroying the Tree because of Woodman's experience, he thought he had to go and find them straight off, so that at least the species would survive. And I'm glad to say he was quite right—they were there.''

"You mean to say," said Cartwright, "that the Tree has been producing People for the last fifteen thousand years without a sexual generation at all?''

"Not necessarily," said Woodman. "There may have been several on this side of the Rift at first, and this Tree may be the last offspring of a small population. It must have been an outlier, if so, because the migration was so firmly set for the west.''

"And there's another tree on the far side which produces females?''

"There are two female trees and three that bear males, but two of the male ones are very old and have few offspring, and none of the seeds have been fertile for at least fifty generations. Apparently not many come to full maturity at the best of times, but this outcross may really save the species.''

"And what exactly is the plan?'' demanded the statistician. "To ferry them across? What will they do when we leave?''

"No," said Jordan. "We don't propose to interfere more than we have to. The tragedy of the whole process was that the People who took the Journey almost certainly died on the way. Twelve miles in the sun, with no water, was too much for them. We propose to provide a green belt—a black belt rather—along the migration route. Tiven is looking into the possibilities—''

Tiven looked up from his slide rule. "Easy as π," he said cheerfully. "We can make the channel in a week, once we get the digger from First Base, and a cooker for concrete, and there are any number of streams which run down to the Waste and then vanish underground. It's just a question of training one of them in the way it should go, and protecting it from evaporation in the first year or two until the vegetation gets thick enough.''

The conversation flowed on. But Ricky, his head resting on the table, was already asleep.

Jordan stood at the edge of the Rift and looked over the embryo river-valley that Tiven had designed. Seedlings had been planted along the channel, in earth transported for that purpose, and were already taking hold. The revolving sun-cutters designed to protect them at this stage and to stop excessive evaporation gave the whole thing a mechanical air at present, but they would be done within a year or two; they were designed to go to dust then, so that even if the expedition had to leave they would not be left. There are places for poorly built things!

Two of the People shot down the cliff a little to one side and disappeared into the shade along the channel.

"Are they off on the Journey?" said Ellen Scott.

"I don't think so. They go singly, as a rule. No, I think . . . look there!"

There were four People now at the end of the line of saplings. Two were presumably the ones who had passed a few minutes before; the other two were linked hand in hand and bore across their shoulders a kind of yoke with a long pod dangling from it. The two from the near side of the Forest had taken the hands of the newcomers and were helping them up the cliff.

"This is the result of your soil report, I think," said Jordan. "Woodman says that one reason for the lack of germination on the other side is the exhaustion of the few pockets of suitable soil. I wonder whether it was the necessity of finding the right soil, as well as of looking after the seedling, that led them to develop intelligence?"

The two newcomers had reached the top of the cliff. They seemed hardly to notice the helpers, nor did the latter seem to expect it. The burdened couple moved slowly along, pausing every now and then to investigate the soil. They stopped close to Ellen's feet and prodded carefully.

"Not here, little sillies!" she murmured. "Farther in."

Jordan smiled. "They've got plenty of time. One couple planted their pod just under one of Branding's tripods; trying not to step on them drove him nearly crazy. He had to move the whole lot in the end. It takes them weeks sometimes to find a spot that suits them."

"Continuing the species," said Ellen thoughtfully. "I always thought it sounded rather impersonal."

Jordan nodded. "The sort of thing you can take or leave," he agreed. "I used to think that you could either explore space or you could . . . well, continue the species is as good a way of putting it as any. Not both."

"I use to think that, too."

"Once it was true. Things have changed, even in the last few years. More and more people are organizing their lives to spend the greater part of them away from Earth. Soon there's going to be a new generation whose home isn't on Earth at all. Children who haven't been to Terrestrial schools, or played in Terrestrial playrooms, or watched the Terrestrial stereos, or—"

"Suffered the benefits of an advanced civilization?"

"Exactly. How do you feel about it, Ellen? Or . . . that's a shirker's question. Ellen Scott, will you marry me?"

"So as to propagate the species?"

"Blast the species! Will you marry me?"

"What about Ricky?"

"Ricky," said Jordan, "has been careful to let me know that he thinks it would be a very suitable match."

"The devil he has! I thought—"

"No telepathy involved. If everyone else knows I love you, why shouldn't he? Ellen—did I say please, before? Ellen, please, will you marry me?"

There was a silence. Depression settled on Jordan. He had no right to feel so sure of himself. Ellen was ten years younger and had a career to think of. He had made a mess of one marriage already and had a half-grown son. He had taken friendliness for something else and jumped in with both feet much too soon. He had made a fool of himself—probably.

"Well?" he said at last.

Ellen looked up and grinned.

"I was just making sure. I'm not quite certain I could take being married to a telepath—which you are not, my dear. Absolutely not. Of course I'm going to."

Ricky, with Big Sword on his shoulder, was strolling along a path in the sun. He saw his father and Dr. Scott return to the camp arm in arm, and nodded with satisfaction. About time, too. Now perhaps Doc. J. would stop mooning around and get on with his work for a change. He'd had Ricky and Woodman's last report on the biology of the People for two weeks without making the slightest attempt to read it, and it was full of interesting things.

Just for a moment, Ricky wondered what it was like to get all wrapped up in one individual like that. No doubt he'd find out in time. It would have to be somebody interested in real things, of course—not an Earth-bound person like poor Cora.

Meanwhile he was just fourteen and free of the Universe, and he was going to have fun.

Big Sword, from his perch on Ricky's shoulder, noticed the couple with the pod. He saw that this one was fertile, all right—the shoot was beginning to form inside it. One of them was an old friend from this side of the Rift, but it was no good trying to talk to him—his mind would be shut. The whole process of taking the Journey, finding a mate and taking care of one's seedling was still a mystery to Big Sword in the sense that he could not imagine what it felt like. Just now he was not very interested. He had nearly a year in which to find out things, especially things about the Big People who, now they were domesticated, had turned out to be so useful, and he was going to enjoy that and not speculate about the Journey, and what it felt like to take it.

Because, eventually, the call would come to him, too, and he would set off up the new little stream to the other side of the Rift where the trees of the Strangers grew. And then he would know. ■

WINGS OF VICTORY
Poul Anderson

OUR PART IN THE GRAND SURVEY had taken us out beyond the great suns Alpha and Beta Crucis. From Earth we would have been in the constellation Lupus. But Earth was 278 light-years remote, Sol itself long dwindled in invisibility, and stars drew strange pictures across the dark.

After three years we were weary and had suffered losses. Oh, the wonder wasn't gone. How could it ever go—from world after world after world? But we had seen so many, and of those we had walked on, some were beautiful and some were terrible and most were both—even as Earth is—and none were alike and all were mysterious. They blurred together in our minds.

It was still a heart-speeding thing to find another sentient race, actually more than to find another planet colonizable by man. Now Ali Hamid had perished of a poisonous bite a year back, and Manuel Gonsalves had not yet recovered from the skull fracture inflicted by the club of an excited being at our last stop. This made Vaughn Webner our chief xenologist, from whom was to issue trouble.

Not that he, or any of us, wanted it. You learn to gang warily, in a universe not especially designed for you, or you die; there is no third choice. We approached this latest star because every G-type dwarf beckoned us. But we did not establish orbit around its most terrestroid attendant until neutrino analysis had verified that nobody in the system employed atomic energy. And we exhausted every potentiality of our instruments before we sent down our first robot probe.

The sun was a G9, golden in hue, luminosity half of Sol's. The world which interested us was close enough in to get about the same irradiation as Earth. It was smaller, surface gravity 0.75, with thinner and drier atmosphere. However, that air was perfectly breathable by humans, and bodies of water existed which could be called modest oceans. The globe was very lovely where it turned against star-crowded night, blue, tawny, rusty-brown, white-clouded. Two little moons skipped in escort.

Biological samples proved that its life was chemically similar to ours. None of the microorganisms we cultured posed any threat that normal precautions and medications could not handle. Pictures taken at low altitude and on the ground showed woods, lakes, wide plains rolling toward mountains. We were afire to set foot there.

But the natives—

You must remember how new the hyperdrive is, and how immense the cosmos. The organizers of the Grand Survey were too wise to believe that the few neighbor systems we'd learned something about gave knowledge adequate for devising doctrine.

Our service had one law, which was its proud motto: "We come as friends." Otherwise each crew was free to work out its own procedures. After five years the survivors would meet and compare experiences.

For us aboard the *Olga*, Captain Gray had decided that, whenever possible, sophonts should not be disturbed by preliminary sightings of our machines. We would try to set the probes in uninhabited regions. When we ourselves landed, we would come openly. After all, the shape of a body counts for much less than the shape of the mind within. Thus went our belief.

Naturally, we took in every datum we could from orbit and upper-atmospheric overflights. While not extremely informative under such conditions, our pictures did reveal a few small towns on two continents—clusters of buildings, at least, lacking defensive walls or regular streets—hard by primitive mines. They seemed insignificant against immense and almost unpopulated landscapes. We guessed we could identify a variety of cultures, from Stone Age through Iron. Yet invariably, aside from those petty communities, settlements consisted of one or a few houses standing alone. We found none less than ten kilometers apart; most were more isolated.

"Carnivores, I expect," Webner said. "The primitive economies are hunting-fishing-gathering, the advanced economies pastoral. Large areas which look cultivated are probably just to provide fodder; they don't have the layout of proper farms." He tugged his chin. "I confess being puzzled as to how the civilized . . . well, let's say the 'metallurgic' people, at this stage . . . how they manage it. You need trade, communication, quick exchange of ideas, for that level of technology. And if I read the pictures aright, roads are virtually nonexistent, a few dirt tracks between towns and mines, or to the occasional dock for barges or ships—Confound it, water transportation is insufficient."

"Pack animals, maybe?" I suggested.

"Too slow," he said. "You don't get progressive cultures when months must pass before the few individuals capable of originality can hear from each other. The chances are they never will."

For a moment the pedantry dropped from his manner. "Well," he said, "we'll see," which is the grandest sentence that any language can own.

We always made initial contact with three, the minimum who could do the job, lest we lose them. This time they were Webner, xenologist; Aram Turekian, pilot; and Yukiko Sachansky, gunner. It was Gray's idea to give women that last assignment. He felt they were better than men at watching and waiting, less likely to open fire in doubtful situations.

The site chosen was in the metallurgic domain, though not a town. Why complicate matters unnecessarily? It was on a rugged upland, thick forest for kilometers around. Northward the mountainside rose steeply until, above timberline, its crags were crowned by a glacier. Southward it toppled to a great plateau, open country where herds grazed on a reddish analog of grass or shrubs. Maybe they were domesticated, maybe not. In either case, probably the dwellers did a lot of hunting.

"Would that account for their being so scattered?" Yukiko wondered. "A big range needed to support each individual?"

"Then they must have a strong territoriality," Webner said. "Stand sharp by the guns."

We were not forbidden to defend ourselves from attack, whether or not blunders of ours had provoked it. Nevertheless the girl winced. Turekian glanced over his shoulder and saw. That, and Webner's tone, made him flush. "Blow down, Vaughn," he growled.

Webner's long, gaunt frame stiffened in his seat. Light gleamed off the scalp under his thin hair as he thrust his head toward the pilot. "What did you say?"

"Stay in your own shop and run it, if you can.".

"Mind your manners. This may be my first time in charge, but I *am*—"

"On the ground. We're aloft yet."

"Please." Yukiko reached from her turret and laid a hand on either man's shoulder. "Please don't quarrel . . . when we're about to meet a whole new history."

They couldn't refuse her wish. Tool-burdened coverall or no, she remained in her Eurasian petiteness the most desired woman aboard the *Olga*; and still the rest of the girls liked her. Gonsalves's word for her was "*simpatico*."

The men only quieted on the surface. They were an ill-assorted pair, not enemies—you don't sign on a person who'll allow himself hatred—but unfriends. Webner was the academic type, professor of xenology at the University of Oceania. In youth he'd done excellent field work, especially in the trade route cultures of Cynthia, and he'd been satisfactory under his superiors. At heart, though, he was a theorist, whom middle age had made dogmatic.

Turekian was the opposite: young, burly, black-bearded, boisterous and roisterous, born in a sealtent on Ganymede to a life of banging around the available universe. If half his brags were true, he was mankind's boldest adventurer, toughest fighter, and mightiest lover; but I'd found to my profit that he wasn't the poker player he claimed. Withal he was able, affable, helpful, well liked—which may have kindled envy in poor self-chilled Webner.

"O.K., sure," Turekian laughed. "For you, Yu." He tossed a kiss in her direction.

Webner unbent less easily. "What did you mean by running my own shop if I can?" he inquired.

"Nothing, nothing," the girl almost begged.

"Ah, a bit more than nothing," Turekian said. "A tiny bit. I just wish you were less convinced your science has the last word on all the chances. Things I've seen—"

"I've heard your song before," Webner scoffed. "In a jungle on some exotic world you met animals with wheels."

"Never said that. Hm-m-m . . . make a good yarn, wouldn't it?"

"No. Because it's an absurdity. Simply ask yourself how nourishment would pass from the axle bone to the cells of the disk. In like manner—"

"Yeh, yeh. Quiet, now, please. I've got to conn us down."

The target waxed fast in the bow screen. A booming of air came faint through the hull plates and vibration shivered flesh. Turekian hated dawdling. Besides, a slow descent might give the autochthons time to become hysterical, with possibly tragic consequences.

Peering, the humans saw a house on the rim of a canyon at whose bottom a river rushed gray-green. The structure was stone, massive and tile-roofed. Three more buildings joined to define a flagged courtyard. These were of timber, topped by blossoming sod, long and low. A corral outside the quadrangle held four-footed beasts, and nearby stood a row of what Turekian, pointing, called overgrown birdhouses. A meadow surrounded the ensemble. Elsewhere the woods crowded close.

There was abundant bird or, rather, ornithoid life, flocks strewn across the sky. A pair of especially large creatures hovered above the steading. They veered as the boat descended.

Abruptly, wings exploded from the house. Out of its windows fliers came, a score or better, all sizes from tiny ones which clung to adult backs, up to those which dwarfed the huge extinct condors of Earth. In a gleam of bronze feathers, a storm of wingbeats which pounded through the hull, they rose, and fled, and were lost among the treetops.

The humans landed in a place gone empty.

Hands near side arms, Webner and Turekian trod forth, looked about, let the planet enter them.

You always undergo that shock of first encounter. Not only does space separate the new-found world from yours; time does, five billion years at least. Often you need minutes before you can truly see the shapes around, they are that alien. Before, the eye has registered them but not the brain.

This was more like home. Yet the strangenesses were uncountable.

Weight: three-fourths of what the ship maintained. An ease, a bounciness in the stride . . . and a subtle kinesthetic adjustment required, sensory more than muscular.

Air: like Earth's at about two kilometers' altitude. (Gravity gradient being less, the density drop-off above sea level went slower.) Crystalline vision, cool flow and murmur of breezes, soughing in the branches and river clangorous down in the canyon. Every odor different, no hint of sun-baked resin or duff, instead a medley of smokinesses and pungencies.

Light: warm gold, making colors richer and shadows deeper than you were really evolved for; a midmorning sun which displayed almost half again the diameter of Earth's, in a sky which was deep blue and had only thin streaks of cloud.

Life: wild flocks, wheeling and crying high overhead; lowings and cacklings from the corral; rufous carpet underfoot, springy, suggestive more of moss than grass though

Poul Anderson

not very much of either, starred with exquisite flowers; trees whose leaves were green—from silvery to murky—whose bark—if it were bark—might be black, or gray, or brown, or white, whose forms were perhaps no odder to you than were palm, or gingko, if you came from oak and beech country, but which were no trees of anywhere on Earth. A swarm of midge-like insectoids went by, and a big coppery-winged "moth" leisurely feeding on them.

Scenery: superb. Above the forest, peaks shouldered into heaven, the glacier shimmered blue. To the right, canyon walls plunged roseate, ocher-banded, and cragged. But your attention was directed ahead.

The house was astonishingly big. "A flinking castle," Turekian exclaimed. An approximate twenty-meter cube, it rose sheer to the peaked roof, built from well-dressed blocks of granite. Windows indicated six stories. They were large openings, equipped with wooden shutters and wrought-iron balconies. The sole door, on ground level, was ponderous. Horns, skulls, and sculptured weapons of the chase—knife, spear, shortsword, blowgun, bow and arrow—ornamented the façade.

The companion buildings were doubtless barns or sheds. Trophies hung on them, too. The beasts in the corral looked, and probably weren't, mammalian. Two species were vaguely reminiscent of horses and oxen, a third kind of sheep. They were not many, could not be the whole support of the dwellers here. The "dovecotes" held ornithoids the size of turkeys, which were not penned but were prevented from leaving the area by three hawklike guardians. "Watchdogs," Turekian said of those. "No, watchfalcons." They swooped about, perturbed at the invasion.

Yukiko's voice came wistful from a receiver behind his ear: "Can I join you?"

"Stay by the guns," Webner answered. "We have yet to meet the owners of this place."

"Huh?" Turekian said. "Why, they're gone. Skedaddled when they saw us coming."

"Timid?" Yukiko asked. "That doesn't fit well with their being eager hunters."

"On the contrary, I imagine they're pretty scrappy," Turekian said. "They jumped to the conclusion we must be hostile, because they wouldn't enter somebody else's land uninvited unless they felt that way. Our powers being unknown, and they having the wife and kiddies to worry about, they prudently took off. I expect the fighting males—or whatever they've got—will be back soon."

"What are you talking about?" Webner demanded.

"Why . . . the locals." Turekian blinked at him. "You saw them."

"Those giant ornithoids? Nonsense."

"Hoy? They came right out of the house there!"

"Domestic animals." Webner's hatchet features drew tight. "I don't deny we confront a puzzle here."

"We always do," Yukiko put in.

Webner nodded. "True. Nevertheless, facts and logic solve puzzles. Let's not complicate our job with pseudo-problems. Whatever they are, the fliers we saw leave cannot be the sophonts. On a planet as Earthlike as this, aviform intelligence is impossible.''

He straightened. ''I suspect the inhabitants have barricaded themselves,'' he finished. ''We'll go closer and make pacific gestures.''

''Which could be misunderstood,'' Turekian said dubiously. ''An arrow, or javelin, can kill you just as dead as a blaster.''

''Cover us, Yukiko,'' Webner ordered. ''Follow me, Aram. If you have the nerve.''

He stalked forward, under the eyes of the girl. Turekian cursed and joined him in haste.

They were near the door when a shadow fell over them. They whirled and stared upward. Yukiko's indrawn breath hissed from their receivers.

Aloft hovered one of the great ornithoids. Sunlight struck through its outermost pinions, turning them golden. Otherwise it showed storm-cloud-dark. Down the wind stooped a second.

The sight was terrifying. Only later did the humans realize it was magnificent. Those wings spanned six meters. A muzzle full of sharp white fangs gaped before them. Two legs the length and well-nigh the thickness of a man's arms reached crooked talons between them. At their angles drew claws. In thrust after thrust, they hurled the creature at torpedo speed. Air whistled and thundered.

Their guns leaped into the men's hands. ''Don't shoot!'' Yukiko's cry came as if from very far away.

The splendid monster was almost upon them. Fire speared from Webner's weapon. At the same instant, the animal braked—a turning of quills, a crack and gust in their faces—and rushed back upward, two meters short of impact.

Turekian's gaze stamped a picture on his brain which he would study over and over and over. The unknown was feathered, surely warmblooded, but no bird. A keelbone like a ship's prow jutted beneath a strong neck. The head was bluntnosed, lacked external ears; fantastically, Turekian saw that the predator mouth had lips. Tongue and palate were purple. Two big golden eyes stabbed at him, burned at him. A crest of black-tipped white plumage rose stiffly above, a control surface and protection for the backward-bulging skull. The fan-shaped tail bore the same colors. The body was mahogany, the naked legs and claws yellow.

Webner's shot hit amidst the left-side quills. Smoke streamed after the flameburst. The creature uttered a high-pitched yell, lurched, and threshed in retreat. The damage wasn't permanent, had likely caused no pain, but now that wing was only half useful.

Turekian thus had time to see three slits in parallel on the body. He had time to think there must be three more on the other side. They weirdly resembled gills. As the wings lifted, he saw them drawn wide, a triple yawn; as the downstroke began, he glimpsed them being forced shut.

Then he had cast himself against Webner. ''Drop that blaster, you clotbrain!'' he yelled. He seized the xenologist's gun wrist. They wrestled. He forced the fingers apart. Meanwhile the wounded ornithoid struggled back to its companion. They flapped off.

"What're you doing?" Webner grabbed at Turekian.

The pilot pushed him away, brutally hard. He fell. Turekian snatched forth his magnifier.

Treetops cut off his view. He let the instrument drop. "Too late," he groaned. "Thanks to you."

Webner climbed erect. He was pale and shaken by rage. "Have you gone heisenberg?" he gasped. "I'm your commander!"

"You're maybe fit to command plastic ducks in a bathtub," Turekian said. "Firing on a native!"

Webner was too taken aback to reply.

"And you capped it by spoiling my chance for a good look at Number Two. I think I spotted a harness on him, holding what might be a weapon, but I'm not sure." Turekian spat.

"Aram, Vaughn," Yukiko pleaded from the boat.

An instant longer, the men bristled and glared. Then Webner drew breath, shrugged, and said in a crackly voice: "I suppose it's incumbent on me to put things on a reasonable basis, if you're incapable of that." He paused. "Behave yourself and I'll excuse your conduct as being due to excitement. Otherwise I'll have to recommend you be relieved from further initial-contact duty."

"*I* be relieved—?" Turekian barely checked his fist, and kept it balled. His breath rasped.

"Hadn't you better check the house?" Yukiko asked.

The knowledge that something, anything might lurk behind those walls restored them to a measure of coolness.

Save for livestock, the steading was deserted.

Rather than offend the dwellers by blasting down their barred door, the searchers went through a window on grav units. They found just one or two rooms on each story. Evidently the people valued ample floor space and high ceilings above privacy. Connection up and down was by circular staircases whose short steps seemed at variance with this. Decoration was austere and nonrepresentational. Furniture consisted mainly of benches and tables. Nothing like a bed, or an *o-futon*, was found; did the indigenes sleep, if they did, sitting or standing? Quite possibly. Many species can lock the joints of their limbs at will.

Stored food bore out the idea of carnivorousness. Tools, weapons, utensils, fabrics were abundant, well made, neatly arranged. They confirmed an Iron Age technology, more or less equivalent to that of Earth's Classical civilization. Exceptions occurred; for example, a few books, seemingly printed from handset type. How eagerly those pages were ransacked! But the only illustrations were diagrams suitable to a geometry text in one case and a stonemason's manual in another. Did this culture taboo pictures of its members, or had the boat merely chanced on a home which possessed none?

The layout and contents of the house, and of the sheds when these were examined, gave scant clues. Nobody had expected better. Imagine yourself a nonhuman xenologist, visiting Earth before man went into space. What could you deduce from the residences and a few household items belonging to, say, a European, an Eskimo, a Congo pygmy, and a Japanese? You might have wondered if the owners were of the same genus.

In time you could learn more. Turekian doubted that time would be given. He put Webner in a cold fury by his nagging to finish the survey and get back to the boat. At length the chief gave in. "Not that I don't plan a detailed study, mind you," he said. Scornfully: "However, I suppose we can hold a conference, and I'll try to calm your fears."

After you had been out, the air in the craft smelled dead and the view in the screens looked dull. Turekian took a pipe from his pocket. "No," Webner told him.

"What?" The pilot was bemused.

"I won't have that foul thing in this crowded cabin."

"I don't mind," Yukiko said.

"I do," Webner replied, "and while we're down, I'm your captain."

Turekian reddened and obeyed. Discipline in space is steel hard, a matter of survival. A good commander gives it a soft sheath. Yukiko's eyes reproached Webner; her fingers lay on the pilot's arm. The xenologist saw. His mouth twitched sideways before he pinched it together.

"We're in trouble," Turekian said. "The sooner we haul mass out of here, the happier our insurance companies will be."

"Nonsense," Webner snapped. "If anything, our problem is that we've terrified the dwellers. They may take days to send even a scout."

"They've already sent two. You had to shoot at them."

"I shot at a dangerous animal. Didn't you see those talons, those fangs? And a buffet from a wing that big—ignoring the claws on it—could break your neck."

Webner's gaze sought Yukiko's. He mainly addressed her: "Granted, they must be domesticated. I suspect they're used in the hunt, flown at game, like hawks, though working in packs, like hounds. Conceivably the pair we encountered were, ah, sicced on us from afar. But that they themselves are sophonts—out of the question."

Her murmur was uneven. "How can you be sure?"

Webner leaned back, bridged his fingers, and grew calmer while he lectured: "You realize the basic principle. All organisms make biological sense in their particular environments, or they become extinct. Reasoners are no exception—and are, furthermore, descended from nonreasoners which adapted to environments that had never been artificially modified.

"On nonterrestroid worlds, they can be quite outré by our standards, since they developed under unearthly conditions. On an essentially terrestroid planet, evolution basically parallels our own because it must. True, you get considerable variation. Like, say, hexapodal vertebrates liberating the forelimbs to grow hands and becoming centauroids, as on Woden. That's because the ancestral chordates were hexapods. On this world, you can see for yourself the higher animals are four-limbed.

"A brain without some equivalent of hands is useless in the wild. Nature would never produce it. The inhabitants are bound to be bipeds, however different from us in detail. A foot which must double as a hand, and vice versa, would be too grossly inefficient in either function. Natural selection would weed out any mutants of that tendency, fast.

"What could yonder ornithoids use for hands?"

"The claws on their wings?" Yukiko asked shyly.

" 'Fraid not," Turekian said. "I got a fair look. They can grasp, sort of, but aren't built for manipulation."

"You saw how the fledgling uses them to cling to the parent," Webner stated. "Perhaps it climbs trees also. Earth has a bird with similar structures, the hoactzin. It loses them in adulthood. Here they may well become extra weapons."

"The feet," Turekian scowled. "Two opposable digits flanking three straight ones. Could serve as hands."

"Then how does the creature get about on the ground?" Webner retorted. "Can't forge a tool in midair, you know, let alone dig ore and erect stone houses."

He wagged a finger. "Another, more fundamental point," he went on. "Fliers are too limited in mass. True, the gravity's weaker than on Earth, but air pressure's lower. Thus admissible wing loadings are about the same. The biggest birds which ever lumbered into Terrestrial skies weighed some fifteen kilos. Nothing larger could get aloft. Metabolism simply can't supply the power required. We've established that local biochemistry is close kin to our type. Hence it is not possible for those ornithoids to outweigh a maximal vulture. They're big, yes, and formidable. Nevertheless, that size has to be mostly feathers, hollow bones—spidery, kitelike skeletons anchoring thin flesh.

"Aram, you hefted several items around this place, such as a stone pot. Or consider one of the buckets, presumably used to bring water up from the river. What would you say the greatest weight is?"

Turekian scratched in his beard. "Maybe twenty kilos," he answered reluctantly.

"There! No flier could lift that. It was always superstition about eagles stealing lambs, or babies. They weren't able to. The ornithoids are similarly handicapped. Who'd make utensils he can't carry?"

"M-m-m," Turekian growled rather than hummed. Webner pressed the attack:

"The mass of any flier on a terrestroid planet is insufficient to include a big enough brain for true intelligence. The purely animal functions require virtually all those cells. Birds have at least lightened their burden, permitting a little more brain, by changing jaws to beaks. So have those ornithoids you called 'watchfalcons.' The big fellows have not.''

He hesitated. "In fact," he said slowly, "I doubt if they can even be considered bright animals. They're likely stupid . . . and vicious. If we're set on again, we need have no compunctions about destroying them."

"Couldn't he, she, it simply have been coming down for a quick, close look at you—unarmed as a peace gesture?" Yukiko whispered.

"If intelligent, yes," Webner said. "If not, as I've proven, positively no. I saved us some nasty wounds. Perhaps I saved a life."

"The dwellers might object if we shoot at their property," Turekian said.

"They need only call off their, ah, dogs. In fact, the attack on us may not have been commanded, may simply have been brute reaction after panic broke the order of the pack." Webner rose. "Are you satisfied? We'll make thorough studies till nightfall, then leave gifts, withdraw, hope for a better reception when we see the indigenes have returned." A television pickup was customary among such gifts.

Turekian shook his head. "Your logic's all right, I suppose. But it don't smell right somehow."

Webner started for the air lock.

"Me, too?" Yukiko requested. "Please?"

"No," Turekian said. "I'd hate for you to be harmed."

"We're in no danger," she argued. "Our side arms can handle any fliers that may arrive feeling mean. If we plant sensors around, no walking native can come within bowshot before we know. I feel caged."

The xenologist thawed. "Why not?" he said. "I can use a levelheaded assistant." To Turekian: "Man the boat guns yourself if you wish."

"Like blazes," the pilot grumbled, and followed them.

He had to admit the xenologist knew his business. The former cursory search became a shrewd, efficient examination of object after object, measuring, photographing, commenting continuously into a minirecorder. Yukiko helped. On Survey, everybody must have some knowledge of everybody else's specialty. But Webner needed just one extra person.

"What can I do?" Turekian asked.

"Move an occasional heavy load," the other man said. "Keep watch on the forest. Keep out of the way."

Yukiko was too fascinated by the work to chide him. Turekian rumbled in his throat, stuffed his pipe, and slouched around the grounds alone, blowing furious clouds.

At the corral he gripped a rail and glowered. "You want feeding," he decided, went into a barn—unlike the house, its door was not secured—and found a haymow and pitchforks which reminded him of a backwoods colony on Hermes that he'd visited once, temporarily primitive because shipping space was needed for items more urgent than modern agromachines. The farmer had had a daughter— He consoled himself with memories while he took out a mess of cinnamon-scented red herbage.

"You!"

Webner leaned from an upstairs window. "What're you about?" he called.

"Those critters are hungry," Turekian replied. "Listen to 'em."

"How do you know what their requirements are? Or the owners'? We're not here to play God, for your information. We're here to learn and, maybe, help. Take that stuff back where you got it."

Turekian swallowed rage—that Yukiko should have heard his humiliation—and complied. Webner was his captain till he regained the blessed sky.

Sky . . . birds . . . He observed the "cotes." The pseudo-hawks fluttered about, indignant but too small to tackle him. Were the giant ornithoids kept partly as protection against large ground predators? Turekian studied the flock. Its members dozed, waddled, scratched the dirt, fat and placid, obviously long bred to tameness. One threshed the air toward a nest, clumsy as a chicken. Both types lacked the gill-like slits he had noticed. . . .

A shadow. Turekian glanced aloft, snatched for his magnifier. Half a dozen giants were back. The noon sun flamed on their feathers. They were too high for him to see details.

He flipped the controls on his grav unit and made for the house. Webner and Yukiko were on the fifth floor. Turekian arced through a window. He had no eye, now, for the Spartan grace of the room. "They've arrived," he panted. "We better get in the boat quick."

Webner stepped onto the balcony. "No need," he said. "I hardly think they'll attack. If they do, we're safer here than crossing the open."

"Might be smart to close the shutters," the girl said.

"And the door to this chamber," Webner agreed. "That'll stop them. They'll soon lose patience and wander off—if they attempt anything. Or if they do besiege us, we can shoot our way through them, or at worst relay a call for help via the boat, once *Olga*'s again over our horizon."

He had re-entered. Turekian took his place on the balcony and squinted upward. More winged shapes had joined the first several; and more arrived each second. They dipped, soared, circled through the wind, which made surf noises in the forest.

Unease crawled along the pilot's spine. "I don't like this half a bit," he said. "They don't act like plain beasts."

"Conceivably the dwellers plan to use them in an assault," Webner said. "If so, we may have to teach the dwellers about the cost of unreasoning hostility." His tone was less cool than the words, and sweat beaded his countenance.

Sparks in the magnifier field hurt Turekian's eyes. "I swear they're carrying metal," he said. "Listen, if they are intelligent—and out to get us after you nearly killed one of 'em—the house is no place for us. Let's scramble. We may not have many more minutes."

"Yes, I believe we'd better, Vaughn," Yukiko urged. "We can't risk . . . being forced to burn down conscious beings . . . on their own land."

Maybe his irritation with the pilot spoke for Webner: "How often must I explain there is no risk, yet? Instead, here's a chance to learn. What happens next could give us invaluable clues to understanding the whole ethos. We stay." To Turekian: "Forget about that alleged metal. Could be protective collars, I suppose. But take the supercharger off your imagination."

The other man stood dead still.

"Aram." Yukiko seized his arm.

"What's wrong?"

He shook himself. "Supercharger," he mumbled. "By God, yes."

Abruptly, in a bellow: "We're leaving! This second! They *are* the dwellers, and they've gathered the whole countryside against us!"

"Hold your tongue," Webner said, "or I'll charge insubordination."

Laughter rattled in Turekian's breast. "Uh-uh. Mutiny."

He crouched and lunged. His fist rocketed before him. Yukiko's cry joined the thick smack as knuckles hit—not the chin, which is too hazardous—the solar plexus. Air whoofed from Webner. His eyes glazed. He folded over, partly conscious but unable to stand. Turekian gathered him in his arms. "To the boat!" the pilot shouted. "Hurry, girl!"

His grav unit wouldn't carry two, simply gentled his fall when he leaped from the balcony. He dared not stop to adjust the controls on Webner's. Carrying his chief, he pounded across the flagstones. Yukiko came above. "Go ahead!" Turekian bawled. "Get into shelter."

"Not till you can. I'll cover you."

The scores above had formed themselves into a vast revolving wheel. It tilted. The first fliers peeled off and roared downward. The rest came after.

Arrows whistled ahead of them. A trumpet sounded. Turekian dodged, zigzag over the meadow. Yukiko's gun clapped. She shot to miss, but belike the flashes put those archers—and, now, spearthrowers—off their aim. Shafts sang wickedly around.

Yukiko darted to open the boat's air lock. While she did, Turekian dropped Webner and straddled him, blaster drawn. The leading flier hurtled close. Talons of the right foot, which was not a foot at all but a hand, gripped a scimitar. For an instant, Turekian looked into the golden eyes, knew a brave male defending his home, fired to miss.

In a brawl of air, the native sheered off. The valve swung wide. Yukiko flitted through. Turekian dragged Webner, then stood in the lock chamber till the entry was shut.

Missiles clanged on the hull. None would pierce. Turekian let himself join Webner for a moment of shuddering before he went to Yukiko and the raising of his vessel.

When you know what to expect, a little, you can lay plans. We next sought the

Poul Anderson

folk of Ythri, as the planet is called by its most advanced culture, a thousand kilometers from the triumph which surely prevailed in those mountains. Approached with patience, caution, and symbolisms appropriate to their psyches, they welcomed us rapturously. Before we left, they'd thought of sufficient inducements to trade that I'm sure they'll have spacecraft of their own in a few generations.

Still, they are as fundamentally territorial as man is fundamentally sexual, and we'd better bear that in mind.

The reason lies in their evolution. It does for every drive in every animal everywhere. The Ythrian is carnivorous, aside from various sweet fruits. Carnivores require larger regions per individual then herbivores or omnivores do, in spite of the fact that meat has more calories per kilo than most vegetable matter. Consider how each antelope needs a certain amount of space, and how many antelopes are needed to maintain a pride of lions. Xenologists have written thousands of papers on the correlations between diet and genotypical personality in sophonts.

I have my doubts about the value of those papers. At least, they missed the possibility of a race like the Ythrians, whose extreme territoriality and individualism—with the consequences to governments, mores, arts, faiths, and souls—come from the extreme appetite of the body.

They mass as high as thirty kilos; yet they can lift their own weight in the air or, unhampered, fly like demons. Hence they maintain civilization without the need to crowd together in cities. Their townspeople are mostly wing-clipped criminals and slaves. Today their wiser heads hope robots will end that need.

Hands? The original talons, modified for manipulating. Feet? Those claws on the wings, a juvenile feature which persisted and developed, just as man's large head and sparse hair derive from the juvenile or fetal ape. The forepart of the wing skeleton consists of humerus, radius, and ulnar, much as in true birds. These lock together in flight. Aground, when the wing is folded downward, they produce a "knee" joint. Bones grow from their base to make the claw-foot. Three fused digits, immensely lengthened, sweep backward to be the alatan which braces the rest of that tremendous wing and can, when desired, give additional support on the surface. To rise, the Ythrians usually do a handstand during the initial upstroke. It takes less than a second.

Oh, yes, they are slow and awkward afoot. They manage. Big and beweaponed, instantly ready to go aloft, they need fear no beast of prey.

You ask where the power comes from to swing this hugeness through the sky. The oxidation of food, what else? Hence the demand of each household for a great hunting or ranching demesne. The limiting factor is the oxygen supply. Turekian first understood how that is increased. The Ythrian has lungs, a passive system resembling ours. He also has his supercharger, evolved from the gills of an amphibian-like ancestor. Worked in bellows fashion by the flight muscles, leading directly to the bloodstream, those air-intake organs let him burn his fuel as fast as necessary.

I wonder how it feels to be so alive.

I remember how Yukiko Sachansky stood in the curve of Aram Turekian's arm, under a dawn heaven, and watched the farewell dance the Ythrians gave for us, and cried through tears: "To fly like that! To fly like that!" ■

THE WAVERIES
Fredric Brown

DEFINITIONS FROM SCHOOL-ABRIDGED Webster-Hamlin Dictionary, 1988 edition:

wavery (WĀ-ver-ĭ) *n.* a vader—*slang*
vader (VĀ-der) *n.* inorgan of the class Radio
inorgan (ĭn-ÔR-găn) *n.* noncorporeal ens, a vader
radio (RĀ-dĭ-ōh, ră-DĒ-ōh) *n.* 1. Class of inorgans 2. Etheric frequency between light and electricity 3. (obsolete) Method of communication used up to 1947.

The opening guns of invasion were not at all loud, although they were heard by many people. George Bailey was one of the many; I choose George Bailey because he was the only one who came within a googol of light-years of guessing what they were.

George Bailey was drunk and under the circumstances one can't blame him. He was listening to radio advertisements of the most verbose and annoying kind. Not because he *wanted* to listen to them, but because he'd been told to listen by his boss, J.R. McGee of the MID network.

George Bailey wrote advertising for the radio. The only thing he hated worse than advertising was radio. And here, on his own time in the late evening, he was listening to fulsome and saccharine drippings on a rival network, at J.R. McGee's suggestion —which George very rightly took for an order.

"Bailey, you should be more familiar with what others are doing. Particularly those of our own accounts which use several networks. I'd suggest that—"

One doesn't quarrel with suggestions and keep a hundred and fifty-dollar-a-week job. But one can drink whiskey sours while listening. One George Bailey did.

Also, one could play gin rummy with Maisie Hetterman, a cute little red-headed typist from the studio. One could do no more than that, but Maisie was worth just looking at across a card table. It was Maisie's apartment and Maisie's radio, but George had brought the liquor.

"—only the best tobaccos," said the radio, "go *dit-dit-dit*—the nation's favorite cigarettes—"

George glanced at the radio. "Marconi," he said.

He meant Morse, naturally, but the whiskey sours had muddled him a bit, so he was nearer right than most people who heard that *dit-dit-dit*. It *was* Marconi, in a way; in, as it turned out, a very peculiar way.

"Marconi?" asked Maisie.

George Bailey, who hated to talk while a radio was going, leaned over and switched it off.

"I mean Morse," he said. "Morse, as in Boy Scouts or the Signal Corps. I used to be a Boy Scout once."

"You don't look it."

George sighed. "Somebody going to catch hell," he said, "broadcasting code on that wave length."

"What did it mean?"

"Mean? Oh, you mean what did it mean. Uh . . . S, letter S. *Dit-dit-dit*. SOS is *dit-dit-dit dah-dah-dah dit-dit-dit*."

"O is *dah-dah-dah*?"

George grinned. "Say it again, Maisie. I like it. I think 'oo is *dah-dah-dah*, too."

"George! Maybe it's really an SOS message. Turn it back on, please."

He turned it back on. The tobacco ad was still going. "—gentlemen of the most . . . *dit-dit-dit* . . . ing taste prefer the finer taste of Golden Harvest . . . *dit-dit-dit* . . . arettes. In the new package that keeps them . . . *dit-dit-dit* . . . and ultra fresh—"

"It's just S-S-S-S," said George.

"Like a teakettle. Or maybe somebody s-s-stutters. But the Golden Harvest people are going to raise— Say—"

"What, George?"

"Maybe it's deliberate, an advertising gag like L.S.M.F.T. used to be. Just a minute till I—"

He reached over and turned the dial of the radio a bit to the right, then a bit to the left, and an incredulous look came over his face. He turned the dial to the extreme right, as far as it would go. There wasn't any station there—not even the hum of a carrier wave.

"Dit-dit-dit," said the radio, *"—dit-dit-dit."*

George turned it to the other end of the dial. *"Dit-dit-dit,"* said the radio.

He switched it off and stared at Maisie, without even seeing her, which was hard to do.

"Something wrong, George?"

"I hope so," said George Bailey. "I certainly hope so."

He started to reach for another drink, and changed his mind. He had a sudden hunch that something big was happening, and wanted to sober up to appreciate it.

He didn't have the faintest idea *how* big it was.

"George, what do you mean?"

"I don't know. But Maisie, let's take a run down to the studio, huh? There ought to be some excitement."

April 5, 1947; that was the night the waveries came.

It was a gay night, except for radio technicians. New York was at its best and gayest and the main stem, which is Broadway, running high, wide and expensive. The streets were full of uniforms, mostly uniforms of men already demobilized—due to recent reduction in the armies of occupation—so recently demobilized that they hadn't taken time to buy civvies. Discharge pay burning in their pockets, they wanted Broadway and they took Broadway; or Broadway took them. Fresh shiploads of them daily.

The gaiety was hectic, but it was a surface gaiety, more so than had been the gaiety of the boom years of 1928 and '29. Workers dead weary from overtime in the reconverted factories trying to supply the peak demand for automobiles and radios and juke boxes and pinball games left the factories for a hasty meal, then went out in their automobiles—with car radios blaring—and spent their overtime pay in the juke boxes and pinball machines. Which, of course, increased the demand for those commodities, which increased the overtime of the factories, which increased the overtime pay, which increased the spending and the demand and— Well, you see what I mean.

It was a vicious circle that would eventually have bitten itself.

But the waveries bit first.

April 5, 1947; that was the night the waveries came.

George and Maisie tried in vain to get a cab, and took the subway instead. Oh yes, the subways were still running then. It took them within a block of the MID Network Building.

It was a madhouse. George, grinning, strolled through the lobby with Maisie on his arm, took the elevator to five and for no reason at all gave the elevator boy a dollar. He'd never before in his life tipped an elevator operator.

The boy grinned. "Better stay away from the big shots, Mr. Bailey," he said. "They're ready to chew off anybody's ears that looks at 'em cockeyed."

"Swell," said George. He left the elevator and headed straight for the office of J.R. McGee, himself. There were strident voices behind the glass door.

"But George," protested Maisie, "you'll be fired!"

"When in the course of human events," said George. "Oh, well, it's worth it. I got money saved up."

"But what are you going to do, George?"

"Stand back away from that door, honey." Gently, but firmly, he moved her to a safe position.

"But what *are* you—"

"This," said George Bailey, soberly.

The frantic voices stopped as he opened the glass door a bit. All eyes turned as he stuck his head in through the crack of the door.

"Dit-dit-dit," he said. *"Dit-dit-dit."*

He ducked back and to one side just in time to escape the flying glass as a paperweight and an inkwell came through the pane.

He grabbed Maisie and ran for the stairs.

"Now we get a drink," he told her.

The bar across from the Network Building was crowded, but it was a strangely silent crowd. Most of them were bunched around the big cabinet radio at one end of the bar.

"Dit," said the cabinet radio. *"dit-dah-d'dah-dit-dahditditdah d'd' dahditddditititdah—"*

Somebody fiddled with the dial. Somebody asked, "What band is that?" and somebody said, "Police." Somebody said, "Try the foreign band," and somebody did. "This ought to be Buenos Aires," somebody said. The radio said, *"dit-dit-dahditititdditah."*

George squeezed Maisie's arm.

"Lovely," he said. Maybe he meant her and maybe not; it didn't matter at the moment.

Somebody ran fingers through his hair and yelled, "Shut that thing off." Somebody did. Somebody else turned it back on.

George grinned and led the way to a back booth where he'd spotted Pete Mulvaney sitting alone with a tall bottle in front of him.

George seated Maisie and himself across from Pete Mulvaney.

"Hello," he said, gravely.

"Hello," said Pete, who was head of the technical research staff of the MID.

"A beautiful night, Mulvaney; did you see the moon riding high in the fleecy clouds like a golden galleon tossed upon silver-crested whitecaps in a stormy—"

"Shut up," said Pete. "I'm thinking."

"Whiskey sours," said George, to the waiter. He turned back to the brooding man across the table. "Think out loud," he said. "We sit at your feet. But first, how did you escape the looney bin?"

"I'm bounced, fired, discharged."

"Shake," said George, "and then explain."

"I told them what I thought it was, and they said I was crazy."

"Are you?"

"Yes," said Mulvaney.

"Good," said George. "I don't care what it is, as long as it's nothing trivial. But what the devil *is* it?"

"I don't know. Space, I think. Space is warped."

"Good old space," said George Bailey.

"George," said Maisie, "please shut up. I want to hear this."

"Space is also finite. You go far enough in any direction and you get back where you started." Pete Mulvaney poured himself another drink. "Like an ant crawling around an apple."

"Make it an orange," said George.

"All right, an orange. Suppose the first radio waves ever sent out have just made the round trip. In forty-six years."

"Forty-six years? But I thought radio waves traveled at the speed of light. In forty-six years they could go only forty-six light-years, and *that* can't be around the Universe, because there are galaxies known to be thousands of light-years away, or maybe millions; I don't know. But more than forty-six, Pete."

Pete Mulvaney sighed deeply. "We," he said, "are in the middle of a super-galaxy which is two million light-years in diameter. That is just one galaxy, a medium-sized one, they tell us. Yes, it's more than forty-six light-years around the orange."

"But—"

"But listen to that stuff. Can you read code?"

"Nope, not that fast, anyway."

"Well, I can. That's early American ham. Lingo and all. That's the kind of stuff the air was full of before *broadcasting*. It's the lingo, the abbreviations, the barnyard to attic chitchat of amateurs with keys, with Marconi coherers or Fessenden barreters—and you can listen for a violin solo pretty soon now. And you know what the first phonograph record ever broadcast was? Handel's 'Largo' sent out by Fessenden from Brant Rock in 1906. You'll hear his CQ-CQ any minute now. Bet you a drink."

"Sure, but what was the *dit-dit-dit* that started what's turned into hash since?"

Mulvaney grinned and then his face went blank. He said, "Marconi, George. What was the first *powerful* signal ever broadcast and by whom and when?"

"Marconi? *Dit-dit-dit?* Forty-six years ago?"

"Head of the class. The first transatlantic signal on December 12, 1901. For three hours Marconi's big station at Poldhu with two-hundred-foot masts sent out an intermittent S . . . *dit-dit-dit* . . . while Marconi and two assistants at St. Johns in Newfoundland got a kite-borne aerial four hundred feet in the air and got the signal finally. Across the Atlantic, George, with sparks jumping from the big Leyden jars at Poldhu and 20,000-volt juice jumping off the tremendous aerials—"

"Wait a minute, Pete, you're off the beam. If that was in 1901 and the first broadcast about 1906, it'll be five years before the Fessenden stuff gets here, on the same route. Even if there's a forty-six light-year short cut across space, and even if those signals didn't get so weak enroute that we couldn't hear them. It's crazy."

"I told you I was crazy," said Mulvaney. "Those signals should be so infinitesimal you couldn't hear them with the best set on Earth. Furthermore, they're all over the band on everything from microwave to ten kilocycles, and equally strong on each. Furthermore we've come five years in two hours, which isn't possible. I told you I was crazy."

"But—"

"Listen," said Pete.

A blurred but unmistakably human voice was coming from the radio, mingling with the cracklings of code. And then music, faint and scratchy and punctuated by *dit-dah*, but nevertheless music. Handel's "Largo."

Only it suddenly climbed in pitch as though modulating from key to key until it became so horribly shrill as to hurt the ear, like an orchestra made up of nothing but piccolos. And kept on going, past the high limit of audibility, until they could hear it no more.

Somebody said, "Shut that thing off." Somebody did, and this time nobody turned the thing back on.

George and Maisie looked at Pete Mulvaney and Pete Mulvaney looked back at them.

"But it can't be," said Pete Mulvaney. "There must be some other explanation. The more I think of it, now, the more I think I'm wrong."

He was right: he was wrong.

"Preposterous," said Mr. Ogilvie. He took off his glasses, frowned fiercely, and put them back on again. He looked through them at the several sheets of copy paper in his hand and tossed them contemptuously to the top of his desk. They slid to rest against the triangular nameplate that read:

B.R.OGILVIE, Editor-in-Chief

"Preposterous," he said again.

Casey Blair, his star reporter, blew a smoke ring and poked his index finger through it. "Why?" he asked.

"Because . . . why, it's preposterous!"

Casey Blair said, "It is now three o'clock in the morning. The radio interference has gone on for five hours and has reached the point where not a single current program is getting through. Every major broadcasting station in the world has gone off the air.

"For two reasons. One: it wasn't doing a bit of good to stay on the air and waste current, no matter what wave length they were on. Two: the communications bureaus of their respective governments requested them to get off to aid their campaigns with the direction finders. For five hours now—since the first note of interference, they've been working with everything they've got. And what have they got?"

"Preposterous," said the editor.

"Exactly. Greenwich at 11 P.M.—New York time—got a bearing in about the direction of Miami. It shifted northward until at 2 o'clock the direction was approximately that of Richmond, Virginia. Now San Francisco at 11 got a bearing in about the direction of Denver; three hours later it shifted southward toward Tucson. Southern hemisphere: bearings from Capetown, South Africa, shifted from approximate direction of Buenos Aires to direction of Montevideo, a thousand miles north. New York had trouble with direction finders; weak indications at 11 were toward Madrid; by 2 o'clock they could get no bearings at all." He blew another smoke ring. "Maybe because the loop antennae they use turn only on a horizontal plane."

"Absurd," said Mr. Ogilvie.

Casey said, "I liked 'preposterous' better, Mr. Ogilvie. It's not absurd; I'm scared stiff. Those lines converge on about the constellation Leo, if you take them as straight lines instead of curving them around the surface. I did it with a little globe and a star map." He leaned forward and tapped a forefinger on the top copy page. "Stations that are directly under that point in the sky get no bearings at all. Stations on, as it were, the perimeter of the Earth get strong bearings in the horizontal plane."

"But the heaviside layer, Blair—isn't that supposed to stop all radio waves; bounce 'em back or something?"

"Uh-huh. It does. But maybe it leaks. Maybe some waves get through. It isn't a solid wall."

"But—"

"I know; it's preposterous. But there it is. Only there's an hour before press time and you ought to turn the observatories on it and get it more accurately. Get *them* to extend those bearing lines. I did it by rule of thumb. Further, I didn't have the data for checking planet positions. Leo's on the ecliptic; a planet could be in line between here and there. Like Mars, maybe."

Mr. Ogilvie's eyes brightened, then clouded again.

He said, "We'll be the laughing-stock of the world, Blair, if we're wrong."

"And if I'm right?"

Ogilvie picked up the phone and snapped an order that sent every rewrite man into his office for orders.

April 6th headline of the New York *Morning Messenger*, final (5 A.M.) edition:

RADIO INTERFERENCE COMES FROM SPACE:
ORIGINATES IN LEO, SAY SCIENTISTS
May Be Attempt at Communication by Beings Outside
Solar System!
All Broadcasting Suspended

RKO and Radio Corporation stocks, closing the previous day at 10⅜ and 11½ respectively, opened at 9¾ and 9½ and dropped sharply. By noon, they were off four and five points respectively, when a moderate buying rally brought each of them back a fraction over two points.

Public action was mixed; people who had no radios rushed out to buy them and there was a boom market in portable and table-top receivers. Those who had radios listened as long as their curiosity enabled them to stand it, and then turned them off. Extraterrestrial or not, the programs were a horrible hash.

Oh, there were flashes—times when, for several seconds at a time, a listener could recognize the voice of Will Rogers or Geraldine Farrar or could catch a flash of the Dempsey-Carpentier fight. But things worth hearing—even for seconds at a time—were rare. Mostly it was a jumble of soap opera, advertising, and off-key snatches of what had once been music. It was utterly indiscriminate, and utterly unbearable for any length of time.

But curiosity is a powerful motive. There *was* a brief boom in radio sets that morning.

There were other booms, less explicable, less capable of analysis. Reminiscent of the Wells-Welles Martian scare was a sudden upswing in the sale of shotguns and sidearms. Bibles sold as readily as books on astronomy—and books on astronomy sold like hotcakes. One section of the country showed a sudden interest in lightning rods—builders were deluged with orders for immediate demonstration.

For some reason which has never been clearly ascertained, there was a run on fishhooks in Mobile, Alabama; every hardware and sporting goods store in that city was sold out of them before noon.

The public libraries had a run on books on astrology and books on Mars. Yes, on Mars—despite the fact that Mars was at the moment on the other side of the Sun and that every newspaper article on the subject stressed the fact that *no* planet was between Earth and the constellation Leo.

And not a radio station on Earth was on the air that morning.

Newspapers were passed from hand to hand because the presses couldn't keep up with the demand. *No news on the radio*—and something big was happening. People waited, in mobs, outside the newspaper offices for each new edition to appear. Circulation managers went quietly mad.

People gathered in curious little knots about the broadcasting studios. MID network doors were locked, although there was a doorman on duty to admit technicians, who were trying to find an answer to the unprecedented difficulty. Some, who had been on duty the previous day, had now spent twenty-four hours without sleep.

George Bailey woke at noon, with only a slight headache. He turned on his radio, and turned it off quickly again.

He shaved and showered, went out and drank a light breakfast and was himself again. He bought early editions of the afternoon papers, read them, and grinned. His hunch had been right; whatever was wrong with radio, it was nothing trivial.

But *what* was wrong?

The later editions of the evening papers had it.

EARTH INVADED, SAYS SCIENTIST

Thirty-six line type was the biggest they had; they used it. Not a home-edition copy of a newspaper was delivered that evening. Newsboys starting on their routes were practically mobbed. They sold papers instead of delivering them; the smart ones got a quarter apiece for them. The foolish ones who didn't want to sell, because the papers had been bought for their routes, lost them anyway. People grabbed them.

The later home-editions and the finals changed the heading only slightly—from a typographical viewpoint. But it was a big change, just the same:

EARTH INVADED, SAY SCIENTISTS

Funny what moving an S from the ending of a verb to the ending of a noun can do.

Carnegie Hall shattered precedents that evening with a lecture given at midnight. An unscheduled and unadvertised lecture. Professor Helmetz had stepped off the train at eleven-thirty and a mob of reporters had been waiting for him. Helmetz, of Harvard, had been the scientist—singular—who had made the first headlines.

Harvey Ambers, director of the board of Carnegie Hall, had pushed his way through the mob. He arrived minus glasses, hat and breath, but got hold of Helmetz's arm and hung on until he could talk again. "We want you to talk at Carnegie, professor," he shouted into Helmetz's ear. "Thousand bucks for a lecture on the 'vaders!"

"Certainly. Tomorrow afternoon?"

"Now! I've a cab waiting. Come on."

"But . . . but—"

"We'll get you an audience. Hurry!" He turned to the mob. "Let us through! You can't hear the professor here. Come to Carnegie and he'll talk to you. Spread the word."

The word spread so well that Carnegie Hall was jammed by midnight when the professor began to speak. By twelve-thirty, they'd rigged a loud-speaker system so the people outside could hear. By one o'clock in the morning the streets were jammed for blocks around.

There wasn't a sponsor on Earth with a million dollars to his name who wouldn't have given a million dollars to sponsor the broadcasting of that lecture—but it was not broadcast on the radio.

The line was busy.

"Questions?" asked Professor Helmetz.

A reporter in the front row made it first. "Professor," he asked, "have *all* direction-finding stations on Earth confirmed your statement as to the change this afternoon?"

"Yes, absolutely. At about noon, the directional indications began to grow weaker. At 2:47 o'clock, New York time, they ceased completely. Until then, the radio waves emanated from the sky, constantly changing direction with reference to the Earth's surface, but *constant* with reference to the point in the constellation Leo."

"What star in Leo?"

"No star. Merely a point in the sky coinciding exactly with the position of no visible star on the most minute charts. At 2:47 o'clock all direction finders went dead, but the signals persisted. They came from *all sides* equally. The invaders were here. There is no other conclusion to be drawn. Earth is now surrounded, completely blanketed, by radio waves which have *no point of origin,* which travel ceaselessly around the Earth in all directions, changing shape at their will—which at the moment seems to be in imitation of the Earth-origin signals which attracted their attention, which brought them here."

"From nowhere? From just a point in space?"

"Why not, sir? They are creatures of *ether,* not of matter. Ether permeates space uniformly. They were, until they were attracted here, at a point in space not greater than twenty-three light-years away. Our first indication of their arrival—rather, the arrival of the first ones, if you want to put it that way—came with a repetition of Marconi's S-S-S transatlantic broadcast of forty-six years ago. Apparently that was the first Earth broadcast of sufficient power to send signals which they could perceive at that distance. They started for Earth then, presumably. It took twenty-three years for those waves to reach them and twenty-three years for them to reach us. The first to arrive had formed themselves, imitatively, to duplicate the shape, as it were, of the signals that attracted them. Later arrivals were in the form of other waves that they had met, or passed, or absorbed, on their way to Earth. There are now fragments of programs which were broadcast as recently as a few days ago . . . uh . . . wandering about the ether. Undoubtedly also there are fragments of the very last programs to be broadcast, but they have not yet been identified."

"Professor, can you *describe* one of the invaders?"

"No more than one can describe a radio wave. They *are* radio waves, in effect, although they emanate from no broadcasting station. They are a form of life dependent upon the movement of ether, as life as we know it is dependent upon the vibration of matter. Life is movement—or at least, life is contingent upon movement."

"They are different sizes?"

"Yes—in two senses of the word size. Radio waves are measured from crest to crest, which measurement is known as the wave length. Since the invaders cover the entire dials of our receiving sets, obviously they can—in imitation, undoubtedly of the waves of ours which they have met—adjust themselves to any frequency, or crest-to-crest wave length.

"But that is only a crest-to-crest length. The actual length of a radio wave is much greater. If a broadcasting station sends out a program of one second's duration, the length of the wave carrying that program is one light-second, or 186,270 miles. A half-hour program is on a continuous wave, as it were, one-half light-hour long, and so on.

"On that basis, the individual . . . uh . . . invaders vary in length from a hundred thousand miles long—less than a second in duration—to about five million miles long—almost half a minute in duration. Each is in constant movement at the speed of light, and presumably that movement is now in a circle about the surface of the Earth. Each wave, as it were, extends many times, or many thousands of times, around the Earth."

"How can that be told?"

"By the length of the . . . ah . . . excerpts from various programs. None are under half a second in duration, none over half a minute."

"But why assume, Professor Helmetz, that these . . . these waves are living things? Why not just inanimate waves?"

"An inanimate wave . . . as you call it . . . would follow certain laws. Just as inanimate matter follows certain laws. An animal can climb uphill, however, or run in circles, or . . . uh . . . climb a tree. A stone can do none of these unless impelled by some outside force. It is the same with these invaders. They are living things because they show volition, because they are not limited in direction of travel, because they can change their form—because they *retain their identity;* two signals never come

Fredric Brown

together on the same radio or conflict with one another. They follow one another, but do not come simultaneously. They do not blend or heterodyne as signals on the same wave length would ordinarily do. They follow laws and rules of their own. They are *not* merely radio waves."

"But, professor, are they intelligent beings?"

Professor Helmetz took off his glasses and polished them thoughtfully. He said, at length, "I doubt if we shall ever know. The intelligence of such beings, if any, would be on such a completely different plane from ours that there would be no common point from which we could start intercourse. We are material; they are immaterial. I do not think there can ever be common ground between us."

"But if they are intelligent at all, professor—"

"Ants are intelligent, after a fashion. Even if one calls it instinct that enables them to do such marvelous things, still instinct is a form of intelligence. Yet we cannot communicate with ants; we shall be less likely to communicate with the invaders. The difference in type between ant-intelligence and ours would be nothing to the difference in type between the intelligence of the invaders and our own. What *could* we have to say to one another?"

The professor must have had something there. Communication with the vaders—a clipped form, of course, of *invaders*—was never established.

Radio stocks stabilized on the exchange. Until, a day after the midnight lecture, someone asked Dr. Helmetz the sixty-four-dollar question and the newspapers published his answer:

"Resume broadcasting? I don't know. Not until the invaders go away, and why should they? Unless, of course, radio communication is perfected on some other planet in some other galaxy, and they're attracted there."

"And if they did go away—?"

"Oh, they'd be back when we started to broadcast again."

Radio stocks dropped to practically zero in an hour. There wasn't any frenzied scene on the Exchange, however; no frenzied selling, because there was no buying, frenzied or otherwise. No radio stocks exchanged hands.

Radio musicians took jobs in theaters, taverns and the like. And failed completely to fulfill the increased demand for talent. With radio out, other forms of entertainment boomed.

Magazine sales boomed. Movies boomed. Vaudeville was coming back. Everything boomed except radio.

"One down," said George Bailey. The bartender asked what he meant.

"I dunno, Hank. I got a hunch."

"What kind of hunch?"

"I don't even know that. Shake me up one more of those, and I'll go home."

The electric shaker wouldn't work, and Hank had to shake it up by hand.

"Exercise; that's what you need," said George. "Take some of that fat off you."

Hank grunted and the ice tinkled merrily as he tilted the shaker to pour out the drink.

George Bailey drank it leisurely and strolled out into an April thundershower. He stood under the awning, and watched for a taxi. An old man was standing before him.

"Some weather," George said.

The old man grinned at him. "You noticed it?"

"Huh? Noticed what?"

"Just watch a while, mister. Just watch a while."

The old man moved on. George stood there quite a while—for no cab went by empty—before he got it. His jaw fell down a trifle, and then he closed his mouth and went back into the tavern. He went into a phone booth and called Pete Mulvaney.

He got three wrong numbers and lost four nickels before he got Pete. Pete's voice said, "Yeah?"

"George Bailey, Pete. Listen, the weather. Notice it?"

"Yes. What's it mean, you want to know. So do I. You tell me. I think it's—"

A crackling sound on the wire blurred it out.

"Hey, Pete. You there?"

The sound of a violin. Pete Mulvaney didn't play violin.

"Hey, Pete. What in—"

Pete's voice again. "Come on over, George. This isn't going to last long. Bring—"

A buzzing noise and then a voice that was not Pete's said, "—come to Carnegie Hall. The best tunes of all come to Carnegie Hall. Yes, the best tunes of all come to Car—"

George slammed down the receiver.

He walked through the rain to Pete's place. On the way he bought a bottle of Scotch. Pete had started to tell him to bring something, and maybe, he figured, that was what it was.

It was.

They poured a drink apiece and lifted them. The lights flickered briefly, went out, and then on again.

"No lightning," said George. "No lightning and pretty soon no lighting. They're taking over the telephone. What do they do with lightning, though?"

"Eat it maybe."

"No lightning," said George. "I can get by without a telephone, and candles and oil lamps aren't bad for lights, but I'm going to miss lightning. I *like* lightning."

Pete Mulvaney leaned back in his chair. He said, "Electric lights, electric toasters, electric hair-curlers, vacuum cleaners. Electric power, and—automobiles and airplanes and Diesel-engined boats. George, do you know no gasoline engine can work without electricity?"

"Huh? For a starter, sure, but can't it be cranked by hand?"

"Yes, but the *spark.*"

"Yes, the spark. Hey, how about these new rocket planes? Those, too?"

"Those, too."

"Movies?"

"Definitely, movies. You couldn't work a projector with an oil lamp. You need concentrated light for that. And sound-tracks—well, that's electricity *per se*."

George Bailey shook his head slowly. "All right, scratch movies. Streetcars. Trucks, tanks, toasters— See what it means, Pete?"

Pete poured another drink. "It means we're going back to the original source of horsepower. Horses. If you want to invest, buy horses. Particularly mares; mares are going to be worth their weight in gold."

"Hey, though, there are steam engines. Locomotives."

Pete Mulvaney nodded. "The iron horse. We'll be back to it for the long hauls, and back to Dobbin for the short ones. Can you ride?"

George sipped his drink slowly. "Used to when I was a kid. Guess I can learn again. Say, it'll be fun. And say—"

"What?"

"Used to play cornet when I was a kid. Think I'll get one and learn again. That'll be fun, too. And maybe I'll hole in somewhere and write that nov— Say, what about printing?"

"They printed books long before electricity. Take a while to readjust the printing industry, but there'll be books and magazines, all right."

George Bailey grinned and got up. He walked over to the window and looked out and down into the storm. A streetcar was stalled in the middle of the block outside. Behind him, the lights flickered again. An automobile stopped, then started more slowly, stopped again.

A neon light across the way suddenly went dark.

He looked up at the sky, and sipped his drink.

"No lightning," he said. He was going to *miss* the lightning.

The changeover, for a wonder, went smoothly.

The government, having had experience of a multiplicity of divided authorities, created one board with practically unlimited authority, and under it three subsidiary boards. The main board, called the Economic Readjustment Bureau, had only seven members and its job was to co-ordinate the efforts of the three subsidiary boards and to decide, quickly and without delay, any jurisdictional disputes among them.

First of the three subsidary boards was the Transportation Bureau. It immediately took over, temporarily, the railroads. It ordered Diesel engines run on sidings and left there, organized use of the steam locomotives and solved the problems of railroading *sans* telegraphy and electric signals. It dictated, then, what should be transported: food coming first, coal and fuel oil second, and essential manufactured articles in the order of their relative importance. Carload after carload of new radios, electric stoves, refrigerators, and such useless articles were dumped unceremoniously alongside the tracks, to be salvaged for scrap-metal later.

All horses were declared wards of the government, graded according to capabilities, and put to work or to stud. Draft horses were used for only the most essential kinds of hauling. The breeding program was given the fullest possible emphasis; the bureau estimated that the equine population would double in two years, quadruple in three, and that within six or seven years there would be a horse in every garage in the country.

Farmers, deprived temporarily of their horses, and with their tractors rusting in the fields, were instructed how to use cattle for plowing and other work about the farm, including light hauling.

The second board, the Manpower Relocation Bureau, functioned just as one would deduce from its title. It handled unemployment benefits for the millions thrown temporarily out of work and helped relocate them—not too difficult a task considering the tremendously increased demand for hand labor in many fields. In May of 1947 thirty-five million employables were out of work; in October, fifteen million; by May of 1948, five million. By 1949 the situation was completely in hand and competitive demand was already beginning to raise wages.

The third board had the most difficult job of the three. It was called the Factory Readjustment Bureau. It coped with the stupendous task of converting factories filled with electrically operated machinery and, for the most part, tooled for the production of other electrically operated machinery, over for the production, without electricity, of essential nonelectrical articles.

The few available stationary steam engines worked twenty-four-hour shifts in those early days, and the first thing they were given to do was the running of lathes and stampers and planers and millers working on turning out more stationary steam engines, of all sizes. These, in turn, were first put to work making still more steam engines. The number of steam engines grew by squares and cubes, as did the number of horses put to stud. The principle was the same. One might—and many did—refer to those early steam engines as stud horses. At any rate, there was no lack of metal for them. The factories were filled with nonconvertible machinery waiting to be melted down.

Only when steam engines—the basis of the new factory economy—were in full production, were they assigned to running machinery for the manufacture of other articles. Oil lamps, clothing, coal stoves, oil stoves, bathtubs and bedsteads.

Not quite all of the big factories were converted. For while the conversion period went on, individual handicrafts sprang up in thousands of places. Little one- and two-man shops sprang up, making and repairing furniture, shoes, candles, all sorts of things that *could* be made without complex machinery. At first these small shops made small fortunes because they had no competition from heavy industry. Later, they bought small steam engines to run small machines and held their own, growing with the boom that came with a return to normal employment and buying power, increasing gradually in size until many of them rivaled the bigger factories in output and beat them in quality.

There *was* suffering, during the period of economic readjustment, but less than

Fredric Brown

there had been during the great depression of the early 1930s. And the recovery was quicker.

The reason was obvious: In combating the depression, the government was working in the dark. They didn't know its cause—rather, they knew a thousand conflicting theories of its cause—and they didn't know the cure. They were hampered by the idea that the thing was temporary and would cure itself if left alone. Briefly and frankly, they didn't know what it was all about and while they experimented, it snowballed.

But the situation that faced the country—and all other countries—in 1947 was clear-cut and obvious. No more electricity. Readjust for steam and horsepower.

As simple and clear as that, and no ifs or ands or buts. And the whole people—except for the usual scattering of cranks—back of them.

By 1951—

It was a rainy day in April and George Bailey was waiting under the sheltering roof of the little railroad station at Blakestown, Connecticut, to see who might come in on the 3:14.

It chugged in at 3:25 and came to a panting stop, three coaches and a baggage car. The baggage car door opened and a sack of mail was handed out and the door closed again. No luggage, so probably no passengers would—

Then at the sight of a tall dark man swinging down from the platform of the rear coach, George Bailey let out a yip of delight. "Pete! Pete Mulvaney! What the devil—"

"Bailey, by all that's holy! What are you doing here?"

George was wringing his hand. "Me? I live here. Two years now. I bought the Blakestown *Weekly* in '49, for a song, and I run it—editor, reporter, and janitor. Got one printer to help me out with that end, and Maisie does the social items. She's—"

"Maisie? Maisie Hetterman?"

"Maisie Bailey now. We got married same time I bought the paper and moved here. What are you doing here, Pete?"

"Business. Just here overnight. See a man named Wilcox."

"Oh, Wilcox. Our local screwball—but don't get me wrong; he's a smart guy all right. Well, you can see him tomorrow. You're coming home with me now, for dinner and to stay overnight. Maisie'll be glad to see you. Come on, my buggy's over here."

"Sure. Finished whatever you were here for?"

"Yep, just to pick up the news on who came in on the train. And *you* came in, so here we go."

They got in the buggy, and George picked up the reins and said "Giddap, Bessie," to the mare. Then, "What are you doing now, Pete?"

"Research. For a gas-supply company. Been working on a more efficient mantle, one that'll give more light and be less destructible. This fellow Wilcox wrote us he had something along that line; the company sent me up to look it over. If it's what he claims, I'll take him back to New York with me, and let the company lawyers dicker with him."

"How's business, otherwise?"

"Great, George. *Gas;* that's the coming thing. Every *new* home's being piped for it, and plenty of the old ones. How about you?"

"We got it. Luckily we had one of the old Linotypes that ran the metal pot off a gas burner, so it was already piped in. And our home is right over the office and print shop, so all we had to do was pipe it up a flight. Great stuff, gas. How's New York?"

"Fine, George. Down to its last million people, and stabilizing there. No crowding and plenty of room for everybody. The *air*—why, it's better than Atlantic City, without gasoline fumes."

"Enough horses to go around yet?"

"Almost. But bicycling's the craze; the factories can't turn out enough to meet the demand. There's a cycling club in almost every block and all the able-bodied cycle to and from work. Doing 'em good, too; a few more years and the doctors will go on short rations."

"You got a bike?"

"Sure, a pre-vader one. Average five miles a day on it, and I eat like a horse."

George Bailey chuckled. "I'll have Maisie include some hay in the dinner. Well, here we are. Whoa, Bessie."

An upstairs window went up, and Maisie looked out and down. She called out, "Hi, Pete!"

"Extra plate, Maisie," George called. "We'll be up soon as I put the horse away and show Pete around downstairs."

He led Pete from the barn into the back door of the newspaper shop. "Our Linotype!" he announced proudly, pointing.

"How's it work? Where's your steam engine?"

George grinned. "Doesn't work yet; we still handset the type. I could get only one steamer and had to use that on the press. But I've got one on order for the Lino, and coming up in a month or so. When we get it, Pop Jenkins, my printer, is going to put himself out of a job by teaching me to run it. With the Linotype going, I can handle the whole thing myself."

"Kind of rough on Pop?"

George shook his head. "Pop eagerly awaits the day. He's sixty-nine and wants to retire. He's just staying on until I can do without him. Here's the press—a honey of a little Miehle; we do some job work on it, too. And this is the office, in front. Messy, but efficient."

Mulvaney looked around him and grinned. "George, I believe you've found your niche. You were cut out for a small-town editor."

"Cut out for it? I'm crazy about it. I have more fun than everybody. Believe it or not, I work like a dog, and like it. Come on upstairs."

On the stairs, Pete asked, "And the novel you were going to write?"

"Half done, and it isn't bad. But it isn't the novel I was going to write; I was a cynic then. Now—"

"George, I think the waveries were your best friends."

"Waveries?"

"Lord, how long does it take slang to get from New York out to the sticks? The vaders, of course. Some professor who specializes in studying them described one as a wavery place in the ether, and 'wavery' stuck . . . Hello there, Maisie, my girl. You look like a million."

They ate leisurely, but volubly. Almost apologetically, George brought out beer, in cold bottles. "Sorry, Pete, haven't anything stronger to offer you. But I haven't been drinking lately. Guess—"

"You on the wagon, George?"

"Not on the wagon, exactly. Didn't swear off or anything, but haven't had a drink of strong liquor in almost a year. I don't know why, but—"

"I do," said Pete Mulvaney. "I know exactly why you don't—because I don't drink much either, for the same reason. We don't drink because we don't *have* to . . . say, isn't that a *radio* over there?"

George chuckled. "A souvenir. Wouldn't sell it for a fortune. Once in a while I like to look at it and think of the awful guff I used to sweat out for it. And then I go over and click the switch and nothing happens. Just silence. Silence is the most wonderful thing in the world, sometimes, Pete. Of course I couldn't do that if there was any juice, because I'd get vaders then. I suppose they're still doing business at the same old stand?"

"Yep, the Research Bureau checks daily. They try to get up current with a little generator run by a steam turbine. But no dice, the vaders suck it up as fast as it's generated."

"Suppose they'll ever go away?"

Mulvaney shrugged. "Helmetz thinks not. He thinks they propagate in proportion to the available electricity. Even if the development of radio broadcasting somewhere else in the Universe would attract them there, some would stay here—and multiply like flies the minute we tried to use electricity again. And meanwhile, they'll live on the static electricity in the air. What do you do evenings up here?"

"Do? Read, write, visit with one another, go to the amateur groups—Maisie's chairman of the Blakestown Players, and I play bit parts in it. With the movies out, everybody goes in for theatricals and we've found some real talent. And there's the chess-and-checker club, and cycle trips and picnics . . . there isn't time enough. Not to mention music. Everybody plays an instrument, or is trying to."

"You?"

"Sure, cornet. First cornet in the Silver Concert Band, with solo parts. And— Good heavens! Tonight's rehearsal, and we're giving a concert Sunday afternoon. I hate to desert you, but—"

"Can't I come around and sit in? I've got my flute in the brief case here, and—"

"Flute? We're short on flutes. Bring that around and Si Perkins, our director, will practically Shanghai you into staying over for the concert Sunday—and it's only three days, so why not? And get it out now; we'll play a few old-timers to warm up. Hey, Maisie, skip those dishes and come on in to the piano!''

While Pete Mulvaney went to the guest room to get his flute from the brief case, George Bailey picked up his cornet from the top of the piano and blew a soft, plaintive little minor run on it. Clear as a bell; his lip was in good shape tonight.

And with the shining silver thing in his hand he wandered over to the window and stood looking out into the night. It was dusk out and the rain had stopped.

A high-stepping horse *clop-clop*ped by and the bell of a bicycle jangled. Somebody across the street was strumming a guitar and singing. He took a deep breath and let it out slowly.

The scent of spring was soft and sweet in the moist air.

Peace and dusk and distant rolling thunder. Thunder, but— ''I wish,'' he said softly, ''there was a bit of lightning. I *miss* the lightning.'' ■

"HOBBYIST"
Eric Frank Russell

THE SHIP ARCED OUT OF A GOLDEN SKY and landed with a whoop and a wallop that cut down a mile of lush vegetation. Another half mile of growths turned black and drooped to ashes under the final flicker of the tail rocket blasts. That arrival was spectacular, full of verve, and worthy of four columns in any man's paper. But the nearest sheet was distant by a goodly slice of a lifetime, and there was none to record what this far corner of the cosmos regarded as the pettiest of events. So the ship squatted tired and still at the foremost end of the ashy blast-track and the sky glowed down and the green world brooded solemnly all around.

Within the transpex control dome, Steve Ander sat and thought things over. It was his habit to think things over carefully. Astronauts were not the impulsive daredevils so dear to the stereopticon-loving public. They couldn't afford to be. The hazards of the profession required an infinite capacity for cautious, contemplative thought. Five minutes consideration had prevented many a collapsed lung, many a leaky heart, many a fractured frame. Steve valued his skeleton. He wasn't conceited about it and he'd no reason to believe it in any way superior to anyone else's skeleton. But he'd had it a long time, found it quite satisfactory, and had an intense desire to keep it—intact.

Therefore, while the tail tubes cooled off with their usual creaking contractions, he sat in the control seat, stared through the dome with eyes made unseeing by deep preoccupation, and performed a few thinks.

Firstly, he'd made a rough estimate of this world during his hectic approach. As nearly as he could judge, it was ten times the size of Terra. But his weight didn't seem abnormal. Of course, one's notions of weight tended to be somewhat wild when for some weeks one's own weight has shot far up or far down in between periods of weightlessness. The most reasonable estimate had to be based on muscular reaction. If you felt as sluggish as a Saturnian sloth, your weight was way up. If you felt as powerful as Angus McKittrick's bull, your weight was down.

Normal weight meant Terrestrial mass despite this planet's tenfold volume. That meant light plasma. And that meant lack of heavy elements. No thorium. No nickel. No nickel-thorium alloy. Ergo, no getting back. The Kingston-Kane atomic motors demanded fuel in the form of ten-gauge nickel-thorium alloy wire fed directly into the vaporizers. Denatured plutonium would do, but it didn't occur in natural form, and it had to be made. He had three yards nine and a quarter inches of nickel-thorium left on the feed-spool. Not enough. He was here for keeps.

A wonderful thing, logic. You could start from the simple premise that when you were seated your behind was no flatter than usual, and work your way to the inevitable conclusion that you were a wanderer no more. You'd become a native. Destiny had you tagged as suitable for the status of oldest inhabitant.

Steve pulled an ugly face and said, "Darn!"

The face didn't have to be pulled far. Nature had given said pan a good start. That is to say, it wasn't handsome. It was a long, lean, nutbrown face with pronounced jaw muscles, prominent cheekbones, and a thin, hooked nose. This, with his dark eyes and black hair, gave him a hawklike appearance. Friends talked to him about tepees and tomahawks whenever they wanted him to feel at home.

Well, he wasn't going to feel at home any more; not unless this brooding jungle held intelligent life dopey enough to swap ten-gauge nickel-thorium wire for a pair of old boots. Or unless some dopey search party was intelligent enough to pick this cosmic dust mote out of a cloud of motes, and took him back. He estimated this as no less than a million-to-one chance. Like spitting at the Empire State hoping to hit a cent-sized mark on one of its walls.

Reaching for his everflo stylus and the ship's log, he opened the log, looked absently at some of the entries.

"Eighteenth day: The spatial convulsion has now flung me past rotalrange of Rigel. Am being tossed into uncharted regions."

"Twenty-fourth day: Arm of convulsive now tails back seven parsecs. Robot recorder now out of gear. Angle of throw changed seven times today."

"Twenty-ninth day: Now beyond arm of the convulsive sweep and regaining control. Speed far beyond range of the astrometer. Applying braking rockets cautiously. Fuel reserve: fourteen hundred yards."

"Thirty-seventh day: Making for planetary system now within reach."

He scowled, his jaw muscles lumped, and he wrote slowly and legibly, "Thirty-ninth day: Landed on planet unknown, primary unknown, galactic area standard reference and sector numbers unknown. No cosmic formations were recognizable when observed shortly before landing. Angles of offshoot and speed of transit not recorded, and impossible to estimate. Condition of ship: workable. Fuel reserve: three and one quarter yards."

Closing the log, he scowled again, rammed the stylus into its desk-grip, and muttered, "Now to check on the outside air and then see how the best girl's doing."

The Radson register had three simple dials. The first recorded outside pressure at thirteen point seven pounds, a reading he observed with much satisfaction. The second said that oxygen content was high. The third had a bi-colored dial, half white, half red, and its needle stood in the middle of the white.

"Breathable," he grunted, clipping down the register's lid. Crossing the tiny control room, he slid aside a metal panel, looked into the padded compartment behind. "Coming out, Beauteous?" he asked.

"Steve loves Laura?" inquired a plaintive voice.

"You bet he does!" he responded with becoming passion. He shoved an arm into the compartment, brought out a large, gaudily colored macaw. "Does Laura love Steve?"

"Hey-hey!" cackled Laura harshly. Climbing up his arm, the bird perched on his shoulder. He could feel the grip of its powerful claws. It regarded him with a beady and brilliant eye, then rubbed its crimson head against his left ear. "Hey-hey! Time flies!"

"Don't mention it," he reproved. "There's plenty to remind me of the fact without you chipping in."

Reaching up, he scratched her poll while she stretched and bowed with absurd delight. He was fond of Laura. She was more than a pet. She was a bona fide member of the crew, issued with her own rations and drawing her own pay. Every probe ship had a crew of two: one man, one macaw. When he'd first heard of it, the practice had seemed crazy—but when he got the reasons, it made sense.

"Lonely men, probing beyond the edge of the charts, get queer psychological troubles. They need an anchor to Earth. A macaw provides the necessary companionship—and more! It's the space-hardiest bird we've got, its weight is negligible, it can talk and amuse, it can fend for itself when necessary. On land, it will often sense dangers before you do. Any strange fruit or food it may eat is safe for you to eat. Many a man's life has been saved by his macaw. Look after yours, my boy, and it'll look after you!"

Yes, they looked after each other, Terrestrials both. It was almost a symbiosis of the spaceways. Before the era of astronavigation nobody had thought of such an arrangement, though it had been done before. Miners and their canaries.

Moving over to the miniature air lock, he didn't bother to operate the pump. It wasn't necessary with so small a difference between internal and external pressures. Opening both doors, he let a little of his higher-pressured air sigh out, stood on the rim of the lock, jumped down. Laura fluttered from his shoulder as he leaped, followed him with a flurry of wings, got her talons into his jacket as he staggered upright.

The pair went around the ship, silently surveying its condition. Front braking nozzles O.K., rear steering flares O.K., tail propulsion tubes O.K. All were badly scored but still usable. The skin of the vessel likewise was scored but intact. Three months supply of food and maybe a thousand yards of wire could get her home, theoretically. But only theoretically. Steve had no delusions about the matter. The odds were still against him even if given the means to move. How do you navigate from you-don't-know-where to you-don't-know-where? Answer: you stroke a rabbit's foot and probably arrive you-don't-know-where-else.

"Well," he said, rounding the tail, "it's something in which to live. It'll save us building a shanty. Way back on Terra they want fifty thousand smackers for an all-metal, streamlined bungalow, so I guess we're mighty lucky. I'll make a garden here, and a rockery there, and build a swimming pool out back. You can wear a pretty frock and do all the cooking."

"Yawk!" said Laura derisively.

Turning, he had a look at the nearest vegetation. It was of all heights, shapes and sizes, of all shades of green with a few tending toward blueness. There was something peculiar about the stuff but he was unable to decide where the strangeness lay. It wasn't that the growths were alien and unfamiliar—one expected that on every new world—but an underlying something which they shared in common. They had a vague, shadowy air of being not quite right in some basic respect impossible to define.

A plant grew right at his feet. It was green in color, a foot high, and monocotyledonous. Looked at as a thing in itself, there was nothing wrong with it. Near to it flourished a bush of darker hue, a yard high, with green, firlike needles in lieu of leaves, and pale, waxy berries scattered over it. That, too, was innocent enough when studied apart from its neighbors. Beside it grew a similar plant, differing only in that its needles were longer and its berries a bright pink. Beyond these towered a cactuslike object dragged out of somebody's drunken dreams, and beside it stood an umbrella-frame which had taken root and produced little purple pods. Individually, they were acceptable. Collectively, they made the discerning mind search anxiously for it knew not what.

That eerie feature had Steve stumped. Whatever it was, he couldn't nail it down. There was something stranger than the mere strangeness of new forms of plant life, and that was all. He dismissed the problem with a shrug. Time enough to trouble about such matters after he'd dealt with others more urgent such as, for example, the location and purity of the nearest water supply.

A mile away lay a lake of some liquid that might be water. He'd seen it glittering in the sunlight as he'd made his descent, and he'd tried to land fairly near to it. If it wasn't water, well, it'd be just his tough luck and he'd have to look some place else. At worst, the tiny fuel reserve would be enough to permit one circumnavigation of the planet before the ship became pinned down forever. Water he must have if he wasn't going to end up imitating the mummy of Rameses the Second.

Reaching high, he grasped the rim of the port, dexterously muscled himself upward and through it. For a minute he moved around inside the ship, then reappeared with a four-gallon freezocan which he tossed to the ground. Then he dug out his popgun, a belt of explosive shells, and let down the folding ladder from lock to surface. He'd need that ladder. He could muscle himself up through a hole seven feet high, but not with fifty pounds of can and water.

Finally, he locked both the inner and outer air lock doors, skipped down the ladder, picked up the can. From the way he'd made his landing the lake should be directly bow-on relative to the vessel, and somewhere the other side of those distant trees. Laura took a fresh grip on his shoulder as he started off. The can swung from his left hand. His right hand rested warily on the gun. He was perpendicular on this world instead of horizontal on another because, on two occasions, his hand had been ready on the gun, and because it was the most nervous hand he possessed.

The going was rough. It wasn't so much that the terrain was craggy as the fact that impeding growths got in his way. At one moment he was stepping over an ankle-high shrub, the next he was facing a burly plant struggling to become a tree. Behind the plant would be a creeper, then a natural zareba of thorns, a fuzz of fine moss, followed by a giant fern. Progress consisted of stepping over one item, ducking beneath a second, going around a third, and crawling under a fourth.

It occurred to him, belatedly, that if he'd planted the ship tail-first to the lake instead of bow-on, or if he'd let the braking rockets blow after he'd touched down, he'd have saved himself much twisting and dodging. All this obstructing stuff would have been reduced to ashes for at least half the distance to the lake—together with any venomous life it might conceal.

That last thought rang like an alarm bell within his mind just as he doubled up to pass a low-swung creeper. On Venus were creepers that coiled and constricted, swiftly, viciously. Macaws played merry hell if taken within fifty yards of them. It was a comfort to know that, this time, Laura was riding his shoulder unperturbed—but he kept the hand on the gun.

The elusive peculiarity of the planet's vegetation bothered him all the more as he progressed through it. His inability to discover and name this unnamable queerness nagged at him as he went on. A frown of self-disgust was on his lean face when he dragged himself free of a clinging bush and sat on a rock in a tiny clearing.

Dumping the can at his feet, he glowered at it and promptly caught a glimpse of something bright and shining a few feet beyond the can. He raised his gaze. It was then he saw the beetle.

The creature was the biggest of its kind ever seen by human eyes. There were other things bigger, of course, but not of this type. Crabs, for instance. But this was no crab. The beetle ambling purposefully across the clearing was large enough to give any crab a severe inferiority complex, but it was a genuine, twenty-four-karat beetle. And a beautiful one. Like a scarab.

Except that he clung to the notion that little bugs were vicious and big ones companionable, Steve had no phobia about insects. The amiability of large ones was a theory inherited from schoolkid days when he'd been the doting owner of a three-inch stag-beetle afflicted with the name of Edgar.

So he knelt beside the creeping giant, placed his hand palm upward in its path. It investigated the hand with waving feelers, climbed onto his palm, paused there ruminatively. It shone with a sheen of brilliant metallic blue and it weighed about three pounds. He jogged it on his hand to get its weight, then put it down, let it wander on. Laura watched it go with a sharp but incurious eye.

"*Scarabaeus Anderii.*" Steve said with glum satisfaction. "I pin my name on him—but nobody'll ever know it!"

"Dinna fash y'rsel'!" shouted Laura in a hoarse voice imported straight from Aberdeen. "Dinna fash! Stop chunnerin', wumman! Y'gie me a pain ahint ma sporran! Dinna—"

"Shut up!" Steve jerked his shoulder, momentarily unbalancing the bird. "Why d'you pick up that barbaric dialect quicker than anything else, eh?"

"McGillicuddy," shrieked Laura with ear-splitting relish. "McGilli-Gilli-Gilli-cuddy! The great black —!" It ended with a word that pushed Steve's eyebrows into his hair and surprised even the bird itself. Filming its eyes with amazement, it tightened its claw-hold on his shoulder, opened the eyes, emitted a couple of raucous clucks, and joyfully repeated, "The great black —"

It didn't get the chance to complete the new and lovely word. A violent jerk of the shoulder unseated it in the nick of time and it fluttered to the ground, squawking protestingly. *Scarabaeus Anderii* lumbered out from behind a bush, his blue armor glistening as if freshly polished, and stared reprovingly at Laura.

Then something fifty years away released a snort like the trump of doom and took one step that shook the earth. *Scarabaeus Anderii* took refuge under a projecting root. Laura made an agitated swoop for Steve's shoulder and clung there desperately. Steve's gun was out and pointing northward before the bird had found its perch. Another step. The ground quivered.

Silence for awhile. Steve continued to stand like a statue. Then came a monstrous whistle more forceful than that of a locomotive blowing off steam. Something squat and wide and of tremendous length charged headlong through the half-concealing vegetation while the earth trembled beneath its weight.

Its mad onrush carried it blindly twenty yards to Steve's right, the gun swinging to cover its course, but not firing. Steve caught an extended glimpse of a slate-gray bulk with a serrated ridge on its back which, despite the thing's pace, took long to pass. It seemed several times the length of a fire ladder.

Bushes were flung roots topmost and small trees whipped aside as the creature pounded grimly onward in a straight line which carried it far past the ship and into the dim distance. It left behind a tattered swathe wide enough for a first-class road. Then the reverberations of its mighty tonnage died out, and it was gone.

Steve used his left hand to pull out a handkerchief and wipe the back of his neck. He kept the gun in his right hand. The explosive shells in that gun were somewhat wicked; any one of them could deprive a rhinoceros of a hunk of meat weighing two hundred pounds. If a man caught one, he just strewed himself over the landscape. By the looks of that slate-colored galloper, it would need half a dozen shells to feel incommoded. A seventy-five-millimeter bazooka would be more effective for kicking it in the back teeth, but probe ship boys don't tote around such artillery. Steve finished the mopping, put the handkerchief back, picked up the can.

Laura said pensively, "I want my mother."

He scowled, made no reply, set out toward the lake. Her feathers still ruffled, Laura rode his shoulder and lapsed into surly silence.

The stuff in the lake was water, cold, faintly green and a little bitter to the taste. Coffee would camouflage the flavor. If anything, it might improve the coffee since he liked his java bitter, but the stuff would have to be tested before absorbing it in any quantity. Some poisons were accumulative. It wouldn't do to guzzle gayly while building up a death-dealing reserve of lead, for instance. Filling the freezocan, he lugged it to the ship in hundred-yard stages. The swathe helped; it made an easier path to within short distance of the ship's tail. He was perspiring freely by the time he reached the base of the ladder.

Once inside the vessel, he relocked both doors, opened the air vents, started the auxiliary lighting-set and plugged in the percolator, using water out of his depleted reserve supply. The golden sky had dulled to orange, with violet streamers creeping upward from the horizon. Looking at it through the transpex dome, he found that the perpetual haze still effectively concealed the sinking sun. A brighter area to one side was all that indicated its position. He'd need his lights soon.

Pulling out the collapsible table, he jammed its supporting leg into place, plugged into its rim the short rod which was Laura's official seat. She claimed the perch immediately, watched him beadily as he set out her meal of water, melon seeds, sunflower seeds, pecans, and unshelled oleo nuts. Her manners were anything but ladylike and she started eagerly, without waiting for him.

A deep frown lay across his brown, muscular features as he sat at the table, poured out his coffee and commenced to eat. It persisted through the meal, was still there when he lit a cigarette and stared speculatively up at the dome.

Presently, he murmured, "I've seen the biggest bug that ever was. I've seen a few other bugs. There were a couple of little ones under a creeper. One was long and brown and many-legged, like an earwig. The other was round and black, with little red dots on its wing cases. I've seen a tiny purple spider and a tinier green one of different shape, also a bug that looked like an aphid. But not an ant."

"Ant, ant," hooted Laura. She dropped a piece of oleo nut, climbed down after it. "Yawk!" she added from the floor.

"Nor a bee."

"Bee," echoed Laura, companionably. "Bee-ant. Laura loves Steve."

Still keeping his attention on the dome, he went on, "And what's cockeyed about the plants is equally cockeyed about the bugs. I wish I could place it. Why can't I? Maybe I'm going nuts already."

"Laura loves nuts."

"I know it, you technicolored belly!" said Steve rudely.

And at that point night fell with a silent bang. The gold and orange and violet abruptly were swamped with deep, impenetrable blackness devoid of stars or any random gleam. Except for greenish glowings on the instrument panel, the control room was stygian, with Laura swearing steadily on the floor.

Putting out a hand, Steve switched on the indirect lighting. Laura got to her perch with the rescued titbit, concentrated on the job of dealing with it and let him sink back into his thoughts.

"*Scarabaeus Anderii* and a pair of smaller bugs and a couple of spiders, all different.

At the other end of the scale, that gigantosaurus. But no ant, or bee. Or rather, no ants, no bees." The switch from singular to plural stirred his back hairs queerly. In some vague way, he felt that he'd touched the heart of the mystery. "No ant—no ants," he thought. "No bee—no bees." Almost he had it—but still it evaded him.

Giving it up for the time being, he cleared the table, did a few minor chores. After that, he drew a standard sample from the freezocan, put it through its paces. The bitter flavor he identified as being due to the presence of magnesium sulphate in quantity far too small to prove embarrassing. Drinkable—that was something! Food, drink, and shelter were the three essentials of survival. He'd enough of the first for six or seven weeks. The lake and the ship were his remaining guarantees of life.

Finding the log, he entered the day's report, bluntly, factually, without any embroidery. Partway through, he found himself stuck for a name for the planet. *Ander*, he decided, would cost him dear if the million-to-one chance put him back among the merciless playmates of the Probe Service. O.K. for a bug, but not for a world. *Laura* wasn't so hot, either—especially when you knew Laura. It wouldn't be seemly to name a big, gold planet after an oversized parrot. Thinking over the golden aspect of this world's sky, he hit upon the name of *Oro*, promptly made the christening authoritative by entering it in his log.

By the time he'd finished, Laura had her head buried deep under one wing. Occasionally she teetered and swung erect again. It always fascinated him to watch how her balance was maintained even in her slumbers. Studying her fondly, he remembered that unexpected addition to her vocabulary. This shifted his thoughts to a fiery-headed and fierier-tongued individual named Menzies, the sworn foe of another volcano named McGillicuddy. If ever the opportunity presented itself, he decided, the educative work of said Menzies was going to be rewarded with a bust on the snoot.

Sighing, he put away the log, wound up the forty-day chronometer, opened his folding bunk and lay down upon it. His hand switched off the lights. Ten years back, a first landing would have kept him awake all night in dithers of excitement. He'd got beyond that now. He'd done it often enough to have grown phlegmatic about it. His eyes closed in preparation for a good night's sleep, and he did sleep—for two hours.

What brought him awake within that short time he didn't know, but suddenly he found himself sitting bolt upright on the edge of the bunk, his ears and nerves stretched to their utmost, his legs quivering in a way they'd never done before. His whole body fizzed with that queer mixture of palpitation and shock which follows narrow escape from disaster.

This was something not within previous experience. Sure and certain in the intense darkness, his hand sought and found his gun. He cuddled the butt in his palm while his mind strove to recall a possible nightmare, though he knew he was not given to nightmares.

Laura moved restlessly on her perch, not truly awake, yet not asleep, and this was unusual in her.

Rejecting the dream theory, he stood on the bunk, looked out through the dome. Blackness, the deepest, darkest, most impenetrable blackness it was possible to conceive. And silence! The outside world slumbered in the blackness and the silence as in a sable shroud.

Yet never before had he felt so wide awake in this, his normal sleeping time. Puzzled, he turned slowly round to take in the full circle of unseeable view, and at one point he halted. The surrounding darkness was not complete. In the distance beyond the ship's tail moved a tall, stately glow. How far off it might be was not possible to estimate, but the sight of it stirred his soul and caused his heart to leap.

Uncontrollable emotions were not permitted to master his disciplined mind. Narrowing his eyes, he tried to discern the nature of the glow while his mind sought the reason why the mere sight of it should make him twang like a harp. Bending down, he felt at the head of the bunk, found a leather case, extracted a pair of powerful night glasses. The glow was still moving, slowly, deliberately, from right to left. He got the glasses on it, screwed the lenses into focus, and the phenomenon leaped into closer view.

The thing was a great column of golden haze much like that of the noonday sky except that small, intense gleams of silver sparkled within it. It was a shaft of lustrous mist bearing a sprinkling of tiny stars. It was like nothing known to or recorded by any form of life lower than the gods. But was it life?

It moved, though its mode of locomotion could not be determined. Self-motivation is the prime symptom of life. It could be life, conceivably though not credibly, from the Terrestrial viewpoint. Consciously, he preferred to think it a strange and purely local feature comparable with Saharan sanddevils. Subconsciously, he knew it was life, tall and terrifying.

He kept the glasses on it while slowly it receded into the darkness, foreshortening with increasing distance and gradually fading from view. To the very last the observable field shifted and shuddered as he failed to control the quiver in his hands. And when the sparkling haze had gone, leaving only a pall over his lenses, he sat down on the bunk and shivered with eerie cold.

Laura was dodging to and fro along her perch, now thoroughly awake and agitated, but he wasn't inclined to switch on the lights and make the dome a beacon in the night. His hand went out, feeling for her in the darkness, and she clambered eagerly onto his wrist, thence to his lap. She was fussy and demonstrative, pathetically yearning for comfort and companionship. He scratched her poll and fondled her while she pressed close against his chest with funny little crooning noises. For some time he soothed her and, while doing it, fell asleep. Gradually he slumped backward on the bunk. Laura perched on his forearm, clucked tiredly, put her head under a wing.

There was no further awakening until the outer blackness disappeared and the sky again sent its golden glow pouring through the dome. Steve got up, stood on the bunk, had a good look over the surrounding terrain. It remained precisely the same as it had been the day before. Things stewed within his mind while he got his breakfast, especially the jumpiness he'd experienced in the nighttime. Laura also was subdued and quiet. Only once before had she been like that—which was when he'd traipsed through the Venusian section of the Panplanetary Zoo and had shown her a crested eagle. The eagle had stared at her with contemptuous dignity.

Though he'd all the time in his life, he now felt a peculiar urge to hasten. Getting the gun and the freezocan, he made a full dozen trips to the lake, wasting no minutes, nor stopping to study the still enigmatic plants and bugs. It was late in the afternoon by the time he'd filled the ship's fifty-gallon reservoir, and had the satisfaction of knowing that he'd got a drinkable quota to match his food supply.

There had been no sign of gigantosaurus or any other animal. Once he'd seen something flying in the far distance, birdlike or batlike. Laura had cocked a sharp eye at it but betrayed no undue interest. Right now she was more concerned with a new fruit. Steve sat in the rim of the outer lock door, his legs dangling, and watched her clambering over a small tree thirty yards away. The gun lay in his lap; he was ready to take a crack at anything which might be ready to take a crack at Laura.

The bird sampled the tree's fruit, a crop resembling blue-shelled lychee nuts. She ate one with relish, grabbed another. Steve lay back in the lock, stretched to reach a bag, then dropped to the ground and went across to the tree. He tried a nut. Its flesh was soft, juicy, sweet and citrous. He filled the bag with the fruit, slung it into the ship.

Nearby stood another tree, not quite the same, but very similar. It bore nuts like the first except that they were larger. Picking one, he offered it to Laura, who tried it, spat it out in disgust. Picking a second, he slit it, licked the flesh gingerly. As far as he could tell, it was the same. Evidently he couldn't tell far enough: Laura's diagnosis said it was not the same. The difference, too subtle for him to detect, might be sufficient to roll him up like a hoop and keep him that shape to the unpleasant end. He flung the thing away, went back to his seat in the lock, and ruminated.

That elusive, nagging feature of Oro's plants and bugs could be narrowed down to these two nuts. He felt sure of that. If he could discover why—parrotwise—one nut was a nut while the other nut was not, he'd have his finger right on the secret. The more he thought about those similar fruits the more he felt that, in sober fact, his finger was on the secret already—but he lacked the power to lift it and see what lay beneath.

Tantalizingly, his mulling over the subject landed him the same place as before; namely, nowhere. It got his dander up, and he went back to the trees, subjected both to close examination. His sense of sight told him that they were different individuals of the same species. Laura's sense of whatchamacallit insisted that they were different species. Ergo, you can't believe the evidence of your eyes. He was aware of that fact, of course, since it was a platitude of the spaceways, but when you couldn't trust your

Eric Frank Russell

optics it was legitimate to try to discover just why you couldn't trust 'em. And he couldn't discover even that!

It soured him so much that he returned to the ship, locked its doors, called Laura back to his shoulder, and set off on a tailward exploration. The rules of first landings were simple and sensible. Go in slowly, come out quickly, and remember that all we want from you is evidence of suitability for human life. Thoroughly explore a small area rather than scout a big one—the mapping parties will do the rest. Use your ship as a base and centralize it where you can live—don't move it unnecessarily. Restrict your trips to a radius representing daylight-reach and lock yourself in after dark.

Was Oro suitable for human life? The unwritten law was that you don't jump to conclusions and say, "Of course! I'm still living, aren't I?" Cameron, who'd plonked his ship on Mithra, for instance, thought he'd found paradise until, on the seventeenth day, he'd discovered the fungoid plague. He'd left like a bat out of hell and had spent three sweaty, swearing days in the Lunar Purification Plant before becoming fit for society. The authorities had vaporized his ship. Mithra had been taboo ever since. Every world a potential trap baited with scenic delight. The job of the Probe Service was to enter the traps and jounce on the springs. Another dollop of real estate for Terra—if nothing broke your neck.

Maybe Oro was loaded for bear. The thing that walked in the night, Steve mused, bore awful suggestion of nonhuman power. So did a waterspout, and whoever heard of anyone successfully wrestling with a waterspout? If this Oro-spout were sentient, so much the worse for human prospects. He'd have to get the measure of it, he decided, even if he had to chase it through the blank avenues of night. Plodding steadily away from the tail, gun in hand, he pondered so deeply that he entirely overlooked the fact that he wasn't on a pukka probe job anyway, and that nothing else remotely human might reach Oro in a thousand years. Even space-boys can be creatures of habit. Their job: to look for death; they were liable to go on looking long after the need had passed, in bland disregard of the certainty that if you look for a thing long enough, ultimately you find it!

The ship's chronometer had given him five hours to darkness. Two and a half hours each way; say ten miles out and ten back. The water had consumed his time. On the morrow, and henceforth, he'd increase the radius to twelve and take it easier.

Then all thoughts fled from his mind as he came to the edge of the vegetation. The stuff didn't dribble out of existence with hardy spurs and offshoots fighting for a hold in suddenly rocky ground. It stopped abruptly, in light loam, as if cut off with a machete, and from where it stopped spread a different crop. The new growths were tiny and crystalline.

He accepted the crystalline crop without surprise, knowing that novelty was the inevitable feature of any new locale. Things were ordinary only by Terrestrial standards. Outside of Terra, nothing was supernormal or abnormal except insofar as they failed to jibe with their own peculiar conditions. Besides, there were crystalline growths on Mars. The one unacceptable feature of the situation was the way in which vegetable growths ended and crystalline ones began. He stepped back to the verge and made another startled survey of the borderline. It was so straight that the sight screwed his brain around. Like a field. A cultivated field. Dead straightness of that sort couldn't be other than artificial. Little beads of moisture popped out on his back.

Squatting on the heel of his right boot, he gazed at the nearest crystals and said to Laura, "Chicken, I think these things got planted. Question is, who planted 'em?"

"McGillicuddy," suggested Laura brightly.

Putting out a finger, he flicked the crystal sprouting near the toe of his boot, a green, branchy object an inch high.

The crystal vibrated and said, *"Zing!"* in a sweet, high voice.

He flicked its neighbor, and that said, *"Zang!"* in lower tone.

He flicked a third. It emitted no note, but broke into a thousand shards.

Standing up, he scratched his head, making Laura fight for a clawhold within the circle of his arm. One zinged and one zanged and one returned to dust. Two nuts. Zings and zangs and nuts. It was right in his grasp if only he could open his hand and look at what he'd got.

Then he lifted his puzzled and slightly ireful gaze, saw something fluttering erratically across the crystal field. It was making for the vegetation. Laura took off with a raucous cackle, her blue and crimson wings beating powerfully. She swooped over the object, frightening it so low that it dodged and sideslipped only a few feet above Steve's head. He saw that it was a large butterfly, frill-winged, almost as gaudy as Laura. The bird swooped again, scaring the insect but not menacing it. He called her back, set out to cross the area ahead. Crystals crunched to powder under his heavy boots as he tramped on.

Half an hour later he was toiling up a steep, crystal-coated slope when his thoughts suddenly jelled and he stopped with such abruptness that Laura spilled from his shoulder and perforce took to wing. She beat round in a circle, came back to her perch, made bitter remarks in an unknown language.

"One of this and one of that," he said. "No twos or threes or dozens. Nothing I've seen has repeated itself. There's only one gigantosaurus, only one *Scarabaeus Anderii*, only one of every other danged thing. Every item is unique, original, and an individual creation in its own right. What does that suggest?"

"McGillicuddy," offered Laura.

"For Pete's sake, forget McGillicuddy."

"For Pete's sake, for Pete's sake," yelled Laura, much taken by the phrase. "The great black—"

Again he upset her in the nick of time, making her take to flight while he continued talking to himself. "It suggests constant and all-pervading mutation. Everything breeds something quite different from itself and there aren't any dominant strains." He frowned at the obvious snag in this theory. "But how the blazes does anything breed? What fertilizes which?"

Eric Frank Russell

"McGilli—," began Laura, then changed her mind and shut up.

"Anyway, if nothing breeds true, it'll be tough on the food problem," he went on. "What's edible on one plant may be a killer on its offspring. Today's fodder is tomorrow's poison. How's a farmer to know what he's going to get? Hey-hey, if I'm guessing right, this planet won't support a couple of hogs."

"No, sir. No hogs. Laura loves hogs."

"Be quiet," he snapped. "Now, what shouldn't support a couple of hogs demonstrably does support gigantosaurus—and any other fancy animals which may be mooching around. It seems crazy to me. On Venus or any other place full of consistent fodder, gigantosaurus would thrive, but here, according to my calculations, the big lunk has no right to be alive. He ought to be dead."

So saying, he topped the rise and found the monster in question sprawling right across the opposite slope. It *was* dead.

The way in which he determined its deadness was appropriately swift, simple and effective. Its enormous bulk lay draped across the full length of the slope and its dragonhead, the size of a lifeboat, pointed toward him. The head had two dull, lackluster eyes like dinner plates. He planted a shell smack in the right eye and a sizable hunk of noggin promptly splashed in all directions. The body did not stir.

There was a shell ready for the other eye should the creature leap to frantic, vengeful life, but the mighty hulk remained supine.

His boots continued to desiccate crystals as he went down the slope, curved a hundred yards off his route to get around the corpse, and trudged up the farther rise. Momentarily, he wasn't much interested in the dead beast. Time was short and he could come again tomorrow, bringing a full-color stereoscopic camera with him. Gigantosaurus would go on record in style, but would have to wait.

This second rise was a good deal higher, and more trying a climb. Its crest represented the approximate limit of this day's trip, and he felt anxious to surmount it before turning back. Humanity's characteristic urge to see what lay over the hill remained as strong as on the day determined ancestors topped the Rockies. He had to have a look, firstly because elevation gave range to the vision, and secondly because of that prowler in the night—and, nearly as he could estimate, the prowler had gone down behind this rise. A column of mist, sucked down from the sky, might move around aimlessly, going nowhere, but instinct maintained that this had been no mere column of mist, and that it was going somewhere.

Where?

Out of breath, he pounded over the crest, looked down into an immense valley, and found the answer.

The crystal growths gave out on the crest, again in a perfectly straight line. Beyond them the light loam, devoid of rock, ran gently down to the valley and up the farther side. Both slopes were sparsely dotted with queer, jellylike lumps of matter which lay and quivered beneath the sky's golden glow.

From the closed end of the valley jutted a great, glistening fabrication, flat-roofed, flat-fronted, with a huge, square hole gaping in its mid-section at front. It looked like a tremendous oblong slab of polished, milk-white plastic half buried endwise in a sandy hill. No decoration disturbed its smooth, gleaming surface. No road led to the hole in front. Somehow, it had the new-old air of a house that struggles to look empty because it is full—of fiends.

Steve's back hairs prickled as he studied it. One thing was obvious—Oro bore intelligent life. One thing was possible—the golden column represented that life. One thing was probable—fleshly Terrestrials and hazy Orons would have difficulty in finding a basis for friendship and co-operation.

Whereas enmity needs no basis.

Curiosity and caution pulled him opposite ways. One urged him down into the valley while the other drove him back, back, while yet there was time. He consulted his watch. Less than three hours to go, within which he had to return to the ship, enter the log, prepare supper. That milky creation was at least two miles away, a good hour's journey there and back. Let it wait. Give it another day and he'd have more time for it, with the benefit of needful thought betweentimes.

Caution triumphed. He investigated the nearest jellyblob. It was flat, a yard in diameter, green, with bluish streaks and many tiny bubbles hiding in its semitrans-parency. The thing pulsated slowly. He poked it with the toe of his boot, and it contracted, humping itself in the middle, then sluggishly relaxed. No amoeba, he decided. A low form of life, but complicated withal. Laura didn't like the object. She skittered off as he bent over it, vented her anger by bashing a few crystals.

This jello dollop wasn't like its nearest neighbor, or like any other. One of each, only one. The same rule: one butterfly of a kind, one bug, one plant, one of these quivering things.

A final stare at the distant mystery down in the valley, then he retraced his steps. When the ship came into sight he speeded up like a gladsome voyager nearing home. There were new prints near the vessel, big, three-toed, deeply impressed spoor which revealed that something large, heavy, and two-legged had wandered past in his absence. Evidently an animal, for nothing intelligent would have meandered on so casually without circling and inspecting the nearby invader from space. He dismissed it from his mind. There was only one thingumbob, he felt certain of that.

Once inside the ship, he relocked the doors, gave Laura her feed, ate his supper. Then he dragged out the log, made his day's entry, had a look around from the dome. Violet streamers once more were creeping upward from the horizon. He frowned at the encompassing vegetation. What sort of stuff had bred all this in the past? What sort of stuff would this breed in the future? How did it progenerate, anyway?

Wholesale radical mutation presupposed modification of genes by hard radiation in persistent and considerable blasts. You shouldn't get hard radiation on lightweight planets—unless it poured in from the sky. Here, it didn't pour from the sky, or from any place else. In fact, there wasn't any.

He was pretty certain of that fact because he'd a special interest in it and had checked up on it. Hard radiation betokened the presence of radioactive elements which, at a pinch, might be usable as fuel. The ship was equipped to detect such stuff. Among the junk was a cosmiray counter, a radium hen, and a gold-leaf electroscope. The hen and the counter hadn't given so much as one heartening cluck, in fact the only clucks had been Laura's. The electroscope he'd charged on landing and its leaves still formed an inverted vee. The air was dry, ionization negligible, and the leaves didn't look likely to collapse for a week.

"Something's wrong with my theorizing," he complained to Laura. "My think-stuff's not doing its job."

"Not doing its job," echoed Laura faithfully. She cracked a pecan with a grating noise that set his teeth on edge. "I tell you it's a hoodoo ship. I won't sail. No, not even if you pray for me. I won't, I won't, I won't. Nope. Nix. Who's drunk? That hairy Lowlander Mc—"

"Laura!" he said sharply.

"Gillicuddy," she finished with bland defiance. Again she rasped his teeth. "Rings bigger'n Saturn's. I saw them myself. Who's a liar? Yawk! She's down in Grayway Bay, on Tethis. Boy, what a torso!"

He looked at her hard and said, "You're nuts!"

"Sure! Sure, pal! Laura loves nuts. Have one on me."

"O.K.," he accepted, holding out his hand.

Cocking her colorful pate, she pecked at his hand, gravely selected a pecan and gave it to him. He cracked it, chewed on the kernel while starting up the lighting-set. It was almost as if night were waiting for him. Blackness fell even as he switched on the lights.

With the darkness came a keen sense of unease. The dome was the trouble. It blazed like a beacon and there was no way of blacking it out except by turning off the lights. Beacons attracted things, and he'd no desire to become a center of attraction in present circumstances. That is to say, not at night.

Long experience had bred fine contempt for alien animals, no matter how whacky, but outlandish intelligences were a different proposition. So filled was he with the strange inward conviction that last night's phenomenon was something that knew its onions that it didn't occur to him to wonder whether a glowing column possessed eyes or anything equivalent to a sense of sight. If it had occurred to him, he'd have derived no comfort from it. His desire to be weighed in the balance in some eerie, extrasensory way was even less than his desire to be gaped at visually in his slumbers.

An unholy mess of thoughts and ideas was still cooking in his mind when he extinguished the lights, bunked down, and went to sleep. Nothing disturbed him this time, but when he awoke with the golden dawn his chest was damp with perspiration and Laura again had sought refuge in his arm.

Digging out breakfast, his thoughts began to marshal themselves as he kept his hands busy. Pouring out a shot of hot coffee, he spoke to Laura.

"I'm durned if I'm going to go scatty trying to maintain a three-watch system single-handed, which is what I'm supposed to do if faced by powers unknown when I'm not able to beat it. Those armchair warriors at headquarters ought to get a taste of situations not precisely specified in the book of rules."

"Burp!" said Laura contemptuously.

"He who fights and runs away lives to fight another day," Steve quoted. "That's the Probe Law. It's a nice, smooth, lovely law—when you can run away. We can't!'"

"Burrup!" said Laura with unnecessary emphasis.

"For a woman, your manners are downright disgusting," he told her. "Now I'm not going to spend the brief remainder of my life looking fearfully over my shoulder. The only way to get rid of powers unknown is to convert 'em into powers known and understood. As Uncle Joe told Willie when dragging him to the dentist, the longer we put it off the worse it'll feel."

"Dinna fash y'rsel'," declaimed Laura. "Burp-gollop-bop!"

Giving her a look of extreme distaste, he continued, "So we'll try tossing the bull. Such techniques disconcert bulls sometimes." Standing up, he grabbed Laura, shoved her into her traveling compartment, slid the panel shut. "We're going to blow off forthwith."

Climbing up to the control seat, he stamped on the energizer stud. The tail rockets popped a few times, broke into a subdued roar. Juggling the controls to get the preparatory feel of them, he stepped up the boost until the entire vessel trembled and the rear venturis began to glow cherry-red. Slowly the ship commenced to edge its bulk forward and, as it did so, he fed it the takeoff shot. A half-mile blast kicked backward and the probe ship plummeted into the sky.

Pulling it round in a wide and shallow sweep, he thundered over the borderline of vegetation, the fields of crystals and the hills beyond. In a flash he was plunging through the valley, braking rockets blazing from the nose. This was tricky. He had to co-ordinate forward shoot, backward thrust, and downward surge, but like most of his kind he took pride in the stunts performable with these neat little vessels. An awe-inspired audience was all he lacked to make the exhibition perfect. The vessel landed fairly and squarely on the milk-white roof of the alien edifice, slid halfway to the cliff, then stopped.

"Boy," he breathed, "am I good!" He remained in his seat, stared around through the dome, and felt that he ought to add, "And too young to die." Occasionally eying the chronometer, he waited awhile. The boat must have handed that roof a thump sufficient to wake the dead. If anyone were in, they'd soon hotfoot out to see who was heaving hundred-ton bottles at their shingles. Nobody emerged. He gave them half an hour, his hawk-like face strained, alert. Then he gave it up, said, "Ah, well," and got out of the seat.

He freed Laura. She came out with ruffled dignity, like a dowager who's paraded

Eric Frank Russell

into the wrong room. Females were always curious critters, in his logic, and he ignored her attitude, got his gun, unlocked the doors, jumped down onto the roof. Laura followed reluctantly, came to his shoulder as if thereby conferring a great favor.

Walking past the tail to the edge of the roof, he looked down. The sheerness of the five-hundred-foot drop took him aback. Immediately below his feet the entrance soared four hundred up from the ground, and he was standing on the hundred-foot lintel surmounting it. The only way down was to walk to the side of the roof and reach the earthy slope in which the building was embedded, seeking a path down that.

He covered a quarter of a mile of roof to get to the slope, his eyes examining the roof's surface as he went, and failing to find one crack or joint in the uniformly smooth surface. Huge as it was, the erection appeared to have been molded all in one piece—a fact which did nothing to lessen inward misgivings. Whoever did this mighty job weren't Zulus!

From ground level the entrance loomed bigger than ever. If there had been a similar gap the other side of the building, and a clear way through, he could have taken the ship in at one end and out at the other as easily as threading a needle.

Absence of doors didn't seem peculiar; it was difficult to imagine any sort of door huge enough to fill this opening yet sufficiently balanced to enable anyone—or anything—to pull open or shut. With a final, cautious look around which revealed nothing moving in the valley, he stepped boldly through the entrance, blinked his eyes, found interior darkness slowly fading as visual retention lapsed and gave up remembrance of the golden glow outside.

There was a glow inside, a different one, paler, ghastlier, greenish. It exuded from the floor, the walls, the ceiling, and the total area of radiation was enough to light the place clearly, with no shadows. He sniffed as his vision adjusted itself. There was a strong smell of ozone mixed with other, unidentifiable odors.

To his right and left, rising hundreds of feet, stood great tiers of transparent cases. He went to the ones on his right and examined them. They were cubes, about a yard each way, made of something like transpex. Each contained three inches of loam from which sprouted a crystal. No two crystals were alike; some small and branchy, others large and indescribably complicated.

Dumb with thought, he went around to the back of the monster tier, found another ten yards behind it. And another behind that. And another and another. All with crystals. The number and variety of them made his head whirl. He could study only the two bottom rows of each rack, but row on row stepped themselves far above his head to within short distance of the roof. Their total number was beyond estimation.

It was the same on the left. Crystals by the thousands. Looking more closely at one especially fine example, he noticed that the front plate of its case bore a small, inobtrusive pattern of dots etched upon the outer surface. Investigation revealed that all cases were similarly marked, differing only in the number and arrangement of the dots. Undoubtedly, some sort of cosmic code used for classification purposes.

"The Oron Museum of Natural History," he guessed, in a whisper.

"You're a liar," squawked Laura violently. "I tell you it's a hoodoo—" She stopped, dumfounded, as her own voice roared through the building in deep, organlike tones, "A hoodoo— A hoodoo—"

"Holy smoke, will you keep quiet!" hissed Steve. He tried to keep watch on the exit and the interior simultaneously. But the voice rumbled away in the distance without bringing anyone to dispute their invasion.

Turning, he paced hurriedly past the first blocks of tiers to the next batteries of exhibits. Jelly blobs in this lot. Small ones, no bigger than his wrist watch, numberable in thousands. None appeared to be alive, he noted.

Sections three, four, and five took him a mile into the building, as nearly as he could estimate. He passed mosses, lichens and shrubs, all dead but wondrously preserved. By this time he was ready to guess at section six—plants. He was wrong. The sixth layout displayed bugs, including moths, butterflies, and strange, unfamiliar objects resembling chitinous humming-birds. There was no sample of *Scarabaeus Anderii*, unless it were several hundred feet up. Or unless there was an empty box ready for it—when its day was done.

Who made the boxes? Had it prepared one for him? One for Laura? He visualized himself, petrified forever, squatting in the seventieth case of the twenty-fifth row of the tenth tier in section something-or-other, his front panel duly tagged with its appropriate dots. It was a lousy picture. It made his forehead wrinkle to think of it.

Looking for he knew not what, he plunged steadily on, advancing deeper and deeper into the heart of the building. Not a soul, not a sound, not a footprint. Only that all-pervading smell and the unvarying glow. He had a feeling that the place was visited frequently but never occupied for any worthwhile period of time. Without bothering to stop and look, he passed an enormous case containing a creature faintly resembling a bison-headed rhinoceros, then other, still larger cases holding equally larger exhibits—all carefully dot-marked.

Finally, he rounded a box so tremendous that it sprawled across the full width of the hall. It contained the grand-pappy of all serpents. Behind, for a change, reared five hundred-foot-high racks of metal cupboards, each cupboard with a stud set in its polished door, each ornamented with more groups of mysteriously arranged dots.

Greatly daring, he pressed the stud on the nearest cupboard and its door swung open with a juicy click. The result proved disappointing. The cupboard was filled with stacks of small, glassy sheets each smothered with dots.

"Super filing-system," he grunted, closing the door. "Old Prof Heggarty would give his right arm to be here."

"Heggarty," said Laura, in a faltering voice. "For Pete's sake!"

He looked at her sharply. She was ruffled and fidgety, showing signs of increasing agitation.

"What's the matter, Chicken?"

She peeked at him, returned her anxious gaze the way they had come, side-stepped to and fro on his shoulder. Her neck feathers started to rise. A nervous cluck came from her beak and she cowered close to his jacket.

"Darn!" he muttered. Spinning on one heel, he raced past successive filing blocks, got into the ten yards' space between the end block and the wall. His gun was out and he kept watch on the front of the blocks while his free hand tried to soothe Laura. She snuggled up close, rubbing her head into his neck and trying to hide under the angle of his jaw.

"Quiet, Honey," he whispered. "Just you keep quiet and stay with Steve, and we'll be all right."

She kept quiet, though she'd begun to tremble. His heart speeded up in sympathy though he could see nothing, hear nothing to warrant it.

Then, while he watched and waited, and still in absolute silence, the interior brightness waxed, became less green, more golden. And suddenly he knew what it was that was coming. He *knew* what it was!

He sank on one knee to make himself as small and inconspicuous as possible. Now his heart was palpitating wildly and no coldness in his mind could freeze it down to slower, more normal beat. The silence, the awful silence of its approach was the unbearable feature. The crushing thud of a weighty foot or hoof would have been better. Colossi have no right to steal along like ghosts.

And the golden glow built up, drowning out the green radiance from floor to roof, setting the multitude of case-surfaces afire with its brilliance. It grew as strong as the golden sky, and stronger. It became all-pervading, unendurable, leaving no darkness in which to hide, no sanctuary for little things.

It flamed like the rising sun or like something drawn from the heart of a sun, and the glory of its radiance sent the cowering watcher's mind awhirl. He struggled fiercely to control his brain, to discipline it, to bind it to his fading will—and failed.

With drawn face beaded by sweat, Steve caught the merest fragmentary glimpse of the column's edge appearing from between the stacks of the center aisle. He saw a blinding strip of burnished gold in which glittered a pure white star, then a violent effervescence seemed to occur within his brain and he fell forward into a cloud of tiny bubbles.

Down, down he sank through myriad bubbles and swirls and sprays of iridescent froth and foam which shone and changed and shone anew with every conceivable color. And all the time his mind strove frantically to battle upward and drag his soul to the surface.

Deep into the nethermost reaches he went while still the bubbles whirled around in their thousands and their colors were of numberless hues. Then his progress slowed. Gradually the froth and the foam ceased to rotate upward, stopped its circling, began to swirl in the reverse direction and sink. He was rising! He rose for a lifetime, floating weightlessly, in a dreamlike trance.

* * *

"Hobbyist"

The last of the bubbles drifted eerily away, leaving him in a brief hiatus of nonexistence—then he found himself sprawled full length on the floor with a dazed Laura clinging to his arm. He blinked his eyes, slowly, several times. They were strained and sore. His heart was still palpitating and his legs felt weak. There was a strange sensation in his stomach as if memory had sickened him with a shock from long ago.

He didn't get up from the floor right away; his body was too shaken and his mind too muddled for that. While his wits came back and his composure returned, he lay and noted that all the invading goldness had gone and that again the interior illumination was a dull, shadowless green. Then his eyes found his watch and he sat up, startled. Two hours had flown!

That fact brought him shakily to his feet. Peering around the end of the bank of filing cabinets, he saw that nothing had changed. Instinct told him that the golden visitor had gone and that once more he had this place to himself. Had it become aware of his presence? Had it made him lose consciousness or, if not, why had he lost it? Had it done anything about the ship on the roof?

Picking up his futile gun, he spun it by its stud guard and looked at it with contempt. Then he holstered it, helped Laura onto his shoulder where she perched groggily, went around the back of the racks and still deeper into the building.

"I reckon we're O.K., Honey," he told her. "I think we're too small to be noticed. We're like mice. Who bothers to trap mice when he's got bigger and more important things in mind?" He pulled a face, not liking the mouse comparison. It wasn't flattering either to him or his kind. But it was the best he could think of at the moment. "So, like little mice, let's look for cheese. I'm not giving up just because a big hunk of something has sneaked past and put a scare into us. We don't scare off, do we, Sweetness?"

"No," said Laura unenthusiastically. Her voice was still subdued and her eyes perked apprehensively this way and that. "No scare. I won't sail, I tell you. Blow my sternpipes! Laura loves nuts!"

"Don't you call me a nut!"

"Nuts! Stick to farming—it gets you more eggs. McGillicuddy, the great—"

"Hey!" he warned.

She shut up abruptly. He put the pace on, refusing to admit that his system felt slightly jittery with nervous strain or that anything had got him bothered. But he knew that he'd no desire to be near that sparkling giant again. Once was enough, more than enough. It wasn't that he feared it, but something else, something he was quite unable to define.

Passing the last bank of cabinets, he found himself facing a machine. It was complicated and bizarre—and it was making a crystalline growth. Near it, another and different machine was manufacturing a small, horned lizard. There could be no doubt at all about the process of fabrication because both objects were half-made and both progressed slightly even as he watched. In a couple of hours' time, perhaps less, they'd be finished, and all they'd need would be . . . would be—

Eric Frank Russell

The hairs stiffened on the back of his neck and he commenced to run. Endless machines, all different, all making different things, plants, bugs, birds and fungoids. It was done by electroponics, atom fed to atom like brick after brick to build a house. It wasn't synthesis because that's only assembly, and this was assembly plus growth in response to unknown laws. In each of these machines, he knew, was some key or code or cipher, some weird master-control of unimaginable complexity, determining the patterns each was building—and the patterns were infinitely variable.

Here and there a piece of apparatus stood silent, inactive, their tasks complete. Here and there other monstrous layouts were in pieces, either under repair or readied for modification. He stopped by one which had finished its job. It had fashioned a delicately shaded moth which perched motionless like a jeweled statue within its fabrication jar. The creature was perfect as far as he could tell, and all it was waiting for was . . . was—

Beads of moisture popped out on his forehead. All that moth needed was the breath of life!

He forced a multitude of notions to get out of his mind; it was the only way to retain a hold on himself. Divert your attention—take it off this and place it on that! Firmly, he fastened his attention on one tremendous, partly disassembled machine lying nearby. Its guts were exposed, revealing great field coils of dull gray wire. Bits of similar wire lay scattered around on the floor.

Picking up a short piece, he found it surprisingly heavy. He took off his wrist watch, opened its back, brought the wire near to its works. The Venusian jargoon bearing fluoresced immediately. V-jargoons invariably glowed in the presence of near radiation: this unknown metal was a possible fuel. His heart gave a jump at the mere thought of it.

Should he drag out a huge coil and lug it up to the ship? It was very heavy, and he'd need a considerable length of the stuff—if it was usable as fuel. Supposing the disappearance of the coil caused mousetraps to be set before he returned to search anew?

It pays to stop and think whenever you've got time to stop and think; that was a fundamental of Probe Service philosophy. Pocketing a sample of the wire, he sought around other disassembled machines for more. The search took him still deeper into the building and he fought harder to keep his attention concentrated solely on the task. It wasn't easy. There was that dog, for instance, standing there, statue-like, waiting, waiting. If only it had been anything but indubitably and recognizably an Earth-type dog. It was impossible to avoid seeing it. It would be equally impossible to avoid seeing other, even more familiar forms—if they were there.

He'd gained seven samples of different radioactive wires when he gave up the search. A cockatoo ended his peregrinations. The bird stood steadfastly in its jar, its blue plumage smooth and bright, its crimson crest raised, its bright eye fixed in what was not death but not yet life. Laura shrieked at it hysterically and the immense hall shrieked back at her with long-drawn roars and rumbles that reverberated into dim distances. Laura's reaction was too much; he wanted no cause for similar reaction of his own.

He sped through the building at top pace, passing the filing cabinets and the mighty arrow of exhibition cases unheedingly. Up the loamy side slopes he climbed almost as rapidly as he'd gone down, and he was breathing heavily by the time he got into the ship.

His first action was to check the ship for evidence of interference. There wasn't any. Next, he checked the instruments. The electroscope's leaves were collapsed. Charging them, he watched them flip open and flop together again. The counter showed radiation aplenty. The hen clucked energetically. He'd blundered some-what—he should have checked up when first he landed on the roof. However, no matter. What lay beneath the roof was now known; the instruments would have advised him earlier but not as informatively.

Laura had her feed while he accompanied her with a swift meal. After that, he dug out his samples of wire. No two were the same gauge and one obviously was far too thick to enter the feed holes of the Kingston-Kanes. It took him half an hour to file it down to a suitable diameter. The original piece of dull gray wire took the first test. Feeding it in, he set the controls to minimum warming-up intensity, stepped on the energizer. Nothing happened.

He scowled to himself. Someday they'd have jobs better than the sturdy but finicky Kingston-Kanes, jobs that'd eat anything eatable. Density and radioactivity weren't enough for these motors; the stuff fed to them had to be right.

Going back to the Kingston-Kanes, he pulled out the wire, found its end fused into shapelessness. Definitely a failure. Inserting the second sample, another gray wire not so dull as the first, he returned to the controls, rammed the energizer. The tail rockets promptly blasted with a low, moaning note and the thrust dial showed sixty per cent normal surge.

Some people would have got mad at that point. Steve didn't. His lean, hawklike features quirked, he felt in his pocket for the third sample, tried that. No soap. The fourth likewise was a flop. The fifth produced a peculiar and rhythmic series of blasts which shook the vessel from end to end and caused the thrust-dial needle to waggle between one hundred twenty per cent and zero. He visualized the Probe patrols popping through space like outboard motors while he extracted the stuff and fed the sixth sample. The sixth roared joyously at one hundred seventy per cent. The seventh sample was another flop.

He discarded all but what was left of the sixth wire. The stuff was about twelve gauge and near enough for his purpose. It resembled deep-colored copper but was not as soft as copper nor as heavy. Hard, springy and light, like telephone wire. If there were at least a thousand yards of it below, and if he could manage to drag it up to the ship, and if the golden thing didn't come along and ball up the works, he might be able to blow free. Then he'd get some place civilized—if he could find it. The future was based on an appalling selection of "ifs."

The easiest and most obvious way to salvage the needed treasure was to blow a hole in the roof, lower a cable through it, and wind up the wire with the aid of the ship's tiny winch. Problem: how to blow a hole without suitable explosives. Answer: drill the roof, insert unshelled pistol ammunition, say a prayer, and pop the stuff off electrically. He tried it, using a hand drill. The bit promptly curled up as if gnawing on a diamond. He drew his gun, bounced a shell off the roof; the missile exploded with a sharp, hard crack and fragments of shell casing whined shrilly into the sky. Where it had struck, the roof bore a blast smudge and a couple of fine scratches.

There was nothing for it but to go down and heave on his shoulders as much loot as he could carry. And do it right away. Darkness would fall before long, and he didn't want to encounter that golden thing in the dark. It was fateful enough in broad light of day, or in the queer, green glow of the building's interior, but to have it stealing softly behind him as he struggled through the nighttime with his plunder was something of which he didn't care to think.

Locking the ship and leaving Laura inside, he returned to the building, made his way past the mile of cases and cabinets to the machine section at back. He stopped to study nothing on his way. He didn't wish to study anything. The wire was the thing, only the wire. Besides, mundane thoughts of mundane wire didn't twist one's mind around until one found it hard to concentrate.

Nevertheless, his mind was afire as he searched. Half of it was prickly with alertness, apprehensive of the golden column's sudden return; the other half burned with excitement at the possibility of release. Outwardly, his manner showed nothing of this; it was calm, assured, methodical.

Within ten minutes he'd found a great coil of the coppery metal, a huge ovoid, intricately wound, lying beside a disassembled machine. He tried to move it, could not shift it an inch. The thing was far too big, too heavy for one to handle. To get it onto the roof he'd have to cut it up and make four trips of it—and some of its inner windings were fused together. So near, so far! Freedom depended upon his ability to move a lump of metal a thousand feet vertically. He muttered some of Laura's words to himself.

Although the wire cutters were ready in his hand, he paused to think, decided to look farther before tackling this job. It was a wise decision which brought its reward, for at a point a mere hundred yards away he came across another, differently shaped coil, wheel-shaped, in good condition, easy to unreel. This again was too heavy to carry, but with a tremendous effort which made his muscles crack he got it up on its rim and proceeded to roll it along like a monster tire.

Several times he had to stop and let the coil lean against the nearest case while he rested a moment. The last such case trembled under the impact of the weighty coil and its shining, spidery occupant stirred in momentary simulation of life. His dislike of the spider shot up with its motion, he made his rest brief, bowled the coil onward.

Violet streaks again were creeping from the horizon when he rolled his loot out of the mighty exit and reached the bottom of the bank. Here, he stopped, clipped the wire with his cutters, took the free end, climbed the bank with it. The wire uncoiled without hindrance until he reached the ship, where he attached it to the winch, wound the lot in, rewound it on the feed spool.

Night fell in one ominous swoop. His hands were trembling slightly but his hawklike face was firm, phlegmatic as he carefully threaded the wire's end through the automatic injector and into the feed hole of the Kingston-Kanes. That done, he slid open Laura's door, gave her some of the fruit they'd picked off the Oron tree. She accepted it morbidly, her manner still subdued, and not inclined for speech.

"Stay inside, Honey," he soothed. "We're getting out of this and going home."

Shutting her in, he climbed into the control seat, switched on the nose beam, saw it pierce the darkness and light up the facing cliff. Then he stamped on the energizer, warmed the tubes. Their bellow was violent and comforting. At seventy per cent better thrust he'd have to be a lot more careful in all his adjustments: it wouldn't do to melt his own tail off when success was within his grasp. All the same, he felt strangely impatient, as if every minute counted, aye, every second!

But he contained himself, got the venturis heated, gave a discreet pull on his starboard steering flare, watched the cliff glide sidewise past as the ship slewed around on its belly. Another puff, then another, and he had the vessel nose-on to the front edge of the roof. There seemed to be a faint aura in the gloom ahead and he switched off his nose beam to study it better.

It was a faint yellow haze shining over the rim of the opposite slope. His back hairs quivered as he saw it. The haze strengthened, rose higher. His eyes strained into the outer pall as he watched it fascinatedly, and his hands were frozen on the controls. There was dampness on his back. Behind him, in her traveling compartment, Laura was completely silent, not even shuffling uneasily as was her wont. He wondered if she were cowering.

With a mighty effort of will which strained him as never before, he shifted his control a couple of notches, lengthened the tail blast. Trembling in its entire fabric, the ship edged forward. Summoning all he'd got, Steve forced his reluctant hands to administer the take-off boost. With a tearing crash that thundered back from the cliffs, the little vessel leaped skyward on an arc of fire. Peering through the transpex, Steve caught a fragmentary and foreshortened glimpse of the great golden column advancing majestically over the crest; the next instant it had dropped far behind his tail and his bow was arrowing for the stars.

An immense relief flooded through his soul, though he knew not what there had been to fear. But the relief was there and so great was it that he worried not at all about where he was bound or for how long. Somehow, he felt certain that if he swept

Eric Frank Russell

in a wide, shallow curve he'd pick up a Probe beat-note sooner or later. Once he got a beat-note, from any source at all, it would lead him out of the celestial maze.

Luck remained with him, and his optimistic hunch proved correct, for while still among completely strange constellations he caught the faint throb of Hydra III on his twenty-seventh day of sweep. That throb was his cosmic lighthouse beckoning him home.

He let go a wild shriek of "Yipee!" thinking that only Laura heard him—but he was heard elsewhere.

Down on Oron, deep in the monster workshop, the golden giant paused blindly as if listening. Then it slid stealthily along the immense aisles, reached the filing system. A compartment opened, two glassy plates came out.

For a moment the plates contacted the Oron's strange, sparkling substance, became etched with an array of tiny dots. They were returned to the compartment, and the door closed. The golden glory with its imprisoned stars then glided quietly back to the machine section.

Something nearer to the gods had scribbled its notes. Nothing lower in the scale of life could have translated them or deduced their full purport.

In simplest sense, one plate may have been inscribed, "Biped, erect, pink, homo intelligens type P.739, planted on Sol III, Condensation Arm BDB—moderately successful."

Similarly, the other plate may have recorded, "Flapwing, large, hook-beaked, vari-colored, periquito macao type K.8, planted on Sol III, Condensation Arm BDB — moderately successful."

But already the sparkling hobbyist had forgotten his passing notes. He was breathing his essence upon a jeweled moth. ■

PETALS OF ROSE
Marc Stiegler

Look to the Rose that blows about us—"Lo,
Laughing," she says, "Into the World I blow,
At once the Silken Petals of my Being
Tear, and my Treasure to the Great Winds throw."
>   —Rosan translation of the Lazarine translation of the
>   English translation of the *Rubaiyat* by Omar Khayyám

SORREL EVERWOOD FELT HIS EARS SLOWLY BEING AMPUTATED; he reached up to adjust the damn strap on his infrared goggles a tenth time. While he was there, he adjusted the coloration control as well.

At last the Rosan he faced looked like the Rosans in xenoanthropological films. Hundreds of delicate cooling fins, the Rosan equivalent of scales or feathers, covered his body. He seemed to be wearing flower petals, petals of deep red laced with a fine network of pink veins. His wide, gentle eyes were violet with flecks of gold. The gold in his eyes matched the gold in his medallion, the medallion of the ruling Bloodbond.

Some of his petals were curled, and turned green toward the edges. *Or Sae Hi Tor must be old for a Rosan,* Sorrell decided before concentrating again on the Bloodbond's words.

"I assure you we'll give you all the help, the highest priorities, available." Or Sae spoke slowly in logitalk for the humans. "Obviously we stand to gain even more from a translight communicator than you do. And I hope that—"

Or Sae rose suddenly from his chair, heading for the exit passage. "I'm sorry," he murmured. "May you die by a . . . rising . . . " He crumpled to the floor.

Sorrel was already moving toward Or Sae. Wandra screamed. The screaming made Sorrel turn, and as he turned he realized what was happening. Thus, when he turned back to Or Sae, he was not surprised to see a pool of green brainblood seeping from Or Sae's head, solidifying into jelly. Nor was he surprised when a sweet, gentle scent, disturbingly like honeysuckle, filled the air.

Sorrel hadn't known he still had it in him to hate; he had been so long so tired and so resigned. But sitting there with the Lazarine, the hate came back to him, along with fear and defiance. "Why me?" he asked harshly, or at least as harshly as he could manage with the fear in his throat.

Balcyrak Kretkyen Niopay blinked slowly. "Because you are the most qualified being in the universe. Isn't that obvious?"

Sorrel said nothing; yes, in some ways it was obvious.

The Lazarine laughed—a resounding sound, which faded slowly. "I'm sorry—I know that for you it's not a laughing matter." A robutler entered; Balcyrak pointed to the serving tray. "Refreshment?"

"Thanks." Sorrel took the warmed liquor glass, containing . . . well, he wasn't sure what it contained, but it was probably costly, certainly good, and hopefully soothing to a dry throat. As he sipped, Balcyrak changed the subject.

"We know how much you hate us."

Sorrel coughed, inhaled sharply.

"And also why. I am sorry about your wife. We are sorry for all who die too soon, regardless of how many Lazarines those sentients may have killed, regardless of how involved we may have been in killing them in return."

Sorrel's wife had been an officer on board a human flagship when Man chose to fight Lazaran, before Man overcame his brooding jealousy. So long ago . . .

"But the work is, in our opinion, too important for historical phenomena, however recent, to interfere. You are the galaxy's foremost authority on Rosans, knowing them even better than they know themselves—in fact, you are the only sentient ever to have transformed an alien culture without force of weapons. That is quite an achievement; it may be said that you are the only successful xenopsychologist ever born."

"Without force of weapons?" Sorrel felt fiery horror. "Millions of Rosans died in the revolution."

Balcyrak waved it away. "But they were killed by other Rosans, the Rosans who could understand the superior regenerative society you offered them. Have you ever read Darwin?"

Sorrel snorted. "I don't have time for reading ancient history."

"Of course; I am sorry to mention it. No matter. The deaths were just a manifestation of the fittest surviving. Because the six-parent religion was superior, it destroyed the four-parent religion. After all, the superiority of six-parenthood inspired you to write your dissertation in the first place. The people of Khayyam are lucky that Prim Sol Mem Brite read it."

"Yeah. But not so lucky he killed so many of his own people because of it," Sorrel frowned. He wanted to argue, but this was neither the time nor the place. "Look. Why don't you go to Khayyam yourself? Why do you need a human as your local overlord?"

The Lazarine frilled his mane in distress. "You will not be an overlord; you will be an associate. Humans are the only beings who can be effective as interfaces between the ideas that originate here and the applied engineering that will originate there. We cannot do it ourselves. It is too . . . painful. For them as well as us." He paused, watching Sorrel, speaking softly. "You've never been to Khayyam, have you?"

Sorrel shook his head. It was an intolerable irony that he should never have visited the planet of the people whose lives he had transformed. He had never met a Rosan in his entire life; he had merely written a dissertation about them, in school, shortly after his wife's death.

And with the dissertation he had caused so many new deaths.

Balcyrak interrupted his thoughts. "Fear not, Man Everwood. You will understand why we can't go ourselves after you've been there a while. After you've become like a Lazarine unto them."

"What?!" Sorrel wrenched forward in his chair.

The Lazarine smiled; he seemed languid, almost uncaring, but then all Lazarine activity seemed languid by human standards. "When you are Lazarine-like, you will understand."

Sorrel realized that Balcyrak was assuming he would take the job, assuming that he would go to Khayyam as Balcyrak's proxy. Even more infuriating, Sorrel realized that Balcyrak was right.

"You'll see," the Lazarine promised.

Wandra took a large gulp from the glass Sorrel had given her; she was still shaken from the death of the Bloodbond. The three humans were back on the ship, though they hadn't yet taken off their coolsuits. The coolsuits made them look like pale, ragged Rosans, as far as Sorrel could tell.

Wandra spoke. "I just don't believe it. I know, I know; everything I had read about the Rosans before coming here warned me about their deaths, and I should've realized that it'd be a casual occurrence." She took another gulp. "But dammit, I still don't believe it. How could somebody be that way?"

"It's simple enough," Cal started with his cool, sarcastic voice. "You'd be that way too if you only had thirty-six hours to live. You don't have time to pay too much attention to somebody else dying."

Sorrel sighed. Cal was going to be a problem; already he was building a shield of cynicism to insulate himself from the wounds this planet could leave. But then, Wandra's hysteria boded ill as well. "It's not quite that simple, Cal. Though the adult phase of the Rosan life cycle lasts only thirty-six hours, they pack a lot more life into those thirty-six hours than most humans pack into a hundred years. The main reason death isn't a cause for grief is that it's so necessary for the children; a Rosan can't, after all, have children in our sense of the word unless his brainblood is preserved for the larval bloodfeast." Sorrel shrugged. "For that matter, the bloodfeast confers a bit of immortality to every Rosan; the bloodchild starts adult life with many of the memories of the bloodparents, and much of the knowledge of the brainparents."

Cal snorted. "Yeah. Immortality. The kids remember everything. Only problem is, you're still dead. Hell, you might as well write a book—that's about as immortal as a Rosan can get."

"And that's probably a lot more immortal than any of us will get," Sorrel said, and immediately regretted its saying; Sorrel, after all, already had that kind of immortality.

Cal stalked from the cabin.

Sorrel watched Wandra pace across the deck, watched her wring her hands in agony. "Yes, Wandra, what do you want to tell me about Cal?" he asked at last.

Wandra paused in mid-stride. "I, uh . . . "

Sorrel nodded his head. "I'm supposed to say that since I'm a psychologist I analyzed you and already know what you want to say. Unfortunately, it would hardly take a psychologist to see that you're disturbed—more disturbed now than you were before Cal left."

She sighed, sat back down. "I suppose you're right. Look, Dr. Everwood—"

"Sorrel," he said, "My name is Sorrel."

"Right. Sorry. Do you know how Cal happened to become a part of this expedition?"

"Not really. I confess I've wondered about it. He doesn't seem like the type to volunteer for a job like this."

"He didn't—not exactly, anyway. He's a flunk. Blew his postdoc thesis at U. of New Terra. Since he couldn't make it as a theoretician, they consigned him to engineering. Apparently that's a big loss of prestige where he comes from."

Sorrel nodded. "Yes, on Narchia it would be. So he came out here to get as far as possible from the embarrassment."

"Yeah."

Sorrel shrugged. "Well, at least he should be successful at getting far enough away. Lord knows, there's nobody here to bother him." Except for Sorrel himself, he realized; his "success" would be a continual insult to Cal. He looked at Wandra; she looked back, knowing his thoughts as he had just known hers. "So who's the psychologist now?" he murmured.

She laughed, the first time since planetfall.

Sorrel stood up. "Let's go back and meet the new Bloodbond. He should be settled in by now; we have lots of business to discuss."

The office had changed little; the Bloodkeepers had taken the remains of Or Sae Hi Tor to the larval gateway, so the next returning larva could take him in bloodfeast. The stacks of papers in the out-slot of the desk seemed larger; those in the in-slot seemed smaller. Tri Bel Heer Te was a member of the current dayspinner ruling bloodline. They directed the MoonBender cavern works during the thirty-six-hour daylight half of Khayyam's cycle, as Or Sae's bloodline ruled during the nightspin half of the planet's revolution.

Tri Bel rose to greet him with a touching of petals along the forearm. The gold, silver, and green medallion of the Bloodbond glinted with splendor. "My children will remember this meeting forever," she said, giving the traditional greeting. With Sorrel, the greeting might well be true; Tri Bel looked upon Sorrel in raptured awe.

Her wide, bright, Rosan eyes were wider than usual, and Sorrel had the uncomfortable feeling that this was how she might look upon a god.

"We will remember you in our books," Sorrel said, using the closest human counterpart of a racial memory. "And even the Lazarines shall sing our songs, should we of Earth and you of Khayyam succeed in our plans."

The awe surrendered to the press of business in just a few seconds—still a long time in Rosan terms. "I wouldn't be surprised. Let's talk," Tri Bel said. The Rosan gestured for Sorrel to take the resting incline at the head of the conference table; Sorrel uncomfortably sidled to one of the others. He wasn't a god, dammit! Why did they have to treat him like one?

Sorrel spoke, as fast as he could, in Ancient Rosan (Ancient Rosan being several years, or hundreds of generations, old); he didn't want to waste any more of Tri Bel's time than necessary. "Do you know what we were discussing with your predecessor?"

"No, I haven't had time to read his lifescription yet."

"The significant information we bring is this," Sorrel ticked off. "The Lazarines have developed a universe-gestalt incorporating methods of faster-than-light communication, methods much faster than sending messages on starships. Cal Minov and Wandra Furenz, the other two humans with me, have translated the Lazarine gestalt into a practical theory. Now all we need is a massive engineering effort, to find a workable implementation of the theories. The Rosans, of course, are the fastest, most efficient engineers in the universe, and the project is so large it'd take any other beings decades of effort. Here on Khayyam we hope to cut that time to less than a hundred generations." Sorrel scratched on his goggles. "When we're done, your descendants will be able to talk to beings on other worlds and receive answers within their own lifetimes."

The Rosan should have been bored with this slow aimless speech—but because this was Sorrel Everwood, the One Parent of the Faith of Six Parents, she was not. Besides, the merits in FTL communication were truly awesome. The merits were especially great for the Rosans, who were isolated on Khayyam by lifespan as well as by distance. Tri Bel's tragic smile seemed a bit human, yet a bit elfin as well. "Man Everwood, again you bring us salvation. How can we repay such a debt?" She shook her head. "Have you spoken with our scientists and engineers? Have they seen the plans?"

"No, we've been waiting for a Bloodbond's authorization."

"You've waited hours, just for a Bloodbond?" Tri Bel's eyes filled with puzzlement, then cleared. "We must arrange for the work to begin. Send Man Minov and Man Furenz to the Bel Dom laboratories at once." She shook herself. "I can't believe you waited hours for authorization!" She moved to her desk. "Your project has Priority 1A, the pick of the engineering pool and all material resources, as well as the right of bloodfeast selections, with higher bloodfeast priority only for Executive Bonds. Further, your techs have fully expanded egg-laying rights. The orders shall be ready within the hour."

Sorrel's head spun; the FTLcom was being backed with resources far beyond his wildest expectations. Bloodfeast selection would permit them to mix and match the brainbloods of the best FTLcom workers in each generation, to selectively shape the chemogenetic skills and blood memories of the next generation even further. And fully expanded egg-laying rights would make positions in the project extremely valuable, since FTLcom workers would be permitted to have more than two replacement eggs, as well as multiple brainchildren and bloodchildren. "Thank you," he said to the Rosan, who was already speaking into the room's transceivers. He listened for a moment, but couldn't understand a word; both because it was modern Rosan, and because Tri Bel spoke impossibly fast. Sorrel left immediately; though Tri Bel never would have dismissed him, Sorrel knew she couldn't work effectively with a god in the room.

There were almost 200 quiet, expectant Rosans listening there in the stone hall. Sorrel cleared his throat. "I want to apologize for the crowding. It looks like our cavern is a bit small for our task. However, a new cavenet is nearing completion, and we've been assured that it'll be ours once it's ready." Sorrel realized it wouldn't make any difference to these students, who would pass into bloodfeast long before the new accommodations were complete. "Anyway, this is Calvin Minov, a spacetime physicist, and this is Wandra Furenz, a topocurve mathematician. Since I know absolutely nothing about faster-than-light communication, or spacetime, or anything that has to do with engineering, I'll give the floor to them."

Cal climbed the low step stiffly, followed by a smiling Wandra.

Sorrel looked at Cal. "Cal, why don't you start off, give them an idea of where we're going, how, and why?"

"Yeah, sure, uh," he turned to the class and froze. Sorrel pressed a copy of the manuscript explaining the theories into his hand—a manuscript that Cal had written. "Just tell them what you know, Cal," he whispered in Anglic.

Cal looked down at the book, seemed to remember where he was, and turned to the lightboard, calling up the first diagram. Sorrel stepped down and examined the roomful of FTLcom students.

They were the best, chosen by Sorrel in consultation with the Chief Geneticist and the Assistant Coordinator of the Bloodkeep; each student had six good parents with backgrounds in science, engineering, or mathematics behind him. The students were young as well, with fat still in their cheeks, not only because young ones would have more time to assimilate more material, but also because only a youth would sit still for the slow ambling ways of humans.

Sorrel turned his attention back to the teacher. Cal, cool and aloof though he might be, was warming to his subject. He talked faster as he went along, and he talked still faster as he realized that no matter how fast he talked his students would keep up with him. In fact, Sorrel knew, the worst mistake Cal could make would be to talk too slowly, for then his students would lose concentration.

Ooops—one of them asked him a question, with such swift sentences he couldn't follow . . . there would be a great deal of adjusting to do. Not to mention the problems it would pose if the humans got too attached to any of the Rosans they taught. . . . At least Cal might be immune to that, but Sorrel could see long, terrible times with Wandra. He'd have to take a very close look at her ego chart. For the first time Sorrel felt that he belonged on this trip, not just because he would awe the natives and make things move swiftly, but because he would be useful as well.

A right arm wrapped itself around his left, and Wandra whispered in his ear. "Well, I think Cal's going to do all right without us. We're planning to take two-hour shifts in the teaching with one-hour breaks after each pair of lectures, so the students'll have a chance once in a while to behave like normal Rosans. How does that sound?"

Sorrel nodded. "We're playing this all by ear, so your suggestion sounds as good as any. We'll see how it goes with this group, and readjust later. I've got a feeling that two or four hours of humans talking is too much at a shot, but we'll see."

Wandra had been gently tugging him out of the room while he talked. Two Rosans in an electric wagon whooshed by with a load of tunneling equipment. Wandra plopped onto the cool stone floor and Sorrel followed, awkwardly falling over her as she dragged him down. She laughed, beautifully, and he laughed as well. She shook her head. "I was getting so tired standing there in the lecture hall, I couldn't wait for a chance to sit down," Wandra said.

Sorrel nodded. "Yes, I've got the feeling all my blood went into my legs. I think we'll have to install a few chairs here and there in strategic locations around Khayyam. Either that, or do some genetic engineering on the Rosans so they need chairs too—that way we can invent the chair for them and make a huge profit, selling cushions."

Wandra laughed again, a wonderful human sound. Rosans knew laughter too, but it was a swift, chirping sound, the laughter of hummingbirds. There was no time for rich melodies here on Khayyam.

Wandra's laughter cut just a bit short. "Were you watching the engineers while you were speaking?"

Sorrel sighed. "Yes, I was."

"They worship you."

"I know."

The silence hung heavy in the still, dry air. Wandra spoke again. "I know you did something special for these people once, but frankly I'm amazed by how they remember you. That was hundreds of generations ago, wasn't it, whatever you did?"

Sorrel sighed. "Yeah, but the Rosan memory is long and fickle."

Wandra just stared at him.

He exhaled slowly. "Especially, they remember their gods."

She nodded. "Brek Dar El Kind said something like that."

"Brek Dar El Kind?"

"One of the students."

"Um." Long pause. "Did he tell you of the Faith of Six Parents?" She shook her head. "Well, it's the main religion of Khayyam. In fact, it's the only religion here in the MoonBenders Cavernwork. The followers of the earlier religion were wiped out here in a war some years ago. Shortly after I finished my dissertation on Rosan culture, as it happens."

"Üm. Coincidence?"

Sorrel clutched his head in his hands. "I'm afraid not. You see, I invented the Faith of Six Parents." He shrugged. "Oh, it wasn't a religion when I invented it, it was just an idea—but when my idea got mixed with real beings on a real planet with real problems, it became a religion." He took a deep breath.

Just then they heard someone—or something—skitter around the corner. The something made sharp clicking steps, much different from the Rosans. "Freeze," Sorrel ordered Wandra.

He turned toward the sound. Sure enough, a krat hunched there, eyeing them hungrily.

The man and the krat looked at each other for a long time, there in the tunnel. The krat's petals were more ragged than Rosan petals, and a vicious scar gouged the length of his left side. The small but tough creature approached.

An electric cart whirred down the passage toward them, and the krat vanished.

Sorrel noticed his hands were shaking, and his brow was damp despite the dustiness. "They really aren't very dangerous," he said, as much to himself as to Wandra. "Usually the krat don't bother adult Rosans. But the Rosans recently started another big extermination push on the krat, and hunger makes them bolder."

Wandra squeezed his arm. "Thanks," she said, before looking him in the eye with some amusement. "You were telling me about your dissertation."

"Ah yes." Sorrel took a deep breath. "I guess I'll give you the whole spiel."

He exhaled slowly. "I'll start with the Rosan lifecycle. Rosans have two sexes, pretty much like humans, except they get along better." Wandra hit Sorrel in the arm, and he laughed. "Anyway, each pair of genetic parents produce several eggs. The eggs hatch in about a year, and the larvae take off into the deserts. These larval Rosans are tough beasts, tough enough to survive repeated exposure to Khayyam's sun. The larvae grow and fight for about two years before returning to the place of hatching. At that time they metamorphose into adults." Sorrel felt Wandra's breath upon his cheek, and enjoyed the warmth of having a woman near again. It had been a long time. "The last act of metamorphosis is the bloodfeast, in which the larva consumes the bulk of the brainblood of its bloodparents. From the bloodparents the larva gets many memories, opinions, and attitudes—foremost are the memories associated with the parents', uh . . . " What was a human equivalent? Sorrel winced. "Their *purpose*, I suppose. Except the *purpose* is also transmitted in brainblood, and it takes generations to change the direction of the brainblood's purpose, even if one of the individuals in the bloodline is fanatically dedicated to a different purpose." Sorrel shrugged. "Anyway, the larva also feasts on a part of the brainblood of the brainparents and receives some of their memories as well—though the brainparent memories are stripped of emotional associations. You could think of the brainparent memories as being collections of highlighted *facts*, and the bloodparent memories as being both facts and *beliefs*." Sorrel chuckled. "Actually, there are theorists who think that *all* memories are passed, even though only a part of the bloodmemories are remembered. But it'd be hard to prove—no Rosan could live long enough to remember that many memories anyway. Especially since the individual Rosan has a photographic memory, as far as his own life is concerned. Just remembering one parent's whole life would be a lifetime affair."

Sorrel stood up, dragging Wandra with him as she had earlier dragged him. "Let's walk." Their direction led away from that of the krat's departure. "Since the larvae always return to their hatch-place for the bloodfeast, genetic parents tended to be the bloodparents as well. Thus there were four parents.

"But after the invention of the shovel, civilization developed inside the caverns, where Rosans could live both day and night. In this new environment the identity of genetic and blood-parents was no longer necessary; in fact, it was a severe hindrance to progress. Since the egg and larval stages last three years, the memories of the great scientists and philosophers missed a hundred generations of civilization between incarnations." Sorrel's voice turned bitter. "That's where my distant, objective eye came into play. I saw something better. You see, if they used a different larva—a larva that reached maturity just as a person died—the person's memories wouldn't have to wait for three years. No, that person's memories could be incarnated the next day." Sorrel shrugged. "The Rosans themselves never saw this possibility. I wouldn't be surprised if there's an instinct for having genetic parents as bloodparents. Not that an instinct was needed anymore—the correspondence of genetic parents with bloodparents was institutionalized in the Faith of Four Parents. The religious leaders, of course, vehemently opposed the six-parent concept."

"So there was a war."

Sorrel nodded. "War isn't common among Rosans—it takes too many generations to make a change that way. Assassination and brainblood-burning are more common. But when they have a war, it's a total war in the finest human tradition." *Like the kind we waged against the Lazarines,* he thought. "The Faith of Six won, of course; no one in the universe can beat the speed with which a six-parent Rosan culture can make advances in experimental sciences like weaponry, because no one else could conduct so many experiments so fast as a series of determined generations of Rosans."

"Which is why we brought the FTLcom here, to be done swiftly."

"Yes." Sorrel looked at his watch. "You know, if you hurry, you'll *still* be late for your part of today's lecture."

Wandra stared at his timepiece, turned and rushed down the tunnel. Sorrel laughed, watching.

Cal never learned their names.

Their faces and their names changed, but their minds stayed the same—as each tech on the FTLcom project died, the Bloodkeepers fed his brainblood to the next,

Marc Stiegler

best returning larva. There was one class for the dayspinners and one for the night-spinners. The minds were constant within those two groups.

Too constant. Day after day Cal would answer the same questions—sharp, insightful questions, but still the same questions. Oh, the Rosans always knew all the facts before they came to class: they read all the textbooks beforehand. With photographic memories it was a breeze. Yes, they knew the facts—but to *understand* and *manipulate* those facts was another matter, and facts without understanding simply wouldn't transmit through brainblood. The brainblood absorbed abstruse mathematics in tiny increments; to produce a clear imprint would require generations of effort.

Sorrel and the Bloodkeepers told him that soon their determined screening and selection of bloodlines would produce engineers who remembered FTL hyperspace mechanics with facility, for whom the brainblood's *purpose* was directed toward this kind of learning. But for now there was a slow, painful learning process.

So Cal would teach. Incredibly swiftly they would learn, and then the new faces would come the next day, having forgotten. So Cal would teach.

Until one nightspin he met Dor Laff To Lin. She was delicate and graceful, even for a Rosan. Her mouth quirked into a laughing smile at the slightest provocation. Better yet, she asked new questions.

New questions! Her brain- and blood-parents had passed their knowledge and their understanding in brainblood, and Dor Laff knew it all. She knew, perhaps, as much as Cal himself, and when she reached midnight age Cal no longer knew answers to her questions. He blustered and flushed at her; she laughed and worked with him. She taught the rest of the class to help him find the answers to her new questions, digging ever deeper into the vitals of the Universe.

Cal had never known a woman with whom he could laugh and work, nor had he ever been a member of a team, a leading member at that: though Dor Laff controlled the discussions, it was Cal's mind that was central; it was Cal's mind that was tapped for knowledge and insights. They pushed him beyond the seeming limits of his creativity, to see new truths, and then they took his truth and ran with it farther and faster, in many directions, than a human mind could go.

But Cal didn't have time to be disturbed by their superiority—for as one group ran off with a new idea, Dor Laff would bring him back to work another track, another direction, to send another group racing in another new direction. Never had he loved so deeply someone who had given him so much.

Dawn approached; the brightness in Dor Laff's eyes was fading, but Cal was too flushed with victory to notice. He half-sat, half-fell to the edge of the lecture platform. Waves of exhaustion caught up with him. "Dor Laff, you're a miracle," he told her in ecstasy.

She knelt beside him and touched his cheek. The gentle petals of her hand brushed across his forehead. "Will you remember me?" she asked.

He looked into her eyes. "Of course I will."

She hugged him. "Thank you, thank you for letting me touch your immortality. She turned. "Good-bye."

He called to her, but she was gone for the moment. The fatigue of thirty hours of concentration took him; he slept.

When he woke, she was gone forever.

" . . . and things are going remarkably smoothly, all in all," Sorrel was saying into his dictalog when Wandra's call came through.

"Sorrel, we've got a problem here," Wandra yelled above the background sound of an angry crowd. "Cal's lost his cool, with a vengeance. We'll be lucky if they don't lynch us."

"Stay calm," he urged on his way out the door. "Be with you in a flash."

The FTLcom cavern had changed a great deal since the last time Sorrel had seen it; corners here and there contained the beginnings of pieces of equipment that would've given Euclid headaches; some were shrouded to prevent glances into the gravwarps being generated. There were nearly 400 Rosans there now, all murmuring to one another. Cal stood before them, cursing and pleading in anguish. "Why don't you remember? Why are you asking me the same thing again? Why do you question me? Listen to me, please!" Several of the Rosans had left their inclines and gathered near the front platform.

A dozen Rosans saw Sorrel enter the room and hurried to him. "Man Everwood, what should we do?" they asked, with reverence in their eyes.

"Nothing," he replied grimly. "Don't let any Rosans touch him. I'm gonna have enough trouble with him as it is." He turned to Wandra. "How tough are you in a fistfight?" Sorrel asked in Anglic.

"Brown belt in modkido. How 'bout you?" She barked a short, tense laugh.

He shook his head. "I'm too old, I'm afraid. I'll distract him; you grab him. Wish we had more manpower, but if the Rosans tried to touch him, he'd really go wild."

"They'd only get hurt, anyway—too fragile," she commented as they moved in on the podium.

"Cal," Sorrel yelled above the noise, "A shuttle just arrived from New Terra! There's a message for you!"

Cal stopped cold. "What?"

Wandra rushed him. He flailed, and Sorrel ran up to assist Wandra. A few minutes' struggle left Cal tired and sobbing.

"Take him back to his cave?" Wandra asked.

Sorrel shook his head. "The ship. Let's surround him with as much humanness as we can. He's suffering classic culture shock."

They picked him up, started him moving out of the cavern. "Classic culture shock? I never heard of anybody frothing gibberish because of culture shock before."

"Well, almost classic culture shock," Sorrel grunted. "You've gotta admit, this culture has a lot of shock in it." He bit his lip, and together they dragged Cal's limp body back to the ship.

Sorrel had never been a practicing psychologist, at least not to the extent of hanging out a shingle and looking for lost psyches. But it seemed to be his main function on this trip; perhaps Balcyrak had known all along that this would happen.

The psychologist took a deep breath, but otherwise retained a professional calm. Apparently this episode had been triggered by the death of a Rosan woman. Sorrel cursed himself for thinking Cal's aloofness would protect him; the aloofness had made him all the more vulnerable, once someone broke through the shell.

At the moment Sorrel was sitting quietly next to Cal, who lay on an accelerator couch pouring forth his soul. Freud would have loved it. Sorrel did not. It had taken great effort even to get Dor Laff's name, and Cal still didn't acknowledge her as his source of pain. "Is that the only problem with the Rosans, Cal? Are you sure?"

Cal nodded. "I can't stand it. Every day I teach the same thing, again and again, and the faces are *different*." The last ended in a howl of horror. "Every day different, never the same person twice." He whimpered, "Please, let me have just one student twice."

Sorrel shook his head. "Don't they remember, Cal? Don't they ever, from one day to the next? Just one thing. Can you remember?"

"Well . . . just a couple of things. Not much. Always the same questions . . . "

Wandra knocked at the open door of the cabin; Sorrel waved her in. "How's he doin', Doc?" she asked, attempting to be light and cheery.

"Cal's as fine as ever, of course. I think we'll spend the rest of the afternoon here, though. Can you manage the courses by yourself?"

She nodded. "You bet, Doc. Stimpills and me, we've got what it takes."

"Yeah, I'll bet. Next Cal will have to take the whole show for two days, while you recuperate."

"Faith, Doc, faith. Catch ya later." She was gone before Sorrel could speak again.

He turned back to Cal. "You were telling me what else bothers you about the Rosans, besides the fact that they forgot every day."

"I was?" Cal twisted his head to Sorrel. "I, uh, I guess there is something else. They don't remember too well, but . . . " Cal's shoulders shook as he sobbed. "They're, they're smarter than we are. I just don't believe how much smarter they are. So fast, so sharp. Every day I say the same things over again, but every day they learn it again in just a matter of minutes." He rolled over, away from Sorrel, and mumbled into the couch, "God, what I'd give to be able to think as fast as they can."

"Would you give your life for it, Cal? They do."

"I know, I know, but . . . " He rolled back over, smiled through the tears. "My old quant prof, Durbrig, used to tell me my problem was that I wanted it all. I guess I still do."

"I guess so, too. I envy you that, Cal. I wish I still had enough hope to dare to want it all." Sorrel stood up. "Stay here until, oh, maybe 5100 hours, and come on back to the cavernwork. Think you'll be all right?"

"Yeah." He smiled, crossed his arms as Wandra would. "Sure thing, Doc."

The new nightspin Bloodbond was different from the earlier Bonds; this Sorrel could tell already, and he hadn't even met the being yet. But so far three other Rosans had gone in to see the Bond, leaving Sorrel to cool his heels for upwards of two minutes—a short but significant wait. Earlier, Sorrel had received immediate service, regardless of how important the other callers were and how precious their time was. It had always made Sorrel uncomfortable before, but now its absence left a trace of anxiety nibbling his mind.

As the third Rosan left, Kik Nee Mord Deth beckoned him. "What, Man, want you?" he asked in peremptory Rosan.

"Equipment," Sorrel replied as smoothly as he could manage. "FTLcom tech bloodmemories firm now. Prototype construction begins. Trouble develops acquiring these items." He held out a list to Kik Nee, who snatched it, skimmed it, and thrust it back to Sorrel.

"Precious items," he commented. "Needed elsewhere."

"Priority 1A on FTLcom," Sorrel replied almost haughtily. That internal haughtiness surprised Sorrel himself. He'd never imagined himself pushing for the prerogatives the first Bloodbond had granted him, but Kik Nee rubbed him the wrong way. "Impediment intentional?"

The Rosan exhaled sharply. "Much work waits," he almost pleaded. "Let it progress. You need not speed, you have time."

And that, Sorrel knew, told the whole story. *You have time,* the Bloodbond knew, and hated. Jealousy haunted the Rosans at last. Sorrel cleared his throat. "I'm sorry. I've not treated you justly." Sorrel moved forward, took an incline. "But that equipment is needed. Without it the project halts. Though I can wait, engineers cannot. I waste not their lives." Sorrel remembered an old analogy, from the Rosan past. "There's an old bit of Rosan poetry—have you read Gesh Lok Tel Hor?"

The Rosan's lips drew back in disgust. "No time for ancient history."

Sorrel shook his head, blushed. "Of course not," he mumbled. "I'm sorry, again."

Kik Nee turned to the next waiting Rosan, who rushed into rapidfire discussion—again Sorrel was embarrassed at how much the Rosans had to slow down to talk to humans. But Sorrel wasn't done here yet. "Equipment?" he demanded in a loud, human voice, over the hummingbird sounds of the Rosans.

Kik Nee turned to him, head slumped ever so slightly. "Yours," he acquiesced.

Sorrel left with much food for thought.

Balcyrak stood with his back to Sorrel, watching the darkening sea, while the wind whipped his fur. Sorrel shivered, though the air was warm—on old Earth, the feeling in this evening air would have meant a storm coming.

Balcyrak turned as Sorrel approached. "You must see a sunrise while you are on Khayyam, Man Everwood. Do you know of them?"

Sorrel nodded. "I am, after all, the expert on the planet, right?"

Balcyrak chuckled. "Then tell me this, expert. From whence did the planet get its name?"

Sorrel tilted his head in thought. "You've got me there. I know it was discovered by a Lazarine, but Khayyam doesn't sound like a Lazarine name."

"It is not. The leader of the Lazarine expedition that landed on Khayyam was an expert, if you will, on Man. Omar Khayyam was one of your own poets. The Lazarine explorer named the planet for the human author who wrote so eloquently of a species similar to the people of Khayyam." He paused, looking again to the sea.

"Yes, Look—a thousand Blossoms with the Day

Woke—and a Thousand scattered in the Clay

And this first Summer Month that brings the Rose

Shall leave Another's gentle Petals, once blown, to lay."

Sorrel cleared his throat. "It does seem apropos, at that."

Balcyrak turned back to the human. "Yes. And now I have a warning for you."

"Oh?"

"Watch out while you are on Khayyam, my friend-to-be. When you arrive, you will be honored, but it will not last. You will prove too alien to them, and a love/hate bond will form. It will prove cyclic. First they will love, then they will hate, then they will love again." The Lazarine's hand clenched and unclenched as he spoke. "Much as Man loves and hates Lazaran," he whispered to the wind.

Sorrel squinted at him. "I see." Sorrel moved to stand shoulder to shoulder with Balcyrak, at the edge of the precipice. "Why is it so important to you that the FTL communicator be ready so soon? Granted, it'll prove valuable beyond price, but why the rush? Why do you need to send people hurtling halfway across known space to get it done so fast?"

Now it seemed that Balcyrak shivered under his thick coat of hair. "I suppose you should know. I suppose it might help motivate you, as well." He paused. "There will be another war between our peoples, Man Everwood."

Sorrel nodded; though currently the peacefulness of Man's relationship with the Lazarines was sickeningly sweet, he knew there was an undercurrent of hatred, a slowly growing group of people who disliked the Lazarines as much as Sorrel himself did. "Who will win?"

"Does it matter? Someone will lose. Someone, Man Everwood, will lose everything. The next war will be a war of genocide. Our wisest consuls have studied carefully, and they know not who will be destroyed, but all agree that one or the other of our species is doomed."

Sorrel paled; he hadn't realized it would go that far.

"We need better communications, Man Everwood. The time it takes for even the

starships to carry messages is too great for your people. Given better communications, and hence swifter understanding, we believe we can avert the war."

Sharp cynicism left a sour taste in Sorrel's mouth. "Communications will avert a war, huh? Just like that." He snapped his fingers. He'd heard that sort of thing before, but only from human dreamers who thought that words had substance. He hadn't expected it from a calm, realistic Lazarine.

"I don't blame you for doubting. Certainly, talk has rarely helped your species avert internal warfare. But this is considerably different." For the first time, the Lazarine's eyes refused to meet Sorrel's. "There is a . . . molding of directions involved. It is difficult to explain." Balcyrak's eyes regained their penetrating intensity. "But I am telling you the truth; communication is the answer." Now his amusement returned as well. "This also is something you'll understand better after working with the people of Khayyam."

Sorrel pursed his lips; Balcyrak's sincerity made a believer of him. "I confess, the urgency of the project seems somewhat greater now than it did a few minutes ago."

"I thought it might. Yes." A particularly strong gust of wind pushed them back from the cliff just as the sun sank beyond the horizon. They turned back to the path. "And remember to see a sunrise while you are there, Man Everwood. It is special indeed."

Sorrel squeezed through the narrow passage into the fresh-cut cavenet. "Whew!" he exclaimed, "that's a small entrance. I didn't even see it at first. You'll have to enlarge it."

The tunneling chief looked upset. "Of course, Man Everwood. The entranceway is always widened as the last step, so our noise and dust disturb the rest of the cavernwork as little as possible."

"Oh. I understand." Sorrel toured the new FTLcom lab facilities with some pleasure. "Well, it all looks pretty good to me, though I don't know anything about the arrangements you need for hyperspace experiments. I suppose we should have Cal and Wandra take a look."

They squeezed back out of the cavenet. Sorrel looked again at the narrow entrance. "Wait a minute. What if we *don't* open it up now?" He pondered for a moment.

The tunneling chief looked upset again. "Why wouldn't you open it?"

"Just in case of emergencies, that's all." He nodded his head. "Chief, these labs are ours to do with as we please, right?"

"Of course."

An evil gleam entered Sorrel's eyes. "Cal and Wandra will probably shoot me for this—the lecture hall is horribly overcrowded, and they need this space now—but I think we'll leave it as is."

The chief's petals fluttered rebelliously.

"Don't widen the entrance," Sorrel said, to make his orders explicit. "We'll open it later. When we want it, I'll have one of your bloodchildren do it for us."

The chief looked like he'd collapse with sorrow. Still he managed to stutter, "Yes, Man Everwood."

Sorrel touched his forearm. "And thanks. You've done a wonderful job. We'll remember you forever."

"Thank you, Man Everwood." The chief's eyes shone brightly again.

All the Rosans are bright, Wandra thought, *but this Sor Lai Don Shee is something special, even among Rosans.*

In fact, he and his descendants could be the key to turning the FTLcom problem into a trivial task. Sor Lai's bloodfeast memories were impossibly crisp, leaving him a perfect understanding of everything his four FTLcom engineering parents had understood.

That was exceptional enough—but then Sor Lai went beyond that. He also learned new things faster than anyone else, he asked the most insightful questions, and he brought new points of view to bear on every problem. In just a few weeks he could have resolved every remaining problem in the final design, Wandra was sure.

But he didn't have a few weeks, and when the second instruction session was over, Wandra didn't want to let him go; she wanted to keep teaching him, to pack as much of her mind into his as fast as she could. She hurried from the platform, worried she wouldn't catch him before he burst from the room in normal Rosan fashion.

But he was not hurrying off with his peers; rather, he was hurrying toward Wandra, and only swift Rosan reflexes kept them from colliding in mid-step.

Wandra gurgled with laughter. "Two minds with one thought," she said. "Would you like to continue our discussions?"

Sor Lai smiled as only a Rosan could smile, with the cheeks lifting gaily and petals fluttering as though in a breeze. "Very much, Man Furenz. I would appreciate it beyond your knowing."

She crossed her fingers at him. "My name is Wandra, Sor Lai. I hate formality."

She had to admit, she liked Sor Lai for more than merely his superior performance. She liked the naive optimism he'd shown early in the day, and she enjoyed watching that optimism develop by midnight age into a mature confidence. He knew that the eccentricities of the Universe could impede progress, or even reverse progress, but never, in the long run, stop progress.

They turned to the cavern passage. "Come with me," Wandra bubbled. "We'll go to my . . . " Wandra bit her lip; there was no word for "home" in Rosan. "We'll go to my place-of-work."

Sor Lai looked puzzled. "Isn't the lecture hall your place-of-work?"

She threw up her hands. "I have many places-of-work. This is a special one."

"I see. I think I understand."

She took him by the arm. "I see a free speedcart up ahead. Race ya!"

Sor Lai won the race, of course, laughing all the way.

* * *

They survived Sor Lai's driving, somewhat to Wandra's surprise, and stopped before the small fountain at the entrance to Wandra's cavern. "Beautiful!" Sor Lai exclaimed. "How many people worked upon this? And what does it do?"

Wandra shook her head. "I built it myself; I'm a sometimes-sculptor. It's not very good, I'm afraid. And all it does is shoot water in the air, from the fairy's fingertips, and collect it again among the green rocks beneath her feet." She turned to flick the pump switch. A thin stream danced up, spiraled down again. Sor Lai bent to touch the smooth stone, amazed. "This is the work of many lifetimes. Joyous." He rose up. "What else do Men do in their immortality?"

Wandra stammered in horror.

"Do not answer. I'm sorry." He came and took her arm. "I must see the rest of your place-of-work." They entered Wandra's home together.

Sor Lai pointed at the walls. "The pictures. Of what are the pictures?" he demanded.

Wandra looked at the scenes of Karly for the first time in weeks. "Pictures of my—" again, there was no word for home— "birth world. I had our ship computer make these up specially—they appear through my infrared goggles to look the way the originals look in normal light—normal light, that is, for a Man. So you're seeing my planet as I see it, more or less."

"These are all pictures of the surface!"

Wandra nodded. "It is gentler on my world than on Khayyam." She looked at the dry-ice-capped mountain towering above the capital and chuckled. "Though not too gentle, I suppose."

Sor Lai looked at another scene, where the sun set over a pink, powdery beach. "Those aren't Men, are they? They're too small."

Wandra followed his pointing finger. "They are almost Men, Sor Lai. They are my children. Humans metamorphose slowly, gradually becoming more Manlike."

"Your children!" He scrutinized the picture. "They laugh with grace. Have you met them? You could have met them, couldn't you?"

Wandra laughed. "Yes, Sor Lai, I lived with them for a long time."

Sor Lai turned back to Wandra. "Do they know your memories well?"

Wandra pondered that. "I suppose you could say they do, at least as Men go. They're more like me than their father, that's for sure. They'll be great mathematicians, someday, not housekeepers like my ex-husband." She shook her head.

Sor Lai turned slowly through the room. "And a love couch right here, in your place-of-work!"

Wandra blushed, though she wasn't sure why; she'd never thought of herself as the innocent type. "Not for a long time, my friend. I use it for, uh . . . You've noticed that Men tire faster than Rosans, haven't you? I rest there. We are unconscious for almost a third of our lives, resting."

"And still you get so many things done." Sor Lai's admiration continued.

By now Wandra's face was burning. "We do our best," she muttered. She turned to her kitchen. "Now, I have to eat something, or I'll die of starvation."

Sor Lai's admiration turned to amazement. "Eat! Like a larva?" he gasped.

"You bet," she agreed. "We don't store enough fat before adulthood to last for the rest of our lives, though sometimes it seems like my body's trying to."

At last Sor Lai was speechless. Wandra cooked, set the table, and started to eat. She talked mathematics continually, until she noticed the horror on Sor Lai's face. She felt uncomfortable. "Listen, do you want me to eat another time?"

"No, not at all," Sor Lai said. To Wandra, he seemed to be shuddering. "It's . . . intriguing."

She looked at him a while, then continued her meal.

"I remember my bloodfeast," he said, petals waving ecstatically. "It is a joy beyond imagining."

"I believe it," Wandra replied. "When we eat, though, it's nothing like that." She had heard of Rosans with keen memories of the bloodfeast ecstasy actually stealing someone's brainblood, to try to eat it—even though the adult Rosan's digestive tract is atrophied. And the ecstasy had to be strong indeed, to risk the consequences—for the stealing of another Rosan's brainblood was punishable by brainblood cremation.

They talked. Wandra finished her meal at last, and the two of them sat upon her bed, still talking. Suddenly Sor Lai clapped his hands and jumped to his feet. "You know, this hyperspace link with sound and video is all right, but the properties of the four-space beg you to generate three-dimensional pictures. Do you have a computer terminal here?"

Wandra was on her feet as well. "It begs you, huh? Well, it never begged me, but if you say so, here—" She marched to her desk and pulled out a keyboard. The wall in front of her lit up, and with quick keystrokes she logged into the Rosan central computer system.

Sor Lai crossed the room to join her. His fingers flew across the keys, and he spoke in machine-gun Rosan as the ideas developed and the machines to implement them took shape. Wandra could only stand and stare. "There," he proclaimed at last. "It's even better than I thought. When the FTLcom is ready, you won't even have to send a ship to deliver the construction plans to people on other planets. We'll be able to project and receive 3-D images all with one transceiver, without any equipment at the other end. Unless they throw a blast screen around your target location or some such thing."

Wandra continued to stare at him. "That's incredible."

He smiled broadly. "Yes, it is, isn't it?"

She laughed. "Even more incredible than a Man who eats even after she becomes an adult."

His smile turned quiet. "No, not as incredible as that."

They hugged each other, artificial coolsuit petals touching honest, living, roselike petals.

For the first time, Wandra became aware of how much thinner Sor Lai was now than when they'd left for her home. She looked at her watch; six hours had passed: the equivalent, in Rosan terms, of almost ten years.

Wandra jerked away. "Sor Lai!" she almost screamed. "We have to get you back!"

"I guess we should, at that," he conceded.

They speeded through the cavenets, as fast as they'd gone before, yet it was too slow for Wandra's concern. She had used up an awesome part of Sor Lai's life, just bringing him home.

Wandra tried to counter her guilt with logic. After all, the time had been productive, hadn't it? And yes, it had been worth it, hadn't it? She hurt nevertheless.

They returned to the conference cavern, where Cal was lecturing. Sor Lai took his place among his fellows, but Wandra couldn't bear to leave. She listened to Cal's lecture absently, looking among the now dawning-aged nightspinners, seeing them for the first time, watching them grow old.

The lecture ended, and a break was taken—a break to work on the two prototypes nearing completion. Wandra hovered by Sor Lai's team. Work ended, and Wandra lectured, and work continued, until dawn.

Wandra fought the tears gathering in her eyes. The curled, green-tinged petals spread inexorably across Sor Lai's body. He smiled at her sadly. "You should leave me now," he whispered. "It's time for me to go, to let my children remember."

"No, let us not waste a minute of life," Wandra choked.

The laughter in his eyes calmed. "I am tired," he said. He settled to the ground. "I'm sorry."

Wandra knelt beside him.

The air turned sweet with honeysuckle, and the flowing blood mingled with a woman's tears.

Sorrel peeked around the corner, into the interior of Wandra's home. "Anybody home?" he asked, watching her lie upon her bed.

She turned to him, tired and distraught. "Hi," she smiled wanly. "I'm sorry I haven't made it in yet. The students are probably better off without me, anyway."

Sorrel slipped in, moved to sit on the edge of her bed. "Are you sick? Did you finally find a bacterium on this planet that knows what to do with our proteins?"

She shook her head.

He nodded. "I understand there was an exceptional student during nightspin."

She nodded.

"I also hear . . . you were rather fond of him."

She rolled away. "God, yes. He was kind, he was beautiful, he was . . . "

"He was all good things. I know. It seems to be a common trait among the Rosans." He rolled her gently over to face him.

"Why do they have to die so soon?" she yelled at him. "Why can't they live like we do, and laugh and love and talk with their children and . . . " She was crying.

Sorrel raised her by her shoulders, held her close. "They can't live like we do because Nature didn't design them to live like we do. Because at the time of their evolving, death at dawn was certain. Why would Nature spend such an effort, giving long life to one doomed to die anyway?"

Wandra started rocking, bringing her legs up into a foetal position. Sorrel stroked her hair. "You remember that krat we saw a while ago, outside the conference hall?"

She nodded.

"I saw it again yesterday."

She looked up. "What? The same one?"

Sorrel shrugged. "It had the same ragged scar on its side."

Wandra's mouth hung open, forming the obvious question.

"The krats have been luckier than the Rosans. When the Rosans moved into the caverns, they found a place free of evolutionary pressures, where they could prosper without menace. But when the krats came, they found the Rosans already here, determined to keep their caves and destroy the invaders. Thus the krats still had evolutionary pressures. Only the strong survived. Nature discovered that longevity would be useful for krats; and the krats earned longer lives through generations of bloodletting.

"But Nature doesn't choose for long life among Rosans, because there is no need —and only need causes Nature to care. Nature doesn't care whether the Rosans survive with grace or joy—Nature only cares that they survive, one way or another. The Rosans can never develop longevity, because they are too good at surviving without it." Sorrel was surprised at the bitterness creeping into his voice. "The characteristics that make them so wonderful and worth saving are the same characteristics that damn them to mere instants of time for all eternity."

"It's not fair," Wandra wailed.

"Fairness and justice have nothing to do with it," Sorrel continued, and this time the bitterness was undeniable. The vision of his children dying on a radiation-burned planet burned his mind. "Nature knows nothing of justice. Only Men think of justice; it is a concept we invented and it exists only when we can create it."

They were both quiet for a long time; finally Wandra spoke. "Isn't there something we can do? Intravenous feeding or something?"

Sorrel shook his head. "That's done under special conditions, but the basic lifetime of the Rosan is built into the cells. Even with plenty of nutrients, the cells just stop metabolizing. It's as if they knew they were supposed to die."

"What about slowing down their metabolisms?"

Sorrel looked her in the eye. "If you could extend your life by a tenth, but to do it you had to cut your ability to live each moment of that life in half, would you do it?"

Wandra sobbed. Sorrel stroked her hair again. "I wish I could say something more soothing." His voice turned gentle again.

Wandra's arms tightened around Sorrel's chest. "Would you . . . stay with me? Till tomorrow?"

Sorrel drew a ragged breath; suddenly, he felt like the old man he sometimes knew himself to be. "I would," he said softly, "if I really believed that, in your heart, you wanted me to." He kissed her on the forehead, disengaged slowly. "I'll see you in a few hours. If you have trouble sleeping, call me." He looked down at her a last time. "Dream well," he whispered as he left.

Kir Bay played with his FTLcom medallion as he spoke. "Well, at least we still have plenty of time left. It'll be hours before the Bloodbond election. It's a shame, though, that the Supremi candidate is certain to win."

Sorrel gasped in horror. "What?!" It had been several days since Sorrel last listened to the Rosan news broadcasts. Now he cursed himself under his breath for not keeping better track; less than a week ago, the Supremi had been just another religious splinter group, with a half-sentence mention in the course of a full spin's broadcasts.

"Is it that important?" the engineer was puzzled. "It's not as if it'll kill the project."

Sorrel rolled his eyes to the ceiling. "Politicians, unfortunately, are even crazier than they seem, Kir Bay. If the Supremi get control of the government, not only will they destroy the project, they'll also destroy you—and I mean burning your brainblood, not just arranging an early death."

It was Kir Bay's turn to gasp in horror. "Are you serious?"

"How closely have you listened to the Supremi plans? They hate humans and everything associated with them. As chief engineer on our project, you're a public enemy in their eyes."

Kir Bay's petals tensed against his body. "I just can't believe it."

"Then come with me." Sorrel consulted Daisy, the starship's computer, on his radcom and found a place where they could hear a prominent Supremi politician speak.

They arrived to find a large crowd mesmerized by the fiery words of a fanatic. Few people saw Sorrel and Kir Bay arrive; those who did drew away from them in contempt, and some of them hissed in fury.

Soon Kir Bay had had enough. "You were right. We're in great danger."

Sorrel pulled him out of the Supremi cavern. "Fortunately I've made some preparations for this, though not as many as I'd planned. Damn! You people move too fast." He sighed. "Listen. Long ago, a special set of laboratories was prepared for the FTLcom project. Just as they were getting finished, I put a damper on the job, and now I'm the only one who knows where they are." He told Kir Bay how to find the narrow entranceway. "Get everybody down there you can—but do it quietly!"

"What about you?"

"I've got an appointment with a Bloodkeeper. I'll catch up with you later." Sorrel shoved him toward the cart, then ran off in the other direction, toward the Bloodkeep.

There was one Bloodkeeper left who still believed in the FTLcom project, one Bloodkeeper whose bloodline Sorrel had nurtured and protected from the Man-hatred that now exploded through the Rosan culture. Sorrel had talked with the current member of that bloodline earlier that nightspin, though he hadn't talked with him about the dangers of Supremi leadership. Sorrel hoped the two of them could work something out to protect the bloodlines they had so painfully constructed.

As he ran, Sorrel listened on his radio to Daisy's translation of the Rosan newscasts. With a sinking heart, he found that Kir Bay had been wrong; they didn't even have hours before the Supremi took control. There was a revolution in progress, and the elections were being pushed ahead of schedule to select the new Bloodbond.

Sorrel leaned against the wall of the tunnel, panting, wishing he'd learned how to drive the Rosan vehicles even though it was crazy for a human to try to drive down the tunnels—men just didn't have fast enough reflexes for Rosan traffic.

Soon he realized that he wasn't going to make it to the Bloodkeep in time, and he interrupted Daisy's incessant reports on the radcom. "Daisy, is there anything you can hook me with to get through to the Bloodkeep? I need to talk to Mai Toam Let Call."

Sorrel listened as Daisy tried various patches into the Rosan communication systems. Finally they linked to the Bloodkeep, and Mai Toam answered. "Thank God you're there!" Sorrel exclaimed. "Have you been listening to the news?"

"Yes." The Rosan's voice sounded grave. "We face trouble, I fear."

"By the galaxyful," Sorrel muttered. "Listen . . . is it possible to, uh . . . jimmy the labels on people's brainblood?"

Mai Toam coughed politely. "It is flagrantly illegal, Man Everwood." His cough gurgled into a chuckle. "It is not, however, unheard of."

"I see."

Daisy's voice filled the line. "I don't wish to interrupt you, gentlemen, but I've heard some news I believe to be important. The selections are over. The Supremi have given orders to capture everyone involved with the FTLcom project."

It had all happened so swiftly! Sorrel held down the fear in his stomach. "Call Kir Bay and warn him. Tell him I'll meet him at the new labs."

Sorrel rushed down the cavernwork tunnels toward the hidden cavenet, giving orders over his radcom all the way. "Mai Toam, quickly! Switch brainblood nametags on the cannisters for Dor Kat, Tey Fin, and Dor Lee with the nametags for other Rosans—Rosans who're supposed to be loyal to the Supremi. Can your bloodmemroies transmit the switches?"

"Probably, Man Everwood, but I'll give you a list for safety. High chance says they destroy my brainblood when ledgers show tampered feast labels."

"Oh my god." Sorrel stopped his running, trying to think of an alternative to losing the Keeper's descendants.

"No fear, Man Everwood. Hope is, to switch my brainblood also. You need remember, whereto I'm switched. Prai Kan Tor Loov will be me renewed."

"Good. I'll remember," Sorrel promised, praying he told the truth. He'd have to write that name down at first opportunity. "Kir Bay, have you stashed the equipment?"

"Yes. All's set."

"Great. I'll be there in—" Sorrel leaped to the landing one level lower, turned right, and ran into four younger Rosans. *The Supremi got me,* was Sorrel's first panicky thought.

"Man Everwood, Kir Bay sent us. We return you to your ship swiftly."

"But—"

The radcom spoke; it was Kir Bay again. "All's controlled here, Man Everwood; your advance planning let us prepare with thoroughness and speed. Thank you. Now, you must return to your ship, where you'll be safe for a few generations."

"But—"

The four Rosans were already herding him back the way he had come.

"Where are Cal and Wandra?" Sorrel demanded.

"Good luck, Man Everwood," the radcom answered obliquely. "May you die by a rising star."

One of the four shepherds answered more directly. "Man Minov and Man Furenz return to the ship. You'll see soon." As they rounded another corner, the lead Rosan jumped back, hitting Sorrel in the chest. "Feign death," he commanded.

Sorrel performed as ordered, slumping into their arms. They carried him around the corner, shouted several rapid sentences at someone. More hands grabbed Sorrel, more words, and he heard many people going with him for interminable distances. His arm was being slowly, agonizingly, dislocated from his shoulder by one of his carriers; but he had no time to worry about that; his concentration was focussed on trying not to breathe. He was not very successful.

At last there was a scuffle. "Run!" someone yelled in his ear, and Sorrel twisted to his feet and ran, following the Rosan leader, not daring to look around to see what was happening. The two of them continued to run till they reached the entrance to the outercave, where the ship lay. Five more Rosans pressed there against a long outcropping of stone, along with Cal and Wandra. Wandra held her finger to her lips, gesturing Sorrel to silence. She whispered, "Guards," and pointed over the outcropping. Sorrel nodded.

The six Rosans held a quiet but rapidfire conference, lasting almost a minute, then split in four directions. There was noise from beyond the outcropping, and a portable sonic pulverizer—designed for crushing rocks during excavation—screamed. "Run for the ship!" Sorrel's Rosan yelled above the din. "Good luck!" He ran in front of the three humans into the open stretch by the slagged landing area.

The weapons there could've killed fully armored Rosan larvae, to say nothing of killing delicate humans, but fortunately the guards were busy. Again Sorrel didn't have time to see how they were being distracted—his goggles obstructed his peripheral vision—but the FTLcom team was doing a good job, and only one guard saw the three humans coming. The Rosan leader leaped at him and knocked him down, but in leaping the leader took the tip of a larva-prod in the chest and started to writhe uncontrollably. Wandra screamed; Sorrel pushed her toward the ship's lock as it swept to ground level. Another sonic blaster wailed, and the three humans dived into the lock, which now swept back up into the body of the ship.

All three were shaking and panting. "We've gotta lift off," Cal gasped, heading for the pilot room.

"No," Sorrel said, "don't. Nothing out there will hurt our asteroid armor. It'd take them generations to haul a main tunnel beamer up here from the bottom levels—and if they did that we'd have plenty of warning." Sorrel was still panting, thinking he talked too much. "Daisy," he breathed at the computer, "Show us the cavernwork entrance."

"Yes, sir."

Cal and Wandra followed Sorrel into the rec bay; everyone collapsed onto his or her favorite recliner, then looked at the vidscreen's view of the entrance. Several Rosans lay in pools of green jelly, including four of the people who had helped them escape.

"Damn," Cal muttered.

Another party of solemn Rosans, wearing the medallions of the Supremi Elders, came into view, to pour smouldering acid on the brainblood of the traitors, the friends-to-humans.

Wandra clenched her fists in horror. "You bastards!" she screamed into the unhearing viewer.

"Viewer off, Daisy," Sorrel commanded.

"I'll kill 'em," Cal swore, heading for the weapons locker with renewed strength. Sorrel leaped up, blocking his path. "You'll only get yourself killed."

"Get out of my way," Cal warned, pushing Sorrel hard.

"Stop, you idiot," Sorrel said in exasperation, then hit Cal three times, twice in the stomach, once in the eye.

Caught by surprise, Cal dropped to the floor. By the time he struggled back to his feet Sorrel was snapping a sleep hypo out of his med kit. Cal tried to dodge, but Sorrel winged him with the hypo. "Moron," Cal muttered as his eyeballs rolled up. Sorrel caught him as he fell. "I'll kill the fiends anyway. Wait till I get up."

But by the time Cal returned to consciousness, the fiends, and the followers, and the vanquished friends, had all already died.

Two days later Sorrel called a council of war. They were sitting in the rec bay, weighing possibilities. "Bring in a battleship," was Cal's first, half-serious suggestion.

Sorrel shuddered. "Right. I'm sure the Rosans work every bit as well under compulsion as Men do."

Wandra bit her nails. "Isn't there some way we can talk with the new leaders?"

Sorrel shrugged. "They know how to reach us—the radcom's in perfect shape. I'm afraid, though, that they're not interested. If I didn't know better, I'd guess they'd forgotten us."

Cal sneered. "What? Forget their God?"

Petals of Rose 275

Daisy rang an alert bell. "We have visitors."

Sorrel looked up. "Are they armed?"

"No."

"Then let's see 'em."

The vidscreen brightened, to show a small party of Rosans. The two leaders, carefully facing away from the cavernworks, proudly bore the medallions of FTLcom techs. "Connect us to the external two-way, Daisy," Sorrel said as he rose. "Hello," he waved to the Rosans. "Glad to see somebody finally came around."

Several of the followers looked away, muttering, touching their shoulders with their hands, then sweeping a half-circle, as in the prayers of the Faith of Six Parents. Even the leaders averted their eyes.

One of them spoke. "Men of Earth, my children will remember this moment forever. We apologize for disturbing you."

"Nonsense, my friends." Sorrel smiled, then whispered to Daisy. "Are you sure they're unarmed?"

Yes, Daisy printed on the vidscreen, invisible to the visitors.

"Why don't you two come in?" Sorrel continued.

They swept the prayerful half-circle. "We'd be honored, Man Everwood."

The lock descended to them, and Sorrel sighed. "It's so comfortable in here, those guys would freeze to death. Daisy, you'd better turn up the heat—" Sorrel turned to his companions— "and we'd better check out our coolsuits again."

They were older Rosans, Sorrel realized when they had come inside the ship. "What time is it out there?" he asked.

"Close to dawn, Man Everwood."

Sorrel nodded.

"As you can see, the blood of the FTLcom is weak, yet still lives."

"I hope that that'll soon change?" Sorrel asked. "Else you shouldn't have risked coming here."

"Yes. During nightspin there's still much danger. But the dayspinners never turned as fanatical, though Supremi attitudes abound. We think you could return to MoonBender during dayspin with little risk."

Cal banged the table. "Great. So we can get the project underway again."

The Rosans' petals drooped. "Not quite so easy. Without at least neutrality from nightspin leaders, any dayspin work would be regularly sabotaged. Further, dayspin leaders wouldn't make a commitment without nightspin assent—the nightspin Bloodbond is more powerful, since more people live in nightspin time."

Sorrel muttered. "So we have to get nightspin authority."

"Yes."

Sorrel got up, started pacing around the room. "Tell me. Would they kill me on sight, if I returned during nightspin?"

The two Rosans spoke briefly, then the one replied. "No, we don't think so—the Supremi religion is still rooted, after all, in the Faith of Six Parents, and they must revere you for that. Now that all's calmer, you might be safe. But Man Furenz and Man Minov concern us; their danger would be great.''

"Good enough. I'll go convince the Supremi leader—what's his name?"

"Kip Sur Tel Yan.''

"Ah. Take me to him, and we'll have priority 1A again before his bloodfeast."

The Rosans gawked. "How?"

Sorrel pursed his lips. "I shall be like a Lazarine unto him," he said grimly. No one understood, and he waved his hands. "Fear not. Kip Sur is putty for my molding. Soon he'll know the FTLcom is the most magnificent weapon the Supremi ever dreamed of." *And Balcyrak will be proud of me*, he thought sourly. He strapped his infrared goggles back into place and departed with the Rosans.

The Bond was old, very old; it was a state Sorrel had seen too many times. But this time that was a good sign. "I have a proposition for you," Sorrel told the Supremi leader.

Rosan facial muscles aren't designed for sneering. Kip Sur gave Sorrel a good imitation. "A weakling from an inferior race brings me a proposition?"

Sorrel drew himself up in anger. "May I remind you that this particular weakling wrought the Faith of Six from Beyond, to make possible your successes of today?"

The Bond's wide, bright eyes radiated anger. Sorrel continued.

"May I remind you that, though you go soon to meet a rising star, I will remain, to make or break the plans you design today."

That got Kip Sur where it hurt; but Sorrel had to move fast, before Kip Sur's agony turned into even more burning jealousy. "Fear not. You have a chance here to touch eternity, for I can protect and assure your plans, if we come to an agreement."

The agony and depression turned to slyness. "What is your proposition?"

"I intend to help you expand into the Universe, to spread the glory and power of the Supremi across the stars."

"You want me to authorize the continuation of the FTLcom project."

Sorrel was again surprised at the speed of Rosan thought. "I don't think you appreciate the values the FTLcom has to offer the Supremi. There are billions of planets out there, hundreds of intelligent species, and the FTLcom will open them all up for you. Think of it! Always before your people have been trapped on this planet, unable to touch any part of the Universe that didn't reach out to touch you.''

The Bond was swept up in a vision of his own. "Of course! Fleets of robot battleships, that we could control from here no matter how far they traveled! At last, to achieve our destiny as conquerors!"

It wasn't exactly the vision Sorrel planned, but it would do. "There's more. With all those conquered species, you'll have plenty of manpower to build colonization ships—ships large enough and stout enough to contain full generations of Rosans, adults and larvae and eggs, so the Supremi could build cities on gentler planets, where growth would not be so slow and painful. Whereas today you can at best fill a handful of cavernworks, tomorrow you could fill hundreds of worlds."

The Bond's slyness now turned to suspicion. "Why would you help us conquer your own people?"

Sorrel frowned. Since he didn't know what kind of a lie to tell, he settled reluctantly on the truth. "The FTLcom will enrich your people's lives, Kip Sur, but I don't think it'll do so in the manner you foresee; I believe the desire to conquer will pass, and Man will benefit almost as much as Rosan from our development."

"You doubt that we, with our superior ability, will one day conquer you? Is not victory of the strong inevitable?"

Sorrel shrugged. "We have a testing here, of your future vision against mine—but in both those futures the FTLcom is crucial. I can accept the dangers in your vision, if you can accept the dangers in mine."

The old Bond relaxed on his incline. "Let the visions compete," he said, and rushed to his desk to prepare orders. "Congratulations, Man Everwood; your FTLcom is now a top priority, even higher than before."

Of course, there couldn't be a higher priority than the old FTLcom priority, but Sorrel thanked the Bond anyway; naturally a prioritization made generations ago wouldn't be remembered in the brainblood.

The Bond turned back to Sorrel, teeth bared in a look of pure evil. "But only the visions shall compete, and neither of us will ever know who was right. Guards!"

The adrenalin surged through Sorrel's bloodstream; his heart nearly exploded as he saw his soon-to-be executioners coming. But despite his rising panic, his brain surged with thought as swift as a Rosan's. He searched the room for a means of escape; he saw the Bond with a clarity given only to those walking the edge of death.

Even as Sorrel watched, the Bond seemed to age. Sorrel had known countless Rosans as they aged—far more than any Rosan had ever known—and in his need, Sorrel foresaw to within seconds how long the Bond would live; it was not much. Sorrel waved for help. "Guards!" he echoed the Bond's request, but with much urgency. He jumped half across the desk, grabbing the surprised Bond in a steely grip; the Rosan struggled, but was no match for Sorrel's strength.

Kip Sur shouted orders to the guards, but Sorrel shouted louder and longer. "The Bond's been poisoned! Send for a doctor immediately! Someone get over here and help me get him to the floor—he's writhing, and I'm afraid he'll hurt himself." Just then the Bond did writhe again, and both he and Sorrel crashed to the floor.

The Bond took a deep breath. "Hate," he spat in Sorrel's face, exhaling hard.

His breath was sweet with honeysuckle.

A guard stood uncertainly over them. "What kind of poison?" he asked.

Sorrel struggled to his feet, shaking his head. "I was wrong; call off the medics." Brainblood spread on the floor. "It was just . . . old age."

"You wish me to feast a larva with the blood of Prai Kan Tor Loov?" The Bloodkeeper scowled at Sorrel. "He is a Supremi Keeper, not an FTLcom tech. Why would you want him?"

Marc Stiegler

"Do we have a 1A priority or not?" Sorrel snapped; he'd already bungled this operation, and the longer the Keeper thought about it the more likely he was to deduce the truth. "The FTLcom tech bloodlines have all been destroyed—your ancestors already took care of that. We're searching for the closest derivatives of those lines. There are only a few bloods with even brainparent histories of FTLcom blood. The computer searches show Prai Kan to be one such."

The scowl did not ease. "You have no jurisdiction over the blood of Keepers."

Sorrel crossed his arms. "Do I have to go to the Bond and embarrass you? Does our priority not tell you the importance of my presence here?"

The Rosan ground his teeth, then at last signed the papers. "He shall join us in the next generation. May you die by a rising star, Sacred One."

The next day Sorrel returned to the Bloodkeep. He found that a smiling face had replaced the scowling one. "My children will remember this moment, Man Everwood," the new Keeper began. "My name is Col Salm Keer Prai."

"Decendent of Mai Toam Let Call?"

The Rosan's eyes danced with laughter. "Are you a member of the Supremi ruling family? If so, then I am not. If not, then I am so."

Sorrel laughed with the Keeper. "How is your bloodmemory?"

"Keen. I have taken the liberty of arranging a number of bloodfeasts for you already. I trust you'll be surprised at how swiftly my bloodmixes bear techs with good memories for FTLcom work."

"I trust also. But there's other blood even more important that you don't know about." Sorrel told him of the secret FTLcom cavern. "The brainbloods of all the techs who died in the labs should still be there. We'll truly have a Renaissance, if you can somehow return their bloods to the system."

Col Salm pondered a moment. "Difficult, but worthy. It shall be done." He looked at Sorrel with the too-common awe of a child. "You've performed a miracle, saving so many of our people."

"Umph," Sorrel still chastised himself for not having done better, but then, it was also true that no Rosan could have done as well. "Yes, the techs have been saved. I just wish I knew what to do about the Supremi, whom I would like not to see saved."

Col Salm's petals waved in agreement. "How sad there are no more politicians or theologians like Prim Sol Mem Brite."

Sorrel looked away. "Yes. Or even like Or Sae Hi Tor." A puzzled thought overtook him. "That reminds me of something I've wondered about for a long time. What ever happened to the brainblood of Prim Sol Mem Brite? I would have expected all the political bloodlines to trace back to the First Disciple of the Faith of Six."

"Didn't you know the fate of the first carrier of your Gospel?" The Rosan must have been stunned by such ignorance; Sorrel blushed furiously. "I'm sorry to be the bearer of these age-old tidings. There was much turmoil in the wake of Prim Sol's revelations. The labels in the bloodkeeps were all either destroyed or switched, by either supporters of the Great Faith or by the traitors who still supported the Faith of Four. The Disciple's brainblood was lost amid the chaos, as were all other people's.''

"Couldn't you trace his lineage after the fact? Surely anyone who had him as a blood- or brainparent would remember, at least for a few generations.''

"Oh yes, many people claimed him as ancestor—far more than any being's brainblood could give feast for.'' He waved his petals in futility. "They say our newer computers could trace back to him, and then back again to modern times, but it would be the work of generations. Several efforts have been made in the past. They failed, long before it even could be determined whether success was possible.'' His petals pulsed in sorrow. "And if found, what value would it produce? His memories are ages too remote to be found again—even the best memories could not bring him back.''

"They couldn't, huh?'' Sorrel clapped his hands in joy. "My friend, I think you've just ended our troubles. Thank you.'' He was quite sure he left the good Keeper quite mystified.

Sorrel was whistling when he barged into Wandra's room on board the ship. "I'm canceling all your lectures for the next few days,'' he said.

"What?'' Wandra whirled away from her dresser to face him. "Who would I be lecturing anyway?''

Sorrel told her about the techs who would soon receive incarnations. "But that's not the best news, and that's why you won't start teaching yet.''

"What could be better?''

Sorrel pulled out a grease pencil and scribbled on the wall.

"Hey! Stop that!'' Wandra tried to pull him away, but he laughed and finished his writing. PRIM SOL MEM BRITE RETURNS, the scribble said.

"I've started putting a few inscriptions like this here and there throughout MoonBender. So the natives can get used to the idea.''

"Have you completely lost your mind? What are you doing?''

"I'm bringing the Faith back to Khayyam. And you and me, lady, we're gonna bring the Disciple himself back to do it!'' Sorrel told her about the great politician/theologian who so many years ago first translated Sorrel's dissertation into the Faith of Six Parents. "So your task, my lady, is to hop onto that computer and find his descendants.''

She shook her head, dazed. "Would you calm down? You're still moving too fast for me. What good will it do to find his descendants? They don't remember anything about him, do they? To say nothing of being like him.''

Sorrel rubbed his hands together. "True, my lady, true. And even the best Rosan memorists can't bring back memories more than a handful of generations old.'' He pointed to himself. "But this ain't no Rosan memorist here.'' His voice turned grim. "No, I'm no Rosan. I'm almost an immortal. And just this once, that 'almost' will be enough.''

Marc Stiegler

It took many days to find a bloodline with a high probability of tracing from the Disciple; and that was just the beginning. "So we believe you are his descendent," Sorrel told the Rosan who had been chosen by fate and technology. "We want to hypnotize you and do a complete memorist retrogression to find his memories."

The Rosan puffed up with pride in his heritage. "I'd love to have his memories," he said dreamily. "Can you do it? I didn't know you could retromemorize that far."

Sorrel grimaced. "Well, you've hit on the problem. You see, we can do it—but you'll never know. If you agree to memorist hypnosis, you'll spend the rest of your life here in trance. Then we'll do the same with your children, and their children, and finally some generation we will find out whether the computers were right, whether the Disciple is the founder of your family."

The dreamy look fell from the Rosan's face for a moment. "It must be very important."

"More so than I can explain."

The Rosan sighed. "What nobler cause could there be, than to give one's life to reunite the Writer of the Gospel with his Disciple, the Parent with his Child? Let us begin."

So they began. Layer after layer of Rosan personalities peeled back before Sorrel's patient yet relentless questing. But each peeling brought him to two bloodparents, two predecessors, and two more possible paths to Prim Sol. Soon Sorrel could no longer peel back through all the parents; he and Wandra were reduced to eking out clues from the Rosan computers and the Rosan minds. With those clues, they fought and considered and guessed and, finally, selected the paths to search.

And the helpful Rosan's children came to them, and stayed, and grew old, and died. Though the Rosans came freely, and rarely complained of their loss, yet with each child and with each child's child the burden of Sorrel's guilt grew. Each day Sorrel cursed himself for a fool; had he known truly the price of the search before beginning, he would not have started, he would say, and Wandra would tap her foot and tell him he was full of it, and soothe him and convince him that it was too late to turn back, that they should not waste the lives of the Rosans who volunteered to help.

And finally they reached back into the time of the Revelation, and a dying Rosan opened his eyes with surprise to tell them, "I remember."

Sorrel paced back and forth in front of the larval Keep.

"You look like an expectant father," Wandra chastised him.

"I suppose in a sense I *am* a father," he replied. "In some sense, he is my creation—both in that earlier time when he rose because of my work, and now because this Rosan remembers his memories because of my efforts." He stopped his pacing. He muttered, "Perhaps together we can do enough good to compensate these people for the wrongs we caused separately."

Wandra snorted. "He certainly ought to be able to do something—with the blood of Or Sae Hi Tor, Dor Laff Toa Linn, Prim Sol Mem Brite, and Sor Lai Don Shee in his mind. Sor Hi Laf Brite should have a medallion with the emblem of Superman on it."

The gate opened, and a newborn Rosan stepped out. Sorrel looked at him with concern; he seemed thin for a Rosan just out of bloodfeast. Would his life be even shorter than normal?

"Sor Hi?" Wandra stepped up to the young being.

"Yes," he said. "You must be Man Furenz." He turned to Sorrel. His voice turned reverent. "And you must be Man Everwood." He stepped forward hesitantly. "Prim Sol always hoped that one day one of his descendants would meet you; I remember, and his memory knows great joy this day." He held out his hand, and the petals of his forearm caressed Sorrel's forearm.

Sorrel choked. "So do I. I'm glad you're here."

Abruptly Sor Hi stepped back, saw people waiting for him. "I must go; the dusking teachers wait for me." He strode off. "I'll see you again soon."

"We should be teaching him," Sorrel grumbled as he and Wandra walked off.

"Like hell. You want to slow him down that much?"

Sorrel didn't say anything.

Wandra giggled. "I think we should doublecheck our arrangements with the prophecies and legends, to make sure everybody finds out that Sor Hi is the one who's been promised." She threw her head back in laughter. From time to time, in the moments when they most needed release from grief over the retromemory treatments of Prim Sol's family, Wandra and Sorrel had traveled through the cavernwork sowing legends. They would tell Rosans of the visions their ancestors had had of the Disciple's return, and speak of omens and portents. Later they found new stories spreading, stories that they hadn't started, and when asked for verification they would give it, thus expanding on someone else's fabrication. The populace was ripe for a Return.

Sorrel chuckled. "Don't worry about people finding out that Sor Hi's the one—the techs have found some advertisers who're just delighted to sell this product. The advertisers, you see, are Believers."

"Wonderful." Wandra rested her head on Sorrel's shoulder.

A group of Rosans hurried by, and Sor Hi was among them. "How's it going?" Sorrel yelled to him.

Sor Hi paused. "It's wonderful. Prim Sol's memories are of the sorrow and hatred between the bloodlines who fought during the Revelation. He knew only of the anger and obstinacy that opposed him. But for me it's different—this time, I am as much a hero as the Disciple was a villain." He breathed deep, then looked at Sorrel. "It is a wonderful world that you and he created," he ended.

Wandra agreed. "Yes, it is."

Sorrel watched him disappear into another passage. "I wish there were something we could do for him."

"There is."

Sorrel looked down at her. "What?"

"Get some sleep, so we can be available later, if he needs us." She snuggled against his arm. "Or maybe do something else. I think we should celebrate. Can I seduce you?"

Sorrel smiled at her. "I'm afraid you may." They headed for the ship. "Let's find out."

Sorrel and Wandra found the FTLcom laboratories almost vacant; what few Rosans were there were busy at communication consoles, not FTL prototypes. Cal sat in the one chair in the room—specifically provided for the humans—with a look of bewilderment.

"I don't know whether to laugh or cry," he sighed. "Sor Hi was here for about six hours, studying our problems. Wandra, did you know we were ditching the hyperspace rotational method because nobody could figure out how to control the timing?"

Wandra nodded.

"Well, at the end of six hours, Sor Hi just looked at it and asked why we couldn't do it one way rather than another, and the solution was obvious." Cal turned to Sorrel. "What this means to you is that we should have an operational FTLcom in just a few days."

Sorrel's jaw dropped open; Wandra jumped up and down and clapped, and hugged both Cal and Sorrel. "Congratulations to all of us!" she exclaimed.

"Yeah," Cal said sourly. "That is, we should have one operational if anyone ever goes back to work. Unfortunately, everybody here's gone bonkers. They can't think of anything except the upcoming Bloodbond election."

Wandra clapped some more. "That's fine, Cal. Who's winning?"

"Who else? The finest mathematical physicist in the universe. The Supremi incumbent doesn't have a chance, unless he can stall the election until Sor Hi is dead."

From his coolsuit Sorrel unhitched his comlink to Daisy. "Well, since everybody else is caught up in the election, we might as well be too."

They listened to the reports. This time it was with more pleasure than Sorrel had felt the last time politics interfered with work, when the Supremi ascended to leadership.

From time to time Sor Hi would return, say polite words to Sorrel and the rest of the humans, then launch into vibrant discussions with his advisors. Each time he returned he was more confident, more mature, more capable. Once the broadcasts told of an assassination attempt on him, but even as Sorrel's hands grew clammy, Sor Hi came bursting into the cavern, reassuring them he was all right. "If nobody tries to kill you, then nobody's taking you seriously," he explained cheerfully. "At least I know that people are interested."

"I want to help him," Sorrel muttered as Sor Hi burst off again in a whirlwind of activity.

"I know. You've said it before. Nobody's going to pay any attention to you," Wandra replied.

Four hours later, Sor Hi returned again. He dismissed his advisors to talk to the humans. "Would you like to be with me in the Hall of Choosing? I would be honored by your presence when the vote is taken."

No offworlder, Sorrel knew, had ever attended a Rosan election. "Thank you," Sorrel said. "We'd be honored as well."

Two two-story platforms rose out of the sea of Rosan faces there in the Hall—an awesome cavern, with as much space as the largest of human spacedomes. On the lower level of each platform the most important advisors of each candidate stood, answering detailed questions for the media, and on the higher level stood each candidate himself, describing his plans, hopes, and dreams, pulling his audience into those dreams and making those dreams their own. The room was filled with talking, listening, reading, and watching, all of which had an intensity that Sorrel had never imagined. Wandra leaned over to him. "You know, you can almost see the information in this room; you can see the knowledge being transmitted in wave after wave."

Sorrel nodded.

Suddenly a hush fell; the voting began at counting booths scattered throughout the Hall.

Then it was over; the loudspeakers announced Sor Hi's victory. An awesome cheer began and ended; Sor Hi gave his inauguration address. It lasted a full minute and a half. A second cheer began—but the noise of a violent explosion shattered the joy. The vibration threw Sorrel to the floor, but he leaped up again even as he realized he was falling. He ran to catch the tumbling body of the new Bloodbond, Sor Hi.

Muscles tore and his back wrenched as Sorrel caught Sor Hi in his arms. Together they fell back to the platform, with Sorrel twisting to protect Sor Hi as much as possible.

Sorrel groaned and rolled over. A Rosan with the medic's medallion leaned over Sor Hi. "He's alive," the medic announced. Sorrel sighed, rolled over again, winced at the new pain in his back, and fell into unconsciousness.

When he rolled over again, he found himself in a comfortable bed, his own bed on the ship. He heard the high-pitched, hummingbird sound of a Rosan chuckling, and opened his eyes to look toward the sound.

Sor Hi lay propped in a cot, looking back at him. "Thank you, Parent. And congratulations. We have won."

"What happened?"

"Another assassination attempt. This one succeeded, but not well enough. I have lived long enough. The Supremi bloodlines have been ordered diluted. And they have no immortal beings to protect their dreams from my orders, as I have you to protect mine."

Sorrel looked at the wounds and bandages covering Sor Hi's body. Yes, the assassins had succeeded all too truly. A wounded Rosan had little time left—his body would burn its layers of stored nutrient in a furious attempt to repair the damage, leading to swift death by starvation.

Sorrel rose slowly and painfully from the bed. "Can I get you anything?"

Sor Hi's eyes drifted absently around the room. "No. I am happy here."

Sorrel searched Sor Hi's face with growing acuteness; the thickness was lifting from Sorrel's mind. Sor Hi's skin was drawn tight against his cheeks; death approached.

" 'May you die by a rising star,' " Sor Hi muttered. "Isn't it funny? Ever since we went into the caves, no one has ever died by a rising star. I wonder what it would be like."

With a horrified sense of awe and wonder, Sorrel looked at his watch. He found what he had somehow already known: the sunrise was coming "Follow me," he told Sor Hi, "I have something to show you."

The top of the ship peeked out from the cavernworks; there Sorrel and Sor Hi found a view of Khayyam in the morning. Now the sun too peeked out from the horizon, and touched the shallow pools of water dotting Khayyam's surface. In that fiery touch the warm water quivered, and bubbled, and broke into boiling. Clouds of steam rose into the purplish sky, condensing into rain as it rose, falling, and boiling again into steam as it neared the surface. Frenzied rainbows danced across those spinning almost-rainstorms, only to disappear as the rains evaporated until the next sunrise.

Sor Hi exhaled sharply. "It is incomparable," he whispered in awe. "My children must remember this beauty for me." He looked at Sorrel. "And they must remember you too." He drew a last hard breath. "I . . . " The surprise of sudden insight entered his eyes. "It's even harder for you," he said. "You . . . must keep on living."

Sorrel sobbed. "Yes, my son." The honeysuckle overtook them, each in its own way.

They found Sorrel there in the nose of the ship, and moved him gently to his own room. For three days he lay there, not speaking, not eating, not moving. He was aware of people when they came to him, he heard them when they spoke, he felt them as they hooked the feeder to him, but he did not care. Deep in its own quiet his mind waited, waited for something to trigger it back to life. Sorrel didn't know what he waited for, and about that, too, he did not care.

On the fourth day they told him the FTLcom was ready. Now they could project a three-dimensional image to Lazara and get one back in return. They told him they were about to make contact with Balcyrak.

It was the trigger his mind awaited. He looked up at them, then rose and followed them to the FTL lab.

* * *

Balcyrak studied him quietly, smiling gently. "Do you still hate us, Man Everwood?"

Sorrel looked down, shook his head, "No. I have walked in your shoes."

"Yes. It is not easy, to be a Lazarine."

Sorrel started to speak, choked, shook his head.

Balcyrak continued. "I want to thank you for all you have done for us. My whole race thanks you, and our civilization shall sing of you, our savior."

Sorrel stared at Balcyrak for a moment, then realized what he meant. Balcyrak had lied earlier. There had been no question of who would win the next Lazaran/Man war, had one occurred. Sorrel had saved the beings who had killed his wife; he did not mind. "I'm glad." He felt weary. "By the way, Balcyrak, there's something I'm curious about—how old are you?"

Balcyrak relaxed in his chair. "Nearly fourteen millennia, I would reckon, by your measure."

Sorrel pondered that. "Just about entering middle age, for someone who lives 25,000 years."

"Yes."

Sorrel sighed. "It would be wonderful, to be almost immortal like you."

Balcyrak sat up, looked sharply at him and through him, as Sorrel started to smile. Balcyrak saw the smile and chuckled. "Yes, almost immortal."

Together they started to laugh, a rich powerful laughter that even the dark universe could not deny. ■

Joel Davis, President and Publisher; Leonard F. Pinto, Vice President & General Manager; Carole Dolph Gross, Vice President, Marketing & Editorial; Leonard H. Habas, Vice President, Circulation; Fred Edinger, Vice President, Finance.

Stanley Schmidt, Editor; Elizabeth Mitchell, Managing Editor; Ralph Rubino, Corporate Art Director; Gerard Hawkins, Associate Art Director; Terri Czeczko, Art Editor; Carl Bartee, Director of Manufacturing; Carole Dixon, Production Manager; Iris Temple, Director, Subsidiary Rights; Barbara Bazyn, Manager, Contracts & Permissions; Michael Dillon, Circulation Director, Retail Marketing; Robert Patterson, Circulation Manager; Paul Pearson, Newsstand Operations Manager; Rose Wayner, Classified Advertising Director; William F. Battista, Advertising Director (NEW YORK: 212-557-9100; CHICAGO: 312-346-0712; LOS ANGELES: 213-795-3114)

ABOUT THE EDITOR

Stanley Schmidt has a varied
background, including formal
training and professional experience
as a physicist. One of
the last writers developed by legendary
editor John W. Campbell,
he was a frequent contributor
to *Analog* before becoming its
editor in 1978.